Partridge Up a Pear Tree
(and Dragons)
Rachel Taylor Thompson

Author's Note

Huge apologies to the peoples of China and Newfoundland, especially of Gander and Trinity, for any unintentional errors on my part or a few small things I had to nudge to make the story work.

Newfoundland is my favorite place on the planet, and you are the most generous, welcoming, kind, chatty, friendly people I have ever met. I didn't meet a single overly gossipy person in Gander, so that part of the story is definitely exaggerated, although I had a woman in a hardware store tell me at length that everyone in the town was in everyone else's business and how great that was.

Also, it's an international crime that I can't buy Ketchup Lay's in California.

~Rachel

P.S. Terms, Acronyms, and Magical Definitions can be found at the back of the book.

Map of Newfoundand

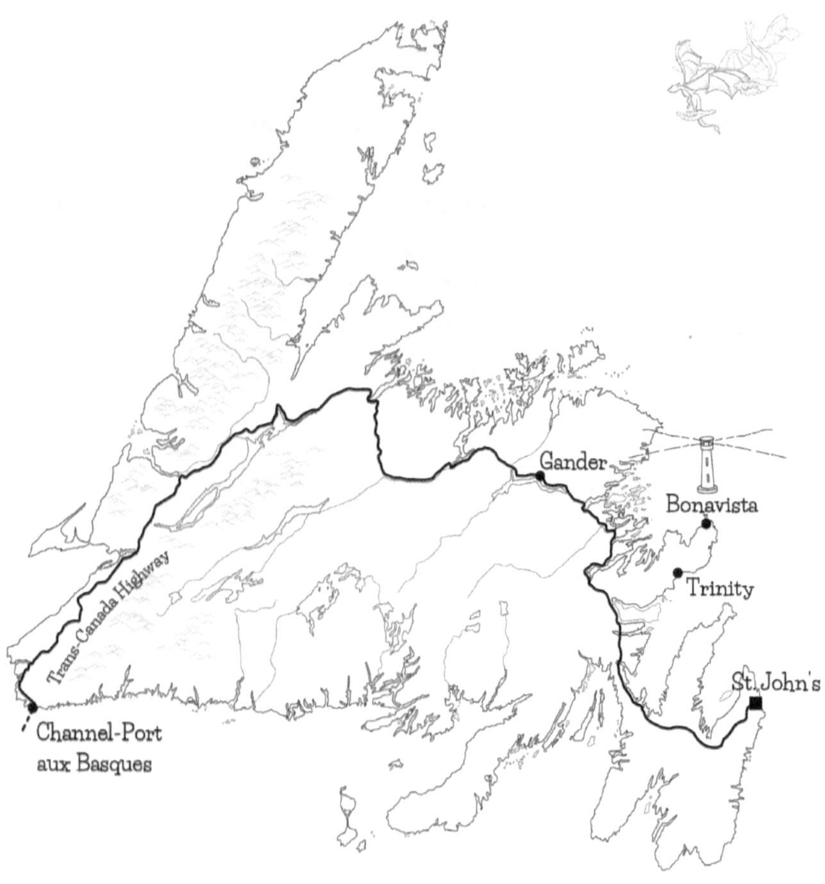

Chapter One

The white note sat crooked on my pillow next to my stuffed penguin from the Falkland Islands. Definitely not from my mother. She only texted. Nor my father. He'd have centered it on the pillow and smoothed the wrinkles from my Norwegian duvet. That left my younger brother, Quentin.

I released a long-suffering sigh and collected the note. The paper was high-quality linen with a weight to it. Quentin had had help.

Ms. Partridge,

I understand you will be relocating to Newfoundland. In connection, I would appreciate a few minutes of your time. Please contact me at the below number.

Aristotle Montague-Smith-Montague

Ummm . . . Aristotle Montague-Smith-Montague, teen heartthrob, Stanford University wunderkind, magic-handler extraordinaire? Randomly reaching out to me, a recent homeschool grad living on the far side of the world?

Not falling for that.

Nor was my family moving to Newfoundland. We'd only arrived in Scotland a month ago and were staying two more. Then I was off to college while my parents and Quentin repatriated to Vancouver for a year.

Quentin and his new Scottish friends were messing with me. The phone number was probably phone-porn or something. I pitched the note in the trash bin and then headed downstairs to snag breakfast and convince Quentin to stop with the games.

Dad and Quentin were both at the table in the dining nook. Quentin, with his blond head ducked over his phone, Dad, with his graying-blond head behind a local newspaper.

Our lodgings weren't half bad this time around. The oak table was sturdy. The chairs matched. The nook overlooked a backyard flower garden that, so far, we hadn't managed to kill. (Our lodgings were provided by the Canadian Magical Sciences Research Council, otherwise known as CMSRC—Mom and Dad's longtime employer.)

"I get the Newfoundland bit," I said, toeing back my seat at the table. "But why Aristotle?"

Just as I went to sit, Quentin kicked the leg of my chair backward. Prepared for his maneuver, I shifted with the movement. One would expect that our nomadic lifestyle meant Quentin and I would be the best of friends. One couldn't be more wrong. That didn't mean I didn't love my brother or see his strengths. He was funny and smart, an amazing athlete, and a great friend. Just also a complete butthead.

Quentin didn't glance up from his phone.

Dad did, lowering his paper to look at me through gold-rimmed glasses. "Josephine, your chair is crooked. You'll drop food in your lap."

I obediently adjusted my seat.

"No dropping food," Mom sang out as she came around the corner from the kitchen. She wore navy coveralls over a woolen sweater, meaning she was headed onto a research vessel for the day. She liked to play at domesticity by providing meals when she was home, but she was way more Marie Curie than Martha Stewart.

Mom nudged my arm as she slid me a plate of food. Four shriveled sausages sat next to a puddle of beans in oil. I smiled at her, ignoring the sour smell. It would taste worse than it looked, but it was important to be nice about these things.

Mom placed a plate in front of Dad, who glanced at it and then got back to his paper. He wore a button-down and a crisp blue tie, meaning he was headed to the research office. He was way more bureaucrat than actual scientist.

"So, Aristotle Montague-Smith-Montague." I tapped Quentin's leg under the table.

Quentin glanced up at me, all wide-eyed innocence. He had Dad's cornflower-blue eyes, as did I, but unlike Quentin and our other siblings,

I'd inherited Mom's unruly brown corkscrew curls. Mom clipped hers short, but I had too round of a face for that. My hair poofed in frizzy curlicues in all directions. Throw in freckles, skin I had to coat in sunscreen even during blizzards, and a dancer's physique, and I looked like a stereotypical Scottish lass. (Which Quentin's friends thought hilarious. Hence the pranks.)

"The famous magic-handler?" Quentin asked. "Didn't you have a crush on him back when Mom was dealing with that arctic dracofox emergency in Siberia? You had photos of him in his underwear all over your room."

"I did not!"

"Not where anyone could see anyway."

I shot him a *you're evil* look. He smirked and returned to his phone.

"Greenland," Dad said a beat late. "*Vulpes draco canidae.*"

Mom patted him on the arm. "That's right, the Vulpes dracos. Maxwell hadn't left for college yet, and he assisted. Such a waste he decided against science. He always had such talent. If I remember right, there was a population emergency in the Vulpes primary food source, and Greenland requested aid from CMSRC—"

"Someone left a note on my bed pretending to be Aristotle Montague-Smith-Montague and implying we're moving to Newfoundland. And to be clear, I had one small photo of him. In which he was fully dressed. And it was while we were in South Africa, not Greenland. Which no one in the British Isles could know unless Quentin told them."

The room went silent.

Outside, a bird tweeted in the flower garden, and a neighbor hollered for a dog named Oswald in a strong Scottish brogue. Mom paused with her fork halfway to her mouth. Dad lowered his newspaper.

Huh?

Their reactions were over the top for my problems with Quentin's friends. Quentin glared accusingly at our parents while turning a slow, furious red.

Oh. Got it.

Mom's and Dad's eyes met across the table. Not guilty, never that, but close.

I cleared away a nervous tightening in my throat. "Before anyone gets upset—"

Quentin shot to his feet, his phone tumbling unnoticed to the floor. "You promised."

"No need to—" I tried again.

"We never make promises," Dad said stiffly.

"Now, Quentin," Mom started in a be-reasonable voice.

Quentin shook his head. "We can't move to Newfoundland. The shuck could take ages to hatch, and then it'll be too late."

"The incubation period is unknown," Dad said. "That being especially true of a shuck containing *Draco marinus* DNA, since there hasn't been one in a good ten thousand years."

"I need to spend my last year of high school in Vancouver," Quentin continued. "I told you repeatedly how much I need it. You did it for Solomon. We went home for Solomon."

Mom placed her fork on the edge of her plate. "Solomon earned a coveted sponsorship from BC Children's Hospital."

"I want to play football." Quentin slammed both fists on the table, making me jump. Family arguments, as compared to us snarking at each other, tended to go nuclear fast. A younger me would dive under the nearest piece of furniture at the first sign of anger. I didn't do conflict well. Or at all if I could help it.

"Newfoundland will have a hockey team," Dad said. "An excellent one, I imagine."

"Football," Quentin insisted, going redder.

"Football," Mom agreed, still being reasonable, which was good.

"Soccer then," Dad said in full-on oblivious mode.

"Quentin wants to play American football," I said to help Dad remember. I kept my voice relaxed, conciliatory, let's-tone-things-down helpful. "There's a league in Vancouver, remember? Quentin already reached out to the coaches."

I felt for Quentin. We had gone home for Solomon to do a Biochemistry program his senior year before college. He'd gone on to pre-med at Georgetown and was currently working on his MD at Duke.

Mom and Dad had been just as supportive of our brother Maxwell even though he'd chosen business over science. He was finishing up his undergrad in Econometrics before beginning a Master of Finance at the University of Chicago.

Our eldest sibling, Desdemona, had gotten parental five-star treatment for both high school and college, anything and everything she'd needed to boost her GPA. Desi'd done her undergrad at Wharton, earned a PhD from Harvard, and was now doing postdoc work in physics at Berkeley with her husband, who was equally credentialed.

I smiled at Quentin so he'd know not everyone was against him.

"Don't smirk at me," he snarled back. "You don't have to waste away in yet another backwater. You get to escape this family and go live your dream life."

I winced.

"Josephine will be attending MIT and majoring in Biological Sciences in the fall," Mom said automatically.

Dad adjusted his glasses. "Josephine will be double-majoring in Neuroscience and Statistics at Yale."

Or I'd do the History program at the University of Toronto.

No need to ramp things up by saying so out loud. Not when all this arguing was hurling me toward an anxiety end zone. Yes, I had a minor anxiety disorder with conflict-induced triggers. No, my parents had never accepted it as a real thing. They looked down their noses at the soft sciences, and I kept my issues as quiet as possible to avoid additional conflict.

I took a deep breath and touched Mom on the sleeve of her sweater. "Maybe we should all—"

Quentin threw up his hands, his voice rising to fill our rental house. "Can't you people even let *this* be about me?"

"Look, Quentin," Mom said, her be-reasonable voice sliding into impatience. Not a good sign. My chest tightened. I gripped the edge of the table, pressing my fingers so hard the grain of the wood imprinted on my bones.

Mom continued, "You shouldn't be surprised that we're being given a new assignment. A seadragon shuck incubating in our own country, it's the research opportunity of a lifetime."

"I specifically asked you," Quentin yelled. "When the egg first hit the news—"

"Not an egg, a shuck." Dad straightened his tie, frowning. Precision was important to him. (On topics he cared about anyway.)

American teenager Sasha Clems had deposited the last ever seadragon egg (or shuck or whatever one chose to call it, since dracos didn't procreate in the normal sense) in a cove on the east coast of Newfoundland. It'd been the talk of CMSRC and the entire world for weeks.

"I asked more than once," Quentin continued. "Each time you said the shuck was too far afield from your lines of expertise for us to be called in."

Quentin was right, but the three of them were now yelling. My heart dread-beat against my lungs, and I glanced desperately at my nearest emergency escape route, the front door.

Mom glared at Quentin. "The Prime Minister's office called."

Dad nodded emphatically. "Your mom and I haven't raised three"—he glanced at me—"I mean four children successfully into adulthood by giving into personal whims. We will honor the requests of our motherland."

I sank further into my seat and tried the five-beat breathing pattern one of my past therapists had taught me. Or had it been four-beat? Maybe three?

Quentin's mouth turned grim. "You promised—"

"We never make promises," Dad repeated loudly.

"You did." Quentin pivoted to me. "Tell them, Joey."

The oxygen whooshed out of my body in a giant explosion of panic. "I . . . I . . . Quentin did ask if we were moving." The words burst from me like shrapnel, full detonation, every direction, no thought, no ability to stop them. "He asked three times. You both said no. No reason for us to do so. Mom's research on the symbiotic parasites of inlet dracos is close to being finished. Dad's planning on spending the time in Vancouver writing his book on draco research ethics and methodology. Of course, CMSRC changes things at the last minute, and this shuck is the very last hope before the extinction of seadragons, but it still makes sense that Quentin would assume—"

"That's enough, Josephine." Mom slammed her plate of untouched sausages and beans onto the table, silencing the room. I collapsed into my chair and pressed both hands to my face, tears pooling like they always did. Why could I never control my mouth? Why, oh why?

Mom continued, *Madame Oblivious* to the level of my distress. "The Prime Minister's office called in every Canadian scientist working for CMSRC. We're all going to Newfoundland. Every single one of us."

What?

A chilled flush, unrelated to my previous failure-as-a-family-member, crept up my chest, making my skin prickle. My preparing-to-gush tears froze. "Did you just say that all Canadian scientists . . ." I enunciated each word carefully. "Every single scientist. Connected to CMSRC. And. Their. Families. We're going to Newfoundland? Together?"

Mom nodded, lowering her voice. "Your dad is taking over as project manager. I'll be heading the team monitoring invasive draco species and parasites."

Quentin laughed. Mean-spirited and ugly and oh-so entertained.

I wanted to kick him but didn't. This couldn't be happening.

"Well," Quentin said with a chortle and a sneer in my direction. "At least I'm not the only one who's totally screwed."

CHAPTER TWO

6 Days Later
Gander, Newfoundland, Canada
Population 12,000. Known as the Crossroads of the World, but for historical reasons only

I normally marched through life with a reasonable amount of confidence. I wasn't a wimp. There wasn't much I hadn't seen or experienced at the international level. I could handle life.

Sort of.

Three things destroyed my and sent me spiraling into anxiety. Avoiding all three was my highest life priority.

The first was the whole people-yelling-at-me thing.

The second was moving. Considering how many times I'd done it (twenty-seven since birth), one would think I'd be a pro. I wasn't. I was especially bad at the part where I packed my belongings into a shipping pod and arrived at a new CMSRC assignment with only what I could cram into two suitcases and a carry-on. I spent the first weeks in a new place waiting impatiently and forlornly for my stuff to arrive. Sounds silly, but a bare bedroom was one of my largest life stressors.

My third was Slade Adler, stepson of Dr. Panozco, a CMSRC draco-geneticist.

Once upon a time, Slade'd been my best friend and romantic obsession. Now I lived in terror that I'd pop around a corner or swing open a door or peek through a window to discover him death-glaring me.

Slade hated me.

Hate wasn't even a strong enough word. Look up hatred in a thesaurus, take the first ten synonyms (animosity, antagonism, antipathy, enmity, hostility, loathing, malevolence, rancor, repugnance, revulsion) and multiply them by a thousand. That was Slade when it came to me.

All made that much worse because I deserved it.

My time stalking him online showed that he was still living with his dad, had finished school, and started a band. Slade was just fine. No reason for him to uproot his life and head to Newfoundland.

Right?

Well . . .

Right, maybe? Because as much as Slade hated me, he loved his little brother, and his little brother would definitely be in Newfoundland with his mom and stepfather. Just thinking about it made my stomach churn like an out-of-balance washing machine on spin.

My first morning in Gander, I left our barren rental house to trek to an insurance agency where my dad wanted me to apply for a job. I was a jittery mess.

Which wasn't Newfoundland's fault. Newfoundland was fine. It was an island somewhat larger than Ireland, only instead of cities, people, and European history, it had rocks, spruce, firs, birches, moose, and ponds in all directions. Our area was pretty in a densely forested way, although the winters were likely hell. Or the opposite of hell, since the average temperature would be well below freezing.

The shuck itself wasn't in Gander, where we were staying. It was two hours east in Trinity Cove. Gander was where the nearest airport was located. CMSRC didn't want family members underfoot, so we were being left here. Also, the town of Trinity was so tiny that it couldn't accommodate even a quarter of us.

So far, I liked Gander. It was practical. A town of strip malls, parking lots, wide streets, and suburbs carved out of thick forest. It was small enough and our rental house central enough that most of the town was walkable. Great for a non-driver. Not so great if Slade was around. It'd be hard to avoid him.

I located the correct strip mall using my phone and walked along the front of the various stores, checking business names and for any sign of Slade. I passed a pizza place with a dark green door and huge front window. Families gathered around the tables inside. None was Slade's. Someone in a blue SUV waved at me. I waved back at the friendly person I didn't recognize, also not Slade.

My Slade-diligence was over the top, of course. Similar to my tendency to not just crack but to panic-explode under pressure, I couldn't help it.

I arrived at the front door of T. Crebs and Sons General Insurance. It was a small place, just a door and window wedged between a dental office and furniture store. A handmade sign on the door read, PHONE ASSISTANCE NEEDED.

Not my dream job.

I mean, I didn't have a dream job. I wanted History as a major because I found people and places and the events that happened to them interesting. Especially the disasters. I was a sucker for a good disaster. (As long as it wasn't happening to me.)

"Hey," a male voice called from behind me. I jerked around in alarm, prepared to find Slade stomping in my direction, smoke coming out of his ears.

It wasn't Slade. The guy couldn't have been less Slade-like if he tried.

"Welcome to the party?" the guy asked with a lopsided, teasing grin. He was tall and lean with brown, wavy hair. His eyes were wide apart and crinkled with humor. His nose was on the large, hookish side, but he made up for it by having the most amazing smile. All sunshine, rainbows, and wide lips.

First impression: Not bad. Cute boys (other than Slade) didn't give me anxiety.

"Is there a party?" I smiled back at him.

"There's a town." He wore khaki shorts and a green T-shirt with an image of a slice of pizza on the front. "Close as you can get 'round here most days. You must be Joey, yeah?" He had a Newfoundland accent, meaning midway between Ontario and Ireland, but also a charming thing of its own.

"You must be Thomas Crebs, insurance agent?" He didn't look old enough to be an insurance agent.

He laughed, warm chuckles that tickled my skin. Definite nice-guy vibes going on here.

"I'm savin' you from old Tommy-boy." He nodded toward the door of the insurance agency. "You're not wantin' that job. Tommy's in his eighties, has five actual clients, and hires pretty girls to sit in front of a phone that never rings for the company."

"Got it, but then how did you know my name?"

His amazing smile widened, and he reached over to tug one of my unruly curls. I started to lean away out of long-standing habit, but then changed my mind and let him do it.

"Cute new girl with wild hair, baby-doll eyes, and freckles? Who else could you be now other than Joey Partridge?"

"Uhhh . . ."

"I'm Mo, by the way. Mo Durand of the Pizza Durands." He pointed back to the restaurant with the green door. "Also known as he-who-knows-all-the-gossip, and that's what we do here. We gossip." He grinned in a boyish, endearing way as if this was all standard.

Which, maybe, it was? Who was I to judge? Would it be wrong to ask if he'd heard anything about Slade?

Yup, totally wrong. Not opening that can of draco worms.

"So where did the gossip describing me as a baby doll come from?" (It wasn't an inaccurate description.)

He tapped a finger to his chin, pretending to ponder. "My mom? Who likely got it from either my aunt or Old Lady Clode, who lives across the street from you. Gander is full of busybodies. Everyone knows everything about everybody, and newcomers are fair game. But me callin' you a baby doll wasn't an insult. You're seriously cute."

"You're seriously good at flirting."

He cocked his head to the side. "I know."

What a beautiful day it was. The sun peeked through the gray clouds. The temperature was pleasantly cool. The flowering bushes outside the dental office filled the air with a sweet scent that tingled my nose. Mo Durand was charming me. Love it!

I slid a step his direction with a quick-but-obvious glance at his shirt. "So, Mo, where should I apply for a job then?" Hint, hint.

"Give me your phone and I'll give you my number so I can send recommendations."

"That's forward of you." I handed over my cell.

"Grand." He ducked his head to type, and a shock of hair fell forward over his eyes. So cute.

"Josephine?" someone hollered from the street. Female voice this time, *Thank the Greek Goddess of Small Mercies.* The last thing I needed was to run into Slade right now. (Or anytime for that matter.)

A white CMSRC pickup stopped in the middle of the road bordering the strip mall, and a petite Asian girl hopped out of the passenger side. She had short-cropped hair styled into a spiky pink fauxhawk and wore a denim jumper. "Joey, it *is* you." She jogged in my direction.

"Lei?" I pasted a welcoming smile on my face.

Lei's mother sat in the driver's seat, watching us from behind mirrored aviators. The Tiens had shared assignments with us several times over the years. Lei was my age. We were friends, sort of. I waved to her mom.

Lei and I did an awkward half-hug, half-tap on each other's backs.

"You just got in, right?" she asked.

"Yesterday. You?"

"Last week. My mom said your family was the last to arrive. I heard you got the worst of the housing options."

"Intro?" Mo asked. He'd been typing into my phone as Lei and I'd hugged, but now handed it back to me.

"Sorry," I said. "Mo Durand, of the Pizza Durands." I nodded toward the green door down the way. "Wait." I turned back to Mo. "You mean, you don't already know who she is?"

He shrugged and snapped his fingers in Lei's direction. "'Course. But I didn't want to be *rude*. Lei Tien, nineteen, attending University of Florida next fall. Mom works for CMSRC in something to do with engineering. Dates girls."

"Nice." Lei looked him over with interest.

"Not a girl." He reversed his fingers to point at himself.

She rolled her eyes. "I meant for town gossip. One never wants to assume about the nosiness factor in new places."

"As I was just tellin' Joey, Gander's plenty nosy but friendly too." He glanced my direction as if wanting to make sure I knew this next bit was less for Lei and more for me. "I'm Mohmmedidrees Alex Hirsch Durand. An unpronounceable, horrid first name. I'm the fourth." He smirked. "Call me Mo. And just for fair play, I'm twenty and a Marketing student at Memorial University in St. John's, home for the summer. Ask about any of that at any point. I'm an open book, especially for cute straight girls I plan to ask out." He gave me another pointed, teasing look.

Lei snorted. "Don't hold your breath. She's taken."

"No, I'm not." I laughed. "Seriously. Not taken."

"Oh, my mistake?" Lei gave me a wide-eyed, innocent look. "I thought you and Slade . . ."

My smile slipped. Horror flattened my happiness. I leaped back a step, rocking my head. "Nope. No way. That ended, and—"

She patted me on the arm all concerned-like, but there was a sparkle in her eyes that said she was baiting me. (So very Lei.)

Lei's mom honked the horn, saving me from having to respond. "Lei, hurry. You're making me late."

"I'll be there in a moment," Lei hollered back. She stepped into Mo's space, standing on her toes as if to speak into his ear, even though the tip of her fauxhawk didn't reach the top of his chest. "Don't you worry," she said in a mock whisper. "Slade lives in Toronto. After Joey got the disintegration of the China expedition blamed on him, he won't come within a thousand miles of her." She turned to wink at me. "Joey, you can thank me later for letting you know you don't have to worry about Slade."

"How about I thank you instead and do it now?" Mo replied. "Since we're all standin' here."

Lei stepped back and shrugged. "Joey will come around to thanking me herself. Being open about life's little issues is just so much better for everyone. Don't you agree, Mo?" She didn't give him a chance to respond but left for the waiting car. "See you at the CMSRC party, Joey."

"Yeah," I replied faintly, feeling like I'd been hit by a speeding car that had then reversed to make sure to get me from the other direction. That was Lei. Prone to randomly running people over.

Mo and I stood next to each other in silence as she drove off.

"Your friend is interesting." Mo nudged me with his elbow.

I nudged him back and forced a grin. "CMSRC kids are crazy. Including me. In a good way. You'll like us."

Mo's eyes twinkled. His generous lips parted to show straight, white teeth. "Aren't you just the nicest person goin'. Along with being cute. And from what I hear, over-the-top smart."

"And in need of a job." Loved the praise, though. Another plus for Mo.

His grin widened. Little dimples appeared in each cheek. "We will be seein' each other again, Josephine Bridget Partridge. Age eighteen. Loves to dance. Received offers from twelve different universities, including four Ivy League, but is keeping which one she accepted close to her heart."

"Uhhh . . ." How *had* he learned all that?

He turned on his heel and walked back to the pizza place. No, not walked but swaggered, as if he was putting on a show for me.

Which, apart from the very real nosiness factor at play here, I loved.

He grinned back over his shoulder. "Don't you worry about old Tommy, yeah? I'll let him know I stole you away. And make sure to check your phone."

Chapter Three

Mo had added himself into my contacts and texted himself so he'd have my number. He'd gotten into my calendar, added a job interview the following morning at Pizza Utopia with *best uncle ever*, and scheduled a six-hour work shift afterward. He'd booked Thursday evening as *date with Mo*, invited himself as a participant, and then, while I'd walked home, sent a list of things we'd do together.

(1) *Mo picks up Joey in oldest, ugliest truck in Gander.*
(2) *Mo and Joey have bland but traditional conversation about the weather.*
(3) *Mo parks at Memorial Park and sets up picnic blanket.*
(4) *Mo feeds Joey homemade meal.*
(5) *Joey is not offended that Mo's mom did the cooking rather than him.*
(6) *Mo tells Joey his life story, including the embarrassing parts.*
(7) *Joey tells Mo her life story, especially the embarrassing parts.*
(8) *Mo and Joey walk around park commiserating about how life sucks (or not).*
(9) *Mo and Joey have PDA moment involving holding hands and longing looks only, because Mo is respectful regardless of whether he is feeling 30 or not.*
(10) *Giant explosion of fireworks.*

Forward much?

I was accustomed to being asked out by guys, as in there being a question and a moment where I got to agree. (I mean, not that it happened constantly or anything. Post-Slade, I'd had three first dates and two assignment boyfriends.)

Mo didn't come off as aggressive or domineering, though. He was more an overeager golden retriever in need of a few more sessions with a trainer. The list could even be seen as sweet. The date sounded great, and my whole leaving-the-last-assignment anxiety would improve if I made friends. Seemed worth it to take a chance and go out with him. Plus, I liked the idea of working at a pizza place.

I arrived at our ramshackle rental house and hopped over the rotten step of the front landing while adding two more items to our shared list.

(1a) Joey brings along homemade dessert, also not made by her.
(9a) Joey uses PDA moment to kiss respectful-Mo on the cheek only.

Boundary set. Hopefully. Since I was terrible at boundaries. I knew I was supposed to set them, wanted to even. It was the enforcement part where I failed miserably. Enforcement always felt like the exact kind of pressure I hated when people put on me.

I texted him.

Me

Send tips for the job interview.

Mo

I'll call you later tonight.

This was going to be fun.

Unfortunately, the rental house I would be spending the summer in wouldn't be. It was a beige two-story with a grayish-green roof, surrounded by weedy grass and a single tree in the back. Other than a rotting wood porch, it was plain and square and in need of a major remodel. The front door was so ancient it took five minutes to get the lock to release, and then the hinges squeaked like a mouse with its tail in a trap.

I added fixing both to my mental to-do list.

Upstairs, my room was depressingly barren. White walls, a twin bed, plain wood dresser, matching desk and chair, a trash bin, and a window facing the tree. On top of the dresser was a blue mug I'd purchased the day before as my Newfoundland memorial. It had *Come From Away* printed on one side. I hugged it to my chest—my version of a security blanket.

That was when I noticed a white note sitting on the bed's pillow.

"Seriously?"

I'd received three more handwritten letters in Scotland from Aristotle Montague-Smith-Montague asking me to call some random number while insisting it wasn't a joke. This was the fifth.

Thank you, Quentin. I let out a long-suffering sigh. (In his defense, Quentin had let me have the larger of the two bedrooms and texted me the number of a dance studio where I could take classes. He wasn't entirely evil.)

I snatched up the note and tossed it into the trash bin. Outside the window, a shiny lavender draco sat in the tree looking at me. A veradraco.

It was small, eagle-sized, making it young, one to two hundred years. It was bright lavender, with a thin neck, pot belly, wings, and pointy tail that rippled back and forth in a mix of cat and cobra. Its scales were smooth and silky, its face snubby and cute, giving it a babyish appearance.

It and I made eye contact through the glass. It blinked its lavender eyes twice and launched for the sky, shimmery lavender wings flapping madly.

"That's weird."

Weird enough that I mentioned the draco to Mom and Dad that evening as we left for the CMSRC party. Dracos didn't interact with people. They avoided us when they noticed us at all.

"There are reports of nontraditional behavior in the area," Mom said as we each stepped over the rotting first step of our rental's porch. She wore a low-cut, red ball gown. "It's believed the American girl who set up the shuck in Trinity Cove did something to rile them. Or possibly the magic-handlers put a spell on the region. CMSRC tried contacting the Handlers' Alliance about the changes, but as usual, they refused to tell us anything."

"Newfoundland has always had a higher than average concentration of verumdracos," Dad said. He wore a tuxedo with a fake red rose in the lapel. So embarrassing, but going all-out when we first arrived at a new assignment was one of my parents' rituals. (It wasn't just the CMSRC kids that were crazy.)

Quentin wore khakis and a button-down, collar open. I wore a white sweater, short tartan skirt I'd picked up in Scotland, and black ankle boots. Not likely fashionable in Newfoundland, but I'd given up bothering with local styles ten moves ago.

"The shuck could be drawing them as well," Dad continued, holding open the door to the CMSRC van that was our family's latest transportation. "The highly respected Dr. Ndlovu wrote a paper about the influence of an incubating shuck on the surrounding ecosystem."

"So I shouldn't worry about it," I inserted before he could overdose us with draco facts. For all that Dad was more of an administrator than an actual scientist, he loved to keep up with scientific discoveries, old and new, and the scientists who made them.

"Oddities are expected," Mom said and ushered Quentin and me into the van. "Nothing to be bothered about."

The CMSRC welcome party was held in a local hall decorated for Blundstones and beer more than red-carpet attire. There were a hundred and forty-seven scientists in CMSRC. That, plus spouses, partners, and children, meant the room was way over capacity. The sit-down tables were full, and a group of younger kids ran around the room playing tag. No one my age that I could see, which wasn't unexpected, as most draco-scientists settled down and turned to teaching as their kids got older. I'd always hoped my parents would do the same.

Mom and Dad made their grand entrance to lots of oohs and aahs as usual. Quentin and I beelined in the opposite direction. I grabbed his arm before he could disappear. "Enough with the letters."

"What letters?"

"Aristotle? The move?"

He squinted. "You mean there really was a letter in Scotland? I thought you made that up to force Mom's and Dad's hands."

"As if. You sure it's not your friends?"

Quentin wasn't a liar, but neither was he on my side. He patted me condescendingly on the shoulder. "Sorry, Sis, but sounds like wyrm-netting to me."

"I wouldn't think . . ." I began, but Quentin strolled off toward the buffet. A distinctive man with a receding hairline in a white lab coat stood there eyeing the food.

Dr. Panozco.

Slade's stepfather.

I blanched and swallowed a lump of panic. He looked just as grumpy and squinty as I remembered him. I shouldn't have been surprised Dr. Panozco was here. Of course he would be. I should've prepared myself for it. I ducked behind a wooden post to scope out who was with him.

I spied Slade's mom. Dark hair, petite build, pretty for a mom, and young. She'd been seventeen when Slade was born.

Behind her was a four-year-old boy in a polo shirt. He stared at his black Chucks as if he'd prefer to be anywhere but here. Slade's beloved little brother, Vinnie.

He had Slade's same thick black hair, angular face, and I-don't-smile dour expression. Vinnie was a total preschool version of Slade. So cute. They'd always been two peas.

My innards went all spin-cycle. It was my fault they'd spent the last year living on separate continents.

But at least there was no sign of Slade. *Thank Eleos, the Greek Goddess of Small Mercies.*

My phone buzzed with an incoming call, and I did a quick parent check. Mom and Dad were over at a table, Mom facing my direction, so I detoured toward the washrooms. My parents had weird rules on phone use in public, but what they didn't know (or bother to notice) wouldn't cause them to get upset.

"There you are," Lei said, heading me off. She wore a skintight knit dress in the same pink as her fauxhawk.

"You look amazing." She totally did.

"Thanks." Lei shoved a glass into my hand.

I shook my head, but took it anyway. My phone buzzed again.

"It's only pop." Lei, at nineteen, could legally drink. At barely eighteen, I couldn't, and the response from my parents if I got caught would be way worse than chatting on a phone in public.

My phone buzzed a third and final time. Shoot.

"You haven't met the twins yet, have you?" Lei asked. "They're out on the patio. I'll introduce you."

"Great idea." The twins were the only other CMSRC kids our age and thus an excellent opportunity for new friends. After the intro, I'd sidle off and call Mo back. I mean, assuming it was Mo who'd rung me.

I followed Lei to a veranda that ran the back length of the building. No twins, just Quentin holding more glasses of pop. Maybe I could ditch him and Lei together to go check my phone?

"Where'd the twins go?" Quentin asked. "Someone said they were out here."

Lei smirked. "Just give up now. You have zero chance with either one."

"Oh, ye of little faith." He smirked. "Partridges have charm."

It was true, we did.

"Fine," Lei said. "Get your butt kicked from here to Antarctica. What do I care?"

"You guys should go look for them," I suggested.

"If they aren't here, they'll be at the fish and chips place down the street," Lei replied. "We were chatting about heading over there before I came in search of you two."

"A night out together." Quentin murmured. "Sounds perfect."

My phone buzzed, and since we were out of sight of our parents, I fished it out of my waistband. Caller ID showed a 709 number, meaning Newfoundland. Since Mo was the only local I knew, the call had to be from him even if it wasn't from his cell.

I stepped away from Lei and Quentin to answer. "Perfect timing. I'd like a single slice of supreme, please. And do you deliver?"

"Hello?" a confused male voice replied. A male voice too deep and old to be Mo.

"Oh, shoot, sorry. I thought you were someone else. I mean, clearly you're someone else. I mean, hello back. Who is this?"

"It's Bob."

Bob? Did I know any Bobs? Maybe back in Arizona? Only the number was local. Oh, wait. Mo's uncle. He must be calling early about the job interview. "Hi, Bob. I can't tell you how excited I am for this opportunity. I've never worked in a restaurant before, but everyone always likes me. I'm sure I'll learn fast if you'll give me a chance."

"Who are you?" the voice asked.

I paused, reevaluating yet again. "Who are *you*?"

"I told you, Bob. Robert Minh Quan. You're supposed to be Josephine Partridge. If you'd just followed the instructions from Aristotle, we wouldn't have this problem."

I jerked the phone down and hit cancel. Then I did a quick glance around in case Quentin had a camera pointed my way to capture me making a fool of myself. Nope, he was badgering Lei about the exact location of the fish and chips place.

Robert Minh Quan was an unusual combination of both draco-scientist and magic-handler. Even more unusual, he'd supposedly died years ago, but Sasha Clems claimed he'd helped her get to Newfoundland. Dead or not so much, there was no way the real Robert Minh Quan would be calling me.

My phone buzzed. Same number. I hit cancel and hurried back to Lei and Quentin. "Lei, have you heard of anyone getting wyrm-netted lately?"

Quentin dropped a not-so-casual hand on my shoulder. "Hey, Sis, let's exit-poste-haste the parental-party and go get food."

I shrugged him off. "No way am I helping you hit on the twins."

"My mom had someone after her in Peru," Lei cut in. "She thought it was the Hungarian magic-handlers. Nothing since. I can't imagine handlers being interested in this assignment. It's a shuck."

My thought, too. Shucks were magically useless to handlers. It was the semis, the progenitors of the shuck, that were invaluable. Handlers used genetically passed abilities to turn semis into spellbooks. The spellbooks both held the magic and let them cast spells.

But semis also held millions of bits of the dead magical-creature's DNA. Combining two into a shuck combined the DNA too. Draco procreation in action.

That was where CMSRC and this assignment came in. It was crazy rare to witness procreation happening, even in the smaller species. There were only a dozen recorded events ever.

A seadragon shuck . . .

Seadragons had been hunted to near extinction in the 1800s. The shuck in Trinity Bay was the DNA of the last two. It was both vitally important to protect the thing and a research opportunity of a lifetime.

For CMSRC, that was. Not so much for the magic-handlers. Only a semis could be turned into a spellbook. Then once the shuck hatched, the millions of draco larvae were so tiny and their magic so weak that they were also useless to handlers. It took between ten years and a hundred for the newborn dracos (depending on the species) to grow big enough for their magic to be worth killing the creature for and collecting. It was illegal to kill magical-creatures regardless, but that didn't stop the magic-handlers from doing it. Hence, the wyrm-netters who tried to phish, scam, and influence draco-scientists into getting them access.

It made no sense for handlers to be contacting me. But other than handlers, who else could it be? I mean, if it hadn't been Quentin leaving those notes on my bed, then a handler using a spell seemed most likely. Especially combined with the phone call. Yikes.

My phone buzzed, and I automatically looked down. This time it read Mo Durand.

I stepped back from the others, putting the wyrm-netter problem aside.

Just as I hit accept-call, Mom in her vivid red dress swept onto the patio.

Her gaze locked on me. She dropped her hands to her hips, and her very red lips turned into an annoyed parent frown. "Josephine Bridget Partridge, I see what you're doing. You will hand over that cell right this minute. We don't use phones in social situations."

Chapter Four

Not only did my mom confiscate my phone, but she spent a loud fifteen minutes lecturing Quentin, Lei, and me on the importance of manners when representing CMSRC. Per Mom, we should be prepared for the King of England or Queen of Bhutan to walk in at any moment. (Yes, she actually said that.)

The moment she finished, Quentin asked if we could go hang out with the other CMSRC kids. Mom immediately agreed and didn't even confiscate Quentin's phone, which left me an opportunity. If I could talk Quentin into it.

"Twenty bucks to use your cell," I whispered to him as Lei led us into the fish and chips place. It was low-lit with a long wooden bar to one side. Glass bottles were stacked along the wall, and the back corner held a pool table. Lighting was industrial steel lamps hanging from the ceiling. Pleasantly atmospheric in a small-town bar way.

"Two hundred and fifty." Quentin scanned the row of booths in the back.

"Twenty-five."

A girl with a river of dark hair stood and waved at us. She wore an A-line chiffon dress in muted green that fit her curves impeccably, and she was so stunningly beautiful that both Quentin and I froze in place and just stared. Magic-handlers did that to people.

Even knowing that, beyond the excessive, magically induced beauty, the twins were just CMSRC kids like us, the extremes of the girl's looks were startling. First impression: More friendly than haughty. I took this to mean she was Tabita Maldonado-Flores, the nice magic-handler twin.

"I'll take that one," Quentin murmured in awe.

I elbowed him in the ribs.

The second twin was Isabella Maldonado-Flores. She stood, but didn't wave or smile at us. Instead, she glared at Quentin. Her gorgeous dark hair matched her sister's in color, but was blunt-cut to her shoulder. She wore a black oversized dress-shirt, black leggings, black combat boots, black eyeliner with wings at the corners of her gorgeous black eyes, and had an oversized black vulture (as in the corpse bird) necklace around her neck. First impression: Red flags in all directions.

CMSRC rumor had it that while they both had the magic-handler gene and had had the standard magic-handler beauty spell performed at birth, they had very little access to spellbooks. Their mom had cut contact with her magic-handling family when she'd married their very ordinary draco-scientist father, leaving them looking the part of a handler but not much being it. They were unlikely to be able to help with my wyrm-netters.

"One twenty-five," Quentin whispered as we walked over. "If you play me up with the hottie in green."

"I heard that," Lei said.

"You going to go fan-crazy on us?" Isabella eyed Quentin and me with an aggressive frown.

Thunk. A red flag whacked me over the head. I pasted a non-threatening smile on my face, but before I could respond, Tabita stepped in, her voice gentle and soft. "Isa, stop. Not everyone is a threat." She turned to me. "Please join us. And don't be embarrassed. We're used to being stared at. Just get over it as soon as possible."

"Meet Tabby and Isa," Lei said, as the twins returned to their seats in the booth. Lei moved to sit by Tabby, but Quentin beat her. Lei rolled her eyes and walked around the other side.

I followed Lei. Once seated, I put my hands up in the universal sign of innocence. "Sorry I gaffed on the staring. I'm usually better than that and won't do it again. I'm Joey, fourth child of the Doctors Partridge."

"And I'm Quentin." He gave an over-the-top chin bob in Tabby's direction. "Fifth and best Partridge. You definitely want to get to know me."

Tabby dropped her gaze to her hands.

Isa scowled. "Back off, buddy."

I forced myself not to stiffen at her tone. "He's just being friendly." I sent Quentin a meaningful look. *Thirty dollars*, I mouthed.

And that was how the evening proceeded as we got to know each other. Quentin hit on Tabby. Tabby got embarrassed. Isa cut him down. Lei ordered a glass of wine, showing off that she was the only one of us old enough to drink. I edged my offer up to seventy-five, tore my paper napkin into tiny stress triangles, and asked as many bland questions as possible to keep the conversation going. (This wasn't a group that was going to end up fast-friends, darn it.)

"Please, Quentin," I said an hour later. "I have a job interview tomorrow. Let me use your phone."

"Interview at the insurance place?" Quentin asked. "Dad will be thrilled."

"Yup." I sifted the pile of napkin confetti through my fingers. Dad was unlikely to notice where I was working.

Quentin turned to Tabby. "I'm trying to find a job coaching kids' sports. Summer camp, something like that. I'm good with kids. You like kids? You could join me."

"No, she can't," Isa stated.

"Joey likes to help out at dance studios," Quentin continued unfazed. "The dance school here is full up, but she's an amazing dancer."

"Just for fun," I quickly added. I'd never stayed in a place long enough for real training. If I managed to get myself to the University of Toronto, I was going to join one of their dance teams.

"We should go out together," Quentin said. "Clubbing, if Gander has one."

Isa glared in his direction. "Dude, just give up already."

"Quentin's a good guy." I sent him a wide-eyed, significant look.

"So good," Lei pointed out, "he refuses to let his own sister borrow his phone."

"That was a joke." Quentin tossed his cell across the table at me. It landed in my pile of napkin shreds, scattering them into my lap. Thank you, Quentin.

Lei took a sip of her wine, making a point of lifting it high so that we'd notice. "You guys ready to get out of here? I'll call for a car."

"They have service in such a remote area?" Tabby asked.

I ignored them and used Quentin's phone to log into our family account. No texts on my line, but I did have three voicemails from an unlisted number.

Unlisted and other oddball numbers weren't unusual in the CMSRC world, where most of my acquaintances lived in far-flung parts of the planet. I put the phone to my ear. The first wasn't Mo, but it also wasn't the guy claiming to be Robert Minh Quan. The voice was female and so loud that I pushed the phone back to avoid ear damage.

"Hi, Joey, this is Sasha Clems." Pause. Then, "No, Ari, she doesn't need a bio. I'm famous. She'll know who I am. Let me—" Laughter. Call ended.

"What the . . . ?" Lei stared at me.

Next message. Same female voice.

"Sorry about that. Certain people won't keep their opinions to themselves." More laughter. "Like I said, this is Sasha Clems, and I'm sure you know who I am regardless of what certain people think. Ignore them and call me back. I'll explain everything."

End of call.

"Joey?" Lei's voice was full of interest.

Next message. "Sasha again. Just in case you don't recognize my name, I'm the one who found a dead seadragon, stole its semis, got my house ransacked, traveled across the continent, did a livestream to sell my semis, but ultimately didn't do so, and instead set the seadragon egg to incubating. I need to talk to you about that. There may be a problem, and Bob needs help, but Ari's been banned from Canada, and I'd draw too much attention if I returned. Call me."

Huh.

It made sense. Aristotle Montague-Smith-Montague, he of my white notes, had helped Sasha Clems get from the west coast to the east. The two of them claimed to have worked with the secretive Robert Minh Quan, a.k.a. Bob, in doing so. According to her social media, Sasha and Aristotle were both back in California now. She'd done a bunch of public interviews and become famous.

That they'd reach out to me was crazy ridiculous. Utterly.

"Do not call," Isa ordered.

"It sounded just like Sasha Clems," Tabby said.

"It did," Quentin agreed.

It had. I'd watched Sasha's livestream and several of her interviews. The whole world had. Still . . . "I don't think—"

"You should call," Lei said right over the top of me.

"You should tell your parents," Tabby said.

"I'd rather not—" I tried again.

"But call the fake-Sasha first." Lei's eyes sparkled with excitement. "Could be fun, right? We're here as witnesses if anything goes wrong."

"No," Isa insisted. "That's a terrible idea."

"Don't you want to find out what fake-Sasha is after?" Lei asked.

"Not at the risk of getting my phone hacked." Quentin leaned over the table and snatched it out of my hand.

Problem solved.

"Whatever," Lei said with a pretend shrug. She'd never been one to lose easily. "Oh, look, Joey." She squinted in my direction. "Here's our ride."

The bells on the entry door chimed, and Slade Adler walked in.

Chapter Five

I flushed hot, then cold, then hot again. Alarm bells worthy of a mega-tsunami sounded in my ears. No way to run for it. Nowhere to go. No time to throw on a life vest of coping methods.

"Surprise," Lei said, throwing up her hands. "Better to rip off the band-aid, am I right?"

"What do you mean?" Isa asked.

Since I couldn't bolt, I froze. So did time and the world, as my emotions, thoughts, and sense of self drained into a horrified puddle under the table.

Slade scanned the room, eyes narrowed, expression flat. Which didn't mean he was mad yet, as he hadn't noticed me. It was just his usual expression.

As I watched him, my alarm morphed into something different. Something fascinated.

It'd been so long, and there he was.

Oh.

So.

Familiar.

And yet different at the same time.

The noise of the bar dissipated into a background hum, and the others at the table faded. My breath slipped out in a wistful sigh. I leaned forward on the table, knocking more of the shredded napkin into my lap.

Even with his painful, like-stabbing-my-own-chest-with-a-knife hatred between us, I'd missed him. Completely, utterly, unconditionally, thoroughly, wholeheartedly, consummately, without qualifications, to-the-depths-of-my-soul missed him. My Slade.

He was still slender and not terribly tall, but his shoulders were wider than I remembered. He'd shaved the sides of his dark hair short, almost buzzed, but the top was longer, falling to one side in a thick, messy curtain. His face was still straight lines and angles with high cheekbones, but that was fuller too. He'd become more of . . .

Well . . .

Himself.

Beautiful and compelling in a never-smiled, furrowed-brows, blank-stare way.

He was dressed in a long-sleeved tee for a band named Earth Crisis, ripped jeans, battered Chucks, and had a dozen black leather bracelets around his right wrist.

Slade's gaze slid to our booth. He walked over, taking in each person one by one.

My anxiety jump-started as if I'd been hit with a defibrillator. I should duck under the table before he noticed me. No, that wouldn't work. I should prepare the best apology of my life. No, I'd tried that, and it'd just made him madder. I should burst into the tears that were already gathering and hope the others would feel so sorry for me that someone else would handle him. Absolutely not. Then they'd see what a mess I was, and that just couldn't happen. (I cried way easily. It was the single thing I disliked about myself the most and was sooo embarrassing.)

Slade's attention settled on me. Hurt flashed through his eyes, followed by the entire list of synonyms for hate plus all related verbs. His frown turned into a curled-lip sneer, his eyes narrowed into lasers of loathing. He folded his arms.

I gulped back a bone-deep apprehension mixed with a longing for things to be different and a heavy, drowning sadness for what I'd lost.

Quentin jumped to his feet, breaking the moment and turning Slade's attention his way. "My bro. Long time."

Thank you, Quentin. (Zero sarcasm intended on my part, even.)

Slade glanced at him and then focused in on Lei.

"I'm not. An effing. Uber." His voice was soft, low, and dead even. If looks could kill, and Slade's came close, Lei would be face down on the table with poison dripping from her mouth.

She smirked. "But I've been drinking." She raised her glass of wine in his direction.

Slade drummed his fingers on his folded arm. He had a serious thing about drinking and driving. Or even drinking at all. If Lei had texted saying she was drunk (which she wasn't), the Slade I'd known would come running.

Lei took a sip from her glass. "Have you met everyone?"

I winced, covered it with a pleasant expression, latched onto the table to keep myself upright, and bit my lower lip.

Slade flicked a glance at Tabby and Isa, his expression unchanged. Lei made the introductions. I shrank in my seat and glanced desperately at the exit sign over the door. Why was Lei doing this? Why, oh why?

"It's a pleasure to meet you." Tabby offered her hand to Slade. He remained unmoving. She lowered it to her lap with an uncertain glance at her sister.

"You're the guy who went to juvie for killing his cousin." Isa met his gaze straight on, challenging, even.

Slade hadn't killed his cousin or been in any way responsible for the car accident that had. He'd spent one night in juvie while RCMP figured that out. It'd happened long before I'd met him, and while he'd trusted me with the truth, he wouldn't care what Isa thought and wouldn't want to be defended. Especially by me.

"Of course, you know Quentin Partridge," Lei jumped in, her voice overtly, obnoxiously, painfully sweet. "And his sister Joey."

I winced again.

"If you want a ride," Slade said, slowly, coldly, his attention fixed on Lei, "I'll be outside. I have seats for four." He turned on his heel and strode off the way he'd arrived.

There were five of us at the table. Phew. I might survive this after all.

"Tabby can sit on Quentin's lap," Lei called out to Slade.

"No, she won't," Isa snapped back.

"Then I'll sit on Joey's." Lei slid my direction, pushing me to the edge of the bench.

"No need," I replied. "I'll walk back to the party."

"You're not walking back to the party," Lei said, way too loudly. "Your dad booked the DJ until 3 a.m. and the music is crap. Besides, you and Slade need to get over yourselves. The six of us are stuck together for the summer, and it's not healthy for you two to be at war."

That was what was behind this?

Also . . .

Slade was here for the entire summer?! I fought a sudden urge to sprint for the nearest washroom. Permanently.

A bell on the front door jangled as Slade shoved it and left.

"We're not at war," I said in the most conciliatory, placatory, disarming voice I could manage. "He just doesn't like me. It's no big deal, and—"

"Why doesn't he like you?" Isa asked.

Lei shoved into me in an explicit command to get out of her way. I leaped to my feet, making the bits of shredded napkin in my lap cascade to the floor. Another of my messes left for someone else to sweep up.

"Lei, please. I can't ride with Slade. Quentin, help me out here."

"This is going to be epic," he said to Tabby. Apparently, his younger-brother helpfulness wasn't as strong as his desire to flirt.

"Be nice to Joey," Tabby said, standing as well. "She's upset and none of this is our business. Joey, I'll go back to the party with you."

"Me too," Quentin announced.

"No way," Isa said. "I told Mom and Dad we'd meet them back home. Took me ten minutes to convince them. We go back now and they'll think something is wrong."

"Perfect, it's settled. Slade will take us home." Lei wrapped her fingers around my wrist, attaching herself to me like one of Mom's parasites.

Five minutes later, I was sitting in the front of Slade's twenty-year-old Honda, with Lei on my lap, and my boots resting on a mound of empty water bottles, several black hoodies, and miscellaneous drumsticks. (The musical kind, not the ice cream).

Slade ignored us as we arranged ourselves. Not even a sneer for breaking his four-people rule or that the most-hated person in his universe had her arm less than a finger's width from his elbow. He kept his attention straight ahead, his jaw clenched, both hands on the wheel. His right palm beat out a rhythm so forcefully it reverberated through the car and my body, pummeling my soul.

My spin-cycle stomach filled with a load of rocks. I tried counting to twelve, matching the numbers to my breathing, but lost track around three.

Slade continued drumming the steering wheel as we pulled out. The leather bracelets around his wrist slid back, revealing the edge of something colorful etched into his skin.

Ink?

He'd done it?

My anxiety lost a tug-of-war to curiosity.

No way. It totally was ink. This was huge. And wonderful. He'd wanted it so bad.

Was it . . . ? Had he . . . ?

Excitement made it hard to stay still, even with Lei's sit bones digging into my thighs. Words, questions, conversation bubbled to my lips. And not just bubbled but fizzed, foamed, and sparkled. Slade and I'd spent months designing the perfect sleeve tattoo in remembrance of his cousin. I *needed* to see the finished artwork.

"Why does Slade hate Joey?" Isa asked from the back seat.

The bubble popped, the fizz flattened, and my excitement sank to drowned-Titanic-level misery yet again. (The real Titanic had sunk not too far from Newfoundland. Just saying . . .)

Slade's pounding on the steering wheel sped up.

"Tell her, Joey." Lei shifted, elbowing me in the shoulder. "It's a great story."

No, it wasn't. "Maybe, we should all—"

"We were in central China," Quentin said, the traitor. "Brought in by the Chinese government because they hoped that this humongous breed of salamander, like twenty-five kilos of slimy reptile, might have a semis."

"I thought China didn't have any remaining magical-creatures," Tabby said.

"They don't," Lei replied. "A fact the government is unhappy about and endlessly trying to remedy."

"Exactly," Quentin continued. "CMSRC was hired to catch one of the reptiles and do tests. But the Chinese official in charge was a real dick. His personal logo resembled a dick, too. Someone, likely one of his own employees, as he was even worse to them than us, used markers on his business card to make the logo even more dick-like. With green herp-ish scabs."

Isa laughed. "Nice one."

"Oh, wow," Tabby said in horrified shock. "That's so disrespectful."

Quentin continued. "The official blamed the scientists' kids. Joey pointed the finger at Slade."

"Cold," Isa said. No laughter this time.

My throat tightened and my face flooded brilliant red, even though Quentin had gone easy on me in the telling. The details were so much worse. I glanced at Slade, who stayed focused on the road, his palm hammering the wheel, the colors at his wrist flashing.

I wanted to fix this so badly, to ease his anger, bring back the boy who'd planned that tattoo with me. The one who for the greatest five months of my life had been my best friend, my favorite person on the entire planet, my addiction, my rock. In China, we couldn't have sat this near each other without touching. He would've glanced over at me every few minutes just to make sure I was there. I would've talked too much and teased him, trying to get him to kiss me.

The car went silent, everyone waiting for me to reply. The weight of their expectations mixed with my longing for Slade and his hatred of me. It densified the air, squeezing my outside edges, shrinking me into myself. My lungs burned. My mouth went dry. Words built in my chest, crushed into each other as I shrank smaller and smaller. One of my many therapists had called these moments *going over emotional threshold*, but it was more like I was crumbling under.

The words piled into each other, compressing into a fragile and pained corner next to my heart.

I cracked.

"I'm so sorry." I touched Slade's elbow. "I never meant to get you in trouble. To hurt you. To get you separated from Vinnie. It just happened. I'm so, so sorry. You have to know—"

He shrugged me off so violently my hand slammed into Lei's chest.

"Just. Shut. Up."

Chapter Six

Day 161 of 162 of the China Assignment
Changde City, Hunan Province, China

"No," I scream as the Chinese MSS officer grabs Slade by the back of the neck and throws him to the floor of the warehouse. Several of the other scientists' kids gasp. Someone is crying.

I'm crying.

Sobs shudder through my body. I can't breathe. The room, the MSS guards, the other scientists' kids, all of it swirls around me, terror feeding a full-blown meltdown. I'm caving in, collapsing.

Slade lies on the ground, silent, unmoving. Four guards point guns at his head.

"You don't understand. It came out wrong." I lunge toward Slade to put myself between him and the guns, but a guard blocks me and shoves me backward. Quentin grabs me around my waist, hauling me out of range.

I still can't stop talking.

"That's not what I meant. There's no connection. He was designing a tattoo, not practicing defacing anything. He's not like that. He didn't do it."

I elbow Quentin in the ribs, needing to get to Slade, but he holds tight. I can't breathe and the world's going hazy. "Don't hurt him. You can't hurt him. Slade, I'm so sorry."

Chapter Seven

Slade's words struck me in my corner of guilt and helplessness, exploding it in all directions. A tremor of physical pain coursed through my body, tears flooded my eyes, my heart shook, my breath came too fast. I fought it, sucking in the humiliation and waterworks, every last bit of it. No way could I fall apart. Not here. Not in front of Slade and the others.

The car went quiet a second time.

Slade dropped Quentin and me off first. I held myself together as I stepped over the rotting porch, battled the front door, and raced up the squeaky stairs. I slammed the door to my empty bedroom, grabbed my Newfoundland mug, slid to the floor, and cried.

And cried.

And cried.

And cried. I was the Three Gorges Dam with a leak. The Bay of Bengal in monsoon season. The kitchen sink of every single rental we'd ever lived in before I replaced the o-rings and washers.

Why couldn't I just keep my mouth shut? Why, oh why?

I pulled the blanket that wasn't mine off the bed and curled it around me on the floor, still holding tight to the mug. The fabric was all wrong, stiff with a chemical odor that made my nose ache.

Slade had trusted me in a way he'd never trust anyone else, and I'd trampled him.

I cried harder.

Eventually, I crawled over to my dresser to hunt up the bottle of pills that would knock me out. I hated taking them, or the anti-anxiety meds Desi badgered me about, as I was prone to side effects. But with my head churning like a waterwheel perched on the top edge of Niagara Falls, I wouldn't be able to sleep without them.

I woke in the morning, stiff, groggy, and with makeup smeared over my face. I dragged myself to the shower but only got a dribble of tepid water that ran down my face like more tears. I unscrewed the shower head and was blasted by a buildup of rust crusties. (I cleaned out the head and took a decent shower afterward.)

It was only when I was back in my room getting dressed that I thought to check the clock.

9:40 a.m.

My job interview was set for 10 a.m. (This was what came of not having my phone!)

I forced away the remains of my Slade-misery, raced through my hair-care routine, opting for a quick braid, and dressed in dark pants and a colorfully striped sweater that was casual enough for a pizza place.

I headed down the staircase, careful to avoid the squeaky steps. The moment I hit the bottom, Quentin stepped around the corner, one hand scratching at his neck, the other guiltily holding out my phone.

"No bargaining?" I nabbed it from him.

He combed his hand through his blond hair, muffing it up. "I was going to. But after all the crying you did last night, it would be cruel. Can you believe Desi is mad at *me* for the whole thing?"

"You told her?"

"She sent you like ten messages on the sibling chat already."

Quentin was the worst snitch ever, and I hated that he'd heard me crying, but at least it had been him and not my parents. Quentin didn't care about my meltdowns. My parents tried to care, but only when unavoidable.

Desi cared. Max and Solomon did as well, but let Desi handle me. The three of them had raised Quentin and me once the five of us were old enough to reject an ever-revolving door of nannies. From then on, Desi had been my self-appointed mental health guardian.

"She's insisting you call her. Which you'll need your phone to do." He shrugged. "I'm sorry, okay? I knew things were bad between you and Slade, but you're such a drama queen I figured it would play out. Then the rest of us would laugh at you, and it'd be over."

"I'm not a—"

"Yeah, you are. And Slade was always super chill. It's why you guys got along so well. That he's now not chill sucks. For you. And for me. Desi says—"

"Whatever." I didn't want to hear what Desi, *Madame Menace*, thought. Also, he was way more of a drama queen than me. *Monsieur Melodramatic.*

I stepped around him toward the front door, but he cut me off. "Look. Slade's got an in with the owner of the most amazing gym in Gander. It's like seriously old school, but it's in a shed behind the owner's house, so membership is invite-only. I was hoping Slade would drop a word for me."

Which Slade would've at one time. It'd been Slade who'd introduced Quentin to lifting weights.

I pushed past him. "Pretty sure I can't help with that."

"Want to go to church with Dad instead? I found a group that's meeting up Sunday morning for rugby, but Mom talked me into church." He said it craftily, way more the brother I was used to.

"How many churches?" I gave an automatic long-suffering sigh.

"Three. It's what I was going to trade for your phone."

"Fine." It was a fair bargain. Dad disliked going to church alone, so the rest of us took turns.

The moment I was outside, I checked my phone. No more texts or calls from Mo or the wyrm-netters. I ignored the sibling chat entirely, as nothing good ever came from there. I did have four texts from Lei.

Lei (CMSRC)

OMG, I'm so pissed at you.

How could you have run off like that?

Seriously, it needed to happen. Rip the band-aid, flush the wound. Slade'll loosen up now.

Lei and Slade had been on the same assignment in Louisiana before Slade and I met in China. I'd texted Lei for information on Slade at first. Then when things between him and me had turned out so great, I'd told her. Okay, I'd told her repeatedly. I'd liked talking about him, and nobody else in my world had known he existed.

> *Everything I did was for your own good. If I'd warned you Slade was in Gander, you would've been all stressy about it, making seeing him even worse.*

That she'd recognized my anxiety around Slade rubbed. I mean, it'd probably been obvious last night, but I still hated people noticing. *Meltdown Joey* wasn't who I was. Or at least it wasn't how I wanted people to see me.

I didn't reply to her, but removed the CMSRC designation from her name in my contacts. (We moved so often that I sometimes forgot who people were if I didn't have reminders.)

I stepped onto the porch as I finished. It buckled under my foot with a crash, sending me sprawling and my phone flying into the weeds.

"I'm graceful," I screeched. "This isn't me."

It was then that I noticed our family's CMSRC van sitting in the driveway with four flat tires. They weren't just pancaked, but slashed. Big gaping tears in the sidewalls.

***

Turned out it wasn't just our CMSRC vehicle that got its tires slashed, but every company vehicle. A total mafia-type hit job on everyone in Gander. Dad was furious, taking the whole thing personally since transportation fell under his jurisdiction. Mom cooked us a late breakfast of barley-eggplant pancakes. (Or at least that's how they tasted.)

This wasn't the first time draco-scientists had been targeted. We were checkerboards for looney-toon conspiracy theorists that liked to throw darts. Four hundred tips had already been called in on the tires, including someone saying they'd seen a UFO last night, another insisting the slasher had poisoned their dog, and several claiming that it was Dover's fault. (Whoever Dover was.)

Yup, that was how things rolled in the CMSRC world. I made a point of mentioning the wyrm-netters. Dad listened but decided it was just another nut-case.

I couldn't head over to Pizza Utopia until RCMP was done, so I texted Mo and then spent the morning doing house repairs. Mo sent me a to-do list in reply.

(1) *Don't worry about work. I've got you.*
(2) *Search King of Gander's Under-25 Social Life.*
(3) *Admire photos of Mo in his crown.*
(4) *Ignore comments on article implying Mo cheated to win. Written by a Durand cousin, you'll note.*
(5) *Text Mo compliments about the photos. Pretty please?*

Of course, I looked and then complimented him in spades.

It was lunchtime before Dad said I could walk over to work. Mo met me three stores down from Pizza Utopia. He wore the same pizza tee as last time, with a beige apron around his waist, and was biting at his lower lip worried-like.

"There's a problem." He drew me back the direction I'd come. A car honked at us, and Mo waved without looking or stopping. "A problem other than some loco decidin' the local tire companies need to have a good sales month. Actually, that's not even true. Buysco Superstore's offering to replace every single popped tire for free. Canadian Tire's matching them. Everyone's horrified this happened, and both Buysco and Canadian Tire are good people."

"Gander is good people. Does your uncle no longer want to hire me?"

"Oh no, not that." Mo gave my hand a reassuring squeeze. "Seriously, no call to worry about a job. I've gotcha there. It's Slade Adler."

I froze mid-step, my Slade-paranoia dropping over me like an ice-bucket challenge gone wrong. Or perhaps right.

Mo kept walking, forcing us to let go of each other. He spun on his heel. "Sorry, sorry. Did I drop that outta nowhere? I should've started by saying your friend Lei told me about the Adler guy goin' off on you."

Thank you, Lei. I frowned.

"Don't be mad," Mo continued. "I wasn't gossipin' about you. Okay, that's a lie. I was, but not to share. Lei picked up a pizza earlier, and I wanted to learn more about you. In a good way, yeah? You're all kinds of deadly awesome. So I dragged out of her how awful that Adler guy is."

"It's fine. I'm flattered you were interested. But Slade's really not—"

"Grand." Mo reached for my hand again. "Five minutes ago, he walked in with his family and ordered an extra-large Donair and a pitcher of Coke."

My gaze jerked toward the front of Pizza Utopia. "Slade's in there?"

"Dark hair, dark clothes, dark expression? Wearin' a tee for a band named Celsius Burns."

"That's his band." I owned the same tee. Crap.

Crap. Crap. Crap. Crap. Crap.

"We'll go 'round to the service door," Mo said. "Then you and I are goin' to do something about him. It'll be fun. Just a small bit of revenge. Something I've pulled on difficult customers we don't want coming back. Trust me, I got this. I can make Slade Adler stay far away from Pizza Utopia and you."

CHAPTER EIGHT

Day 161 of 162 of the China Assignment
Changde City, Hunan Province, China

The moment I'm back in our apartment and my parents are done yelling at me and each other, I grab my penguin, my blanket, and my framed photo of Slade, Vinnie, and me, and ball myself up on the floor between my desk and dresser to call Slade.

He's home. Mom said MSS dropped him off not long after delivering Quentin and me. It's the single thing that held me together while my parents yelled.

I fumble trying to pull up his number. Finally, his phone rings, and I rub my wet face on my sleeve to calm myself.

He doesn't answer.

He always answers when I call.

Always.

Which must mean Dr. Panozco has taken his phone.

I get his voicemail.

"Slade, I'm so sorry." I pause to choke on a sob, my words coming fast. "I don't know what happened. I didn't mean to talk so much, to get you in trouble. Please, Slade, you have to call me. Please. Just call me when you can and tell me you're okay."

When he doesn't respond, I call again. And then text. I go back and forth between the two, so that the moment he gets his phone back, he'll have proof of my remorse.

Fifty texts and so many voicemails that I shut down his account later, Mom walks in.

"Pack up," she says. "We're being kicked out of the country. Flight leaves first thing in the morning. Until then, you aren't to leave the apartment. MSS is watching."

"Is Slade okay?"

She shakes her head, my question irrelevant to her.

The moment she leaves, I hunt up binder paper and a pen to write Slade a letter, telling him how worried I am about him and how horrible I feel about us being sent away. How I don't want him to be blamed. How I know this is all my fault. The letter ends up seven pages long and quotes To Kill a Mockingbird, Persuasion, Fahrenheit 451, and Wuthering Heights. Hopefully, he'll read it, see my desperation, and write back.

"Quentin?" I ask, going into his room. He's on his bed, his attention on his phone. "How much do I have to pay you to get a letter to Slade?"

Chapter Nine

Mo took me around back to a gravel-strewn alley half-blocked by a big rig being emptied of furniture pallets with a forklift. Pizza Utopia was the fourth store down and had a large leafy tree with a picnic bench outside.

"So, about this plan—"

"Here's where we take breaks," Mo said as we passed the picnic bench.

"I'd rather just wait out here until Slade's family leaves on their own."

"I've got you, Joey Partridge. I'll even try not to swamp you again, which my best friend tells me I do to people." Mo tugged me through the back door and into the kitchen, where I was hit by warm, yeast-soaked air. In any other moment, the kitchen would've smelled delicious, but right now it was too much.

Just like Mo going all golden retriever with its eye on a just-thrown ball. (Maybe, he'd be *Monsieur Manic-puppy*?) At the same time, I liked that he recognized his own faults and was working on them. That was admirable. "What if instead we—"

"Hey, Uncle Gerald," Mo called out to an older guy chopping mushrooms a thousand kilometers per hour on a stainless-steel counter. Behind him, a massive brick oven roared.

"Hey there, b'y," Uncle Gerald said in a thick accent without looking up. (*Thank Eleos*. At the speed he was chopping and the size of his knife, I worried for his fingers.)

I had to put a stop to Mo's plan. Somehow. Slade didn't deserve to be targeted. I was the bad guy here, not him, and guaranteed Mo's plan would backfire and make things worse.

My phone buzzed. My brother Maxwell. Likely calling to get the gossip about the slashed tires. I hit decline. "Can we maybe—"

Mo led me through the kitchen to a hall and then a cluttery office holding a computer desk, chair, and a thirty-something guy related to Mo. (Same height. Same large, hookish nose. Same super-friendly smile.)

Mo nodded at him. "Uncle Charles. Joey Partridge. Proper introductions all 'round."

I pasted on my most winning smile and answered his questions about my background and availability. I tried to draw the conversation out in the hopes Slade would leave before we were done. Uncle Charles announced I was hired and handed me a packet of paperwork to complete and a Pizza Utopia tee. The whole thing took five minutes. Aghhh!

"C'mere," Mo said the moment Uncle Charles left the office.

"About the Slade thing, I'm grateful you want to help, but he's really not a bad person, and there's no need to put yourself out."

"It's no trouble." Mo motioned me over to a wall covered in white vinyl blinds and pulled the cord, giving us a view of the restaurant's dining space.

And Slade.

Who was seated with Dr. Panozco, his mom, and Vinnie at a table on the other side of the glass.

I dropped to a crouch, my fingers pressing into the cold of the floor tiles to keep from collapsing.

"He can't see you." Mo dropped down next to me. "It's a mirrored window."

My body didn't care. I froze up like the rental's back door before I'd WD-40ed it. My phone buzzed again. Max again. I managed to hit decline without falling over.

Mo touched my shoulder. "That guy really gets to you."

"He doesn't. It's all good. I was just taken by surprise. But let's not do anything to antagonize him."

"You know what I heard? Only one person connected to CMSRC didn't get their tires slashed. One. And that with the vehicles parked in garages and everything. Guess who?"

I leaned into the wall, glancing longingly at the door to the kitchen. "No way is Slade the slasher."

"You can't be sure."

I could. Slade wouldn't do something like that. Not even to me, at his angriest. Also, there was a logical explanation for the tire situation. "It's his own car, not a CMSRC vehicle. He must've driven up from Toronto. Everyone else has company vehicles."

"Still's suspicious. The one person who treats you like crap, and he escapes punishment."

"I don't know that the slashing was a punishment. Likely it was politically motivated." I forced myself up to my knees.

"Don't ruin this for me." Mo puffed out his chest. "I'm tryin' to pull off a protective male act to impress you with my manliness." He curled his arm to show off a bicep that might've been impressive if I hadn't spent months of my life drooling over Slade's.

I poked Mo's arm anyway. He was putting in effort here, and stupid as it was, I didn't want to diminish that for him. "Spectacular. But you don't need to—"

"Excellent progress."

My phone buzzed. Number three for Max. Number three decline.

Mo patted me on the shoulder and stood. "Here's what's goin' to happen. I'll take care of that Adler guy. You watch through the window. I swear he can't see you, yeah?"

"I don't want—"

"I'll dribble a pitcher of pop into his lap, and he'll stomp out lookin' like he peed himself. The security cameras will pick it up, and we'll mock him later. All of which that Adler guy deserves."

"Really, he doesn't—"

My phone buzzed yet again. A text this time. I automatically glanced at it.

Max

Would you please answer?

Mo stepped past me and left. No . . . !

Me

I needed to stop Mo. I *had* to.

Only, the thought of going out there, facing Slade so soon after last night, kept me in place. It was all I could do to peek over the edge of the windowsill.

Slade wore a Celsius Burns tee just like Mo had said. It had a sideways skull resting on crossed hands, as if dead and asleep. I'd never worn mine, not once, but Slade forming his own band was such a milestone I'd had to have one, even though the band was so new they were only doing covers. (Also, there was a good chance no one but me got the name.)

Slade popped open a box of crayons for Vinnie to choose a color. His mom sat across from him, her attention on Dr. Panozco. Dr. Panozco's mouth moved, shooting angry, rapid-fire words at Slade.

My stomach twisted into a pretzel flattened by a steamroller coated in broken glass. Dr. Panozco had a history of yelling at Slade.

Vinnie chose a green crayon. Slade slid out a blue one. Together, they went to work on Vinnie's placemat.

Dr. Panozco's mouth continued to snap open and closed. He shook his finger in Slade's direction.

Further out in the room, Mo headed toward the drink fountain with an empty pitcher. Sweat broke out along the back of my neck. I had to do something.

Max

Either you answer or I call the parents and tell them you secretly enrolled yourself in the University of Toronto and paid the $500 deposit.

Mom had enrolled me and paid the deposit for MIT. Dad had for Yale. Desi did the same for Berkley. Until this exact moment, I'd thought no one knew about U of T. I wasn't ready for them to find out, and Max didn't make idle threats.

A good enough excuse to flee?

No. I had to save Slade.

Max

Right now, Joey. I've got class in ten minutes.

I crawled over to the door and then jumped to my feet, prepared to run out into the dining room to . . .

Do . . .

Something.

Stop Mo. Distract him. Create a scene of my own that drew attention in my direction.

Including Slade's.

My body refused to go there. It was too much, a cliff edge teetering beyond *emotional threshold*.

Instead of the dining room, I bolted the other direction, through the kitchen where Uncle Gerald was now chopping peppers, and out the back door.

***

I was a horrible person. A chicken incapable of looking at the road it needed to cross. A glass neither half-full nor half-empty, but cracked down one side and leaking. A tree that not only fell silently in the woods, but landed in a campfire, scattered the cinders, and set the forest ablaze.

No wonder Slade hated me.

Outside Pizza Utopia, the forklift still unloaded furniture boxes from the truck, backing up with a *beep, beep, beep* that was only slightly louder than the thumping of my guilty heart. I collapsed on the picnic bench and dropped my head onto the table, trying to breathe and hold back tears.

My phone buzzed. This time I answered it, my hand shaking.

"Hey, Little Sis." Max, of course.

"Make it quick." Focusing on him and the call helped. Anything to not think about what was happening inside that restaurant. "I'm at work." (Sort of.)

"Look, I understand Aristotle Montague-Smith-Montague has been trying to reach you."

I choked on my own spit, gagging and coughing in surprise. "How do you know that?" But the answer was obvious. "Quentin told you."

I glanced at the forklift driver and then at the restaurant door. I wanted this conversation overheard about as much as I wanted to end up a Yale neuroscientist or witness Slade's humiliation.

"Actually, no. Aristotle himself—"

"You're being contacted by wyrm-netters too?"

"Would you just listen," Max growled out.

"Wyrm. Netter."

"There are no wyrm-netters. Aristotle is Aristotle. He's been my roommate at Stanford for the last two years."

The forklift returned to beeping. The driver picked up a sofa-sized box that listed to one side, an accident waiting to happen.

"Who are you and how did you get my brother's phone?"

He sighed. "Ask me something no one else would know."

"Where were we living when Desi left us for college?"

"Ghana."

"How about when Solomon left us?"

"South Korea."

"And the year Mom and Dad separated, and we had two households?"

"Bora Bora, then Papua New Guinea. Easiest move we ever had."

Okay. So this really was Max. "You're roommates with Aristotle Montague-Smith-Montague and didn't tell anyone?"

"He asked us not to, especially our sisters. Look, I've got two minutes before class starts, so listen up. Aristotle got hold of the CMSRC assignment docket and recognized Mom and Dad's name as being related to me."

"Then why didn't he call them? Why didn't you?"

"Have you met our parents? Robert Minh Quan tried reaching out to CMSRC, but—"

"Wait? That really was Robert Minh Quan who contacted me?" And, of course, that meant Sasha Clems would be real too. "No way."

"Mr. Quan needs help and is too paranoid to trust just anyone. Sasha talked him into a teenager since he trusted her and it worked out. She and Ari picked you because of me. Look, I gotta go, but stay put. I just texted Ari your GPS coordinates. Mr. Quan will be by in a moment, okay? And don't tell Mom and Dad. CMSRC blew Mr. Quan off. He's paranoid, feels burned, and doesn't want anyone official knowing he's around."

"I—"

Max hung up.

"—don't like this."

Something squawked above me in the tree, and I glanced up. A lavender draco dropped to the picnic table in front of me, wings spread, tail swishing. The same lavender draco from the branch outside my room.

Ummm . . .

What?

It fluffed its shiny wings like a girl billowing a skirt. Then it rose on its hind legs and deposited something small and black from its front claw to the table.

A USB drive?

The forklift beeped again.

The draco shot up into the sky in a burst of energetic flapping.

Was this a joke? Dracos didn't do things like this. (Only with Sasha Clems, they had.)

I picked up the drive. Blazed across one side in handwritten red letters were the words TOP SECRET.

Subtle much?

In the background, something made a shrieking, metal-on-metal crunching bang. The forklift still had its unbalanced box perched on the tines, but the driver had backed into the big rig. The perfect metaphor for my life.

The door to Pizza Utopia blew open, and Mo burst out, an elated grin on his face. "Best Bad-Busboy routine I've ever done. Just wait until you see the video."

Chapter Ten

Day 162 of 162 of the China Assignment
Changde City, Hunan Province, China

Slade isn't at the airport when we reach our departure gate. His mom, stepdad, and younger brother are. When I ask, Dad says Slade was packed off to his father in Toronto the night before.

It's Slade's worst fear come true.

Slade is not okay.

Because of me.

But also, it explains why I can't reach him.

CMSRC dumps us at my grandparents' house in Vancouver. The moment we arrive, I steal into their bedroom and use the house phone to call him.

I dial his number, holding the receiver so tight my knuckles turn white.

It rings. Once. Twice. And then stops.

I take a deep breath, fighting for calm.

"Yeah?" Slade's soft, familiar voice. My best friend's voice.

I burst into tears. Words gush out of me so fast, not even I understand them. "I'm so sorry. They took you away from Vinnie, and it's my fault, and—"

Click.

He hangs up.

And then I get really, really scared.

Chapter Eleven

I flat-out refused to watch the video, and when Mo pushed it, I threw his phone into the icemaker's bin. I didn't want to tick him off, though, especially as whatever Lei had said seemed to have convinced him Slade was some kind of monster. Meeting Slade in person had likely reinforced this, since Slade kept people at a distance by being threatening and scary. From that perspective, Mo's desire to protect me could be considered white-knight-ish.

I smiled at him and teased him while I confiscated his phone. In revenge, he hid my phone behind the bags of flour in the pantry.

From there on, I let myself have fun.

Sort of.

Or not really. Forgiving Mo was easy. I was an excellent forgiver. Not picturing Slade sitting there with Vinnie while being yelled at and waiting to be humiliated was much harder.

It wasn't until I was back home in my depressing bedroom and had collected my blue mug for reassurance that I considered the problem of the USB. I didn't want to look at it. Really, really didn't want to. I plugged it in.

It contained two documents. I clicked on the one titled READ THIS FIRST.

CONFIDENTIALITY NOTICE

By accessing, reading, or disseminating the contents of this or any further materials provided by Robert Minh Quan, Josephine Bridget Partridge acknowledges and agrees to hold the information contained herein confidential and privileged. Failure to adhere to these terms will result in legal action and financial damages.

Thank you for your cooperation.

Uhhh . . .

Wow?

With my inability to keep my mouth shut under pressure, I was the last person anyone should trust. I clicked on the PDF named READ THIS SECOND anyway.

Dear Ms. Partridge,

I write to you regarding an offer of employment. Key responsibilities include legwork in and around Gander and Trinity, Newfoundland, use of your connections within the draco-scientific community, and regular reporting of evidence collected via a secure method.

I glanced up at a *tap, tap, tapping* at my window. The lavender draco was perched outside again. The side of its snout pressed to the glass so that its eye bugged out.

"Can I help you?" I asked it.

It pulled its eye back and tapped several more times with a front tooth. I went over and struggled with the latch of the window to shove it open. There was no screen (shocking!), so the draco jumped onto the sill, cocking its head like a dog might do. Its tail whipped back and forth in the air.

"You aren't supposed to want anything to do with me," I said to it. "You know that, right?"

It cocked its head even farther, turning its face ninety degrees. Then it righted itself and threw its head up and wings wide in alarm, smacking the frame of the window.

The steps of the rental's staircase squeaked.

"Josephine?" Mom called.

"Hide!"

The draco launched itself back outside, and I slammed the window shut.

Mom pushed open the door without waiting for an invitation. "Did your father talk to you?"

"Not yet." I slid over and shut my laptop. (This wasn't even about Bob. It was just second nature to hide what I was doing from my parents.)

"CMSRC hired a car to drive a few of us to Trinity tonight so we can continue setting up the research stations. I'm going. Your dad is here until Sunday, when a bus arrives that will begin a daily circuit. I'll keep the family calendar updated with our locations. Text me if anything comes up. Questions?"

"Nope." Quentin and I were accustomed to parental abandonment.

Mom reached over and ruffled my curls in an attempt to be affectionate, even though I hated having my hair touched. (She meant well. Doting didn't come naturally to her.)

"Could you take a look at the dresser drawer in our bedroom?" she asked. "It's stuck."

"Sure."

"Both your dad and I appreciate how much you do for us, Josephine. You've become a lovely young woman. Ready for college." She smiled at me, her eyes bright, tender in her own way.

"I'm ready." I smiled back. "Hey, Mom? I was hoping I could talk to you a moment? About something I've been thinking about lately."

"Slade Adler?"

My breath hiccupped in my chest. I'd hoped to bring up U of T.

"It's okay," Mom said. "Dr. Panozco warned us he was here. We didn't want to make a big deal of it, but Desi called and said you'd had a run-in."

Desi was *such* a menace. She'd filled our sibling chat with questions about Slade too. I was ignoring her.

My parents had never liked Slade. Nor had they known what'd been going on between him and me in China. They'd thought I was his tutor, which we'd encouraged. When things had ended, Mom and Dad (and Desi) had blamed Slade for everything, including the mess I'd become for several months afterward.

"Desi says she can find you someone to talk to if needed," Mom continued. "We don't want a repeat of last time. Not when your dream of MIT is just months away."

"Thanks, but I'm good."

She pressed her lips together, fighting between showing more motherly concern and a need to be her usual forceful self.

"I mean," I jumped in to make it easier on her, "I appreciate that you worry about me, but I'm fine. It's not like I'll see Slade much. When I do, I'll stay far, far away."

Mom nodded and grinned. "For MIT."

"Right."

The moment she left, I closed my eyes and ran through the first twenty digits of pi. Once done, I reopened the window for the draco and returned to the email.

The goal of your employment is to determine if and how someone may or may not be attempting to interfere with the incubating Draco marinus shuck. The veradracos and I are concerned for its safety. Due to my own personal limitations, I am unable to pursue the matter myself. Additional information will only be provided after the agreement has been signed.

In addition, my and the dracos' involvement must remain confidential. If a suspect and proof of a crime are confirmed, you will notify the authorities and protect the shuck in such a way that I and the dracos stay anonymous.

Your salary will meet the minimum level required by the Province of Newfoundland and Labrador. However, should the investigation end well, you can pursue media attention and additional financial opportunities at your own discretion.

The media attention on its own was a deal-killer. CMSRC employees and family were supposed to keep so far under the radar we resembled overfed puffins trying and failing to fly ourselves out of the ocean.

Nor did I need money. My parents had been saving for my (and each of my siblings') impressive college careers since birth.

And if the shuck was in danger, that was call-the-Armed-Forces serious. Or call the newspapers. Or call Greenpeace. The last person anyone should be calling was me.

To accept this offer, click on the below document-sign link and complete the nondisclosure agreement. Upon your signature, you will be sent a secure cellphone delivered by Ramoth, whom you've already met. She'll be your primary direct contact.

"Ramoth?" I looked to the lavender draco. Dracos didn't have names. Or genders. Biologically even. This was well known. Sasha Clems had named the giant one that had helped her, but the consensus of the entire planet was that it was an affectation of hers, not a thing. Apparently, the entire planet was wrong.

Ramoth hopped up on her back legs. She was cute in a charming, childish way. Her color and her mannerisms did seem feminine. Which was another oddity to add to my mental list. I'd never once heard anyone say dracos had mannerisms.

"Hi, Ramoth. I'm Joey."

She looked me right in the eyes and batted her lashless lids. Then she hopped down to the floor and poked her head into the trash bin.

"I should be freaking out right now. Why am I not freaking out?"

As if she understood me, Ramoth did a half-leap, half-fly to my bed and flicked her forked tongue my direction. Two small puffs of orange flame popped out of her nostrils, each the size of a lit match.

So cute.

But not a reason to accept Bob's job offer.

Even apart from the publicity issue and my inability-to-keep-my-mouth-shut issue and the seriousness-of-the-situation issue, I had zero experience being a private investigator or whatever it was Bob wanted. And while I liked that Max was behind me in this, my parents wouldn't be. My parents would freak if they found out and do so right when I was trying to butter them up about U of T. (My personal issues were way less important than the extinction of a foundational planet species, but there I was.)

"Bob needs to find someone better."

***

Ramoth must not have liked my answer. She became my personal draco-shadow, showing up outside the hardware store on my home repair shopping expedition, on my visit to the local dance studio, on my walks to and from Pizza Utopia, on my breaks, and outside my window pestering me to let her in anytime I was home.

Pressure much?

"You're going to be seen and linked to me."

She sat on my bed watching me get ready for Sunday churches.

"This is a bad thing. CMSRC has minimal-disturbance protocols. I'll end up in trouble."

Ramoth flicked her tongue and snorted flames. (Yes, I'd replaced the batteries in all seven of the rental's smoke alarms in case of fire accidents.)

"I'm dead wrong for what Bob needs. He should ask one of the researchers. Or if it has to be a teenager, then Lei. Or the twins. Or even Quentin. Okay, not Quentin. But surely there's someone else."

I applied gloss to my lips, wanting to look good for my outing with Dad. I wore a loose, gauzy dress that was a tad short, but the weather outside was summer-gorgeous, and I loved sunshine and fresh air on my legs.

Churches could also be great ways to make friends.

It wasn't about that for Dad, of course. His goal was a quality organ that lacked anyone who could properly play it.

"No following me, 'kay?" I put my hands on my hips and looked down at Ramoth, aiming for a firm expression. Ramoth flicked the tip of her tail back and forth like she was mimicking my (fake) stern vibe.

"Josephine, are you ready?" Dad called up the stairs for the tenth time.

I grabbed a pair of ballet flats but paused before heading to the door. "None of this even makes sense. Why does Bob want *me*?"

"Josephine?" Dad called again.

Ramoth lifted her head, stretching her neck its full length.

"Please, just stay here. Pretty please?"

She glanced at the window. Guaranteed she would follow.

"The All Angels congregation seems the most promising," Dad said as we walked out the front door. I stepped carefully over the porch steps. I'd replaced the broken boards, but the memory of its collapse hadn't faded.

"Three manual case from the 1920s," Dad continued. "Most of the pipes are original." He wore a suit and his good-luck shoes, off-white oxfords polished to a high shine. Dad had strong opinions about dressing for church, one of his rituals.

"That does sound promising," I replied to be encouraging.

Church number one (not All Angels) was a disappointment. The building was rundown, and not in a charming way. The organ was single-manual and out of service for broken stops. Also, there wasn't a person present under sixty.

We stayed for the service anyway. Dad was a full-on atheist, but showing respect was important to him.

The moment we left, I spied Ramoth sitting on a fencepost bordering the parking area.

I grabbed Dad's arm. "Look!" I pointed dramatically in the opposite direction.

Dad turned. "At what?"

"Oh, nothing. I meant it as an exclamation."

He blinked his eyes at me in bewilderment.

I did my usual and started talking. "Solomon told me that the University of Toronto has fantastic science programs for undergrads." Solomon had never once mentioned U of T, but Dad missed conversational details like an ostrich, head-first in a hole, missed lions.

"U of T is the top medical research university in Canada," Dad said.

"It's the best university overall. And the cost is way cheaper than a US school. Both you and Mom have contacts there."

"It could be a good choice for collaboration opportunities for Solomon," Dad said, picking up the wrong thread of what was important here. "Dr. Panozco taught there recently. If Solomon needs a recommendation, I'm sure he'd be happy to give one."

Dr. Panozco had taught at U of T several years ago. Slade's mom had been the Draco Sciences department secretary. It's how they'd met. Not that any of that was relevant to what I was trying (badly) to accomplish here, but my brain rambled when under stress. "You should ask Dr. Panozco his opinion on U of T. I'm sure he has glowing things to say."

"He preferred Yale. Did you know he, like me, did his undergrad at Yale? Speaking of Yale, have you looked at the admission checklist yet? I forwarded it to you several weeks ago."

And there went the conversation. Dad rattled on about Yale until we arrived at our next church. Ramoth landed in a tree out front. A turquoise draco the same size joined her.

Reinforcements?

Great.

They looked down at me with their heads identically cocked. I made a cutting motion with my hand across my neck. "Please go away."

"What?" Dad asked.

"Nothing. I mean, we should hurry inside. The services must be about to start."

Ramoth waved her front claw and snapped her jaw, mimicking me. The turquoise draco disappeared into the leaves of the tree.

The second church was also disappointing. The *organ* turned out to be a Yamaha keyboard and speaker. The pastor offered to let Dad play it, but Dad declined with a disdainful sniff. The congregation was even older than the last church.

No sign of the dracos when we left. Which meant Ramoth was lying in wait somewhere.

All Angels was plain on the outside, weathered-looking with a peaked gray roof, white siding, tall steeple, and stained-glass front doors that were propped open. The sound of a piano playing "How Great Thou Art" drifted out. An excellent sign. Dad walked faster.

Ramoth winged in to land on the corner of an eave, my own little lavender gargoyle. I fake-glared at her.

Something white drifted down from the roof. A feather?

Nope. A piece of paper similar to the ones I'd found on my bed. I nabbed it before it could hit the ground.

Up on the eave, Ramoth shook her shoulders and ruffled her wings. A woman in a tweed suit pointed upward. "What a cute little dragonette. It's been a while since I've spotted one in town."

I hurried Dad inside while unfolding the note.

Ramoth likes you.

That was it. Nothing on the back. Just those words. The writing, the same as before.

Okay? I liked her too.

Dad beelined through the vestibule and past the other churchgoers seated in the pews of the nave. (A number were my age this time!)

The entire front wall of the church was embedded with silver pipes nestled into white wooden pipe racks. The console, also white, sat to one side against light blue walls. Super pretty in a contemplative way. Not that contemplation was what Dad cared about. I liked it, though.

A woman in a crocheted pink shawl plunked out "Nearer my God to Thee" on an upright piano. She hit a wrong note, and I winced. Provided the organ was in working condition, the pastor would likely be thrilled with Dad's offer to play for their Sunday services in exchange for practice time when he was in town. (Dad was really good.)

Before Dad could corner the pastor to convince him of this, the music faded to a halt. Dad did an abrupt turn and settled onto the nearest pew.

I sat next to him. Lei slid in on my other side.

Crazy thing, but I wasn't even surprised to see her. It was just that kind of day.

I shoved the white note into my pocket.

"We need to talk," she whispered.

Dad gave us both disapproving looks.

Lei cleared her throat. "If you'd just answer my texts."

"Control yourself, Miss Tien," Dad whispered.

"Later," I whispered to her, and then to keep from upsetting Dad, I gave my full attention to the pastor.

Or at least I pretended to.

I preferred the more formal churches like this one, the restfulness of the services, especially. The music and the pastor's voice usually made the hamster in my head leave off running in its wheel and take a nap. Today, I missed the entire sermon and ignored the music in favor of worrying about that note and whatever it was Lei was here to hassle me about. (Or more likely, who.)

The moment the service ended, Dad jumped to his feet and exited the far side of the pew to accost the pastor. I turned to Lei to get whatever was coming over.

"An opportunity has arisen," she announced. "With Slade."

"Lei . . ."

"Just hear me out."

"Slade hates me." I stepped over her to exit the pew.

Lei followed me down the aisle. "You need to change his mind."

"Why do you even care?"

"I don't."

We passed through the vestibule where several people stood behind a table with coffee and cookies. I nodded a polite greeting at them and kept going. A teen boy held the exterior door for us. He had trimmed blond hair that was smoothed down and parted to the side, a long face, and glasses. Super cute in a nerdy, quiet way.

First impression: Possible friend opportunity. If I didn't already have a kind of thing going with Mo, I might've even been interested. (Yes, I'd prefer to focus on a random cute boy rather than Lei and her obsession with Slade.)

The boy handed us each a flyer for youth group. We kept walking.

No Ramoth outside.

Yet.

Lei directed me to the lawn. "My mom hired Slade to drive me to Trinity tomorrow. I'm taking a suitcase to her because of the fire and—"

"What fire?" That thought was immediately overrun by another. "Wait. Slade forgave you for forcing me on him?"

Lei shrugged. "He doesn't hold grudges for things like that."

My heart gave a dull, wounded thud in my chest. "The fire?" I muttered to change the subject.

"One of my mom's new spectrometers shorted and started a kitchen fire in her Airbnb. No injuries, but it's a mess. I'm surprised your mom hasn't asked you to bring her stuff too, as she was staying in the same place. Everyone's clothing is toast."

"Pun intended?"

Lei scrunched her eyebrows together and gave me a blank look, not getting my joke, which was lame anyway.

"My dad's heading to Trinity tonight. He'll handle it."

"Come anyway," Lei said. "This is your chance to be normal around Slade. I won't bring up any of the awkward stuff, and then you'll—"

"No." I stepped back from her, putting up my hands as if to ward off evil, which this totally was. (Although if I looked at the situation from a positive direction, it was possible Lei really thought she was helping.)

A high, thrumming squawk sounded from somewhere in the sky, like one of the shorter organ pipes slowly going bad. A draco squawk.

Both Lei and I looked up.

Ramoth skimmed over our heads, dropping something our direction.

Another note?

I grabbed Lei's arm to distract her. "When it comes to Slade—"

Lavender chunks of draco dung splatted all over Lei's runners. An overwhelming smell of sulfur mixed with refuse attacked my nose. Ramoth bolted.

Lei shrieked and jumped from one foot to the other. "That draco just pooped on my new shoes!"

I backed away from her, pinching my nose. Yes, the odor was that bad.

From out of nowhere, a white note landed on my head. I grabbed it while Lei frantically wiped her feet on the grass.

Answer your phone.

"I just bought them last week," Lei screeched, continuing to hop around, oblivious to the note. "I'm going home, but you *are* coming tomorrow."

No, I wasn't.

Lei dashed off in the direction of her rental.

My phone buzzed with an incoming call.

Chapter Twelve

Twelve days after the China Assignment
Vancouver, Canada

"Joey, you aren't okay." Desi leans against the doorframe of my grandpa's office, back lit by a square of blinding light. She flew up from Berkeley after Quentin tattled that I wasn't leaving the house. My parents believed me when I said it was lingering jetlag. Not so much Desi.

I lay curled on a sofa bed under a scratchy blanket. The blinds are pulled, the room as dark as I can get it. I called Slade fifteen more times. In response, he blocked me, Quentin, and my grandparents' house phone. I'm not okay at all.

"I'm fine," I tell Desi.

"No. You aren't." She comes farther into the room, a blond, equally competent version of our mother. "You discovered boys and latched on to the first messed-up one you could find. Mom and Dad were too oblivious to notice, and the rest of us too late to stop it. You got sucked in and became overly emotionally dependent."

"That's not what happened."

"It's exactly what happened. It ended badly, and you got hurt. But Joey, you're sixteen. It was always going to end. Trust me, you'll find someone else. Someone better for you."

She's wrong, I'm not her, and Slade isn't exchangeable. He's the ground beneath my feet, my rock, my everything. I pull the blanket over my head.

Desi tugs it down. "You're depressed and need to talk to someone. I'll find a therapist."

I don't need to talk to some stranger. I need to talk to Slade.

And then it strikes me.

Slade and I need to see each other in person, where we can look at each other face-to-face and touch. He'll never resist forgiving me if I can touch him.

Chapter Thirteen

I didn't answer the call.

Nor did I listen to the voicemail that the caller left. Nor the second voicemail. Or the third. Or fourth.

Guaranteed the caller (Bob, Sasha, or Aristotle, possibly all three) would hard sell me on signing Bob's contract. Since I lacked the talent for surviving human steamrollers and other such flattening equipment, better to avoid the lot of them.

Only when my phone buzzed with a text, I automatically looked down as always.

Unknown Number

> *It has to be you because Ramoth has decided she likes you.*

"There are plenty of other people in this world for you to like," I said to the open sky outside of the church, even though Ramoth had disappeared after the poop incident. I returned inside to see what could be done about freeing the poor pastor from Dad's attention and getting us out of there. Halfway through the vestibule, my phone buzzed again. I looked again.

Unknown Number

> *Ramoth convinced the other dracos and the shuck to like you too.*

Which made no sense at all. Even if Ramoth had convinced her turquoise friend that I was a decent human being, the shuck was an egg. It didn't have the ability to like or dislike someone.

I heard Dad's voice in conversation with another person. Not the pastor.

Dr. Panozco?

It sounded just like him. Uhhh . . .

I promptly got another voicemail.

I powered off my phone to end the arm-twisting and peeked cautiously into the nave. Dr. Panozco and Dad sat in the back pew facing each other. I couldn't see Dad's face, but Dr. Panozco wore a frown and a white lab jacket. I stepped back so they wouldn't see me, but stayed to eavesdrop. (Second nature for Partridge kids.)

"Why does canceling the bus service make any difference?" Dad asked, sounding confused. "It leaves us stranded in Gander until the tires are replaced."

"At fifteen grand a day?" Dr. Panozco snapped back. "All spent on a single shuck that we can't even examine up close. How many water samples need to be taken? How many people are needed to run pH tests or scan the ocean floor with Dr. Tien's spectrometers?"

"Geraldine has hopes for finding some new parasitic organisms. And we want to monitor for other draco species in the area."

Dr. Panozco huffed. "Better if our resources go to more important research and we leave the shuck alone."

It all sounded just like Dr. Panozco. More than once, my parents had complained about him adjusting the CMSRC budget to get more money for the projects that interested him.

"Once the research vessels arrive—" My Dad started.

"Once the research vessels arrive . . ." Dr. Panozco said, cutting Dad off. So rude. "We'll verify that the shuck is where Sasha Clems left it. Then that's it. Nothing more to do since we can't go near the thing."

"But the bus—" my dad started, still sounding more confused than objecting.

Dad needed to object.

I needed him to object.

Mom needed her suitcase of clothing. If he didn't object, get that bus back on schedule, and go to Trinity himself . . .

I shuddered. I'd rather face a category 5 tornado (or listen to the voice-mails from the Aristotle/Sasha/Bob combo) than take Mom's suitcase to Trinity with Lei and Slade.

Dr. Panozco continued. "I'm right on this. None of what we're doing here is scientifically relevant. All these people. All this money, and it's a PR stunt. CMSRC is being used to make the politicians look good. I won't have it."

"The government would never—"

"Of course they would."

I hadn't previously thought about it that way, but Dr. Panozco was right. Calling in all CMSRC personnel was crazy overkill. Most assignments had two or three CMSRC scientists mixed with researchers from other countries. But gathering us all together did make it look like the shuck situation was under control. I'd also heard that the attention was bringing in hefty donations to our program and getting grants approved.

"I told Geraldine I'd bring her additional clothing," Dad said. "She's counting on me. The bus must be rescheduled for tonight."

Exactly what I wanted to hear.

"No," Dr. Panozco answered, firm and decided. "Dr. Tien has hired my stepson to take her daughter down with her belongings. Send one of your children as well. And . . ." he paused, and when he spoke again, his voice was hard and low, "send your daughter. Slade has been told several times that it's past time he apologized to her for his behavior in China. Send them together. You make sure she goes. I'll make sure he expresses his regrets."

Noooo . . .

***

There was no way Slade would ever apologize to me. He didn't owe me an apology. He knew it. I knew it. There was no danger of an apology ever happening.

But being told he *had* to apologize would tick him off.

Which I was going to get to face.

Turned out Dad, who barely knew Slade, really liked the idea of him apologizing to me. The more I protested, the more insistent Dad became.

I gave up and texted Mom to ask if Lei could take her bag. When Mom didn't respond, because turns out Mom's phone had been destroyed in the fire, I begged Quentin to go in my stead behind Dad's back. Quentin refused as he'd gotten a job at a kids' sports camp and started in the morning.

I holed up in my room to plan out an outfit for dying slowly over a two-hour drive. Ramoth showed up, tapping her tooth against the window. I let her in, too worn out to do anything else. She flew to my desk, snatched up my phone, and threw it at me. I looked at her in confusion. She looked at the phone.

Oh. Got it.

Apparently, she understood the concept of *unplayed voicemails*.

"I can't. Believe me, I really, really can't." I sniffed, fighting tears.

She cocked her head and scrunched her eyes so that her upper lids pointed to the ceiling. Made her look disappointed in me. I hated people (or dracos) being disappointed in me. Disappointment was a younger sibling to anger and yelling and rejection.

I collapsed onto my bed and told her about Slade and why I was so upset and the list of several thousand disasters that could happen if I drove with him. Once I'd talked myself out, I took a sleeping pill, grabbed my blue mug, and curled up on my bed. Ramoth perched on the back of my chair, watching me. (She'd better not decide to poop indoors.)

The next morning, I walked over to Lei's rental, pulling Mom's suitcase. Ramoth followed overhead, throwing small rocks in my path for unknown reasons. If she was trying to hit me, her aim was terrible.

"Is there something I can do for you?"

No response.

My outfit had turned out great. Skinny jeans low on my hips, a cropped white cami that showed off my belly, an unzipped wool fisherman's sweater, and runners on my feet. I'd even spent extra time turning my hair from its usual half-frizz into ringlety curls.

Not that any of it would matter.

This was a second Halifax Explosion in the making.

Ramoth was still pestering me with badly thrown rocks when I arrived at Lei's rental. "I promise to listen to the voicemails tonight," I called up to her, "if you'll go hide somewhere Lei can't see and stay there."

Ramoth bolted for a tree, burying herself in the leaves.

That'd been suspiciously easy.

Lei stepped out of her rental with her mom's suitcase and handed me a lime green wristband that matched the new green color of her fauxhawk.

"Put it around your arm. Then anytime you're about to say something that will upset Slade, snap it against your skin. The pain will distract you."

Not a bad idea.

Slade's faded Honda came into view. I took a sharp, panicked breath. Lei reached over and snapped the wristband.

"Owww," I yelped. "That hurt."

"Worked, didn't it?"

It had.

Or at least it did right up until Slade got out of the car. Today's tee was for The Tragically Hip. He'd tied the front of his hair back so that the fade on the sides was super obvious. It made him look edgy and smoldering in a Slade kind of way. Back in China, I would've run my fingers through the shaved parts just to get a feel.

I twisted my fingers around the handle of Mom's suitcase. Lei snapped the wristband again, and I yelped again.

"Just act natural. Be yourself. He liked you once. We need to get you both back to that." Lei grabbed her mom's stuff and headed down the drive. I followed, my stomach doing an improv swing dance with every step. Ramoth poked her head out between the leaves of the tree, looking pointedly at the car and Slade.

I stopped mid-step.

No.

No. No. No. No. No.

Please not now. Not him. Not more poop.

"Hey," Lei said to Slade.

"Hey." He went around the back of the car and popped open the trunk.

I shook my head frantically at Ramoth and pointed at my cellphone. If she did a single thing to him, I *wasn't* listening to those voicemails.

She ducked back into her tree, *Thank Eleos.*

Slade hefted Lei's suitcase as if it was packed with feathers, the muscles of his upper arms going super defined with the motion. Nice!

"Hey," I said softly.

He ignored me.

Right.

Tension twined around my bare midriff and innards. I snapped the wristband as Slade packed up Mom's suitcase and slammed shut the trunk. Ramoth did a draco scream.

"Joey, you should sit—" Lei started, but I rushed to the back seat before she could finish and force me up front. Once in place, I snapped the green band so many times my wrist went numb.

Slade got in and started the car. Lei took the passenger seat, turning in his direction. I waved goodbye to Ramoth to be polite.

"Did you hear," Lei said, "that Joey got into MIT, Yale, Columbia, Cornell, Berkeley, and—"

The car filled to overflowing with the screaming-singing of AC/DC. That I recognized the music was due to Slade. He really loved old-school metal bands. And nu metal. And death metal. And avant-garde metal. Pretty much anything and everything that had the word metal in it, and the angrier the better. *Thank Eleos and Her small mercies* for the overwhelming sound of metal. Conversation was officially impossible.

Lei gave Slade a sideways glance of annoyance and then pulled out her phone to entertain herself. I did the same but didn't open mine. I couldn't. Not with Slade so close. His ink was fully covered by the sleeve of his tee, but his eyes were right there in the rearview mirror.

I loved his eyes, even when they were crinkled into his habitual frown. The color was unusual, a feathery walnut transitioning outward to sparks of darker brown.

Celsius Burns's promo photo was of all five members against a white wall. Slade's eyes had come out the most amazing honey gold. Every once in a while, when I was sunk particularly low about what'd happened and missing him, I apologized to that photo while staring into his golden eyes.

They looked the same color in the mirror.

I snapped the wristband. No way did I want to get caught staring at him. I took another quick glance anyway. And then another.

The drive to Trinity was lovely. Newfoundland was built like a piece of paper that had been scrunched into a super-tight ball and then re-flattened as best as possible, before being layered with trees and all the low spots filled with water. The cove holding the shuck was shaped like a face down, ragged 2 that connected to the Atlantic. All of it just gorgeous.

We passed through an RCMP checkpoint where we each had to provide our CMSRC Family IDs. This wasn't normal, but also not unexpected given the importance of the shuck. There was a camp of over a hundred RCMP personnel here to protect it and keep tourists and other looky-loos out.

The trees gave way to rocky, grassy hills with square houses painted in vibrant hues of green and blue and mustard and red. The town of Trinity was straight from an 1800s seafaring novel. Tidy, windswept buildings. White picket fences. One-lane roads. Cemetery with lots of leaning headstones. Population one hundred and ninety.

The shuck sat several kilometers away at the top of the 2, so security was minimal in the town itself. The road ended in a short wooden pier where two CMSRC research vessels bobbed gently against their moorings. They must've recently arrived, as the day before, Dr. Panozco had implied everyone was still waiting on them.

Slade stopped next to a restaurant bordering the dock where everyone here from CMSRC was gathered for a luncheon. We'd made it. And without anything bad happening at all.

I jumped out of the car and was hit by a breeze, the soft *lap-lap* of the ocean against the shore, and the call of gulls. No people around, but chatting voices came from the direction of the restaurant. Slade removed our suitcases for us. (Yes, I admired his muscles again.)

"I'll wait here." He looked at Lei, still ignoring me.

Lei and I pulled our suitcases toward the restaurant. Slade got back into his car and shut the door.

"You could've at least tried." Lei gave a massive sigh. "He would've turned the music down if you'd said it hurt your ears."

"He'd likely have turned it up."

"You have such a bad attitude."

The restaurant was small, decorated with beams scavenged from ships and vintage seafaring wares, and held only a handful of CMSRC employees since everyone else was stuck in Gander. Mrs. Tien hurried over.

No sign of my mom.

I took a sharp breath. Guaranteed she was out by the shuck, and to reach her, I'd have to ask Slade to drive me. Kill me now. (Slade would likely want to.)

"Your mom's finishing up on the research vessel." Mrs. Tien took her suitcase from Lei.

I brightened. "At the dock? I'll head there."

Phew.

I pushed Mom's suitcase against a wall and headed toward the dock and the research vessels covered in antennas and other such equipment sticking out in all directions.

Slade had turned off his music and rolled down his window. His arm rested on the sill, his hand beating out a rhythm only he could hear. I crossed to the far side of the road, my way of being courteous, mannerly, diplomatic, and distantly polite. A heavy sadness drizzled through me at the necessity of doing so.

We'd only had five months together, but they'd been the best five months of my life. It was hard to put into words just how important Slade had become to me. If only I could find a way to apologize, ease his anger, and—

The world exploded in a massive whoosh of cracking sound and light and heat and pressure. I flew backward, my feet ripped from the ground, and slammed back-first to the road. The world exploded a second time, and my head struck the pavement with a thump that propelled my brain into my eyeballs. The world faded to black with small pinpricks of bursting lights around the edges. Like really tiny stars. Pretty!

I studied them, trying to figure out what had just happened.

Maybe I was dead . . . ?

"Jojo, talk to me." The words were insistent and arrived in Slade's voice.

Using the nickname he'd given me in China?

I loved that nickname!

Yup, I must be dead.

I watched the blinking stars. They didn't seem to have a pattern to them. I liked patterns. It's why I was so good at math, even though I hated math. I'd *rather* be dead than take any more advanced Calculus classes.

"Pulse is steady. You're breathing. Don't try to move, 'kay? I need to figure out where the bleeding's coming from."

"Deceased," I murmured as Slade's fingers ran lightly through my hair, caressing my scalp. He was one of the few people I didn't mind touching my hair. Or pretty much any other part of me. "Buried. Done for. Perished. Expired. Pushing daisies. Liquidated."

"Scalp wound." Slade let out a relieved sigh. "You'll need stitches. But it won't kill you."

"Sorry to disappoint."

The stars spun in a circle, revolving faster and faster. Was this the pearly gates? Any afterlife where Slade wasn't yelling at me couldn't be hell.

"Jojo, what's the date?"

"November 15th." If this was heaven and I got to relive my time with Slade, I knew exactly when I wanted to go. "Bank of the Jinbianxi Creek. You paid Quentin to take Vinnie for a walk. We're sitting under a tree near a stream, and I'm utterly terrified even though this was my idea. You reach over, run your fingers down my face, and kiss me for the first time. You're so gentle. It's the most perfect moment of my life."

Slade made a choking noise, like he had a wishbone stuck in his throat. "I meant today."

Today? I fought to remember, but the stars were too much of a distraction. "Mmmm . . . Sunday . . . maybe?"

"Right," he said very matter-of-fact. "Concussion. Stay still. I'm going to check the rest of you."

He pulled my sweater open and skimmed his hands down my sides and over the bare skin of my middle. His touch tickled pleasantly.

"You were always the best kisser," I mumbled, as he moved to my right arm and then my left. I always talked too much to Slade, but it's okay. He'd once said he liked that about me, and he was a great listener. "Better than Bayani. Or Duarte in Brazil. Duarte played bari sax, but he was terrible. I bet you could pick up a sax and you'd be better than him. Duarte was a great boyfriend, but you're definitely the better musician. And kisser." I sighed. "My brain hurts."

He ran his hands down my legs. "Other than the back of your head, you seem to be in one piece. The head's going to get worse."

"We could try kissing to see if that helps."

"You talk too much."

"That's what I just said!" Or had I? Maybe I'd just thought it. Also, Slade was supposed to like my rambling. He'd once told me so. This was confusing. I tried to flutter my eyes open, but my lids stuck.

"Is she alive?" someone not-Slade yelled. It was my mom, actually, and for reasons I couldn't quite remember, relief swept through me that she was here. "What happened?" she demanded.

Great question. I started to turn her direction, but Slade locked me in place with a hand on my chest. "Don't move. You could still have a spinal injury."

"She broke her spine?" my mom screeched.

"We're treating it as a spinal injury." Slade's voice went all calm and authoritative in a way I'd never heard from him before. "Until we know otherwise." It was also a lot of words for him in front of my mom.

I tried opening my eyes again, but the stars had glommed together into a massive ball of painful light that rose and subsided in pace with my heartbeat. A heartbeat that also pulsed in my ears. I latched on to the hem of Slade's tee, balling my fist to hold on. "I'm fine." The words reverberated painfully inside my skull, making me suddenly, violently want to vomit.

"You're not fine," Slade said.

I swallowed hard, fighting to keep my stomach in place. No way was I upchucking in front of him.

Which thought led to the realization that I wasn't dead, this was actually happening, and I'd asked Slade-who-hated-me to kiss me.

Bile rose in the back of my throat. I jerked over onto my side, knocking Slade away so that I could bend forward.

Slade lunged to support me from behind, one hand under my head. "I told you to hold still."

I gagged and heaved and shook, but nothing came out. This was still my worst nightmare come true. (But at least my spine was intact.)

Slade swept my hair out of the way, still supporting me. The moment I was done heaving, he drew me backward until I rested against his chest, my body between his knees, one of his arms around my shoulders, the other around my waist.

I leaned into him, the most familiar move of my life. We'd sat like this a million times. It was like coming home. (Not that I'd ever had a home or even really experienced one.)

I pried open my eyes against the blinding light.

Slade and I sat circled by CMSRC scientists and restaurant employees. Beyond them, where there once had been two gray-colored research vessels, was now water, smoke, and half a scorched pier, all of it littered with flaming chunks of metal. The acrid stench of burning petroleum permeated the air.

"They blew up," I said, stupidly.

Slade tightened his arms around me.

I jerked my gaze toward my mom. "You were supposed to be on that boat."

Slade breathed into my hair, even, steady, intentional, as what must've happened became suddenly real.

My mom shook her head. "I left just minutes ago. I was around back, unpacking the trailer. Whoever did this waited until no one was on board."

"They were watching us," Mrs. Tien said. "Probably still are."

I looked wildly around, my head throbbing and my stomach dizzy.

Slade was like a rock, my rock. His chest rose and fell against my back, the heat and the steadiness of it holding me together. I matched my breathing to his, just like I used to do in China, and clutched his sleeve.

Mrs. Tien stepped closer. "They knew we were having this luncheon and that we'd all be inside and the vessels empty. Someone worked hard to make sure no one got hurt."

Just like someone had gone to an effort to cancel the bus from Gander so that my father and most of the other scientists wouldn't be here when it happened?

No.

Nope.

No way. That was an errant, non-useful thought that I should never have had and that needed to go away immediately. It was probably the result of my pounding head.

Only it wasn't.

I became suddenly aware that a pebble was jamming into my left butt cheek. My wrist, where I'd snapped the wristband, ached. Slade's hand rested against my bare belly, his thumb stroking back and forth, sending tendrils of warmth spiraling around my skin.

I should've been over the Moon, Mars, and Jupiter that we were touching. Instead, I slammed my eyes shut and tightened my hold on his sleeve.

No way could Dr. Panozco be involved in whatever had just happened. Just the thought made me want to hurl again. It was ridiculous. I was totally reaching.

"Pain getting worse?" Slade murmured into my ear.

Pain, as a description, didn't even cover it. Foreboding, prognosticating-disaster, handwringing, gut-deep anxiety was much more accurate.

CHAPTER FOURTEEN

Eight weeks after the China Assignment
Toronto, Canada

The outside of Slade's dad's building is rundown and dirty, with trash spilling from an overflowing bin onto the sidewalk. The ground-floor store has several FOR LEASE signs in the window that have faded from red to a mottled orange. (No judgment. My family has lived in way worse.)

My mom was asked to speak at a U of T seminar right before we leave for our new assignment in the Philippines, and I talked her into taking me along. Finally, I have my chance to see Slade in person.

I'm a nervous wreck. I can't eat. I haven't slept well in forever.

This has to work.

I buzz Slade's dad's apartment on the street-side intercom, the sound painful in my ears. I'm prepared to beg him to let me in, but the door pops unlocked. That's a good sign, right?

The building has no elevator, so I climb the staircase to the third floor, practicing my apology.

Everything will be fine. He won't be able to resist me in person.

I knock on his door, the sound light, my hand shaking.

The door opens.

Slade.

Right there in front of me.

So familiar in a Black Sabbath tee, his dark hair pushed to the side, his mouth in its habitual frown. I choke up. I've missed him so much.

His eyes flicker with surprise before lowering into a dark glare. He swings the door shut in my face.

I block it with my foot. "Please, Slade. You have to listen to me. You just have to."

He hesitates and lets me push the door open but also crosses his arms, blocking me from entering. His expression is grim. His eyes narrowed. His jaw clenched.

That's how he tends to look. It doesn't have to mean anything.

"I'm so sorry," I start, but all the perfect words I prepared disappear into a jumble of whatever wants to get out first. "It just happened. I wish it hadn't. I wish I'd kept my mouth shut. You were so worried about Dr. Panozco sending you away, separating you from Vinnie, and it's my fault, and I'm so sorry. Please. I told everyone who would listen that you were innocent. The Chinese police, my parents, CMSRC, everyone, but they didn't believe me. They thought I was lying. You have to know how very sorry I am."

He stares at me, silent and forbidding. All very Slade.

"Please. Would you let me come in? Let me apologize?"

"I never want to see you again."

"I'm so sorry—"

"Go away, Jojo." His voice rises with heat. The cords of his neck show in sharp relief under his skin. He grips the door so hard, it looks ready to crumble.

Slade is always calm. Always. And cool. He never gets upset. Ever. Or yells.

He gets louder and snarlier. "Stop hounding me. Stop trying."

I flinch with each word.

"Please, Slade." It bursts from me with a renewed desperation. I reach forward to touch his sleeve. We spent so much time touching. "I need to know—"

"I don't care what you need." He shoves my hand away.

I begin to shake. My heart races. My breath comes in short, loud bursts. I plow on anyway.

"You have to forgive me. You just have to. I'm begging you."

He slams his fist into the wall next to the door.

I jump.

The sheetrock gives. Slade jerks his hand free, and blood streaks his knuckles. Everything about him screams violence, fury, hatred. Uncontrolled and savage. As opposite to the boy I know as humanly possible.

He's a stranger.

Red flags everywhere.

Someone so deadly and dangerous that my throat caves in, my heart stammers and trips, panic churns in both my head and stomach, and for the first time since the day we met, I'm afraid of him. I try one more time anyway. "Please . . ."

"Leave. Me. Alone."

The last of the air expels from my lungs in a single burst as if he's hit me like he had the wall. Tears well in my eyes. I know he sees them.

Slade refolds his arms. A drop of crimson falls from his knuckles to the floor. His lip curls in a sneer.

I know in this moment that I'll never fix this. This stranger, this Slade, is not the boy I love. This Slade hates me in a way I didn't even realize existed.

I turn on my heel and rush down the stairs and out of the building.

I return to the hotel where my mom and I are staying, shut myself in the washroom, and cry harder than I've ever cried in my life. I cry until I'm hysterical, can't breathe, lose all sensation in my body, think I'm going to die, and finally pass out on the floor next to the toilet.

Chapter Fifteen

The nearest paramedics were over an hour away, and the 911 operator said my injuries weren't serious enough to call in a helicopter. Trinity's RCMP officers decided Slade should drive me to the hospital in Gander.

I took the passenger seat, a white bandage around my head to control the bleeding. Lei and my mom sat in back. Slade played a string of slow, relaxing songs set to ocean waves and chirping crickets. When I finished the first bottle of water he handed me, he wordlessly gave me another. Every time I closed my eyes, he nudged me with his elbow.

This was the Slade I knew. My best friend.

However . . .

All his lack of animosity would take a nosedive into the foulest gutter of the dirtiest city I'd ever been to if I pointed a finger at his stepfather. Especially a false one, which guaranteed it would be since that was how my life worked. And since Slade'd been with me at Trinity, he'd be pulled into my false accusation. The whole China cataclysm would get re-dredged. Slade'd be blamed and lose any hope of being with Vinnie. It'd be all my fault.

Which was beyond paranoid.

But not that paranoid. Not after China.

And yet . . .

If the bus had been canceled to keep everyone in Gander, then the tires must've been slashed for the same reason. The situation was too serious to stay silent. Those explosions could've killed my mother, and the shuck did seem to be in danger.

I couldn't do nothing.

Which left a growing headache and . . .

Bob.

Slade stayed with us at the emergency room while I got an official diagnosis of a mild concussion, a strip of the back of my head shaved, and eight stitches. (I had so much hair that the loss of a strip was pretty much negligible.)

After we collected a bottle of heavy-duty pain meds, Slade drove us to our rental and walked us to the front door. Ramoth sat across the street, watching with her head cocked in interest.

Mom went in. (Yes, I'd fixed the sticky lock.)

"Thank you," I said to Slade, keeping my eyes on his chest where a streak of blood was smeared across his tee. Another thing I'd ruined for him.

"Sure."

I waited, hoping for more, something like *let's be friends*, or *I just realized I don't hate you after all*, or the entirely improbable *let's drop everything and make out*. I got nothing, but his lips were straight rather than their usual stern downturn.

No way was I messing that up.

***

Voicemail #1: "Hey Joey, this is Sasha Clems. In case you haven't noticed, the dracos are learning. It started with Bob and a spell gone wrong that lets him participate in the way dracos communicate. I won't bore you with the details. Every time Ari tries to explain it to me, I fall asleep. Anyway, Bob started communicating with dracos twenty-ish years ago. He set rules on what he said to them, but that all fell apart when they helped me. Well, that and the books. Ari thinks Bob reading them books was the real game-changer, but doesn't want to hurt my feelings by saying so."

Voicemail #2: "Not long after I left the shuck in Trinity Cove, the dracos started complaining to Bob that people were sneaking in at night to see it. This stopped once RCMP got security set up. Only then it started up again, and the shuck told the dracos who told Bob who told Ari." Pause. "Ari says to tell *you* that the shuck is not sentient, it's magical." Another pause. "Don't question this. If you do, Ari will give you a two-hour lecture that you'll walk away from more confused than before. Personal experience on my part. So no to sentience, yes to magic. More importantly, if the shuck is telling the dracos something is wrong, then something is definitely wrong."

Voicemail #3: "Which is why Ari and I talked Bob into reaching out to CMSRC. When they ignored him, he put CMSRC at the top of his suspect list, which is more about being snubbed than because he has any proof. Anyway, next Ari and I talked Bob into you as someone with access to both CMSRC and Trinity, and whose family was still in Scotland when the problems started. When the CMSRC tires got slashed, we almost changed our minds about bringing you in because we don't want anyone getting hurt, but by then Ramoth had decided you're the best thing since Anne McCaffrey wrote her first *Dragonriders of Pern* book, which, yes, Ramoth named herself after.

"I can't tell you how big it is that she likes you. The dracos put up with Bob. They like that he reads to them and explains the human world, but they don't really like him. The shuck, back when it was a semis, never liked me at all. Maur still regularly asks if he can fly to California and eat Ari."

Voicemail #4: "Somehow you charmed Ramoth. She had Bob explain the concept of *friendship*, and now every single draco in Newfoundland insists you're the only human they will work with because you're their friend and the rest of the humans are not. So please, sign Bob's contract. The dracos won't accept anyone else."

Voicemail #5: "One more thing. Ari says to tell you that your modeling of the concept of *distractions* to the dracos was likely a bad idea. We're pretty sure Bob did a terrible job of explaining how you kept your dad from noticing them. So sorry about your friend's shoes. Bob had a talk with Ramoth about that, but since she successfully made Lei Tien leave, it's highly unlikely Bob got through. Ari also says to be careful overall what you teach them. They tend to pick up the wrong lessons. And remember, sign Bob's contract. Please."

CHAPTER SIXTEEN

Day negative 1 of 162 of the China Assignment
Air China Flight 063
Vancouver International Airport

"Hey, can I squeeze by you?" I say to the boy in the aisle seat after shoving my carry-on into the overhead bin. Quentin, Mom, Dad, and I are last-minute additions to the flight and have middle seats scattered around the plane. Middle seats are the worst.

The boy doesn't answer. He's about my age, is dressed in a retro Iron Maiden tee, has headphones over his ears, and is staring down at his phone, avoiding engagement from other passengers.

Fair enough. I've used that tactic myself.

I still need to get past. I tap him on the shoulder. He takes his time looking up, and I shift from one foot to the other. "Middle seat." I point at the place I need to go.

He doesn't make eye contact or remove his headphones but does stand so I have space to shimmy past. Once we're both seated, he closes his eyes and folds his arms. Everything about him says, don't mess with me. A clear line in the airplane aisle I have no intention of crossing, and not just due to plane etiquette. It's been a while since I've met someone so covered in red flags.

I'm bored, and fifteen minutes after we take off, my earbuds die. The charger is in the front pocket of my carry-on, which is in the overhead bin. (Rookie mistake.) I glance at the boy. He hasn't stirred, not even a tiny shift. No way am I disturbing him.

I play with my phone, put on some lip balm, and eventually pull out my school tablet and open my Calculus homework. I hate math, but it needs to be done, and no one in my family has ever received less than an A in a STEM subject.

Two hours later, I can't take any more math. I'm also reasonably sure the boy next to me is fake-sleeping since he hasn't head-slumped a single time.

I really want a look at his face. There's something compelling about him in an edgy, dangerous way. (I could be wrong about this. I have very little experience with boys that don't share my DNA.)

To distract myself, I trade my tablet for a CMSRC brochure on China. I skip past all the cultural stuff and go to the phonetic dictionary to do a quick memorization of the common words of civility.

"You're CMSRC?"

I swing around at the soft, even voice.

The definitely not-sleeping boy looks at me from clear brown eyes. Startling clear, even, especially against his pale skin, dark hair, and lashes.

His face is just as interesting as I'd thought. His nose is thin. His mouth blade straight. His cheekbones and jaw, defined. Not what I'd normally call attractive. He's kind of grim, actually, both rough and sharp at the same time. Shark-like. As if getting too close to him wouldn't just cut flesh but tear.

His dark brows quirk up in challenge at my studying him. His upper lip curls into a sneer.

More red flags.

"Shì de," I reply anyway.

Chapter Seventeen

The voicemails were a lot. I listened to them seven times to make sure I got everything. Ramoth perched on the back of my chair and nodded her head at important points.

What I didn't do was freak out.

No trouble breathing, no tension in my muscles, not even excess saltwater in my eyes. Since no one was yelling at me, disappointed in me, or leaving me, my anxiety was uninterested in the situation, and my *emotional threshold* so distant it was like searching for the eastern end of the Great Wall of China from Prague.

Honestly? I liked Sasha Clems. I almost, but not quite, regretted not taking her calls in the first place.

I signed the contract.

Nothing happened other than Ramoth snorted tiny flames of joy and whipped her tail back and forth.

Nothing happened the next day either. Or the next. This was likely because my new pain meds made me drowsy, and the ER doctor suggested I sleep them and the concussion off. Which I did, and Ramoth witnessed. She only left my side in those moments when Quentin or one of my parents thought to check on me.

Bit anti-climactic.

In my awake periods, I told Ramoth about the explosion and how great Slade had been. I didn't tell her my speculations on Dr. Panozco or that one of my primary motivators was to prove he wasn't involved. Seemed best to keep that to myself.

I heard through my parents that not much changed at Trinity other than RCMP going Parliament Hill-level security and putting watches on nutters worldwide. I told this to Ramoth so that she could inform Bob.

Mo called daily, keeping me entertained and telling me not to worry about work. He also texted to see if I wanted to postpone our date.

Dating was one of the things that had helped me after China and Toronto. My family had transferred to Cebu City in the Philippines, and Desi had badgered me into meeting people. (Better said—meeting boys.)

For once, she'd been right in her advice. Focusing on others rather than my Slade-misery had slowly made things better. After a couple of tries, I'd met Bayani, a shy, sweet guy who'd just been through a breakup himself. We'd hit it off, and even though he hadn't been Slade, we'd liked each other.

Leaving him for a new assignment in Brazil had been tough, but I'd almost immediately met Duarte. Duarte had been the opposite of Bayani (and Slade). He'd been high energy and a terrible sax player but hadn't cared as long as he was having fun. He'd loved to dance and had taken me out almost every night. We'd spent our time together at clubs with his extensive group of friends. Our first kiss had happened on his boat moored under a huge tree.

Duarte also hadn't been Slade, but he'd kept me too busy to get stuffed up in my own head.

I replied to Mo with a giant flashing *Let's Go For It* GIF.

Dating Mo had the side benefit of him being he-who-knew-all-the-gossip. Mo was potentially a resource, and our date an opportunity for digging.

On the evening of our outing, I took a ton of non-drowsy painkillers to manage my headache and guilted Quentin into making Nanaimo bars for dessert. (Quentin was the only person in our family who made food that wasn't better off in a compost pile.)

Mo arrived in an old truck that, back in its heyday, would've been green. Now it was a faded yellow, had a large Pizza Utopia label on the door, and an 'In Cod We Trust' sticker on the back. Just as Mo's original to-do list had promised, it was indeed the oldest vehicle I'd seen in Gander. The driver's door shoved open with a groaning creak.

"Where's the party?" He wore a navy tee and khaki shorts. His hair was tousled. His expression huge and happy and puppy dog-ish. Just looking at him left me more energized than I'd felt in days. (Admittedly, I'd been asleep most of that time.)

"No party on this street," I replied, smiling back. "We definitely want to go elsewhere."

He laughed and pulled my hair to the side to examine my injury. "Man, I'm sorry you got hurt. This is supposed to be the friendliest place goin', not the most dangerous. I apologize from the lot of us."

"Not your fault, but feel free to make it up to me anyway."

"That a challenge?"

"If you want it to be."

His eyes sparked with excitement. "Grand. I never turn down a challenge."

"Game on then."

"Done, but this needs to be a multi-date challenge. Making things up to Joey will take some planning. No complainin' when I ask you out again."

"Never." And I meant it.

Mo laughed, grabbed my hand, and led me to the passenger side of the truck. Once there, he put a shoe on the side and used both hands to yank on the door handle. It opened with a clunking pop. (Several spritzes of WD-40 would likely help.)

I added the Nanaimo bars to a basket sitting in the center and climbed in. Once I was settled, Mo slammed my door so hard it rattled my teeth, which were way too close to the ache in my head that I was trying to suppress. I winced.

"Sorry," he yelled as he trotted around the front of the truck. "It won't stay closed otherwise." Mo climbed in, buckled in, and after several tries, convinced the engine to start.

"So, who does local gossip say blew up the boats?" I asked, since it was the obvious thing to talk about, even if I hadn't been fishing for info.

"Same people who slashed the tires. Other than that, gossip is split four ways."

"Four suspects?"

"Four groups of suspects. There's the rich lookey-loos, which seems unlikely, but there's been a bunch of them comin' and goin' on their yachts outside Trinity. There's also the developers who want to turn the seadragon birth into a commercial enterprise. Then the anti-dragon agitators, for obvious reasons, yeah? And the scientists themselves, although no one has a half-sane reason for them."

"Definitely not the scientists." The rest of his information was helpful.

I'd heard about the lookey-loos. Yachting up to Trinity to stare at the cove that held the shuck had become a thing for them. They weren't allowed into the cove itself, although they kept trying to slip in. In fact, some of the visitors observed by the dracos could be them. I made a mental note to tell Bob.

The anti-draco groups were regulars at major CMSRC projects. They liked to protest against CMSRC, magical-creatures, and magic-handlers under the mistaken belief that magic was evil, given to the world by whatever version of wicked-incarnate they feared, and destroying humanity. They were loud, but generally harmless.

"Tell me about the developers." This was the first I'd heard of them.

We drove past the Gander International Airport. Mo turned down a street for a memorial park on the far side.

"They want to rebuild an old, closed-down theme park near Trinity and turn it into a draco-destination with ATV and boat tours, draco-themed hotels, that kind of stuff. Locals are dead against it, and nothin' is happening with the Mounties in charge. I heard that since the blowup, RCMP tightened things right up."

"I heard the same." A group of developers might see preservationists like CMSRC as obstacles, but blowing up research vessels? Not sure how that helped them. It was still something. I added them to my list for Bob. "What about a guy named Dover?"

Mo gave me a puzzled look as we drove down a bumpy, gravel road.

"CMSRC got several calls blaming him."

Mo's eyes lit with a sudden humor. "That's just someone messin' with you."

Now it was my turn to look puzzled.

"Dover's Fault? Get it? The fault that runs under Lake Gander. It's the go-to culprit for everything."

Got it. I laughed and shook my head.

Mo stopped the truck with a lurch in a gravel parking lot. "The party is here. Or at least our party. Party of two, just for you. Come, my child."

I exaggerated a groan at the horrendous endearment but also smiled at him.

Mo battled my door again. This time I helped by shoving from the inside with my shoulder. It gave with a sudden clunk. Mo staggered backward, fighting to stay on his feet.

"My hero." I let out a saved-princess sigh and hopped down.

"This way." He grabbed the basket and a blanket from the truck and led me down a path through the forest to a small, cleared area near Lake Gander. (And its fault, apparently.)

Trees towered above. A beach of rounded stones sloped gently downward. The descending sun sparkled on the water. Somewhere in the distance, a woodpecker *peck-peck-pecked*, and a soft breeze caressed my skin and made the trees rustle.

All of which presented a problem.

Every single one of my first kisses had happened in a pretty location with trees and water. Four boys total, although the second had been barely a peck and maybe shouldn't count, and Slade's was worth ten if not a hundred of the others.

Still . . .

Four similar locations.

Four first kisses.

It was a thing.

Mo was great. I liked him. Maybe someday. Not today. Today was *way* too soon.

How bad of a date would I be if I asked if we could sit somewhere else? Like in his truck?

On the other hand, it's not like he knew about my first-kiss location ritual. I was overthinking things and made a conscious decision to let it go. There would be no kissing happening here.

Mo flung out the blanket to catch the air and spread it wide. Once it settled to the ground, I stretched out the corners until it was square. I'd just finished when a shadow crossed over the top of our heads.

Please be a seagull. Or osprey. Or Canadian goose. Or even a bald eagle.

It wasn't.

Ramoth did an aerobatic roll through the trees to land on a branch where she was clear-as-day visible.

I quickly sank onto the blanket, facing her, spreading out so Mo was forced to put his back in Ramoth's direction. Ramoth threw a walnut-sized pine cone at me. I caught it and tossed it aside.

The moment Mo bent to unpack our meal, I mouthed a desperate plea to her and clasped my hands together in what she'd hopefully understand as begging. She leaped backward several trees and perched behind a bushy green shrub. *Thank you,* I mouthed.

While we ate, I told Mo all my best living-abroad, moving every five-to-six-months horror stories to entertain him. This was also the best way to make sure he was aware of my ever-revolving expiration date without me directly talking about it. Which I didn't do. Period.

"What's something most people don't know about Newfoundland?" I asked, both to let him have a turn to talk and in the hopes of bringing the conversation back to the explosions.

Mo launched into a story about polar bears hitching rides on ice sheets, spotting the Newfoundland coast, and swimming over to take up residence until Fish and Wildlife sent them back to where they belonged.

He was a great storyteller, but polar bears were not what I was looking for. To keep the conversation going, I told him about the penguins in the Falkland Islands. I tried to use that as a jumping-off point to bring up tourism overdevelopment, but Ramoth kept distracting me with more pine cones. She was clever about it, picking moments when Mo wouldn't notice.

"Newfoundland seems like a great place to grow up," I said in another attempt to turn the conversation as we finished up Quentin's dessert. (Which was delicious!) "I mean, since popping car tires and blowing up boats aren't the norm."

"Definitely not when someone gets hurt."

"So, if someone was blowing things up, they'd be careful to make sure there were no injuries?"

He gave me an odd look.

Right.

Odd question. I smiled flirtily at him. "That was a joke. Bad one."

Ramoth rustled her wings loud enough to make me look up. She sat back on her haunches and lifted her front leg. A drawstring black bag the size and shape of a cellphone hung from her front claw.

Now?

No. Not now. The moment Mo looked away, I violently shook my head at her. She could wait until I was back at the rental.

She swung the bag in a circle, whacking it against a branch.

"You hear that?" Mo started to turn Ramoth's direction.

"Nope. Don't hear a thing." I nudged his leg with my hand to distract him. (No wonder Ramoth had picked up the concept of *distractions*. I did it a lot.)

Mo's eyes widened with surprise at my nudge. A pleased smile slid across his face. He covered my hand with his own.

Oopsss . . .

Total wrong message sent.

He looked deep into my eyes.

I automatically looked back.

He leaned in until we were inches apart. His eyes sparkled. The corners of his lips quirked. I resisted an urge to squirm (or bolt). My vision blurred. He became more blob than boy, and my headache thumped in complaint.

And there was my perfect excuse to exit myself from this unintentional, deeply uncomfortable, romantic moment we (or at least he) seemed to be having.

"Hey, my head's starting to hurt. I think I left my pain pills in your truck. Could you run up and grab them?"

"Your head's botherin' you?" Mo didn't leap to his feet in a heroic effort to help me as hoped but pressed his brows together in concern. He also leaned back, which stupidly made me feel guilty. It wasn't his fault I'd unintentionally led him on.

"Concussion." I pointed at my forehead.

"I thought you were better."

"I am."

"Not if you have a pounder." He bit at his lower lip.

"I'm fine, really. I just need to take a couple more pills."

"I'd better get you outta here." Mo jumped to his feet, his tone filled with worry. "Joey, I'm so sorry."

"I didn't mean we should leave." I tugged on the edge of his shorts to encourage him to sit back down. Which was counterproductive to my no-kissing goal, but he seemed genuinely shaken. No way did I want him getting upset. "I want to talk more. About Newfoundland. And all the interesting people that live here. Like you."

"Remember my list? The one that ended with a giant explosion of fireworks?" He took my hand, pulled me to my feet, and began folding up the blanket.

Ramoth lobbed the black bag at Mo's head. I twisted sideways, pretending to have lost my balance, and knocked into him but caught it no problem.

Mo grabbed me around the waist to hold me steady.

"Sorry, sorry. Moment of clumsiness." I shoved the bag behind my back. Yes, there was definitely a phone inside.

He tightened his grip. "I meant the fireworks thing literally. The airport has a problem with dragons layin' on the tarmac after dark, and there's a plane arriving tonight. The airport's goin' to set off a bunch of fireworks to move them along. If your head's already hurting, we got to get outta here."

***

Ramoth totally could've waited to give me the cell. It wasn't like I would've talked to Bob in front of Mo anyway. Ramoth just liked to cause trouble.

She flew into my room the moment I returned home and perched on the back of my chair, cleaning her claws with her forked tongue as if nothing unusual was going on at all.

"That my date with Mo got ruined is entirely your fault," I said as sternly as I could manage. "Friends aren't supposed to ruin things for each other. Friends are supposed to be supportive."

She cocked her head and blinked her eyes all innocently.

"If you want to be my friend, you need to be nice to me. Which means not throwing things at me or messing up my dates. And I'll be nice to you too. If there's something you need from me, I'll do my best to give it to you."

She gave a charming little shake of her wings. No idea what that meant.

"Fine, I give up." I flopped backward onto my bed. "Ramoth, you're too cute and I'm terrible at boundaries."

I powered on the bright yellow phone from Bob, and a fingerprint symbol appeared on the screen. I touched my thumb to it, and then when a text screen popped up, I typed out the info I'd learned from Mo, figuring that this was what I was supposed to do. Five minutes after I hit send, the phone lit up with an incoming call.

"Took you long enough." Bob's voice was deep and gruff. I recognized it from our previous conversation. He also sounded peeved and was much better at it than me.

My shoulders stiffened. "I just got home."

"Ramoth says you've been off playing at a park. What are you, five?"

I reached for my Gander mug. Not sure what I'd been expecting, but him being mad at me wasn't it. "I'm actually—"

"No, don't answer that," he snapped. "I know your age. More importantly, I want you to listen."

"Of course. I'm here to help." I said it in my best conciliatory voice. Had I offended him somehow? Did he not like me? He didn't even know me. "But could you not yell at me?"

He made a sharp *hmph-ing* sound. When he spoke, nothing in his voice had changed. "The night before those draco-dolts got their dinghies blasted into a million pieces, four men took a rowboat onto Trinity Cove."

I sat up on the bed, crisscrossing my legs, the phone in one hand, the mug in the other. This was good. Great, even. Dr. Panozco had been in Gander. "Who was it?"

"If I knew that," Bob barked, "I wouldn't need you, would I? One of the dracos saw the boat and the men. They were dressed in black with hoods on. They pulled the rowboat out of the water, put it in a shed, and drove off in a white sedan. Or possibly a green sedan or a beige one. Dracos aren't good with human objects. Could also not have been a sedan, although the draco insists it had four wheels and stank, so definitely motorized. This also may have occurred a couple nights in a row, as several other dracos claimed to have seen the same thing after the first came forward. It's impossible to tell if the additions were telling the truth or repeating the story, as they don't get the difference between fiction and fact. Either way, you're going to look into it."

"Absolutely. The dracos know where the rowboat is stored?"

"Bingo. The girl is smarter than her SAT scores make her out to be."

He didn't have to be so rude. I'd done nothing to deserve his meanness. (Also, I'd gotten a 1560 on my SATs. Nothing to be embarrassed by. At all.)

Bigger problem. "I don't have a way to get to Trinity. I don't have a car." I held my breath, waiting for him to skewer me for that.

"I'll rent you one."

"I don't have a license."

The line went quiet.

Ramoth reached down to play with the top handle of my dresser, swinging it back and forth so that it clanged.

The silence stretched uncomfortably long.

Too long.

"You could ask a draco rather than me," I finally said. "Ramoth's extremely capable."

She batted her eyes and flipped the tip of her tail, looking pleased by my compliment.

"I want pictures," Bob growled. "Their front claws don't have the flexibility to do more than carry objects. Maur can fly you out there."

Maur was the very large draco that had helped Sasha Clems.

"Dracos will do that?" My voice hitched with surprise. But also, flying with a draco? That would be so cool.

"You'd be the first. I'd have to come up with something for you to ride in and impress on him the consequences of letting go. Dracos recently discovered the joy of throwing objects. If I explained—"

"No." I said it firm and final. "I'll find a ride on my own."

"That does seem the simpler solution."

Chapter Eighteen

Day negative 1 of 162 of the China Assignment
Air China Flight 063
Destination: Beijing

"I don't speak Chinese," the boy says in a soft, slow voice while I rack my brain trying to figure out who he is. CMSRC is a small organization. Very few people know it exists. He must be connected somehow, but I know every CMSRC family member between the ages of twelve and twenty-five.

But not him. I'd remember someone as intimidating as him. My worst nightmare.

I still have to be friendly. (It would definitely be unfriendly to point out that it's Mandarin, not Chinese.)

"Are you American?" I know most of the US kids too.

"Canadian."

Then it strikes me. "Oh, wait. Did your mom marry Dr. Panozco last spring? My parents attended the wedding." And came home saying Dr. Panozco would have his hands full with his two new stepsons. According to Mom, the elder stepson showed up wearing a tee and ripped jeans instead of a suit. (Admittedly, my mom had worn a white, strapless, formal gown, also entirely inappropriate for someone else's wedding.)

"Yeah." He packs a 1930s Dust Bowl lack of enthusiasm for the happy event into the single word.

"Welcome to the CMSRC family."

He looks at me, his gaze steady, his mouth straight, his brows furrowed. Nothing about this boy is even slightly inviting, but since he's new to CMSRC and the rollercoaster expat life, I have a moral obligation to charm him. Also, I just believe in being nice. It's what I do. "What's your name?"

"Slade Adler."

"Joey Partridge."

I let the moment hang, hoping he'll take a turn with our conversation.

He doesn't, just keeps looking at me as if I'm missing a major facial feature or something.

"Where's home? Mine's supposed to be Vancouver, but other than a year when I was nine, we only go to visit my grandparents."

"Toronto."

"My mom speaks there at conferences occasionally. I've been to the airport and the university."

"What music do you like?" he asks abruptly. So abruptly that it occurs to me he isn't good at this. Small talk, that is. It doesn't come naturally to him, but for some reason, he's making an effort with me. My cheeks pink with pleasure, and I say the first thing to pop into my head, as usual.

"Taylor Swift."

I wince.

The headphones, the band tee, the question itself, all of it announces loud and clear that he's one of those music-expert type people. The kind who can recite lyrics to any song and only listens to esoteric bands. He's going to skewer my choice. "She's really fun to dance to." My cheeks deepen from pleased-pink to full-on-embarrassed-red.

He purses his lips, but calmly. As if he's paying close attention to what I said and thinking it through.

I tense.

"Good choice." He lifts his chin in my direction. "She's talented. Have you heard Light's 'Little Machine'? You'd like it too." He slides off his headphones and places them on my head, smoothing my curls out of the way all careful-like and without a single pull. "Listen."

And I know.

Right there and then, as an excellent female singer croons into my ears, I absolutely know. Something I've always hoped to happen but never has before.

Slade Adler is going to be my best friend. I'm going to be his. We're going to be inseparable, and it's going to be wonderful. I saw red flags where there weren't any. He isn't a shark. He's a guppy.

Chapter Nineteen

I couldn't ask Mo to drive me to Trinity. He wouldn't be able to get through the security checkpoint. It had to be someone with a CMSRC Family ID.

Slade would have an ID, but no way. Lei didn't drive, so she was out. Neither did Quentin.

Which left Tabby and Isa. They'd both mentioned that they drove. Whether they had access to a car with functioning wheels, I had no idea. I also needed a reason for the trip, especially as the GPS coordinates Bob sent were closer to the shuck's location than the town of Trinity. I needed an excuse to go out there.

I played with a couple of ideas out loud while taking a damp cloth to Ramoth after she knocked over a can of soda I'd left on my desk and got her tail all sticky. She slithered against the cloth in pleasure, making humming noises and occasionally puffing out smoke.

By the time she was clean, I had a single Joey-is-bonkers-crazy idea. Sometimes the bonkers ideas were the ones that worked, and at least Isa and Tabby, as part of CMSRC, were used to crazy.

The next morning, I fixed Mom's stuck dresser drawer, changed out the filter on the heater, downed a full dose of non-drowsy painkillers, and snuck out of the house while Ramoth wasn't looking. (Ten bucks said she followed me anyway.)

It was a thirty-minute walk to the Maldonado-Flores rental, which was fine. I passed a large brick community center, two aircraft-outline statues that doubled as jungle gyms, and numerous houses. People waved to me from passing cars as I walked. I waved back. One woman with a minivan full of kids pulled over to ask if I needed a ride. Living in a friendly town was awesome.

No Ramoth either. Surprising.

I passed the local Buysco Superstore, skirting around the parking lot. Just past the store entrance, fifty or so protesters stood in a group holding signs and bullhorns. I detoured their direction to see what was up.

A guy in a knit vest held a sign that said 666 in giant red letters. A woman held one that read, *Extermination is the Answer. Why let them breed more?*

An anti-draco rally?

Perfect.

Because . . .

Suspects!

Also, so glad Ramoth wasn't here. I wouldn't want her seeing this.

The man holding the bullhorn looked familiar. He was tall with slicked-down hair and wore a white shirt and suit pants. The pastor from All Angels church? Yup.

The blond boy who'd given Lei and me flyers for youth group was there too. He held a handwritten sign that read, *I saw a beast rise up out of the sea, and upon his heads the name of blasphemy.*

Bummer. No way could I befriend someone who disliked dracos.

Gander was an odd place for them to be protesting. Then again, they were unlikely to be allowed anywhere near Trinity. I took pictures with the yellow phone, making sure to include a sign that said, *Hell: Where the wyrms don't ever die.*

Pretty blatant. (Yay!)

I took a few more pictures and then kept walking. No need to get myself or my interest in them noticed.

Tabby and Isa's family had gotten a cutesy sky-blue house as their rental. The street address was framed in a giant wooden sunflower attached to a front portico bordered by flowers. Very homey. Lucky.

I knocked. Isa opened the door and immediately frowned. Tabby slid around her and invited me in. Isa blocked the door before I could enter. I quickly explained what I needed.

"You want a ride out to Trinity for closure?" Isa asked, sounding rightfully skeptical.

"So I can perform one of my life rituals." I linked my hands together behind my back and lied through my teeth. "When bad things happen, I have a ritual I do. It sounds silly, but it totally works. I go somewhere near the location, apologize for my part in whatever happened, and offer a formal farewell to the bad moment. Since the explosion happened at Trinity, I need a ride down there. But I don't want my parents to find out. They tend to overreact when I do these things." (Or not notice, definitely one of the two.)

"That's weird."

It totally was.

Tabby nudged Isa on the side. "Be nice to Joey. Rituals are good things."

"They are," I agreed.

"Sounds like you need a therapist." Isa raised her brows in challenge.

"I had a therapist. That's where I got the idea from." I'd had a bunch of therapists come and go in my life. Desi'd find me one, I'd get comfortable with the person, and then it'd all fall apart when we moved and time zones or schedules or something else didn't match up.

"I'll drive you to Trinity," Tabby offered.

"No, you won't," Isa instantly replied.

Tabby ignored her and placed a hand on my arm. "Our mom's CMSRC car just got repaired this morning, and she's been encouraging us to hang out with other CMSRC kids. I'm sure I can borrow—"

Isa gave her an evil sneer. "You told Mom we'd go on that interpretive forest hike with her today."

Tabby wilted. "I did."

"Tomorrow?" I asked. "I'm not scheduled to work until five."

"I have a dentist appointment in the morning," Tabby said.

"You're not changing your appointment." Isa rolled her eyes.

Tabby smiled at me and then shot her sister a knowing look. "Isa's free, and she owes me a favor. She'll be happy to do it."

Isa rolled her eyes a second time, looked at her sister, and then begrudgingly nodded.

***

Having dragged a promise to pick me up the next morning out of Isa, I returned to the rental house to find a beefed-up pickup parked in the drive next to our CMSRC van. (Which still had four slashed tires. It made zero sense that the twins' mother's car had been fixed while my parents' van was still flat, but that was CMSRC for you.)

The truck was navy with blacked-out windows, lots of chrome, and had a logo on the side that said 'Rickett Brothers and Sons' in a distinctive, swirly font and a drawing of a huge crane knocking into a building.

A developer?

If the developers were interested in Trinity, my dad, as project manager, was their best CMSRC contact to schmooze. There was an opportunity here.

If I wanted it.

Which, of course, I did.

I peeked into the cab of the truck, being careful not to touch it in case it was alarmed. The tinting was too dark for me to see much.

Ramoth dropped from the roof of the house with a loud squawk.

"Just give me a few minutes," I called up.

Lavender poop cascaded from the sky, hitting the front windshield of the truck.

"Ramoth!" There was a good chance she'd been aiming at me. "Sasha Clems said you'd been told not to do that anymore."

Ramoth bolted for the sky.

"We're so talking about this later." I hurried around the side of the house. Dad would invite the visitors to the kitchen for tea and coffee. In good weather, like today, we kept the kitchen window cracked in preparation for Mom's (or Dad's or my) attempts at cooking.

Too easy.

From the exterior, the kitchen window was chin-high. I slid underneath it to listen in.

Three voices. Dad, a man, and a woman. I slowly rose up to take a peek. The kitchen table was offset from the window, so they'd be unlikely to notice me.

Both the man and woman had overly styled brown hair and wore business suits. The man spoke fast and loudly, waving his hands a lot. Something to do with politicians and a hope for a better Newfoundland. The woman tapped long scarlet fingernails against the table.

First impression: Smarmy. But that didn't make them inherently bad people.

I pulled out the yellow phone, hit voice record, and slid it onto the sill.

"We all agree," the man said, "that if the crowds are there, if people are sneaking in anyway, let's charge them. Nothing big, not a carnival, not Niagara Falls. Tours. One yacht a day to start. Three buses out of St. John's. Everything high-end with stops at restaurants and souvenir shops."

"I don't think—" Dad said.

The loud guy didn't pause. "The shuck is a gift, something rare and special to be protected. Help the economy, save the dragons. That'll be our message. My partners and I are prepared to take it to the world. Hell, in this sense, we've got the same goal as the scientists. There's no money to be made if we kill the damned thing. Then all we've got is a graveyard."

"CMSRC will never allow—"

"They will if it helps their coffers. Then once the shuck hatches, we'll go big. Make Trinity a destination for draco-tourism. CMSRC, as the draco experts, can take a part. It'll be an income stream for you, and what government agency isn't endlessly thinking of its bottom line? We've got some big names working with us. Political and industry. At the national level. This is going to happen."

The conversation continued at length. Dad didn't cave, but he also didn't say much. Eventually, it wound down, and the man took Dad by the hand in a strong shake. "I'm so glad we're on the same page. This is going to work out."

Dad again said nothing, but the moment the front door shut, he gave a long-suffering sigh.

I waited before going around to the front. No need to witness the developers' highly negative reactions to Ramoth's gift on their windshield.

Once they were gone, I found Dad in the kitchen, bleaching the Formica tabletop while wearing pink plastic kitchen gloves.

"Hey, Dad."

"There was a stain," he said.

"I'm sure you got it. Did we have company?"

"More developers." He paused in his disinfecting to study me. "Josephine, you've got a spot on your shirt."

I brushed at a minuscule spot on my tee. It stayed put. Shoot. I loved this tee. I'd bought it in Brazil. Hopefully, I could get the spot out. "I'll go change. Have there been many developers dropping by?"

Dad returned to scrubbing the table. "These were the first to show up in person. Why do any of these people think the commissioner of CMSRC will listen to me?"

Because they'd done their homework, and the commissioner did listen to my dad. Dad was great at his job.

I left Dad to it and snuck upstairs to go do some intel gathering on the Ricketts. Only when I opened my door, my room had been hit by a typhoon. My bras and panties and socks were scattered everywhere. My drawer of tees was upended. All the hangers and clothes from my closet were on the floor. My blue mug was knocked on its side.

Ramoth lay belly-up in the middle of my bed, the tip of her tail twitching with draco attitude.

"This is not okay."

She gave me a side-eye glare.

"We're supposed to be friends."

She jumped up, righting herself, and snorted flame at me. A narrow, pencil-length stream this time.

"Fine. I'm sorry for leaving you behind. Can you not do that with the fire? It's dangerous." I righted my Gander mug, checking it for damage. "And okay, I'll admit that sneaking off without you wasn't the best way for me to demonstrate friendship, but neither is pooping nor making a mess of my room the best way to handle being upset."

She cut off the flame and sat back on her haunches.

I lectured Ramoth on manners and communicating emotions while cleaning my room. Once done, I sat down at my laptop. She remained on my bed, keeping a close eye on me, as if waiting for me to do something she didn't like again. Sigh.

Geoff and Layla Ricketts. Married couple. Owned a butt-load of touristy businesses around Newfoundland and Nova Scotia. Restaurants. Craft Beer. Bus Tours. Boat Tours that advertised Puffins, Whales, and Icebergs. Deals with cruise lines.

I made notes on them and the protesting church people. I couldn't see any leads to follow up on but sent it all to Bob along with my Isa-plan as proof I was doing my job.

***

"So, what's really going on?" Isa asked as I climbed into her family's Nissan Micra the next morning. Music played in the background, a lilting, high-pitched female voice.

Ramoth had stayed in my room after I'd explained to her what I was doing, that Trinity was too far for her to fly, and that I'd tell her every detail of my day once I got back. She'd seemed accepting of this, or at least she neither pooped on me nor threw anything. (I'd hidden my mug in the bathroom cupboard regardless.)

"This trip really is so that I can get closure," I said in a friendly voice as we drove off. If we were going to spend most of our day together, it seemed a good idea to win Isa over. I'd even made a list of twenty conversation starters to help. "Hey, this is Allie X singing, right? Great choice. Have you seen her in concert? My sister got me tickets to Mitski for my birthday last year."

"Lucky you," she replied flatly and changed the music to Drake.

Next . . .

"You guys were in Argentina before here, right?"

"Yup." She pushed her hair behind her ear.

"How was the living?"

"Better than some, worse than others."

"I know that feeling. But at least you speak Spanish. I've never learned any of the local languages beyond the necessities."

"I don't speak Spanish." There was zero inflection in her voice, and definitely no invitation.

I winced and put an extra boost of friendliness into my voice for the next item on my list. "So as twins, did you and Tabby ever try to pass for each other?"

She yawned, big and fake and without covering her mouth.

Did she have to make this so hard? I tried five more items on my list before giving up and letting an awkward (for me anyway) silence reign.

Two deeply uncomfortable hours later and after passing through not one but three RCMP checkpoints, we made it to Trinity. Our CMSRC Family IDs got us through all the security, but the guard at the last one informed us that the area was being patrolled by ATVs and drones and to not leave the paved roads. Fair enough.

We passed the hook of land sticking out into the cove where Sasha Clems had done her livestream. Weird to think of the shuck nestled somewhere down in the dark water, incubating its precious inhabitants. (And magically aware of what was going on around it.)

Hundreds of buoys with Keep Out signs crisscrossed the land and water in all directions. We were just past the last of them when Isa slammed on the brakes and swung us sideways into someone's driveway.

I launched forward, the seatbelt catching me. "What—"

"Hide if you don't want to be seen."

I got the barest glimpse of a white CMSRC truck coming at us from behind, full throttle, engine roaring. I dropped to the center of the car. So did Isa. We crashed into each other, my shoulder, her head.

"Owww!" we both yelped at the same time. (At least it wasn't the reverse, my head, her shoulder. No need to antagonize my healing.)

The truck raced past us.

I sat back up, rubbing my newest sore spot. Isa stared out the window but not toward the disappearing vehicle. A grouping of fifteen dracos circled over a forested area. Big dracos, giraffe-sized and larger and colored in the full spectrum of the rainbow. They looked to be circling right where my GPS was leading us.

"Don't even try to tell me that's coincidental," Isa said.

"Totally coincidental. Also unrelated, random, accidental, a fluke, bad-happenstance, and the opposite of fate."

"Right," Isa replied, all well-duh. (She was way too perceptive for my sanity.)

A huge, as in the torso was the size of a Learjet, mustard-yellow draco dropped down above the others.

"Isn't that Maur, the draco that helped Sasha Clems?" I asked. "Must be something big going on. But not anything to do with me. I mean, how would that even be possible?"

Isa turned to face me, her brows together, her eyes narrowed.

I tensed.

"Who are you working for?" she demanded. "The Canadian magic-handlers? The Americans? Not the Mexican Americans as my Nana would've warned me. Scottish? That's where you lived last, right?"

"No magic-handlers," I said quickly. "Other than you and Tabby, I don't know any. I've met like three my entire life. Seriously. I have no connection to magic-handlers." (If I didn't count Bob. And . . . err . . . Aristotle Montague-Smith-Montague via Sasha Clems.)

Isa pulled the car back onto the road. "The only reason I believe you is because if there was a magic-handler within a hundred kilometers, I'd know."

I let out a small, forced, defensive laugh. "Let's just head to where the dracos are circling, see what's up."

"As if I didn't already realize that was our goal."

We turned off the main road for a smaller one leading into a treed area that pushed out into the cove. I used my phone to follow the GPS coordinates. The houses here were less historical and more utilitarian than the ones in the town. No people around either, but that was to be expected. Any locals not being employed by CMSRC would've been relocated elsewhere until the shuck hatched.

Isa slowed at a white saltbox with brown trim. The CMSRC truck was parked on the left. A large shed sat to the right.

My phone made a loud you-have-arrived chirp.

"Another non-coincidence?" Isa asked dryly.

"Fat-finger mistype. Park a couple of houses down. Then we'll sneak back to watch the dracos." I hesitated. That had sounded pretty suspicious. "No need to let CMSRC see us. I have to do this for closure, but I didn't tell my parents I was coming out here. I'd rather not get grounded."

"R-iiii-ght. That's what you're worried about." She did as I asked and parked behind a hedge where the car wasn't noticeable. The CMSRC personnel wouldn't bother us as long as they didn't see us, since CMSRC protocol said they had to stay indoors or in vehicles when big dracos were about.

Isa got out. I texted Bob.

Me

Why are dracos here?

Isa headed into the trees toward the house. I followed.

Bob

What dracos?

Hold on.

Ramoth told Maur to keep an eye on you. Now he's insisting on helping. The others follow him. Get used to it.

Great, Bob was even snarly in texts. And thank you, Ramoth, for making this harder than it had to be. I should've known something was up when she stayed behind without fussing.

Me

Help with what?

"What are you doing?" Isa stopped where the tree line ended near the back of the brown-trimmed house and its shed.

"Texting a friend."

"Who?"

"A guy from town I just met. He's really great."

"Now?" she asked incredulously. "You're kind of ditzy, aren't you?"

I smiled as if she was joking. She wasn't, and tension crawled up my spine like a millipede wearing cleats. Why couldn't Tabby have been the one to drive me?

"Let's sneak over to the shed," I said. "Better view from there, and we can hide inside while I take care of my ritual."

She gave me an unimpressed eyebrow raise and turned not to the shed but to the cove. "The dracos moved out over the water. Marking something? The shuck? Is there anything you want to tell me?"

"Not about the shuck," I said quickly. "Or the dracos. Or why they might be circling in just that spot near this particular house."

"R-iiiii-ght."

The millipede did a quick about-face and bolted to join the rest of the tension points churning in my stomach. I started for the shed, mentally hunting through my list of conversation starters again. Something to lighten things up. A joke. Humor. I came up blank.

Isa followed me, glowering.

The side of the shed facing the water had two doors, a giant, roll-up one and a regular one. Both were locked.

"You know what would be nice right now?" I said, going for friendly, casual, and hopefully humorous. "An open-sesame spell."

Isa turned inch-by-inch my direction and shot me a death glare worthy of Slade.

My respiratory system turned to ice. The kind with jagged, crystalline edges that shredded my lungs. Wrong thing to say. Based on her expression, waaayyy wrong. "I— I— I—"

"Don't talk to me about spells," she growled.

"I'm so sorry," I blurted. "I didn't mean it. I shouldn't have said anything. It was a joke. I just wanted to ease the tension between us. I should've known that you'd think me mentioning magic was offensive. Although how I should've known that, I have no idea, since I know nothing about spells. Or you. I was just trying to be funny. But I totally overstepped. I get that, and just when I'd been working so hard to get you to like me. But clearly, I screwed up. And now you hate me. I'm so, so sorry. I really didn't mean anything by it."

She sneered. "What is wrong with you? Can't you ever stop talking?" She turned her back and walked around the corner of the shed.

I slumped against the locked door, banging my head in the process. "Ouch."

As if on cue, the yellow phone buzzed.

Bob

Maur says to bring the rowboat down to the water. He wants a look but there isn't enough space for him to get close to the shed.

Chapter Twenty

Day 2 of 162 of the China Assignment
Changde City, Hunan Province, China
Urban Population: 1 million

The day after we arrive at our new apartment, I decide to distract myself from the vast emptiness that is my latest bedroom by going to see my new best friend, Slade. Our families are the only Canadians and native-English speakers on the assignment, so we've been booked into the same ten-story building, two floors apart. I take the stairwell down and knock on his door.

"Hello, Josephine," his mother says. She has Slade's coloring and is really young for a mom, if also every bit as serious as Slade. She wears a yellow eyelet dress, and her hair is braided down her back. There's something odd about her. I can't put my finger on it, but on the ride from the airport, she watched Dr. Panozco and never once looked at Slade or his little brother.

"Is Slade around?" I ask, giving her a winning smile.

"He's asleep."

It's currently noon.

"Jetlag, huh? Can I wake him? I thought I'd take him shopping, help him get on the local time zone right away."

"Sure." She yawns and motions me in. Vinnie is face down on the sofa, completely out.

Their apartment is the same as ours, which means small and barren, other than a few pieces of rented furniture. Slade has the tiniest of the three bedrooms. Quentin has the same one in our apartment. I peek in to find him crashed on his back on a narrow bed, wearing a tee for a band named Voivod and sweats. His arm is thrown up over his head, his eyes are closed, and his lips are parted. Hard to miss that Slade's totally ripped. Like wide shoulders and sculpted arms.

"Nice," I murmur and sit down next to him. He's not Mr. Universe big or anything like that. He's just really fit. I give him a gentle shake on his shoulder. "Hey, Slade, wake up."

He opens his eyes and stares at me with a furrow between his dark brows. Then he drops his hand on my bare knee and runs it up my thigh to my hip. He pushes his fingers into the waist of my shorts and tugs me toward him. It all happens so fast I don't react. The look in his eyes is intense and laser-focused. I've never seen anything like it before.

"You," he whispers.

Butterflies go wild in my stomach, and I give a nervous half-laugh, shoving his hand away. "Slade!"

The furrow between his eyes deepens. He blinks, and then his eyes flare abruptly wide. A look of horror crosses his face. He scrambles backward and leaps from the bed, knocking into me with his leg and sending me tumbling to the floor.

I laugh again while he presses his back against the wall as far from me as he can get. Which, in the postage-stamp room, means we could still reach out and touch each other if we wanted.

I don't.

And he doesn't.

Instead, he glances frantically around as if he has no idea where he is or who I am.

I climb back onto his bed. I should be as horrified as him, but he's doing such a fine job of it for both of us that I just can't. Besides, I've already decided we're besties, even if that look in his eyes was more than friendly.

"I was dreaming," he announces slowly, word-by-word, as if struggling to turn his thoughts into language. "We're in China. You woke me up. Where's Vinnie?"

"Vinnie's in the living room with your mom. I did wake you up, and I'll make a point of not doing that again."

***

Changde is confusion and chaos. Or at least the part we are living in is, which is outside the nicer tourist areas or newer, wealthier areas. There are kids in school uniforms, delivery drivers on mopeds weaving between traffic, cars, carts, people in all directions, and street vendors calling out wares and prices. All of it's squashed down into streets running between tall apartment buildings. It's fun and charming and I love everything about it. This is where Slade and I will begin our new friendship.

We end up taking Vinnie with us. Slade puts miniature sneakers on his feet and finds a little boat hat to cover his head. The moment we walk out of our building's elevator, Slade swings Vinnie off the ground onto his shoulders in a practiced move. He stops me at the glass doors to the street, looking at me all intent-like.

"I'm sorry for before," he says slowly, carefully, a bit choppily even. He has a furrow between his brows again. "Really sorry. I'd never . . . I'm not that guy."

I laugh. He's so funny. "No worries. I've already forgotten the whole thing."

Liar. No way am I forgetting that. No one has ever looked at me the way he did. I'm not going to forget it. I'm going to savor it. Daily. Until I'm dead.

No need for him to know that.

He nods, accepting my words at face value. "It's just . . ." He glances to the glass door and the chaos beyond. "I'm not this either."

I pause, not sure what he's talking about.

He presses his lips together and stares at me, frowning. Waiting for me to get it.

I don't.

He chin-nods toward the busy street. "I've never been anywhere. Except Toronto. And now Louisiana."

Oh, got it.

This, too, I find totally cute and funny. I can't imagine what it'd be like to stay in one place your whole life, where things and people are always the same.

Actually, it sounds nice.

I pat him on the arm. "Don't worry. As long as you download the translation app and the AI guide, you'll be fine."

He looks at me as if he has no idea what I'm talking about, and then the moment we step outside, he locks onto my upper arm as if afraid of losing me.

"Where are we going?" he asks as we skirt around a man selling seaweed patties from a cart. Slade isn't much taller than me, so he says it right into my ear.

"Outdoor marketplace. It's not far."

"Why?"

"I have a ritual whenever we move to a new assignment. I have to buy a knick-knack for my room. A memorial, you could say, or maybe my proof of life. Every time I add another item to my collection, I'm adding to who I am as a person. I'm adding the China me."

He doesn't say anything. Good thing, since my explanation, while being true, doesn't make all that much sense. Also, I'm babbling, which annoys people.

We crisscross through traffic, and he holds so tight to my arm that my elbow aches. I pull his hand away and twine his fingers between mine so that we're still connected. His grip is warm and firm, but not too firm, and the inside of his thumb has a rough spot. I've never held a boy's hand before, and I like it. I like him.

China is an exceptional assignment.

CHAPTER TWENTY-ONE

Since tears weren't really an option with Isa and the dracos present, I counted from one hundred backward, made it to ninety-six, forgot where I was, and took a deep breath.

"I think I've found a way in," Isa called. "Since this shed seems to be why you dragged me out here." She sounded slightly less irritated than before. That helped too.

I found her with her hand cupped against a dirty glass window, peering in. I copied her. Inside was a wooden rowboat. Bingo.

"The window's not locked," Isa said. "We just need to find a way to slide it over." She pushed with her hands, but it didn't budge. I grabbed a stick, wedged it between the frame of the glass and the casing. A good tug just so, and the glass shifted over enough to get my fingers in. From there, the window slid easily.

Isa boosted me through. It wasn't graceful, but I made it, coating my hands and clothing in dust along the way. I brushed myself off as best I could and let Isa in through the door.

"Hey, look at this cool rowboat," I said in an attempt to make my examination of it slightly less weird. "I always wanted a rowboat."

The boat was painted red on the outside, white on the inside, made of heavy wood, and was totally empty. Just an open hull with benches, no obvious clues at all. I ran my hand down the side, and powdery red paint joined the covering of dust on my hands. I searched for a name or any distinguishing marks. Nothing. I took photos and videos anyway.

Isa watched me as if I was nuts.

The rest of the shed was filled with fishing equipment, all tidily stored and in much better condition than the boat. Crab traps, coils of rope, drying racks, and buoys were stacked along one wall. I collected a particularly small trap from the floor and put it with the rest, aiming to look casual. Unless Bob sent a way for me to gather fingerprints or something, there wasn't much here to be discovered.

Isa pulled out her phone and took a photo of me standing next to the rowboat. "I take it you aren't the one who stole it?"

"Stole what?"

"Are you hoping for the reward money? It was only a couple hundred bucks."

"I have no idea what you're talking about."

Isa rolled her eyes.

"No, really. No idea."

"That *is* the stolen boat in the flyers around Gander, correct?" she asked.

Ummm . . .

What?!

"Here's the thing." Isa took another photo of me. "Your closure story is stupid, and you made the whole thing up to get me to drive you here. I'm not a tattler, and I don't care what you've gotten involved in except for one thing. My dad works out here too, and I'm not letting you do anything that might end up causing harm to him or the other scientists just because you got suckered into some wyrm-netter's scheme."

I took an alarmed step backward. That was the conclusion she'd come to? (Actually, I could see why.) "No. Never. I—"

"I told you not to call that phone number. Tabby told you. As did Quentin."

"I didn't. I wouldn't." And I hadn't. They'd always contacted me.

The sunlight coming through the open door disappeared, and the most unbearable smell wafted through the shed. Like dead fish mixed with a leaking sewer line spewing sulfur.

"Don't want to tell me what's going on, fine," Isa continued, for once not noticing the obvious. She stood with her back to the door, and unlike me, her nostrils must not have been sensitive. She put her hands on her hips. "Whatever the wyrm-netters want with this boat, you're not going to do it. The dracos are already riled up, and I'm not letting you get drowned or eaten or scorched on my watch."

A massive yellow eye peered in on us through the door. An upside-down eye. Maur must've done contortions to get his head through the trees.

Every individual hair on my body stood on end. And this was knowing Maur wasn't here to hurt us.

"Dragon," I screeched.

Isa frowned and turned to look. "Well, great. As if this wasn't bad enough already, now I'm going to have to save us. If my mom finds out, I'm so dead." Isa lifted her hands in the air, balled her fists, and drew her brows together with a sudden, concentrated rigidity.

"Don't hurt him!" I said in a strangled yelp. I didn't try to stop her. No way. Interfering with magic seemed a terrible idea.

"Get ready to run," Isa replied calmly, considering her body vibrated with tension. (Or magic.)

She snapped her fingers, and a shock of energy that I could neither see nor hear but felt burst from her body. Maur's upside-down eye disappeared. A tree cracked, then another and another. Then a massive splash of water and a booming, unhappy roar.

Isa and I bolted for the car.

***

The good news? We didn't get attacked by angry dracos on our rapid journey out of Trinity.

The more good news? Isa was so freaked out about whether her mother's wards would know that she'd used magic that she didn't interrogate me further. (What exactly wards were or how they worked, I had no idea. I would've liked to have asked, but no way.)

The bad news? Ramoth waited for us when we got back to my rental and proceeded to poop not just on the front window of the car but also the back. Pretty sure the only reason she didn't poop on Isa and me was because her digestive system ran out. Yup, she was mad again, which meant she'd heard about the Maur incident. Isa was still so busy freaking out about her mother that she made one small comment about pissing off all the local dracos and left it at that. Isa was seriously afraid of her mom.

Luckily, Ramoth didn't take out her ire on my room. Instead, she paced back and forth on the floor, her wings half-spread, her tail snapping, clearly making a point.

"Is Maur okay?" I asked, sheepishly.

She pointed her snout to the sky, her lower jaw dropping to expose pointy teeth, and gave me an annoyed side-eye glance. I took that to mean he was fine, but that his health wasn't her point.

I made a quick trip to the washroom to retrieve my mug. I needed it. "It all happened super-fast, and Maur scared us." Or at least me. "Isa reacted, and I didn't know what to do."

Ramoth turned her head away and gave a little snort of smoke. No flames, but there was enough sting in her expression to make it clear she was disappointed in me.

"Fail on my part, I know. I'm so sorry, Ramoth. Please tell Maur how sorry I am. It won't happen again."

She tilted her head my direction in a human-like nod and then relaxed her tail down to the floor.

"I don't want the dracos mad at me, especially not you, 'kay? I'll tell you everything that happened while I send the photos to Bob."

She leaped from the chair to my bed and brushed her wing against my arm, batting her eyes. I was forgiven.

My photos got me a call. Bob wasn't just a little angry, but over-the-top-growly-and-loud angry. That led to me blurting everything that had happened in about three breaths, adding in what Isa had said about the boat being stolen. Yes, tears ran down my face as I did it. Ramoth touched one with her forked tongue, a comforting gesture. I pet her glossy scales and put my arms around her, clinging to her the same way I did my memorials. She seemed to appreciate this as much as I did.

I apologized multiple times, and Bob calmed down enough for us to agree that my next step would be to search out the stolen boat flyers. This should be easy since Pizza Utopia had a board, and I was scheduled to work tonight and the next morning.

Bob told me that he was preparing dossiers on the developers and the pastor of All Angels. As soon as he had them done, he wanted me to read through them.

I'd just ended the call and mopped up my face when my regular phone buzzed.

> *I found something for your verbal-garbage outbursts. It's an app.*

Attached was a link.

Me

> *Appreciate the gesture, but why are you doing this?*

Lei

> *Click on it.*

Me

> No

I changed into my Pizza Utopia tee, put on mascara and gloss, and fixed my hair into a French braid to hide the stitches at the back of my head. (Hair growth was going great. My hair could beat bamboo in a growing contest.)

My phone buzzed again.

Lei

> *You know I'm majoring in psych, right? I have to write a case study essay for one of my classes, and the school Reddit board says the teacher likes students to take extra initiative. Since you have problems when it comes to Slade that are totally measurable, could you click on the link and let me write about you?*

I hated that she knew Slade stressed me out. At the same time, she did struggle academically, and looking up a teacher's expectations to pre-prepare was something my elder siblings had all recommended. Not that I had. Still, being supportive of Lei was the nice thing to do, and considering how much effort she was putting into this, it did seem as if she was trying to assist me. I hesitated, then clicked on the link. It took me to an app whose byline read, *Help to Sort Things Out.*

And didn't that just sound all tele-mental-healthy. Yuck. No way.

I put my phone in my pocket and left for work.

When I arrived at Pizza Utopia, Mo wasn't there, which made for a long shift. Also, none of the flyers posted on the board were about missing boats. On my walk home, I kept an eye out for flyers on street signs or electrical poles. Nothing.

The next morning, I took a circuitous route to work for more sign opportunities. Still nothing, but Mo was at Pizza Utopia, and when I walked in, his face bloomed with the biggest, most welcoming, friendly, flirtiest smile I'd ever seen.

Considering everything that had happened in the last couple of days, having someone be glad to see me felt wonderful.

"I've been waitin' for you, Curly Girly."

I forced back a wince at the horrific nickname. But hey, I didn't need him to be perfect, just nice.

"Would you be interested in a second try at my making-up-to-Joey challenge? Uncle Charles gave us both next Friday off, on a condition."

"What's the condition?"

"Don't laugh." He rubbed at the back of his neck and bit his lower lip as if suddenly nervous. Totally pretend. Especially when he ruined it by tilting the corners of his lips upward again. "We gotta go check out the local theater group. Aunt Brenda and two of my cousins from Grand Falls are in it. And it's *Carrie: The Musical.* As in Carrie from the Stephen King book."

"That sounds great." In a way equally fun and horrific.

"Grand. It will be. I promise."

Several hours later, I was in the kitchen loading dirty pizza platters into a quick-wash industrial cleaner. I'd tried to get new info out of Mo about either the pastor or the developers but failed, or at least I got nothing that Bob's dossiers hadn't contained.

The pastor's name was William Forester, and he was from a long line of Newfoundlander anti-draco activists. A group on the island had formed an organization a hundred years ago because they thought the larger-than-normal draco population a nuisance and a danger to people. Pastor Forester led the Gander chapter. He had no criminal history. He was married, had three kids, had led All Angels for thirteen years, and enjoyed hunting, fishing, and curling.

The developers were more recent additions to Newfoundland. They'd arrived fifteen years ago from Halifax and built two houses. A summer one on a pond outside Gander and a mansion outside of St. John's. They'd spent the intervening years making money every way they could. No kids. Hobbies were vacationing in the Bahamas (her) and cryptocurrency (him). No criminal records, and their companies all had A+ ratings with the Better Business Bureau.

"Hey, babe, c'mere a sec," Mo called out from the front counter. "My best friend wants to meet the super awesome, deadly gorgeous, way-too-good-for-me girl I keep tellin' everyone about."

"Compliments make my world a better place." I tossed a clean dishrag at him. He grabbed it, looped it around my neck, and towed me out to the dining area.

"Stella, meet Josephine." Mo released me in front of a girl our age sitting at one of the tables. "A.k.a. Joey. A.k.a. hot girl that Mo is crushing on."

"Enough already." I said it teasingly but also meant it.

I recognized Mo's best friend. She had straight black hair and a round face. "You teach at Tutu and You Too Ballet. I saw you demonstrating for a class. You're good." She had been. Even more, if we had dance in common, she was a definite friend possibility.

"You came by last week," Stella replied, looking me over.

Mo pressed me down into a seat. "Stella's majorin' in biz admin at St. John's. We've been best friends since Grade Two, share an apartment during the school year, and keep an eye out for each other. Her people are Mi'kmaq, but believe it or not, my family arrived in Newfoundland a full hundred years before hers."

"Mo!" Stella glared at him.

He gave her a sheepish grin. "Her mom hates it when I tell people that. The Mi'kmaq are originally from Labrador."

"I hate it when you tell people. You have no boundaries."

He rubbed the top of her head, ruffling her hair affectionately. "Stella's right. I don't have boundaries, but she loves me anyway and keeps me in check."

She relaxed back into her seat and pushed his hand off her head in a way that said this happened regularly and she wasn't really upset. "Since Grade Two."

"Since Grade Two," he agreed.

Stella was awesome. I was so going all-in on winning her over.

Mo returned to work, and Stella and I chatted about the studio, dancing, and Gander. Mo had excellent taste in friends.

Right as Stella was inviting me to come to her intermediate jazz class, the kitchen's delivery bell rang. Mo had his hands full delivering a pizza, so I jumped to my feet. "Back to work."

"Come by the studio when you can."

"I absolutely will."

The bell rang again as I headed through the kitchen and past Uncle Gerald slicing onions. "Impatient much?" I grumbled as I opened the back door.

And came face-to-face with Slade.

I froze, a cement wall of panic displacing the air in my lungs.

"Hey," I managed in a shivery whisper.

His eyes flashed with surprise. "Hey."

When he didn't then glare or sneer, I slowly relaxed into the part of me that remembered what had happened at Trinity and that things weren't as bad as before.

He wore a long-sleeved beige uniform with a swirly logo embroidered on the pocket. Weird. I'd never seen him in anything but a band tee before. Behind him in the alley was a matching beige delivery truck with a logo on the side that read RBS Brewery Depot.

"*You* got a job delivering *beer*?"

He coughed into his fist as if embarrassed. "Mostly it's pop. But yeah. Panozco recommended me, and I need the money. It's a job."

"It's a job," I repeated back to him.

He nodded.

This was good, meaning he and I having a normal conversation. Not just good, but amazing. Grand, even, as Mo liked to say.

I became aware of the sun shining down on my skin, the brilliance of the green leaves of the tree just outside, the happy chirping of small birds jumping between the branches, just how solid the world was. I opened my mouth to say something else. Something witty or charming or pretty much anything to keep the conversation going. Easy words. Natural words.

No words?

I went totally, utterly, tongue-dead-on-the-floor-of-my-mouth blank.

Slade stayed silent as well, but that wasn't unusual.

A guy in the same beige uniform lowered the lift at the back of the delivery truck. Slade and I continued to look at each other. Awkwardly.

Slade tugged on the sleeve of his shirt, leaving a dusting of red on the beige fabric as if his hands were dirty. "You got a job too."

"Yup," I managed.

"Head's better?"

"Yup." A flustered heat crawled up my chest and neck that matched the stain on his hands. (But he was trying. And without any yelling. I needed to try too.)

Silence again.

Heat prickled my skin. I should've prepared in advance, made flashcards. I was great at memorizing flashcards. Why hadn't I made flashcards? And why was I freaking out here?

"Well . . ." Slade glanced at me. "I've got deliveries."

"Yup."

From this moment forward, I was officially nixing that word from my vocabulary.

Slade turned to go back to the truck.

The moment his attention was no longer on me, the world got a little cooler, the sun a little dimmer, the birds chirping in the tree not so cute. "Slade, I . . ."

He immediately turned back.

"Hey, babe." Mo came up beside me in the doorway. "Thanks for handling the delivery. I've"—he stiffened—"got it from here." His tone went cold in a very non-Mo way.

The second delivery guy walked over, pushing a handcart of boxes. "Mohmmedidrees, my man. Is this the girl you've been going on about?"

"Best girl ever." Mo threw an arm over my shoulder. Slade followed the movement with his eyes, but the rest of him stayed still.

"Gorgeous, amazin', too good to be true, too good for me," Mo continued, his voice edged with challenge.

I casually stepped out from under Mo's arm, but he slid his hand down my spine to rest it against my lower back, keeping us in physical contact, making a statement.

Slade's mouth curled into a sneer. His eyes narrowed. His nostrils flared as if he smelled something rotting. "Nice."

It was then that I remembered Slade and Mo had met before.

***

I didn't cry.

Not when Slade walked away without looking back. Not when Mo congratulated himself on solving the Slade problem. Not when I tried three times to tell Mo that Slade was a great guy once you got to know him.

At the end of my shift, I walked home, still without crying, but it was a near thing. Twice, I pulled my phone out to text Slade and explain that I hadn't asked Mo to spill pop on him. Both times I only stopped once I was staring at his contact information.

I'd been so close. So, so close. Before Mo had interrupted, Slade and I'd been communicating. (Sort of.)

I wanted to hate Mo for interrupting, like get really, really mad at him. Only Mo seemed to see Slade as a mix of Joseph Stalin, Genghis Khan, and Vlad the Impaler, and my trying to refute this as me being overly nice. If Mo's viewpoint had been correct, then everything Mo'd done would've been heroic. I couldn't bring myself to criticize him for protecting me from Vlad the Impaler.

I returned to the rental house, intending to rush upstairs to release a St. Lawrence River of misery but paused at the mailbox next to the front door. It was overflowing with mail, an unusual occurrence since we never gave anyone the address of our rentals. I pulled out the pile, most of which was letters and envelopes from various local companies. Developers. The largest envelope was from the Ricketts. Same logo with a crane knocking into a building and the distinctive, swirly letters RBS that . . .

I hiccuped an inhale that turned into an exhale and then stalled.

The same swirly letters RBS that had been embroidered on Slade's beige shirt.

I went suddenly overly warm. Ramoth squawked high and low and then high again, although she wasn't anywhere I could spot her.

I dropped the stack of letters on the porch, shaking my head. "No, no, no." Slade is not involved in this. "No, no, no."

Even if the delivery truck had been more than big enough to move a rowboat.

And Slade had wiped off a red residue from his fingers that could've been the same powdered paint I'd gotten on mine.

"Negative. Absolutely not. I refuse. I decline. I object. Never."

Slade had said Dr. Panozco had gotten him the job.

I slid down against the front door to the porch, dropping the envelopes everywhere and pressing the tips of my fingers to my eyes. "No way. Nah. Nay. Nix. Thumbs down. Not happening."

As if in response, the world beyond my closed eyes went dark.

"What are you doing?" Lei asked from somewhere above me.

I jerked in surprise.

She stood with her hands on her hips. Her fauxhawk was now navy with sparkles.

"Dying slowly of theasaurical immolation," I muttered.

"There's an app for that." She crouched down next to me and gathered up the envelopes. "Did you try it?"

"Synonym self-assassination?"

"You clicked on the link, right?"

"Love the new hair color," I mumbled, giving up on word-drama and dropping my chin to my chest.

"You're avoiding the app because you know it'll work." She handed me the now tidy stack of letters.

Actually, it wouldn't. Thanks to Desi, I'd done enough tele-mental health programs in the past to know they weren't my thing. "Fine. I'll try it."

"Today?"

"Today."

"Good." She tugged me back to my feet. "Since I'm being so thoughtful toward you, you now have an obligation to help me as well, don't you agree?"

"Sure?" Although, wasn't the whole point of the app that I was already helping her?

"There's this girl. Gay, cute, local, and going to a party at some abandoned house on Friday. I need an invite. You need to get me one. From Mo. Who's sure to know about the party. He can take us both."

"He and I already have plans Friday." I told her about *Carrie: The Musical.*

"Mo will take you to the party after. I've heard it's an annual thing, and everyone under the age of twenty-five within a two-hour drive attends. There's a DJ, so there'll be dancing, which you love. You can pick me up after the play."

"Mo drives an ancient pickup. Three in the front is going to be tight."

She pressed her lips together, considering. "Get me the address. I'll convince the twins to drive me out. I'm not missing this opportunity."

"The twins don't seem like partying-types, and their mom is super strict."

"You do your job," Lei replied, "I'll do mine."

Chapter Twenty-Two

**Day 3 of 162 of the China Assignment
Changde City, Hunan Province, China**

There's a soft knock at the front door of our apartment. I jump to go answer it, since Quentin is off playing basketball with our next-door neighbor, Yuze, and Dad left a few minutes ago to meet up with the local Chinese MSS officer. I thought Mom went with him, but she beats me to the door.

"Is Joey here?" Slade asks, stumbling over my name and speaking super slow and choppy. "My online teacher. He suggested. I ask her to tutor me. With my math. And English. Even though. I'm a year ahead."

"She's—"

"I'd love to tutor you." I rush over to save Slade and pull him toward my room. "I'm an excellent tutor."

"Door open," Mom calls loudly. I shut it three-quarters of the way. The walls are so thin, we won't have much privacy either way.

Slade puts his school tablet on my desk and looks curiously around my space, which I love even though there's not much there. Bed, dresser, nightstand, and chair, same as his. The picture frame I'd bought on our shopping trip the day before sits on the dresser with a selfie of Slade, Vinnie, and me inside. The perfect China memorial.

He picks it up.

It's the only decoration I have, which, for once, is more than enough. Especially with Slade standing there.

"Do you ever go by anything other than Joey?" He speaks softly and stumbles on my name again. I'm starting to think he has a speech thing going on. I'd noticed it on the plane, but I also did most of the talking. It's more than he's just quiet. When he does speak, it's slow and in short phrases, *as if he has to work through what he says. If there's anyone other than me around, he hardly speaks at all.*

"Josephine, but only my parents call me that. What's wrong with Joey?"

"Joey is my drum instructor. He's fifty. And looks like Steven Tyler." He gives a soft laugh.

I blink in surprise since he's usually so serious. The humor is another cute thing about him, even if I don't understand it. My heart does several quick tumbles.

"What would you like to call me?"

"Jo?"

"Jo's the uncle I'm named after. He's a dental surgeon in Edmonton." I give a fake shudder.

"Jojo then? It's got a rhythm."

"A tautonym," I say. "Tautonyms are inherently rhythmic."

"Jojo, Jojo, Jojo." He says it as if trying it out on his tongue. He nods as if he likes the taste.

Which makes me smile so hard my cheeks ache. "Jojo, it is."

***

Day 5 of 162 of the China Assignment
Changde City, Hunan Province, China

My phone says it's 3:41 p.m.

Every day from noon to 4 p.m., Slade practices his drums. Or his fake drums anyway. They're this big stand with multiple padded rounds sticking out and several foot pedals that don't hit anything other than silencers.

He kicks me out for practice. He says I'm too distracting, a compliment that fills me with more warmth than a thousand beaming suns.

Slade's obsessive about practicing. According to his mom, he'd be at it ten, twelve hours a day back in Toronto. He played percussion in his school band, in a regional student orchestra, and for a local theater company. Any chance he got, he also played with his dad's friends and bands that could get an under-nineteen into their venues. (Which means a lot of jazz backup bands. He seems to think this was a good thing for some reason and liked Louisiana for the music.)

Today Slade's mom ventured out to the market for the first time, using the exact instructions I'd given her. I wait for the clock to make it to 3:45 p.m. and sneak over to their apartment. I find Vinnie rooting around the sofa, which is covered in a tower of blankets and pillows and towels. I wave at him before walking on my tiptoes to Slade's room.

He sits on his drum throne with his headphones on. He's got sticks in both hands, feet on fake pedals, and his eyes are closed. I move a pile of laundry and sit on the floor, wrapping my arms around my knees.

Everything about him moves both crazy fast and effortlessly as he creates a rhythm and then breaks it, going off on horribly complicated fills. It's both precise and graceful, considering he's forcefully whacking things with slimmed-down tree branches. He's really good.

I go all warm and gooey.

Slade never teases me or mocks me. He takes everything I say seriously, even when I blather on and on. Slade is a rock.

I've never had a rock before. Having a rock changes everything.

"Jojo, you're not supposed to be here." He doesn't open his eyes or pause in his playing.

"I wouldn't miss this for the world. Do you take requests?"

***

Day 12 of 162 of the China Assignment
Changde City, Hunan Province, China

I lay on my back on my bed, my head and hair draping over the side to the floor. Three Days Grace plays in the background. Slade's on the floor doing sit-ups. He's as fanatical about strength training as he is about practicing drums.

Part of this is that he's image-conscious. (He totally uses hair-blackening shampoo.) Part is that strength training improves his endurance for drumming. (Drumming also being the point of having an image.)

I roll onto my belly. "Tell me something you've never said out loud before."

"Like what?" He starts doing pushups. Several minutes later, he finishes and leans back against my bed, my cue that he's ready for more talking. I take a chance and press my cheek against his arm, which is hot and bulgy

from the exercise. He doesn't object to my touching him, which fills me with delight.

"Tell me your greatest secret, your biggest dream."

He's the most intensely private person I've ever met, and I have to drag information out of him.

I already know his favorite band is Tool, and he hero-worships Tool's drummer. I know that several pairs of his jeans have rub marks in the back pockets because in Toronto, he never went anywhere without a pair of sticks shoved in there. I know his dad is a session musician, bass guitar, and that Slade grew up in the Toronto music scene, even going on tour with his dad at times. I know he had a tough childhood, pulled back and forth between his mom and dad, who divorced when he was two but then endlessly got back together and broke up again. I know Vinnie is his full brother, and Slade's life mission is to make sure Vinnie has a better childhood than he did. I know he really hates Panozco, has no idea why his mom married the guy, and is doing everything he can to keep both of them happy anyway, so that he can raise Vinnie himself.

I also know he had his first girlfriend at age fourteen. I'd like to know more on this, but he went all silent when I asked.

"I'm going to have my own band," he finally says. "And we're going to make it."

I burst out laughing.

He jerks sideways as if I slapped him. Which breaks the contact between my cheek and his arm, darn it.

I sit up, waving my hands frantically. "No, no, no. I'm not laughing at your dream. I'm laughing because it's not a secret. It's the most dead obvious thing about you. Of course, you're going to have a band. Of course, you're going to make it. Those are givens."

He swivels around on the floor to look at me, one eye squinting. "Actually, Jojo. They're not."

"I mean, not tomorrow. You'll have to put in a bunch of work. But I've never seen anyone as focused and dedicated as you. And that's saying something coming from my family. Seriously, you're really good. You'll make it."

He stares at me as if I've lapsed into Mandarin.

So I babble on.

"It's magical when you play." It is. I sneak into his practice sessions fifteen minutes before he ends every day to pester him into putting on music and playing along to songs I like. "If I feel that way, other people will too. Musicians will line up to be in your band. Once you have them producing the greatest music ever, people like me will keep you at the top of our playlists on repeat."

He continues to stare at me.

"I talk too much, don't I?"

"I like that about you." He doesn't stop staring.

"Don't you think you'll make it?"

He shakes his head. "I'll make it. It's just . . ." He hesitates, struggles for the words. "No one else. Has ever. Thought so. Too."

Chapter Twenty-Three

Once Lei left, I sent photos of the envelopes to Bob, making no mention of Slade, and texted Mo to get info about the party.

Then I went around tightening the screws on all the door handles. Since I had the screwdriver out, I also went to work on the legs of the kitchen table, the chairs, and everyone's bedframes. (I wasn't freaked out by Slade's connection to the developers or anything.)

Ramoth followed me around, so I told her all about Lei and the assignments we'd shared, bringing out all of Lei's good points in the hopes of avoiding any more poop incidents. Talking about Lei led to Slade and China. I told Ramoth how much I'd loved him and still missed him. I even told her how China had ended. She paid rapt attention and gave me consoling looks at the bad parts, so I started over at the beginning. Since kissing was likely outside of her understanding, and there was no way to talk about Slade without mentioning it, I did a brief overview focusing on the importance of the perfect spot for a first kiss.

I'd just finished checking my dad's office for random loose screws when my phone buzzed.

Mo

Seriously? Lei told you about the party??? I wanted to surprise you.

Me

Apologies on her behalf.

Mo

When we get there, can you act all surprised anyway? I was looking forward to that part.

Me

I won't let you down.

Mo sent a GPS link. I forwarded it to Lei.

I moved on to reorganizing my closet while explaining to Ramoth what had happened with Slade and Mo at Pizza Utopia and why the whole thing was so upsetting from the Slade perspective but also chivalrous from the Mo perspective.

With no more excuses to hide away at the rental, I headed out in search of flyers for the missing boat. Ramoth followed me, doing a great job at keeping her distance and being unobtrusive. She really did seem to be learning.

No boat flyers at Canadian Tire nor the library nor the local RCMP station. I hit up the Arts and Cultural Center, Foodland, and then Buysco. Where I hit the flyer jackpot. Or at least I found a flyer with the word STOLEN and a photo of the red boat posted on a large board in Buysco's entry. In the photo, the boat sat on blocks on a lawn. Inside were three guys. One wore a green Buysco vest. The second wore a red Canadian Tire jacket. The third was an older guy with a fluffy white goatee in a suit. Under the photo was a handwritten note, *This is no longer funny. Reward for information. Talk to Thaddeus in Electronics.*

I took a photo of the flyer, sent it to Bob, and went in search of Thaddeus. I found him shelving earbuds.

"Hey there," I said. "Great shirt."

He was a couple of years older than me, several inches shorter, had shaggy, cut-me-now hair, and wore a brown shirt embroidered with baby-blue pineapples under his Buysco vest. First impression: Nerdy goofball. Not a bad combination.

His face lit up in a friendly grin. "Aren't you the girl Mo's so in love with?"

I blinked in surprise. Seriously?

"I'm Joey. Mo and I just met." I would've preferred to keep my questioning anonymous. (Possibly wishful thinking from the start.)

"Well, then you work fast, Joey, because Mo's crazy for you. What can I help you with?"

"I need a . . ." I gave a quick glance around Electronics for something inexpensive. "PopSocket."

"Over here." He led me to the cellphone aisle. "Mo's a great guy. Any girl would be lucky to have him." He held up a PopSocket with a skull and bones on it that made me think of Slade's band.

I quickly chose one with a rainbow-spouting unicorn. "I like this one. Aren't you the guy who got your boat stolen? I saw the flyer."

He gave a gurgling laugh. "Now there's a Mo story."

"Mo stole your boat?"

"Seven of the eight times." He pulled out his phone and showed me the same photo that was on the flyer, enlarging it so the people were more visible. "See? That's him."

The guy in the Canadian Tire jacket did look like a younger Mo with a buzz cut. I swallowed down an uneasy, surprised laugh. All my walking around town and Mo was my best lead? "Stealing your boat is like a thing?"

"Used to be, back in high school. The first time, Mo left it in Gander Lake wrapped in caution tape. The second time, he left it upside down on our school principal's car. The last time, he hung it from a parkin' lot light at Canadian Tire. That was everyone's favorite. Pretty much won the competition."

Hmmm . . . None of this seemed connected to Trinity or useful to me. "In what sense was it a competition?"

"Canadian Tire? Buysco? Mo worked for one, I worked for the other. In revenge, several of us kept stealing his truck."

"Ah, got it." Sounded just like Mo. "I take it Mo is not the one who stole the boat this time around."

"Nope. It would've shown up already if he had. Besides, if Mo had done it, he would've used his truck. The night it disappeared, one of my neighbors saw the getaway vehicle. Not his."

I took a sharp breath with a sudden foreboding. "What did it look like?"

"Delivery Truck. One of the bigger ones. Light-colored."

✳✳✳

I went home, collapsed onto my bed, and downloaded Lei's app with shaking hands. Because . . .

Well . . .

The reason was so obvious I wasn't going to think about it. At all.

The app asked me to clarify which category of my life I wanted to improve. Options were professional, health, or relationship. I clicked on professional.

Time frame for fulfillment? Twenty-four hours (preferably less).

Best possible outcome? I proved Slade wasn't involved with the rowboat theft or any other recent disasters.

Feelings about a positive outcome? Extreme relief bordering on euphoria, ecstasy, bliss, rapture.

The app told me to close my eyes and do a visualization of the exact moment of the positive outcome and imagine the success flowing through my body.

I tried.

And got an image of Slade, his hands covered in red paint, standing next to the RBS truck, sneering at me.

***

"Quentin?" I followed him out the front door of the rental early the next morning. He wore board shorts and a yellow tee that read *Camp Gander Sports: Teamwork Makes the Dream Work.*

"You're on church duty today, right?" I asked.

Quentin didn't answer. I went with Ramoth's technique, picked up a pine cone, and threw it at his head.

"Hey!" He glanced over his shoulder, pretending to just now notice me. Totally fake. "What was that for?"

"Today is Sunday? Dad?"

"You trying to arrange a trade?"

"I'll go if you'll get me Slade's work delivery schedule without letting him, or anyone else, know I want it."

"If you're thinking of doing the whole apologize-your-heart-out thing again, don't. You're just humiliating yourself."

So aware.

I had to do something, and no one, especially Slade, would think twice about me hunting him down to apologize. It was the most straightforward way to scope out the back of that delivery truck. Also, I wanted an excuse to visit All Angels again, so a deal with Quentin was a double win. Or sort of a double win. No part of me, not even my wisdom teeth, which I'd had removed when I was thirteen, wanted to approach Slade.

Quentin walked past me down the drive.

"I'll not just take church duty but get you an invite to a party. Abandoned house. Everyone under twenty-five going. Even Lei and the twins." (Maybe.)

He spun back my direction. "Seriously? Why didn't you open with that?"

I hadn't thought of it yet. "Will you get Slade's schedule?"

"I'll see what I can do." He walked off, leaving me standing on the porch.

***

Church was uneventful, which was disappointing as I'd been hoping for something momentous (if unlikely) to occur that made it one hundred percent certain that Pastor Forester was the bad guy rather than Dr. Panozco or Slade.

Pastor Forester wasn't there. Nor did Dr. Panozco put in an appearance. I made three attempts to engage Dad about U of T. Dad used each to turn the conversation to Yale. (He played beautifully, though. Dad on an organ was like having angels in the room.)

The next day, Mo spent our shift at Pizza Utopia dropping hints about the party and flirting with me. It was fun. He was fun. He even told me the same stories Thaddeus had when I asked about the missing boat, adding in that every time the Buysco guys stole his truck, they loaded the bed with things like fish guts or chicken dung.

On my walk home, I spied Pastor Forester and his picketing friends. Same bullhorn. Same signage. Same cute, blond boy in the crowd.

I took more photos, trying to be casual about it. The boy caught me, and we made eye contact. He immediately slid to the back of the group.

That was weird.

But also kind of suspicious? Maybe? Hopefully?

Or . . .

Since the cute boy had no idea I was investigating anti-draco activities, maybe he just didn't like me for some reason. The thought made my stomach churn. He didn't even know me. He might not even know who I was. (Nope, scratch the last. This was Gander.)

When I returned to the rental, Quentin sat at the kitchen table scarfing down a bowl of ramen. "Thank me at any time. Groveling will work. As will cash disbursements."

Crap. He'd succeeded. "You got Slade's schedule?"

"Even better, I got an invitation to work out with him at the shed gym." Quentin did a bicep curl. "You can ambush him when we leave. Which, don't say I didn't warn you, is just going to make him angry and you cry."

A truer truth had never before been stated. Still . . . "A visit to a gym wasn't what I asked for."

"Only because it didn't occur to you."

"I can't talk to him in front of other people, not even you. I need to run into him casually, like while he's out doing deliveries." The delivery truck being a mandatory element.

"My plan is better."

"I'll go to church with Dad for the rest of the month if you'll just get me his schedule."

"Entire summer."

Oh. Got it. I gave a long-suffering sigh. "You totally have his schedule, don't you?"

Quentin shrugged all fake-innocent and wolfed down a spoonful of ramen. "Vinnie's enrolled in pre-K sports camp. Slade delivers the drinks every morning and stops to chat with him. The schedule was just sitting there on a clipboard, so I snapped a photo."

***

According to the photo Quentin texted me, Slade's shift the next day began at 8 a.m. with loading up at a warehouse out by the airport. At 9 a.m., he stopped by the sports camp and then delivered north of Gander, followed by a lunch break at noon. In the afternoon, he delivered in Gander itself. Perfect.

Sort of perfect.

Actually, not really perfect at all.

I'd rather rub a bar of soap against my eyeballs or dunk my hair in used motor oil or time-travel back to Europe during the Black Plague than do this.

I dressed casual but cute. Navy leggings, hoodie with a penguin on the front, black Ugg boots, hair in two French braids.

The schedule didn't give exact delivery times, just the order of drop-offs. Of the list, my best option was the Goose and Gander Grill located in another strip mall. The back entrance of the strip mall was kitty-corner to the front parking lot of the hardware store. Weird setup, but Slade wouldn't think twice about bumping into me outside a hardware store.

When I arrived, I did a quick trip inside for bathtub caulking and then settled onto a pallet of potting soil out front. Ramoth was on the roof of a building across the street, far enough away that, should she be noticed, no one would connect her to me. (I'd have to remember to praise her for this choice later.)

"You all right, m' love?" An older man in a flannel shirt and rubber boots asked on his way into the store.

"Great, thanks. Just waiting for my mom. Love your shirt."

A moment later, a woman with three kids came up. "Hey, you're Mo's girlfriend, yeah? You need a ride? I've got space."

I was so not anyone's girlfriend, but the woman was smiling, so I didn't refute her. "I'm good. My mom's just running late. Your baby is super cute."

The stops and inquiries continued. Even the store manager came out (twice!) to check on me. Another hour of this, and Stella walked up.

"You need a ride?" she asked, right on cue.

"Waiting on my mom."

A beige delivery truck with a swirly logo pulled into the lot.

Finally!!! (Sort of.)

Stella sat down next to me on the potting soil, which gave me an idea. A good one. One that might get me a look into that truck without putting myself through another skewering since Slade would be less likely to take me down in front of someone he didn't know. Especially if I didn't do anything to upset him.

I chatted with Stella about Tutu and You Too while the truck backed up to the delivery entrance of the grill with a loud *beep-beep-beep*. She gave me recommendations for a couple of classes to try, all sounding great. The door of the truck cab opened.

"Hey Stella, want to go with me to meet an old friend of—"

"Isn't that the guy from Mo's video?" Stella interrupted while staring at Slade. "The one who messes with you? Mo told me to run interference if that guy ever showed up. Want me to go scratch his eyes out?"

And there went my brilliant idea.

***

My last chance of the day was a car dealership.

Gander had a lot of dealerships, most of them right in a row. Luckily, the one I needed was next to a steel building with trees. I took up watch from there, making a point to stay out of view of the street to avoid helpful Ganderites.

The dealership was a squat building with glass windows on three sides and cars for sale parked in rows all the way around. A portly salesman stood out front smoking.

The beige RBS truck arrived within minutes. It backed up to the side door of the dealership, loudly *beep-beep-beeping* again. I slipped into the first aisles of cars, staying low and working my way closer vehicle-by-vehicle so that I wouldn't be seen. I heard the back door rolling upward and the whine of the truck's lift. I peeked through the window of an SUV to get a look. Slade was riding up the lift. No sign of his coworker.

Hmmm . . .

Maybe if I snuck around the backside of the delivery truck while Slade was inside the building, I could get a look without him realizing I was ever there. Worth a try.

I continued to sneak between vehicles, taking regular looks at my goal through windshields and windows. The moment Slade pushed a full handcart into the building, I ran for the truck. Right as I made it to the back corner, the passenger door opened and Slade's coworker jumped to the ground. "Hey, Mo's girlfriend, yeah?"

Crap. Crap. Crap.

"Joey," I muttered. Not that Mo's oversharing or my having a name of my own was my biggest problem in this exact moment.

"That's right," he said. "Weren't you just over at Gander Hardware chatting with Stella Jeddore? Are you stalking Slade or something?"

"Definitely not stalking. I just need a word." More craps. Hundreds of them. Thousands even. I'd been so close.

"Heyo, b'ys," a male voice said from behind me. I swung around to find the salesman joining us. He tossed his cigarette to the ground and toed-it into oblivion while offering me a too-welcoming smile. "I'm Lewis. Can I help you with somethin'?" He paused. "Oh, eh, aren't you Mo's—"

"Girlfriend," I said quickly, just to get it over with.

Of course, that's the moment Slade came back outside.

"Hi," I said weakly.

He frowned and walked past me to the back of the truck.

A sad, hurt weight settled on my shoulders. Even worse, all the things I so desperately needed him to hear coalesced in my throat. A giant ball of apology for upsetting him, for China, for Mo, for existing. I whacked my fist into my sternum, but it didn't matter. The pressure was building. The words were coming.

At least this once, I'd get something out of my humiliation.

Slade pushed the handcart onto the lift.

"Can we have a minute?" I managed to the coworker and salesman. "I owe Slade an apology and—"

"Don't bother," Slade said over his shoulder, his tone cold.

"Young love." The salesman lit up another cigarette.

"Isn't she supposed to be with Mo?" the delivery guy asked.

Right. I was.

I mean, I wasn't.

What a mess.

I joined Slade on the lift.

"Seriously, Jojo?" Slade's eyes narrowed. He pressed his lips into an unhappy frown. The lift rose with a whine that grated on my ears. (Winch needed oiling.)

"I didn't mean for it to happen. Mo thought he was helping me. I swear I didn't ask him to spill pop on you or embarrass you. I don't want things to be bad between us anymore."

"Fine. I forgive you."

"I know I screwed up in China. And here. And constantly, but I—" I paused as his words sank in. The lift came to a jarring halt, and I shifted to keep my balance. "Wait. You forgive me?"

"That's what you want to hear, right?"

"I . . ." Was it? "Yes?"

"Good." He turned the handcart to move past me.

I cleared my throat. "You forgive me for China too? Or just the thing with Mo?"

"All of it," Slade said, evenly, disinterestedly. "You done? I need to get back to work."

"Right. Of course. You're at work, and I shouldn't be pestering you. Bad timing." The lift was in the air, so I couldn't actually leave.

I sucked my lower lip between my teeth, watching him as he wheeled the handcart into one of the aisles between the storage racks in the back of the truck. An inappropriate and wildly wrong urge to touch him settled over me. I followed him, sliding between the racks. (Once upon a time, a dark crevice would've been a total invitation to attack him.)

The racks.

They were welded into place.

No way would the rowboat fit inside. And there was a big red stain under one of them as if a powdered drink had spilled.

That must've been what I'd seen on Slade's hands before.

There, I had it. *Thank Eleos for her many mercies.* Of course, Slade wasn't involved with the rowboat. Slade, for all that he worked to scare people off, had always been a rule-follower. How could I have even considered otherwise?

The euphoria promised by Lei's app didn't hit. Instead, I watched Slade heft boxes onto the handcart while wishing I could run my fingers through his hair.

He tensed, not liking me watching him.

"You truly forgive me? We can be like casual acquaintances now or something?"

"Sure." He pushed the handcart my direction, forcing me to back out of his way.

"You're not just saying that to get me to go away?" I shifted to keep my balance as the lift jolted downward.

"Nope."

The lift whined to a stop. I got off. Slade started for the building again. His right shirtsleeve was pushed back, showing a smidgen of the colorful design on his wrist. Dragon scales? I so wanted it to be, and the urge to touch him became nearly unbearable.

Slade halted and turned to look at me. The corners of his lips pointed straight down. "Question."

Yes! "Anything."

"If you didn't want your boyfriend to screw with me, then why didn't you stop him?"

"He's not . . ." My mouth went dry. "I mean . . ." My pulse rapid-fire ticked in my veins. Sweat broke out on the back of my neck. I stared at Slade, paralyzed by the question, his frown, the massive kettle of simmering anger behind it that made *me* need a release valve. Words built anyway, a staggering, painful pile of words.

Slade turned his back and walked away before I could let them loose.

CHAPTER TWENTY-FOUR

Day 15 of 162 of the China Assignment
Changde City, Hunan Province, China

I push Vinnie's stroller toward the gym where we'd left Slade two hours ago. Slade's so lost when it comes to China that he won't leave the apartment without me to guide him. He also won't leave Vinnie home alone with his mom. He hasn't explained why this is, and I haven't seen anything to indicate an obvious problem, but Slade's really protective of his brother. It took me fifteen minutes to convince him that we'd be fine going to a kids' playland without him.

Now he's standing outside the gym, his arms crossed, headphones around his neck, scanning the busy street back and forth as if waiting for an imaginary attack. Pedestrians give him a wide berth. Other than a group of girls, that is, who are totally checking him out.

I wave. He spots me but doesn't relax.

"Jojo? Someone's following you."

I glance around but don't see anyone out of place. "It's probably MSS. My dad warned me that might happen. No biggie as long as we don't do anything suspicious. It's happened a few times in other countries too."

He nods but stays stiff and takes my hand in his. Which makes me go all gooey. Also, a just-spent-several-hours-lifting-weights Slade is . . .

Well . . .

Wow.

Just wow.

Next-level.

With his free hand, he swings his brother out of the stroller and up onto his shoulders. "Thanks. For taking care of Vinnie."

"It was fun. Right, Vin?"

Vinnie nods. He's a super quiet kid.

Slade told me that he'd been the same at that age. He was held back in kindergarten for it, so even though Slade and I are only a year apart in school, he's two years older.

Also, Slade's still super quiet. Pretty sure I'm right about him having a speech thing going on. He hasn't offered an explanation, and I haven't asked, as I don't want to upset him if he's sensitive about it. He has tells, and not just that his words get slow and choppy when he's struggling. The furrow between his brows is a dead giveaway. Also, he gets little wrinkles on each side of his mouth, and sometimes his gaze goes far away as if he's focusing on an inward battle. My guess is that his inability to call me Joey is related. He's also yet to attempt a single word in Mandarin.

But he does talk to me. And it's getting easier and easier for him to do so. He also really likes my nickname. He says it all the time, even though we're usually alone and there's no question who he's talking to. I think the tautonym aspect appeals to the drummer in him.

Slade takes the now-empty stroller from me. I loop my hand through his arm and pat his bicep. His skin is toasty and underneath is like granite. Yum!

Our next stop is a noodle house where we pick up food for Quentin and our neighbor, Yuze. The four of us hang out regularly, and I'm tutoring Yuze with his English. I'm also helping Slade in every subject and prodding Quentin along in biology.

Back at the apartment, Slade sets everything up in the kitchen, and we all serve ourselves. Yuze offers Slade and me the sofa, but Slade gives him an upward chin-nod and takes the floor. (He never says a word in front of Quentin or Yuze.)

There isn't really room for me on the floor, but I fold down next to Slade anyway, and shift sideways to lean my back against his side. He hesitates, glances quickly at Quentin and Yuze, and then puts his palm face up on my knee. I slide my hand into his.

***

Day 23 of 162 of the China Assignment
Changde City, Hunan Province, China

"And after India, we moved to Peru. That's where I bought the bell. It called to me from the vendor's stand. The statue of the Greek Goddess Eleos is from the Falklands, which makes no sense as a local tribute, but I just had to have her. Also, that's where I got my penguin. Every one of my memorials spoke to me. It's how I pick them. Slade, are you even listening?"

"India, Peru, the Falklands, all of your things speak to you. Your memorials are what make you, you."

We're in the kitchen of his family's apartment. I'm taking apart the sink faucet to figure out why it won't stop leaking. (Guaranteed it's the o-ring. Always is.)

Sum 41 plays on Slade's speaker. Slade sits behind me at the table, his left foot bouncing as if tapping a drum pedal. He's supposed to be putting together his To Kill a Mockingbird essay: "A Deconstruction of Atticus Killing the Dog in contrast to Tom Robinson's Death." Or as he titled it before I'd forced him to fix it: "Dying Dog versus Dying Man."

Instead of schoolwork, he's looking at drum kits online. Sometimes I get the feeling Slade wasn't a very focused student before me.

"Am I talking too much?" I ask, moving closer to him. My family's shipping pods arrived last night. I can't seem to stop telling him about my stuff.

"You have a great voice." He glances up at me. "I like listening to you."

Warmth, pleasure, delight, happiness, effervescence flood my body.

"Plenty of people find me annoying." I'm totally fishing for another compliment.

"Their loss."

I grin wildly.

Our gazes catch and hold, and I see it again, that look he gave me on our first morning in Changde, all focus and intensity and heat. We both go still. Butterflies gather in my chest, their fluttering keeping my heart going. Goosebumps prickle my skin.

"I like you. Jojo," he says abruptly.

"I like you too."

He shakes his head and frowns. "I have. Since the first moment. You're funny. And kind. You help people." A crease forms between his eyes. He's having to work to speak and the words come slow. "You're not afraid. Not of anything. You're happy. And confident. I've never known. Anyone like you. You're perfect."

A grin spreads across my face. The butterflies go wild.

Then I pause.

His words are the most wonderful, flattering, exquisite thing anyone has ever said to me. Especially since Slade doesn't flatter or flirt or fawn. Slade's always sincere.

He's also wrong. He only thinks I'm brave and adventurous and happy and perfect because he's never seen me cry or fall apart or be the girl who can't cope.

And no way will I ever let him.

Chapter Twenty-Five

To-do list from Mo for our next date.

(1) Mo picks up Joey again in oldest, ugliest truck in Gander.
(2) Mo admires Joey, compliments everything about her, and takes selfies to prove such an awesome girl agreed to go out with him.
(3) Joey tells Mo how good he is at flattery and considers complimenting him back.
(4) Mo and Joey suffer through local theater group.
(5) Mo and Joey may or may not pay more attention to each other than the stage.
(6) Mo and Joey drive to epic party.
(7) Rest of the evening to be determined.
(8) Based on Joey's preferences.
(9) Mo is open to suggestions, especially suggestive ones.

It was overall a great list. Fun and flirty in all the ways that I liked about Mo. It even had a healthy dose of him going overboard as usual. I wrote back:

(8a) Joey and Mo dance at party. A lot. Because Joey loves to dance until she's too exhausted to do anything more than collapse.

Boundary set. Hopefully? Badly?

My plan was to use the party to hunt down the blond boy from church. Since he was local and under twenty-five, he should be there. I'd work up a casual conversation and charm him. It was past time to figure out what was going on there.

The morning of the party, our family's shipping pods arrived. I showed Ramoth each of my memorials as I unwrapped them. I told her their stories as I placed them in their special places on my dresser.

My sandalwood elephant from India went in the far-left corner. My Capiz Flower from the Philippines, next to it. Then my Scottish stuffed wool heart, my mini statue of the Greek Goddess Eleos, and my plastic mango-on-a-stick from Mexico. I placed my Newfoundland mug front and center, since it was new. On and on it went.

My last memorial, the framed photo of Slade, Vinnie, and me, I shoved into the lowest drawer. Usually, I took my time with it, lingered a bit, let myself remember how good things had once been. I couldn't handle that today. Ramoth craned her head around, trying to see the photo anyway. I closed the drawer.

Mo showed up right on time, thank goodness. For once, I was the one in need of a distraction.

I wore a short denim skirt, a cream cami with tiny pearl buttons down the front, and a powdery soft, baby-blue sweater. Great outfit for dancing. Mo wore chinos and a flower-patterned button-down. Perfect for a casual date.

"Where's the party? No. Don't answer. Tonight, I know the answer, and the hottest girl in Newfoundland and Labrador is goin' there with me." He looked me over appreciatively, pausing at where my sweater slipped off my shoulder.

I fixed it and smiled at him. "You look pretty great yourself. Who would've thought you'd pull off flowers so well?"

"I know, right?" He struck a pose, one hand behind his ear, the other on his hip.

As we drove to the theater, I brought up the boat theft again, fishing for new leads. He told me about the time he hid it under a stack of firewood. Took him hours of work, but it also stayed lost for a good week before the homeowner noticed. Funny, and I complimented his ingenuity and dedication. But not helpful.

Once at the theater, he helped me from the truck and then grabbed my hand, twirling me around so that my back was tucked against his chest. "Selfie time." We both went all out, making faces and playing it up while he took pictures.

"I like this one," he said once we were seated inside.

The photo *was* pretty perfect. Me, leaning against him, his arm wrapped around my waist, both of us laughing. Pictorially, we made a great couple.

"Social media?" he asked, nudging my arm.

"Way too soon. Question for you, though. I met this guy a couple of weeks ago when I went with my dad to church. You know he plays the organ, right? My dad, not the boy. I was wondering if you knew him."

Mo stiffened and jerked sideways, his attention going past me to the front of the theater.

"Joey, I'm so sorry." His voice was clipped and sharp. "If I'd known, I wouldn't have brought you here."

"What's wrong?" I glanced around. The pit band was entering from a side door. First, a woman with a cello. Then a guy with a sax. Then Slade, wearing a dark shirt and tie, his hair in a tidy ponytail, carrying a quiver of sticks.

Ohhh . . .

I swallowed hard and slid down in my seat.

"How didn't I know?" Mo asked, sounding put out. "I'm supposed to know everything, and the play's been in the works for months. How is this possible?"

"Slade's really good at picking up new music." I half-whispered it just in case Slade could hear. He was too far away to do so, but my paranoia had walked right in with him.

"No one's that good," Mo grumbled.

"Slade is. He's done theater gigs in the past. As long as he practices a few times and studies the drum chart on his own, he could easily do it. He's really talented."

"Grand." Mo frowned.

Right. Overly complimenting Slade to Mo was insensitive on my part. I squeezed Mo's hand and touched his arm in apology. "Let's just watch the show so that you can report back to Uncle Charles that we followed orders. We'll sneak out at the end before the houselights come on. He'll never know we were here."

Mo nodded and, in a deliberate move, draped his arm around my shoulders. The weight pushed me forward in my seat. Totally uncomfortable, but he seemed upset, so I couldn't bring myself to say anything.

***

I gave Mo all my attention on the drive to the party to make up for having spent the entire play watching Slade while hiding it from Mo. Yes, watching Slade hurt like being attached to a medieval torture device. Yes, Slade behind a drum kit was still slices of heaven raining down to Earth.

By the time we arrived at a large clearing full of parked cars, Mo'd let the Slade sighting go and was back to his usual cheery self.

Not sure what I'd expected when it came to a party at an abandoned house, but I was blown away by what I got. Pickup trucks with huge tower lights in their beds were staged around the edges. People were everywhere, sitting in camp chairs around several bonfires, hanging out around a line of kegs, dancing in front of a huge speaker on the house porch that blasted the Dave Matthews Band.

The abandoned house had all its windows and doors and appeared in decent condition, if in need of fresh paint. A line of Porta-potties backed up to trees on the far side. The whole thing was noisy, rowdy, and perfect for dancing.

Even better, I spied the blond boy almost immediately. He stood at a table holding a pyramid of packaged snack foods, attempting to add a family-sized bag of Ketchup Lay's to the munchies monolith.

I prodded Mo on the side. "Hey, who's the guy standing by the food?"

Mo started to turn, but Lei came running our way, Quentin, Tabby, and Isa following.

"Joey!" Lei threw her arms around me. "Yay, you're here! Joey's here, everyone."

She reeked of soggy bread left in a plastic baggy to rot in the sun. A.k.a. beer. My nose wrinkled. (It was Slade who'd first pointed out the connection between beer and mold. Not that I was thinking about Slade.)

"Love your dress," I said to Lei, determined to be positive anyway. She wore a beige mini with a mesh top. Her fauxhawk was brilliant orange. "Do you all know Mo?" I did quick introductions.

Lei crashed into my side. "Do you know Stella Jeddore? She's supposed to be here, but I can't find her and there's no cell service."

"You know Stella?" I rubbed at my complaining nose.

"She's on her way," Mo said to Lei. "She said you were hot, if that helps."

Stella was Lei's cute girl? Unexpected. (Stella *was* totally cute. And Lei *was* totally hot.)

"So, Joey—" Isa started.

I pulled Mo away from the group and toward the snack pyramid before Isa could bring up anything I didn't want to talk about, a.k.a. Trinity, Maur, or her belief that I was working for wyrm-netters.

Unfortunately, my quarry had disappeared.

"Hey, who's the blond guy who brought the Lay's?" I asked Mo.

"Goin' to need a bit more detail than blond and chips, babe." He headed to the kegs and poured himself a beer.

I could've used some water, but there wasn't anything but beer available, which sucked. I picked up an empty cup just to have something in my hand. "Shall we dance?"

"I'm in charge of the game room." He put his hand on my lower back and turned me toward the house.

"Games aren't really my thing. I'll go . . ." My words trailed off as I spied a guy I didn't recognize in a suede jacket struggling to push a large black case on wheels. The case had a label on it that read Celsius Burns above a stylized sideways skull resting on two clasped hands as if dead and asleep.

Seriously?

Twice in one night?

This couldn't be happening.

Slade jogged over to help the guy pushing the case. He'd changed from his professional-musician attire of earlier to an I'm-in-a-band-and-edgy outfit of black ripped-up jeans and an unbuttoned shirt over a Cancer Bats band tee. His hair was loose, the top curtaining the side of his face, and he had nickel-sized steel hoops in his ears.

Piercings!?

We'd never discussed him getting piercings. They suited him.

He turned and looked right at me, frowning but not with surprise. His gaze dipped to the cup in my hand. I flushed and upended it to show him it was empty and dry. Not that it was any of his business.

He flicked his gaze to Mo, who was half turned the other direction. Mo took that moment to down his beer. Slade returned to pushing.

I winced. Even more, my plans to dance the night away ground deeper into the dirt with every turn of the wheels of the case holding Slade's kit. No way could I dance. No. Absolute. Way.

But at least Mo had missed the entire interaction.

"Where's the party!?" Mo yelled as we entered a living room filled with an elongated table, three sofas, ten chairs, and five times that number of people.

"Mo's the party!" a girl with her arms around two very drunk guys yelled back.

Someone tried to hand Mo another beer, but he turned it away. Then he cleared the table and set up six triangles of red cups. Another girl leaned into me. "Mo's the best. You're so lucky to be with him."

"Definitely lucky," I replied, aiming at and mostly hitting a note of sincerity.

An hour later, we were still there, and I was feeling the opposite of lucky, cursed even.

Mo was a great game-meister. He kept things moving and entertaining. When two guys started screaming at each other over a missed shot, he jumped in to separate them and calm things down. I ducked to the back wall.

He kept his drinking to a minimum but seemed content to spend the entire evening inside, which was pretty much the last place I wanted to be. Or second to last. Very last would be wherever Slade was.

I waited until Mo was between games and tapped him on the shoulder, "Hey, I'll be right back, I'm going to hit up the toilets."

"I'll walk you."

I held up my hands to block him. "Appreciated but not needed. Girl thing."

Outside, the majority of people were slowly moving toward the back of the house, where I could hear Slade and a couple of guitars warming up. I sent a mental plea to the heavens that my blond boy wasn't interested in music and headed over to scope out the crowd around the kegs and food.

No blond boy there, so I meandered over to a group settled in chairs around a small bonfire. Also, no blond boy, but a guy in a green toque pulled me into a conversation about Pizza Utopia that led to an invitation to join him and his friends. I almost asked about the blond boy, but then he called me Mo's girlfriend. I quickly left.

The next group I approached was a rinse and repeat, only it was a girl who brought up Mo. The third time, I started to get annoyed. Loved how friendly everyone was, but seriously? I was going to have to have a talk with Mo about this. (Eventually.)

I kept hunting for the blond boy, but the pickings got thinner as more and more people moved to the back of the house. Unless I was willing to do so as well, my chances of finding him were getting low.

I headed to check in with Mo.

Slade began playing, going at it alone on a tom, swift and loud. The beat was so intense, so furious, it reverberated off the building, the cars, even the trees. I halted in my steps because furious wasn't a euphemism. His anger was palpable with every strike as he played the opening of "A Certain Romance" by Arctic Monkeys.

Anger at me.

It'd always been like this between us when he played. It got worse if I danced. No way could I go back there. Not even to lurk and hunt for the blond boy.

The volume and tempo increased as the guitars joined in. Then the music exploded in every direction, a vicious, personal punch to my gut. His emotions pummeled my soul.

Which was when Isa walked up.

"Hey," I said, only because I had no choice.

A singer launched into the lyrics. He wasn't half bad, if not as good as the vocalist from Celsius Burns. (I mean, I'd only ever heard Celsius Burns perform via cell-recorded online videos, and I was biased.)

"Lei sent me to find you," Isa said. "She wants you to dance with Stella."

"Shouldn't she dance with Stella?"

"Like I care." Isa fingered a large vulture charm around her neck. There was something threatening in the motion.

"I'm going to go hang with Mo."

"This party is stupid, and I want out of here. But Tabby won't leave Lei, and Lei won't leave at all until you dance with Stella."

"I'm saying *no* to that."

"The only reason I didn't tell my parents about the wyrm-netters was because Trinity was too far away for my mom's wards to link me to what happened to that draco. She never found out what I did, and I don't want her to. But I bet I could come up with a new story about you, the wyrm-netters, and Trinity to get you in trouble. If you want me to refrain, you're going to go out there and dance." Isa lowered her chin, her eyes narrowing to displeased slits, her voice dangerously cold. "Right now."

***

The band played from a portable stage backed up to the house and consisted of a couple of guitars, a keyboard, Slade at a jet-black kit with two bass drums that was triple the size of the one we'd bought in China, and a vocalist. After Arctic Monkeys, they moved on to a song by the Killers.

Maybe with the size of the crowd, Slade wouldn't notice me?

Of course, he'd notice me. He always noticed me.

Which made me feel helpless. To him. To Isa. To Lei. To the music pounding into my skin. Something within me, a small nameless organ tucked in next to my useless appendix, suddenly went hard. It wasn't the usual stiffening and collapse due to nerves. This was less quivery fear, more frustrated desire to do something about all these people pressuring me.

So I'd dance.

I'd ignore Slade and his anger and go all-in on the magic, sorcery, seductiveness that was his playing. Screw the repercussions for once. (Bad idea. Bad. Bad. Bad.)

I spotted Lei and Stella to one side of the throng near the speakers and slid into their circle, grabbing each by a hand and lifting their arms up. I didn't even bother looking for the blond boy. He'd have to wait. The music rolled through me, pulling me in, moving my body with no conscious thought, just sensation.

Quentin, Tabby, and Isa joined us. The band moved on to Franz Ferdinand.

It was everything I could've hoped for. The energy and the heat and the blasting sound. I ditched my sweater, so I only wore my skirt and cami and the cool night on my steaming skin.

Stella pulled me into an improv-at-a-raging-party version of swing. So fun. So good. I tossed my hair and sang at the top of my lungs for the pure joy of doing so.

And then Slade noticed me.

I heard it in his playing. A spike in his anger and then something else. Something intense and tantalizing replacing it.

I should make a run for it.

Protect myself.

Hide.

I didn't. (Terrible idea. T.E.R.R.I.B.L.E.)

He filled me, thrummed through my muscles, raced up my veins, overflowed me with the sense of him. Of us.

The first time this had happened, things had gone nuclear explosion between us and turned into a make-out session that only stopped because someone threw a chair at Slade's head.

I kept dancing.

He kept playing.

The *we* of it built song by song until I had to look at Slade. A Sherman tank aimed at Normandy couldn't have stopped me.

He sat on his throne, his arms flying, his whole body in action, his sticks near invisible. Sweat dripped down his face. He tossed his head, strands of black hair whipping backward.

Over the top of the other people, the music, and his kit, our eyes met.

Time slowed.

Sound disappeared.

Everything and everyone fell away until it was just him and me. The way we'd been in China, at our best and closest.

A seed of something soft and tender swelled within me, unfolding petal by petal into an achingly beautiful, entirely familiar, gooey warmth.

Chapter Twenty-Six

Day 42 of 162 of the China Assignment
Changde City, Hunan Province, China

I arrive first and take a seat on a step in our usual spot. The place where we meet when our apartments are too full of our families. Slade slides in behind me so that I can lean against him. He wraps his arms around me, and we twine our hands together, our favorite way to sit.

He rests his forehead against the back of my head but says nothing.

Pretty sure Dr. Panozco has been lecturing him again, lecturing being an understated term for what occurs. I don't know why Slade's mom doesn't put a stop to it, but from what I can tell, she never does.

Slade won't talk about it. He takes whatever is thrown at him, absorbs the punches, and then goes so deep within himself that the rest of us no longer exist, keeping it all bottled inside.

I get an idea. Something I've been saving for just the right moment, and that is sure to knock him out of his dark place and back to me.

"Slade?"

"Hmmm?"

"We should start kissing."

He startles, just as expected.

I grin, loving his reaction. "Not right this moment. We need to plan ahead, set things up just so, pick a romantic spot." I squeeze his arm. "It has to be *just right. And outdoors. Somewhere pretty. Near water, maybe. It'll be my first kiss."*

He clears his throat as if suddenly uncomfortable about something. "Jojo . . ."

I pat his hand, as I'd anticipated this. "I know it won't be yours. I'm sure you've been kissing girls since you were a toddler, but that's a good thing. Means one of us will know what they're doing. I'll take care of the timing and location. You handle the actual kissing. You don't mind, do you?"

I swivel around to look up at him, pretending I don't already know what his answer will be.

Based on the laser-focused look he gives me, he's good with his assignment. He's also entirely distracted from whatever happened with Dr. Panozco.

***

Day 47 of 162 of the China Assignment
Zhangjiajie National Forest, Hunan Province, China

The time is now, and I'm utterly terrified. Why, oh why, had I thought kissing Slade would be a good idea? He's the best friend I've ever had, the proverbial yin to my yang, my rock. What if the two of us kissing ruins that?

What if I'm terrible at it? What if I'm so awful he can't stand to be my friend? What if he compares me to all the other girls he's already kissed and I fail?

We leave the city for the mountains. Slade, Quentin, Vinnie, and I, because Slade won't leave Vinnie and Quentin insists on joining us.

We follow a trail running along a creek to a perfect, romantic, private little glade. There's soft light, leafy trees with moss, the burble of water, privacy, and the cool scent of green things. I set out a blanket, making sure it's spread straight all the way to the corners.

We eat lunch with our siblings. I'm nervous, but Slade is his usual calm self. Afterward, he gives Quentin cash to take Vinnie for a walk up the creek. (Slade totally has Quentin figured out.)

We sit together with our backs against a boulder. The warmth of him presses up and down my side. My tremors of utter terror vibrate against his. This is going to be a disaster. I'm going to ruin everything. He's going to hate kissing me.

"Jojo, you need to calm down. I'm not going to attack you."

"Pretty sure you're supposed to want to attack me."

He laughs softly, deep in his throat. A delicious sound, because his laughter is so rare. I should be reassured, but the tremors get worse.

"Of course, I want to attack you. I've wanted to attack you since the first moment I laid eyes on you. But I'm not an idiot. I'm not going to do that." He says it calmly, easily. He never has trouble talking to me anymore.

"What if I'm scared?"

Slade shifts so that we're facing each other. He studies me all intent-like. "Yeah, that's kinda obvious."

Heat rises under my skin. I try to look away, but he cradles my chin between his thumb and pointer finger so I can't. With his other hand, he presses my palm over his heart.

"I've got this," he murmurs.

Should I purse my lips? Close my eyes? Lean into him? My tremors increase. "Slade—"

"Stop thinking."

"I can't. I—"

He hums my name. Even and velvety and rhythmic. "Jojojojojojojo." He strokes my face. His chest rises and falls under my hand. I match my breathing to his. My lashes flutter down.

"There," he murmurs.

He leans into me and brushes his lips against mine. Not a lip-mash like in the movies. Nor a quick peck. It's more of a hint, a suggestion, a test, a tease, a whisper, an introduction.

His lips are soft, and I part my mouth automatically. He brushes against me a second time, so gentle, so easy, just the lightest touch. A feather of breath and warmth that ripples across my skin, down my body, and into my toes.

I slide my hands up his chest to his shoulders and around his neck. He's so solid, so entirely there.

The next time his lips touch mine, they stay.

Yeah . . .

I was an idiot to have been afraid of this.

Chapter Twenty-Seven

The moment the last song was announced, I fled the dance floor. Quentin, Tabby, and Isa had already taken off. Stella was driving Lei home, so the three of us had kept dancing.

I wanted to touch Slade. To throw myself at him. Drag him off into the dark and devour him.

Tell him how I felt.

"Help me find my sweater," I announced in a panic. I had to get out of there.

We searched the area where I thought I'd left it. Nothing.

Shoot, I really liked that sweater. It was special. All my clothing was, and for reasons I couldn't put into words, I needed the comfort of that sweater right this minute.

The music stopped.

"Let's check the front." I bolted around the side of the house.

Mo walked toward us, his hands in his pockets, smiling. Mo. My ride out of here, away from Slade and the overwhelming sensations still running under my skin. I raced straight at him.

"I'm glad to see you too." Mo threw his arms around me, lifting me off the ground, crushing the air from my chest.

"Can't. Breathe."

"Sorry, sorry." He put me down but kept his arms around me, a huge, happy grin on his face. A dollop of guilt added itself to the rest of the muddle of feelings battling it out inside me. I'd forgotten about Mo until now.

Also, he reeked of musty, moldy bread.

Gross.

I ran my hand up his chest to push myself free, but he must've taken it wrong as he bent me backward. He did it so fast that I threw my arms around his shoulders and clung to him to keep from crashing to the ground. Which, from his perspective, must've seemed an additional invitation because he went all-in, mouth first.

First impression: He tasted like wintergreen. Great that Mo had thought of mints.

Second impression: This wasn't a romantic location for kissing. There were people everywhere. A light glared in my face. Lei complained to Stella in the background.

Third impression: Mo's mouth was too big. He overwhelmed me, and not in a good way. He didn't take his time like Slade always had, but hurried the kiss, creating a mashing, grinding sensation. On a scale of zero-to-Slade, Mo was a 1.5. Maybe a 2.0, if I was generous.

Fourth impression (which should really have come first): Even if I'd accidentally made Mo think I wanted to kiss him for a second time now, I absolutely, utterly didn't want to be doing this.

"And we're outta here," Stella announced.

"Maybe we should—" Lei started, but Stella cut her off.

"Mo's got her now."

They left.

I wiggled around to get my hand up Mo's arm and leverage myself so that I could turn my head away. "Time to stop!"

Mo immediately straightened and let me go. I stumbled sideways at the sudden release and leaned on him to steady myself.

A slow, satisfied grin spread across his face. "You're amazing, my party girl."

I pushed away. "Mo," I said as sternly as I was capable, so not all that sternly. "Next time, ask first."

"Next time?" His eyes sparkled.

Crap.

"Let's take a walk 'round the lake. Head over to Lover's Rock. It's a lovely grand kind of night."

No, it wasn't and not if I could help it. I waved my hand at his flower-print shirt. "Did someone dump a beer down your front?"

"Yeah. But that was hours ago. I'm sober, I swear. I drank a total of two beers."

I looked him over. He didn't appear drunk. He just stank. I pointed at my nose. "Super sensitive, but I'm also really tired. Could we just go home?"

Mo's smile fell. His shoulders slumped. His eyes drooped like a kicked puppy.

Which made me tense up. In no way had he been trying to force anything by kissing me. Not really, and he'd stopped the moment I asked. He just really liked me. In trade, I was making him feel bad, which I *absolutely* didn't want to do.

Before I could come up with a way to talk him back up without encouraging any more kissing, a chubby-cheeked guy shoved a garbage bag into my hands. "Mo, you and your girlfriend are on cleanup."

"Actually, I'm not his—"

"Got it." Mo took the garbage bag from me. "Cleanup first. It'll go fast if we all pitch in. Then home, yeah?"

I nodded with relief and let the girlfriend thing go for the moment.

An hour of recycling collection later, with no sightings of Slade, the blond boy, or my sweater, Mo said we'd done enough. (Yes, I made Mo look for my sweater. It was that important.)

Right as we finished, the generators running the tower lights cut out. Mo turned on his cellphone, and we headed to his truck. Out of nowhere, another light came on, shining right at us, blindingly so.

"What the hell?" Mo halted.

Standing in front of the truck with a black industrial flashlight pointed our direction was Slade.

I choked on my own inhale. Not now. Please, please, not now. Not when I was still raw from the dancing. Not with Mo witnessing.

"How much. Have you had. To drink?" Slade's voice was edged, the words choppy, his lips tight, his eyes slits, the crease between his brows obvious even in the low light.

"Nothing," I stuttered around a loss of air. "I'm not a drinker. You know that, and my dad has the nose of a bloodhound. My parents would kill me if—"

"I meant him." He did an angry chin-nod at Mo.

Right.

I was an idiot.

I should've seen this coming from miles away. Even if he hated me, Slade would never let me go home with someone who'd been drinking.

Mo grabbed my hand and towed me around Slade.

Slade stepped into our path. His nostrils flared, likely at Mo's smell. The crease between his brows was joined by ones around his mouth. "You're not. Driving her. Home."

"Not your decision, dude." Mo pulled out his keys and jangled them challengingly in Slade's direction.

Slade blocked the truck door. "Jojo? Do you drive?"

"No." I shivered. The temperature was dropping fast.

"You aren't. Getting. In that truck. I'll take you home."

Mo swung around. He radiated tension but plastered on a cheery smile. "I haven't had a beer in hours. I'd never put the deadliest girl in Newfoundland in danger." He turned to me. "Tell this douche to go to hell. You don't have to put up with this crap from him. I've got you."

Slade crossed his arms. "Jojo. I'm not. Giving you. A choice."

I glanced between the two of them. I had to do something. Stop this. Calm things down. End the conflict. Somehow.

The pressure built.

"Babe?" Mo pressed.

Slade stared at me.

I broke. "Mo, I'm so sorry. I have to go with Slade. He utterly and completely hates me. Like pure loathing. But he feels really strongly about driving under the influence. Even if you'd had just a sip of beer, he'd worry. He might even follow us. I know you don't understand, that it makes no sense, but I have to go with him. There's a history here."

"A history." Mo rammed his keys into his pocket, not taking his eyes off Slade. "I got that."

Great. Now Mo was going to be mad at me too.

"I'll see you at work tomorrow night?" I asked, desperate to fix this, to stop Mo's anger.

"I'm scheduled for lunch shift."

"I'll call you."

"C'mon," Slade said coldly. "Let's get this over with."

***

"You're shivering," Slade said as he opened the passenger door of his car for me.

I was shivering, only it had nothing to do with the temperature.

Since this was actually happening and not a setup for a JFK situation, I had to stay calm. And distant. And silent. And not do a single thing to annoy him or make him yell. (So wish I'd thought to bring Lei's wristband with me tonight.)

Slade placed his flashlight on the car roof to remove his outer shirt.

"You don't have to do that," I said quickly. "Then you'll be cold, and I've ruined enough of your night and your life for one evening. You shouldn't have to sacrifice for someone you hate. It's my problem, not yours, and I'll be fine. It's not that cold. And we'll turn the heater on. That'll work."

So much for silent.

"Take it." He handed me the shirt.

I did.

Stupid of me, but I couldn't help but admire the way his Cancer Bats tee hugged his chest and shoulders. And his biceps. Where it ended. Because it was short-sleeved.

I paused.

There it was, totally exposed. Brilliantly colored even in the low light. Slade's sleeve tattoo.

"You did it." I grabbed his hand, cupping his palm in mine.

He didn't respond but also didn't object, so I ran my fingers up his arm, tracing a wooden branch that twined around dragon scales so intricate they looked real. Ramoth's weren't even that gorgeous.

"It's amazing. How long did it take?"

"Forty hours. Because of the detail. And the shading." His voice was soft and even, quiet but no longer struggling. Very much the Slade that'd been my best friend. I bent to look closer. Each dragon scale shifted in color from green to blue to purple, giving them layers and depth. The design was complex and complicated. I spotted a dragonfly worked into it, and then a bee, flowers, and a butterfly.

I traced the branches, enjoying the warmth of him, the solidness of the muscles under his skin, the familiarity of his veins.

"Oh, Slade," I whispered, my eyes prickling with emotion. "It's perfect. And beautiful. And so you. It matches."

My words pleased him. He liked me liking his ink. I knew this the same way I'd known about his anger when he'd been playing his drums.

He gave a quick shake of his head, making the steel hoops in his ears swing, and I longed to touch those too. They were another thing new about him in need of exploring.

"We should go." He said it quiet but firm.

I jumped backward in embarrassment, dropping his arm, breaking the connection.

He turned to the car and shoved several water bottles and a Tim Horton's bag from the front seat to the back. I slid into his shirt, reveling more than I should in wearing his clothing. Once we were driving, he turned on Taylor Swift's *The Tortured Poets Department*, keeping it low, barely audible. We didn't talk. He beat out a light rhythm on the steering wheel as he drove.

It was . . .

Not stressful.

No pressure either. Just him and me. Comfortable with each other in the way we'd been comfortable in China.

I wanted to tell him about my evening, just rattle it all out. Watching him at *Carrie: The Musical*, what I'd experienced dancing, how bad I felt that he was stuck with me again, how much I wanted to keep exploring his ink and also his hoops, how I hadn't liked kissing Mo, or that everyone kept calling me Mo's girlfriend.

I'd never once called Slade my boyfriend.

It was true. Bayani and Duarte had been boyfriends. Mo wanted to be one but wasn't.

Slade had been my . . .

Well . . .

My everything.

We hit the lights of Gander.

"I don't hate you," Slade said, the words low, barely audible.

I turned to him, taken by surprise. "What?"

He did a chin-nod and drummed the steering wheel in a four-beat pattern. "You said I hated you. I don't. Or I did. For a long time. But I don't anymore."

"I don't hate you either." It was a dumb thing to say since I never had hated him. I stared at a dirt smudge on the dash in front of me. It was in the shape of the front half of a shoe, as if the last occupant of the car had rested their foot there.

"You take life lightly," he continued. "It's one of the things I liked about you before, that I still like about you. You're happy, and your happiness is contagious."

"Really?" The barest spark of hope flickered to life. He was being straight this time and not just trying to get rid of me.

His hand on the steering wheel stilled. "You're happy because you don't have real problems."

"That's not true. I've got problems. You've met my parents."

"They fight a lot. But it's not . . ." He paused as if searching for just the right words.

I tensed.

This wasn't the two of us working things out, him forgiving me. He was busy sharpening a knife to slice my chest wide open. The red flags were all there and waving in my direction.

"Maybe we should just—"

"Your biggest life problem is picking which expensive American school you want your parents to pay for."

"That's not my biggest problem." Only I couldn't tell him about the Bob situation. Nor my anxiety about conflict, and that I fell apart whenever anyone yelled at me. It's one of the few things I'd never talked to him about. I'd never wanted him to see me that way. I still didn't.

"I no longer hate you," he continued. "But this game you're playing—"

"I'm not playing a game."

His lip curled in a sneer. "Jojo, you spent all night dancing for me and then ran off with some other guy."

I stared at his profile in surprise. I hadn't run off with Mo. I'd ditched Mo and run off with him. Unless . . .

"You came after me." Little bubbles of crazy-happy joy birthed a flurry of butterflies in my chest. In the next moment, a dark, dropping stone of horror smushed them to pulp. "After you stopped playing. You came after me." And found me on the receiving end of Mo's terrible kissing.

Slade's hand flattened on the steering wheel. "Of course I came after you. When in the history of your games have I not?"

"It wasn't a game. I didn't mean for that to happen." It hadn't occurred to me that it would, that he would. If it had, I definitely would've waited for him and—

"Right." He said it dismissively.

"No, I mean it. Isa blackmailed me into dancing with Stella, and then it was just so fun that I gave in and enjoyed myself. I wasn't trying to get to you." Only I was lying. Maybe it hadn't been a game, but I *had* been dancing for Slade. Of course I had. I'd known what would happen the moment I'd gone out there. "I left before you stopped playing. I was afraid if I didn't that I would attack *you*. But then Mo found me and he's a really nice guy and—"

Slade cut off my blurting, his voice back to cold and hard. "Fine. You didn't mean for it to happen. But that's the thing, isn't it? You never mean for these things to happen. But they do." He ran a hand through his hair in frustration.

The knife, icy sharp, sliced a ribbon from my navel to my neck.

"Even if you weren't with that boneheaded guy, I can't do this." He took a breath. It shook as if he was troubled by his own words. "You're not a bad person. I get that. But you don't look past the moment. You never see the bigger danger. You never saw what I was experiencing in China. You still don't really see me."

The knife slid through skin and muscle and ribs. I fought to breathe around the cold metal in my chest.

"I don't hate you, but I need you to stop." He didn't yell. He was calm about it, Slade-calm. "I need you to hear that stopping is what's best for me. I'm done. I've been done for a long time."

My heart cleaved in two. Tears gathered in the back of my eyes. I was going to fall apart. Toronto-fall apart. My *emotional threshold* collapsing under its own weight.

The tears built. A sob fought its way up my throat. My chest tightened, and the first tear escaped down my cheek.

That was the moment I recognized it.

Not the tear, although I was plenty familiar with those when it came to Slade, but the shoe smudge on the dash. It had a flat place and then a swirl with a small circle. I'd seen this pattern any number of times before. It matched my dad's lucky shoes exactly.

The tears dried up startlingly fast, and I straightened in my seat. There was no good reason for my dad to have been in Slade's car. None.

"Did you recently loan out your car?" I asked, abruptly.

Slade shot me a confused sideways glance.

Right, we were discussing all the reasons he didn't hate me but thought I was a shallow game player who he was long done with. (He so totally hated me.)

This was more important.

"Did you?" I pressed.

"Panozco borrowed it last night. He used my entire tank of gas. Why?"

It'd take a lot of gas to get to Trinity and back. Why would my dad and Dr. Panozco need to drive out to Trinity at night?

Chapter Twenty-Eight

Day 51 of 162 of the China Assignment
Changde City, Hunan Province, China

Here's what kissing Slade teaches me about Slade.

He has music running inside his body. His heart beats to it, his blood flows on it, it slips out of his fingers and hands and his lips. When we kiss, he tunes his music to me. It's the greatest experience of my life. It's addictive, and I want every bit of it. Of him.

We sit in the stairwell of our apartment building like we usually do. Only closer.

"Jojo, we're going to get caught." He whispers it into the side of my neck.

"Ummm, hmmm." I kiss his ear, since it's the easiest part of him to reach.

He pulls back to look at me. "Don't you think getting caught's a bad thing?"

"Not really." Mostly because I don't think we will. I kiss the corner of his lip, trying to raise it into a smile.

He pulls back even more. "Your dad looks at me like I'm pond scum."

I'd hoped Slade hadn't noticed that. My parents tended to only like people who fit in at Mensa conventions. "No, he doesn't."

"Yeah, he does." Slade takes me by the shoulder so I'm forced to look at him.

I sigh. "Well, you'll just have to forgive him since you look at everyone except Vinnie and me as if you're about to commit murder. And besides, my parents are completely oblivious. They won't notice anything unless Quentin tattles, and I'm paying him off."

Slade takes my hands in his and presses them under his chin. "Jojo, I know you like me, but nobody else does. Most people think I'm a screwup. Your parents for sure, and Panozco's just looking for a reason to get rid of me. If your family objects to any of this. To us. If Panozco finds out. I'll get sent back to my dad and separated from Vinnie."

Seems a little far-fetched. I mean, what about his mom? I still get a weird feeling around her sometimes, but I have yet to see anything actually wrong.

Slade's looking at me all worried-like, and I hate that, so I nod to make him happy. "Let's set some rules so we don't get caught, 'kay? Rule #1. I won't pressure you into kissing me in the stairwell."

He sighs in relief. "No more kissing in the building. Definitely not in our apartments. And no kissing at all when your parents or Panozco are in town."

***

Day 65 of 162 of the China Assignment
Changde City, Hunan Province, China

We're in a city park. Slade and I sit on a stone bench. Vinnie roots around in a broad-leafed bush for plastic Bluey figures that Slade hid for him to find. It's their favorite game.

The park is pretty with shade trees embedded in stone walkways, a pond with ducks, even rose bushes behind our bench. A man does tai chi in the distance, and a Chinese auntie watches Vinnie with a longing, friendly smile on her face.

Slade hasn't spotted the auntie. They're sweet and mean no harm but are drawn to Vinnie, which freaks Slade out.

Slade wears his headphones, a Pearl Jam tee, and jeans with torn-up knees. I draw a daisy in black pen on his kneecap. He twitches and squirms and pushes my hand away. His gaze goes to my mouth, and we stare at each other for a long moment.

He won't kiss me in public. He's so guarded, reserved, low-profile that he likes everything kept private. (Which, since he also doesn't like me to kiss him in our building, means I have to sneak kisses whenever and wherever I can get away with it.)

I steal his headphones and hold them up to my ears. He's listening to "Poison" by Alice Cooper.

"Here, read this to me." I hand him my school tablet with his latest English book open. He's got an essay due that I'm having to push him to work on. Interestingly, reading out loud doesn't trigger his speech struggles.

He cocks his head my direction. "I know what you're doing."

"Read it to me anyway."

He does a quick check on Vinnie and spots the auntie. For once, he doesn't run over to collect his brother. Instead, he takes the tablet, glances over the part I highlighted, and gives me a pained look.

"Just do it."

"'You pierce my soul,'" he reads super dryly. "'I am half agony, half hope. Tell me not that I am too late, that such precious feelings are gone forever. I offer myself to you again with a heart even more your own than when you almost broke it.'"

I'm suffused with warmth and joy and sap and mush, even if he's so dry he sounds mad.

I reach over and twirl a lock of his hair through my fingers. His eyes glow with an inner, humored light as he hands the tablet back. "Very romantic." He plucks a red rose from a nearby bush and uses it like a drumstick, tapping me on the arm. The auntie glares at him.

"It's beautiful." I snag the rose and quick kiss him on the lips, just because I can.

***

Day 67 of 162 of the China Assignment
Changde City, Hunan Province, China

I'm on Slade's unmade bed, leaning against his pillows and wearing his socks. He's sitting on his throne behind his practice kit even though he's supposed to be putting together his Persuasion essay. His laptop sits open behind him, and he keeps going back and forth between a percussion website on the screen and hitting his drum pads. He isn't practicing. He just can't not tap out a rhythm if there's a stick and a pad (or a towel or furniture or occasionally me) available.

Miles Davis plays in the background. Not Slade's usual style.

"Is something wrong?" I ask.

"Take a look." He swivels my direction, which I use as an excuse to slide onto his lap.

"Jojo . . ." His eyes go wide, but he doesn't push me off.

"Your mom never comes in here." She's got to know, though. I try to be discreet, but I have a hard time keeping myself to myself around Slade. Best guess is that she doesn't care, but Slade does, which is important to me.

I use my foot to push us around so we're facing his laptop. Slade wraps his hand around my waist, and I snuggle into him.

He isn't looking at a percussion website after all but the Chinese version of Craigslist. More specifically, he's looking at a beat-up beige acoustic drum kit for sale. One I've seen him checking out any number of times before.

He clears his throat, making his chest rumble against my back. "It looks terrible. But the heads are decent, and I can afford it."

"You want to buy it?" I ask, surprised. "Where would you put it? Even more, where would you play it?"

"I don't know. I just . . ." Slade picks up a drumstick with his free hand and beats out a soft rhythm on my leg. "I do want to buy it. Will you help me?"

"Of course."

Chapter Twenty-Nine

CMSRC vehicles all had GPS trackers, so the most likely reason for Dad and Dr. Panozco to have taken Slade's car was if they were doing something they didn't want CMSRC to know about.

Only no way would my dad work against CMSRC or the shuck. The popped tires? The blown-up boats? Dad? The idea was ridiculous, absurd, ludicrous, preposterous, nonsensical, asinine, fatuous, insane.

Or at least it was until I added the adverb *unintentionally* to the conversation.

Dad was the best of the best when it came to things that interested him. Logistics, finances, managing things, cleanliness, extreme order, his personal research projects, and playing the organ. With those, he was focused, dedicated, Ghandi-on-his-salt-march committed. My mom handled all the things Dad ignored.

I could absolutely see him being pulled into some underhanded scheme without realizing what was going on. Being pulled in by Dr. Panozco, even.

There was another aspect to this that didn't occur to me until I was lying in bed having just finished giving Ramoth a brief outline of my evening, less the Dad-shoe connection, while rubbing her itchy spot behind her left wing. (She was oddly uninterested in my stories for once, although it was also now near morning, so possibly she was as tired as me.)

Why had Dad been wearing his lucky shoes?

He wore them when he was headed off to play the organ, even if he had special *made in Belgium* organ shoes for the actual performance. He wore them when he was nervous about something, such as going church to church to try to find an organ. Sometimes he wore them to formal events, although he hadn't done so for the CMSRC party. He definitely wore them in public speaking situations, which he hated above all things.

I couldn't see any of that applying now, but it was a clue. I stewed about it while falling asleep.

"Josephine," my mom called through my bedroom door, not enough hours later. "I'm starting brunch. Join us in twenty."

I rubbed my eyes and sat up. My entire body complained, and I crashed backward onto my pillow, curling around my stuffed penguin.

Two dracos perched on my desk chair, watching me.

I blinked to make sure I wasn't having vision problems. I wasn't. Also, they were different colors.

One was lavender Ramoth. The other was a turquoise draco. The same turquoise draco that'd joined her during Dad's organ hunt. It had droopy whiskers around its snout like an overly long mustache, making it appear male.

"Hey, Ramoth." My voice came out crusty. "You've got a friend. Could one of you ask Bob if anything unusual happened at Trinity two nights ago?"

Ramoth cocked her head in her usual way. The turquoise draco gave me a chin tilt that reminded me of Slade.

I couldn't think about Slade.

Thank Eleos that the shoe smudge had distracted me. (I mean, sort of.) If I dwelled on Slade and the things he'd said, what it meant, how if I'd just not let Mo kiss me, then the night might've ended differently, it'd be Toronto all over again. I never wanted a repeat of Toronto. Never, ever, ever. Toronto had been the worst day of my entire life. Worse even than the incident in China.

Ramoth jumped from my chair to my desk, sending my phone clattering off its charger and to the floor. The turquoise draco did a wing lift and flap, pointing at the phone.

I collected it, wishing I could go back to sleep. (Downside of epic parties.)

Seventeen texts, social media notifications in the three digits, and two voicemails.

Uh-oh.

I went for the voicemails first.

"Joey!" Lei yelled so loudly I held the phone away from my ear and gave Ramoth and her friend apologetic looks. Lei's message was from an hour after I'd last seen her. "How could you kiss Mo like that? Are you crazy? Stupid? Crazy stupid? Did you not notice Slade watching you all night? He drooled, Joey. Ravenous, stalking-wolf-like drooled."

Ramoth made a pleased hooting noise. The other draco hissed and shot twin flames in her direction.

Lei kept going, dropping her voice. "But hey, could you not tell Stella I told you all of this? She has some concerns about you dumping Mo. Which you are going to do, and I don't want that to mess up me and her."

Lei's voice went back up. "But come on, Joey. Slade's your soulmate. You just need to get real with him and—"

I hit the delete button. I just couldn't.

Also, I already was *real*. Completely *real*. Last night had been *real*.

The second voicemail was from an unknown number, meaning Sasha Clems.

"Hey, Joey. Ari and I both think you're doing a fantastic job. Like, really, a million times better than we hoped. Bob thinks so too but won't admit it. With that, Ari feels an ethical responsibility to warn you about something. You've probably noticed that Ramoth hasn't been following you around as much as before. Well, she actually has. The dracos just figured out how to turn themselves invisible to do it."

I looked at the two on the back of my chair. Ramoth lifted her wings in a draco version of a shrug.

"I know, I know," Sasha continued. "Totally wild. Dracos are not supposed to be able to use magic. Ari thinks it's because Bob read them a book with an invisible dragon that convinced them that it was possible, so they figured out how. Several of them have been turning themselves invisible and following you everywhere, like non-stop. Consider yourself warned."

Bummer that I'd missed Sasha's call. She seemed really great.

"Did you follow me to the party last night?" I asked Ramoth.

She craned her head to rub her snout on her wing, giving me a cheeky, proud glance out of the corner of her eye. I took that as a yes.

No wonder she'd been uninterested in my recap. She'd witnessed everything that'd happened.

Maybe I should've been pissed about this, but I wasn't. Invisible draco snoops. Felt about right. And totally *real*. Especially as the antonym of getting real was getting fake, which I wasn't. (That I was now feeling sensitive was all Lei's fault. Plus, I could use a few more hours sleep.)

I flipped over to my texts.

Amber (Arizona – friend from dance class)

He's gorgeous! Tell me everything!!!

Bayani (Philippines – boyfriend)

I'm happy you've found someone, but I still really miss you.

MariCarmen (from Spain, met in the Philippines -- scientist's kid)

Didn't Bayani give you that sweater?

Desi

Answer my questions on the sibling chat, Joey. Now.

With a sinking feeling that I knew what they were talking about, I opened up my social media and immediately groaned. Front and center was a giant photo of Mo and me outside of the theater. The picture that I'd specifically told him not to post.

He'd added a big red heart around us. The caption read: *Hottest girl ever lost this sweater at the party last night. The thief can either drop it at Pizza Utopia or face the wrath of her guy. You may or may not get a reward.*

I groaned again. (Can't say Stella hadn't warned me about his lack of boundaries.)

Ramoth bobbed her head in agreement. The other draco curled her lip, as if I was being too harsh.

"Okay, fine," I said to the turquoise draco. "From a certain perspective, I'll agree that it was a sweet thing for Mo to try to find my sweater. Especially when I made such a point of wanting it back and I ditched him for Slade. His heart's in the right place, but I specifically told him no on the photo. And yes, Bayani bought the sweater for me."

Ramoth leaped from the chair to my bed, her eyes wide with interest.

"I'll tell you all about Bayani another time, he's—"

Before I could finish, fireworks flashed a rainbow of colors across the screen of my phone and giant red letters announced I had a new-and-very-important notification. My Slade alarm.

Ummm . . .

What?

I stared at it, dumbfounded. I'd set it up right after China, but it'd never once gone off. Not ever.

Now he texted me?

I glanced around, half expecting Quentin to jump out from behind the door and *gotcha* me. Nothing happened. It was just the two dracos and I, and they were both staring with their heads identically cocked in interest.

Slade Adler (DO NOT CONTACT. You've been blocked. If you do it anyway, you'll feel worse than you already do.)

Are you okay?

What?

"Brunchtime, Josephine," Mom yelled from downstairs.

Right. Food. It was likely to be awful. I'd compliment it anyway, and a family meal was an opportunity to feel Dad out about Slade's car. No idea how I was going to do that, especially since I failed abysmally every time I tried to talk to him, but I had to do it anyway.

"Be right down," I called.

I looked at Slade's text.

Three words.

Meaning unknown. (Beyond the obvious.)

I didn't want to answer. Too risky. Another opportunity to get myself skewered.

That was what was *real* for me.

Only it was Slade. I'd been waiting for a text from him since China.

Me

I'm fine.

***

Downstairs, the table was fully set, even if the floral plates were mismatched, the utensils different sizes, and the glassware actually coffee mugs. Dad was reading the local newspaper. Quentin had his head bowed over his phone. Mom was busying herself in the kitchen. All dead normal.

"Morning." I sat next to Quentin. He didn't attempt to kick the chair out from under me for once.

"Afternoon," Dad replied, without looking up.

"Hey," I said, "is the family calendar up-to-date?"

Dad lowered his paper and studied me through his glasses. "My schedule is synced, yes. Has your mother not been keeping hers current? Is there an issue?"

Quentin mouthed something in my direction I couldn't understand.

"No issue," I said quickly, since Dad seemed intense about it and the calendar was one of the things they fought about. "I just like to keep track of when you guys are in Trinity." I watched Dad carefully for a reaction.

He folded the paper into exact quarters and placed it next to his plate. Mom thumped a hot skillet onto the table with a hefty dose of force, way more than was needed.

I glanced at Quentin, who mouthed words at me again. I again couldn't understand him.

Mom nodded my direction. It was stiff. "Quentin said you went to a cultural event last night."

Quentin gave me an imperceptible nod. Safe topic.

"Yup," I agreed. "Very cultural."

"First Nations?" Dad asked and then glared at Mom. "I've wanted to take in a festival myself."

"Me too!" I announced a little too loudly, because it was becoming increasingly clear that they were on the verge of a raging argument. There was no predicting these things or even understanding them. Every once in a while, it just happened, and it'd been a while. "One of our new friends is—"

"Did you know," Dad cut in, "that Yale has a Native American cultural center?"

"MIT has ninety-eight instructors who are Nobel laureates," Mom whipped back so fast it was clear she'd been waiting for the opportunity.

"Yale's endowment is twice the size of MIT's," Dad announced.

Oh no, oh no, oh no. Not since Toronto had there been an argument about me.

I scooped up a good helping of scrambled eggs with broccoli from Mom's skillet, even though they had an odd glossy sheen. "Looks fantastic." I took a bite.

Quentin mouthed at me again. Again, I got nothing.

Dad glowered at Mom. "Yale has the more rounded academic program."

"Nobody beats MIT for STEM."

I wasn't ready for this. I'd thought I had more time so that I could work on them separately. (I could just hear Slade sneering over my *biggest life problem.*)

I latched on to the edge of the table with both hands.

"Dr. Budnik, one of the foremost experts on draco neuropathology and someone I admire immensely, teaches at Yale." Dad launched into Dr. Budnik's credentials.

Mom ruffled my curls. "Josephine," she said, all forced, honey sweet, "you know your father and I will be fine with whatever school you choose. It's a major decision, and it's yours to make."

"Of course it's her decision," Dad interrupted. "No one goes to Yale by force."

Mom slammed her fist on the table next to my plate.

I jumped.

Quentin kicked me under the table and mouthed more words. This time I got it. *Do. Not. Pick.*

He flashed his phone in my direction. Our sibling chat was open, which meant one or more of our older siblings was listening in on the conversation. I leaned forward to bury my face in my hands and focus on intaking air that suddenly seemed heavier than the single bite of Mom's brunch currently residing in my stomach.

"Elbows off the table," Dad snapped.

I straightened.

"Josephine, sweetheart, it's time for your decision," Mom said.

"We're waiting," Dad agreed.

Tears gathered in my eyes as the pressure became too much. "I'm tired and this is all really sudden, and I don't know what I want to major in at either Yale or MIT, and it's a lot of money to spend when I don't know, and I appreciate what you guys are doing for me, but you've got really high expectations and—"

"She should go to the University of Toronto." Quentin said it all weird while looking at his phone.

Both my parents turned to stare at him.

So did I.

"Why U of T?" Mom asked.

Because Toronto was where Slade lived.

I'd never had the thought before, not once, not even while I was secretly looking at the U of T website or putting together my application. My goal had always been a school where I could major in something just because it interested me, join a dance team, make long-term friends, and stay put forever. U of T was the obvious choice for all of those, and it was more likely to get Mom and Dad's support, since it was the best school in Canada, and Mom lectured there occasionally.

Slade was still the bigger reason.

Which was stupid. And useless. A terrible motive to pick a college. U of T wouldn't change anything, and Slade wouldn't want me there, especially after last night.

"It's a good school," Quentin said, reading from his phone.

"You do want to go to U of T?" Mom asked, puzzled, like we were discussing something over-the-top outlandish, like taking a gap year or attending a community college or moving to Mars.

"It's not Ivy League," Dad said dismissively. "Do you realize what you'd be giving up by not going to Yale?" He reached for a helping of broccoli-eggs and nodded at my mom. "Or even MIT?"

Oh, got it.

This wasn't about me. This was about my elder siblings getting my parents to stop fighting each other by uniting against what they'd both consider an inferior choice. My choice.

I shrugged as if that didn't hurt. There was zero I could do about it. "It's just an idea. I really do see myself somewhere more impressive. I'll do some more research and pick one soon."

(Which wasn't me avoiding getting real. Not. At. All. No way. Never. Nope.)

***

When I didn't hear back from Bob on my Trinity question, I sent him a text on the yellow phone. Then I walked over to Pizza Utopia for my shift. I got called Mo's girlfriend a lot, which I tried to put a stop to, but everyone seemed to think I was joking when I did it.

Mo wasn't there, for which I was deeply grateful, and not just because of the girlfriend thing. I hadn't called him as promised. Or texted. Or done a single thing to put him in his place about that photo. I just . . .

Didn't want to.

Because I was no longer into him.

At break-time, I grabbed a slice of Hawaiian pizza and headed to the picnic table out back. Mo drove up in his truck. (Such was my life.)

I resisted an urge to collapse face-first on the table in exhaustion. Instead, I looked upward at the tree. No sign of Ramoth but guaranteed she was invisibly there to witness whatever was about to happen.

Mo got out of his truck, but slower than usual. His hands were shoved in his pockets, and he didn't call me any stupid nicknames, make any jokes, or do anything else Mo-ish. He slid in next to me at the picnic table, straddling the bench so he faced me. His expression was serious, his mouth held in a frown.

Not having anything better planned out, I started blurting.

"I'm so sorry for last night. I made you unhappy, and I didn't mean to. It was a mess. I was a mess. Going with Slade was me taking the easy way out, but I hurt you, which I shouldn't have done."

"Joey, I'm the one who's sorry."

"No. I'm sorry. It was all me, and—"

He put his hand over my mouth to shut me up. "My turn. I owe you an apology, yeah? Not the other way around." He dropped his hand. "I really hate that guy, and I was jealous. I still shouldn't have gotten into it with him. Especially not in front of you. Babe, I'm sorry I put you on the spot and made you pick one of us. And before that, I'm sorry I stayed in the game room rather than with you. I know you love to dance, but I'm a terrible dancer, so I asked Stella to take you out. I should've just told you that, but I was embarrassed. And after seeing that Adler guy at the play, I should've asked around to make sure he wasn't showin' up at the party, but it didn't occur to me to do so. I sometimes miss things and come on too strong. I'm sorry about that, and for the drinkin'. I really did only have two beers, but I'll never put you in a bad position like that again." His eyes brimmed with apology and sincerity and goodness. "If you'll agree to go out on another making-up-to-Joey date, that is. Can I get another chance?"

A lumpy thickness built in my throat, a jumbled mix of confusion and anxiety because he was putting pressure on me, but also . . .

A really stupid, probably inappropriate, and totally selfish happiness.

I was the one who did the apologizing and worrying over how someone else felt. Being on the receiving end for once was heavenly.

"I got your sweater back," he continued, his voice a mix of hope and pleading. "And my mom wants me to bring you to a family shed do. It'll be horrendous. Thirty people at least, but Uncle Charles will let me work a split shift so we can go if I close up after."

There was a raucous shuffle of leaves above us and the sound of something, possibly a draco tail, bludgeoning a solid object, possibly another draco. I looked up but nothing was visually amiss. Mo stayed focused on me.

He was a good person in his own boundary-less, over-the-top way. I liked that he was so honest about himself. But I didn't want to date him anymore, and I definitely didn't ever want to kiss him again. Most of all, he wasn't Slade.

Not that I could tell Mo that. Especially not right now, when he was being so nice and had admitted he was jealous of Slade. No way. "Of course, you can have another chance."

(This wasn't me avoiding getting real any more than dealing with my parents had been. Nope. Not at all. Absolutely no. This was me being as kind to him as he was being to me and keeping us both in happy mental places.)

Chapter Thirty

Day 69 of 162 of the China Assignment
Changde City, Hunan Province, China

Changde doesn't have a metro, so it takes us three different bus lines to get to the drum kit seller's place, Slade holding tight to my hand the entire way. He hasn't gotten used to China, and the bus system overwhelms him.

We'd had Yuze make all the arrangements for today's visit. I'd wanted him to come along, but his parents had said no.

We get off in front of a faded yellow three-story building with a traditional Chinese roof. It's rundown, with metal fencing around the exterior balconies and drying clothing strung between the windows. I've lived in way worse, find the place charming, and am not bothered. Slade glares at it and a group of older men as if we're about to be attacked. A group of girls totally check him out anyway.

Super glad I'd talked him into leaving Vinnie behind. One less thing for him to freak out about.

"This is important to you," I say to Slade to distract him as we follow the instructions on my phone to the correct entry to the building.

He does an upward chin-nod.

"Why?"

"Have you ever . . ." he starts.

I wait, giving him the space to work out what he wants to say.

". . . needed something. Needed it so badly that it eats at you. You're not right without it. You just have to have it. Because otherwise you're only half yourself?"

I know exactly what he means.

"I need to play. Really play. Not just on the practice pads. I need to create sound. It's who I am."

"Like my memorials are who I am." I step in closer to him, lifting on my tiptoes to give him a small kiss, even though we're in public and it'll make him uncomfortable. "I like who you are. I like who I am when I'm with you."

I haven't had a single meltdown since the day I met Slade. Not one.

Slade needs to play the drums.

What I need, even more than my memorials, is him.

***

Day 71 of 162 of the China Assignment
Changde City, Hunan Province, China

We're in my room. Slade sits on the floor. His tablet rests on his thighs, open to a PreCalc practice exam he isn't taking. I'm on my bed, my leg hanging down next to his arm, my Physiology assignment on my tablet.

The pieces of his new drum kit are stacked in the back corner and shoved under my bed since he can't fit it and his practice pads in his room. Quentin is out with friends, so we're alone in the apartment. "Misery Business" by Paramore plays in the background.

Slade's left hand beats a slow rhythm against the floor with one of his sticks. His right hand taps the top of my bare foot. Doubt he's aware he's doing either. He's deep in himself thinking, and not about math.

"I could set up with the buskers," he muses. "Join one of them, even."

"Dr. Panozco would freak if he found out you were playing on the street. Besides, it takes two buses to get to the tourist district. That's a lot of moving your kit back and forth." It'd taken us three trips to get it all home.

Unsurprisingly, owning the drum kit hasn't filled his need to make sound, and the one time he played around on the snare while in the building, Yuze came running to warn us his parents objected.

I slide onto the floor next to him and run my fingers over his arm, tracing one of his veins until he squirms and turns my way. I wrap my arms around his neck and distract him for several minutes.

"Jojo," he murmurs in warning, pulling back.

"Fine." I lean my head against his shoulder. "Would the university have a place you can play?"

"I checked. I'd have to enroll."

"What's the noisiest place we've passed in Changde so far? Maybe we could ask if you could play there?"

Slade turns and looks at me, his gaze pausing on my mouth, but he doesn't kiss me.

I pout encouragingly.

"What I need," he says and looks past me at the stack of beige drums, "is a club. One with soundproofing. That's empty during the daytime. Jojo, you're brilliant."

I grin. "Of course I am." Even if the idea is his and not mine.

Chapter Thirty-One

Still nothing from Bob, although I gave Ramoth and her turquoise friend a firm lecture on the importance of silence when doing invisible surveillance. Then I told them the story of my dating Bayani, including the time he'd surprised me with a trip to the most gorgeous waterfalls hidden in a tropical forest. He'd given me my beloved sweater, and we'd had our first kiss. Telling a nostalgic story of something and someone that had gone right cheered me up.

The next morning, I tried to engage Dad again on our walk to All Angels for church services. Yes, Dad wore his lucky shoes. Yes, I kept glancing at them.

Dad turned our conversation to Yale. The state-of-the-art laboratories, the impeccably organized class schedules, and a guy named Aldo Leopold, who'd graduated in the early 1900s and went on to develop the first protections of draco habitat. Dad really admired him.

"Have you spent much time with Dr. Panozco lately?" I asked when he paused for breath.

"Dr. Panozco not only did his undergrad at Yale but taught there as an adjunct for two years."

And that was that.

The moment we arrived at All Angels, Dad hurried to the organ console and switched from his lucky shoes to his organ shoes, all entirely normal. We were early and no one else was around, so I browsed the brochure table with an interested look on my face in the hopes that Pastor Forester would show up. He didn't, although other people trickled in, including the blond boy.

I waved. His eyes went wide with alarm.

So suspicious.

I started in his direction.

Only Dr. Panozco, Slade's mom, and Vinnie were right behind him. The boy brushed past them. Slade's mom nodded in my direction. "Hello, Joey."

"Hi, Mrs. Panozco." I smiled at her, but her attention was already past me and on her husband, who was heading to a front pew. I looked down at Vinnie. His hair was combed to the side, and he had a frown on his face that made him look like a Shrinky Dink Slade. "Hey, Vinnie. Do you remember me? I used to play with you in China."

He glared and bolted past me.

So apparently a no.

I took a seat behind them anyway and made a silent plea that Dr. Panozco would randomly say something that would answer all my open questions and clear both Dad and himself. Long shot, I know.

Pastor Forester walked up to the pulpit, and I sent a plea his direction to drop a random admission of guilt or something else equally as useful. Even longer shot. The blond boy returned and sat on the far side of the nave, as far from me as possible.

None of my pleas came true, but Dad's playing was over-the-top fantastic as always. (He'd double majored in music performance for his undergrad. At Yale.)

The moment the service ended, the blond boy bolted. I followed. Lei, of all people, cut me off in the vestibule. "We need to talk."

"At church? Again?"

"You didn't return my voicemails or texts."

"The Panozcos are here," I said, lowering my voice. No way did I want her going all Joey-plus-Slade in front of them.

"You don't get to blame me for bombing with Slade. That was all on you. I couldn't have set it up better. Did you not use the app?"

"Let's go outside."

She planted her feet and frowned. "Stella thinks you're going to dump Mo for Slade. Convince me that she's right."

I did a quick glance around to verify Slade's mom wasn't near. "Lei, you need to drop this. Slade and I talked. He straight-out said he's not interested in me."

"And you believed him?" She ran a hand over her fauxhawk, ruffling it backward and then letting it roll into place hedgehog-like.

"He was pretty clear."

"Man, you guys are both bad at this. Look—" Lei started, but the blond boy walked up, interrupting us. His face was flushed, and he fidgeted back and forth before shoving a folded piece of paper at me. "You should come," he mumbled while looking at his shoes. "I can drive you if you want. Text me."

I did a double-take. "What?"

The boy turned and stumbled backward, retreating as quickly as he could without flat-out running. I started to follow, but Lei hauled back on my arm.

After all those times he'd avoided me?

What.

Had.

Just.

Happened?

Lei grabbed the paper from my hand. It was a flyer for youth group, just like last time. Handwritten on the top was *Brady Forester* and a phone number.

"Seriously?" Lei jiggled the paper as if she was going to rip it in half. I yanked it back and shoved it behind my back.

"Slade, I'm willing to compromise on," she said with a snort. "But you don't get to mess up my romance with Stella by dumping Mo for this guy."

***

Brady Forester. What were the chances he wasn't related to Pastor Forester? It was a great lead.

The moment Dad and I got home, I texted Brady saying I'd love to go to youth group and requesting the offered ride. I even added a variety of happy emojis to make it clear how excited I was pretending to be. (Or actually was. If for different reasons than he might expect.)

From the back of my desk chair, the turquoise draco lashed his tail at Ramoth. Ramoth threw out her wings, whacking the turquoise draco and knocking both of them backward. Wings and legs and tails and small bursts of flame went everywhere.

My desk chair had become their favorite place to hang out, but there wasn't room for both of them to perch comfortably without bumping into each other, so we kept having incidents.

"Not in the direction of my memorials!" I jumped to put myself between the excited dracos and my treasures. My origami star from Japan would never survive a flame battle. "I'm going to kick you both out of my room if you don't stop." Which sounded good, but was likely impossible to enforce, especially with their tiny flamethrowers at the ready, and my long-standing habit of not following through on my threats.

The yellow phone rang. Ramoth gave up the chairback and hopped over to my bed, ending the dispute. I patted the top of her head. "See? Everything's better if we're all just nice to each other."

"What do you think might've happened on Thursday at Trinity?" Bob demanded the moment I answered and before I could get in a cheery greeting to butter him up.

"A friend said someone borrowed his car. It's probably nothing, but I thought I'd ask."

"Which boy?" Bob asked.

"What?"

"From the party. Mohmmedidrees Durand or Slade Adler?"

"How do you know about them?"

Ramoth flipped her tail in a circle, looking pleased with herself. The other draco strutted back and forth on the back of the chair.

Right.

I sat down on my bed next to Ramoth and scratched her favorite spot under her wing, which made her preen. She rubbed her claws on my side (gently) as if trying to return the favor.

"Ramoth and Temeraire," Bob continued, "that's the blueish-green one, are your assigned watch-dracos."

"I figured."

"No. I'm not telling her that."

"What?"

"I'm not telling her that either."

"Are you even talking to me?" I asked, confused.

Ramoth leaped onto my chest and puffed out two little flames.

"Ramoth!" I pushed her backward. "My hair is flammable."

"Fine, I'll tell her," Bob grouched via the phone. "The dracos are divided on which boy you should choose. Ramoth, Maur, and the shuck like the Adler boy. Saphira, Norberta, Balerion, Temeraire, and the rest prefer Mohmmedidrees, primarily because he's a local and smells like pepperoni. There, are you happy?"

"What?" I said for the third time. My life was quickly taking a turn down *Really Strange Road.* "I don't even know that many dracos. And can you make them stop following me when I'm not doing any investigating?"

"You think I haven't tried?" he snapped back. "You think I enjoy interpreting your soap-opera teenage life to a bunch of nosy dracos? Thank you, by the way, for putting me in the position of needing to explain male possessiveness and territorialism. As if I didn't have enough problems."

Ramoth rubbed her head against my arm, catlike, and then turned to shoot flames at Temeraire in a clear challenge. I'd been claimed.

I laughed. Or better said, snickered. It was really more of a snicker. Not even Bob's cranky attitude seemed all that bad when lined up against the craziness of my draco situation.

"Maur says to tell you that nothing unusual occurred at Trinity two nights ago other than the RCMP's patrols, the usual CMSRC watchers, and a few Elitists trying to sneak through."

"Elitists?" I asked, fighting more snickers. "Why are the lookey-loos still interested?" I hadn't previously considered them as suspects.

Temeraire leaped to join Ramoth and me on the bed. I reached to pat him, but he sidled sideways and then whipped around to grab one of my curls in his mouth, stretching it out.

"Hey, that hurts." I pulled my hair free. Temeraire bumped hard into Ramoth, sending her careening to the floor.

Territorial indeed.

"Someone started a rumor that bathing near the shuck works as an anti-aging elixir and takes twenty years off skin care. It's not true. People are idiots, but the Elites keep trying to sneak through to take a bath anyway. Do you know how cold that water is?"

"Hmmm . . ." No way would Dad or Dr. Panozco fall for something like that.

Ramoth beat backward across the floor until she was under the window and then, in another burst of draco energy, launched herself at

Temeraire. Both of them went tumbling in a bundle of wings and claws and smoke.

"Also," Bob continued, "Maur says the shuck's glowing. The shuck denies this is happening, but Maur reports that it's lying and the glowing is so strong it's lighting up the water in a way that is quite appealing. In teenage parlance, it looks *cool*, but can only be seen at night."

Was it wrong that I wanted to see the glowing shuck at night too? It did sound cool. That the shuck did things like lie and pick a side in my love life was somehow making it feel like another draco friend.

Either way, no way would Dad and Dr. Panozco sneak out to Trinity to see the glowing shuck. They could go while already down there, and there'd be no reason to be secret about it or borrow Slade's car.

Nor could I see either Dad or Dr. Panozco stealing Thaddeus's rowboat or doing something physically strenuous like rowing it them-selves. If they'd wanted to go secretly out on the water, they'd at least have stolen a boat with a motor. Not that I could see either of them knowing how to work a motorized boat either.

I still had nothing.

Bob sent me the names of a couple of locals that may or may not have connections to Trinity and asked me to get a feel for them. Two were more developers who had sent letters to Dad. One was a plumber, which was great since Quentin's and my toilet wouldn't stop running, even after I'd replaced the fill valve. The last was Pastor Forester.

I told Bob about Brady and said I'd start there.

Mom and Dad left for Trinity a few hours after church. The moment their CMSRC van pulled away, I headed to their bedroom for some snooping. Dad was so tidy it seemed unlikely I'd find anything useful, but snooping was another time-honored Partridge tradition.

I checked their closet, then dresser, then nightstands. I was rooting through Dad's drawer when Quentin walked in. Shoot. I hadn't realized he was home.

"What are you doing?"

"Borrowing something to read." I snatched up the top of Dad's TBR pile. Based on the title, it was a biography of a long-dead draco-ge-neticist. "I'm just that bored."

"Want one of my Shonen books?"

"Sure." I followed him back to his room, where he gave me an entire series. Every once in a while, Quentin was a pretty great brother.

"Desi wants you to call her," he said as I was leaving, "since you aren't responding to her texts. She's worried you're going to end up committed to a mental hospital again."

Ugh. "I was never committed to a mental hospital."

Which he knew.

I'd gotten a forty-eight-hour psych hold in Toronto after my mom found me unconscious on the washroom floor, and Desi'd convinced her I'd hurt myself intentionally. I hadn't. I'd just passed out. But when I'd come to, I'd started crying again and couldn't stop. The doctors drugged me up, did a bunch of tests that showed I was reasonably okay, and sent me home. Afterward, there'd been a massive family blowup where Desi had demanded Mom and Dad send me to live with her. They'd refused, *Thank Eleos.*

"I'm fine," I said.

"Don't tell me. Tell Desi."

Siblings were the worst.

Quentin left to go hang out with his sports friends, and I finished up my parents' bedroom without finding anything of interest. From there, I moved to Dad's home office, which was mostly empty. Only thing worth investigating was the shredder. It had a side-bin full of papers, all tidily stacked waiting to be cross-hatched at a later date.

I shuffled through the stack.

Junk. More junk. Even more junk. Notice from CMSRC about retirement benefits.

Something hit the window behind me with a crack. I jumped.

Ramoth was outside, madly flapping her wings and bobbing up and down in place.

"Aren't you supposed to be invisible? Someone is going to see you." Dad's office faced the street. I tried to open the window anyway, but it wouldn't budge. (Project for another time.)

Ramoth rammed into the glass again.

"Ramoth, I thought we were past this. Go wait in my room. I'll . . ." I glanced around Dad's barren office, trying to think of something, anything I could use to distract her. Nothing appeared, so I went with what she'd like. "I'll meet you there in a few minutes and tell you more about Bayani. And Duarte. I dated Duarte too, and have some great stories about him that you'll love. Our first kiss was in a boat under a tree with crickets chirping."

Ramoth zipped away. Disaster averted. I returned to shuffling through Dad's shred pile. More junk mail. Another CMSRC notice. And a check for seven hundred and fifty thousand dollars payable to Dad.

From Ricketts Brothers and Sons.

Chapter Thirty-Two

Day 85 of 162 of the China Assignment
Changde City, Hunan Province, China

"It's a horrible story. Both indecipherable and insufferable." I throw Slade's paperback of Fahrenheit 451 at his chest, hitting his Iron Giant tee.

He catches it. "It's a masterpiece. You just don't get it."

Louis Armstrong plays in the background. For unknown reasons, Slade thinks Armstrong's music goes well with the book. A book he likes so much he made me find a real copy for him.

"Whatever. The book's just bad. You should pick a different one. Both Jane Eyre and Wuthering Heights are on your English list. Let's read one of those."

We're in his room. His mom went shopping for dinner ingredients as Dr. Panozco is coming back this afternoon, and she wants to do something special for him. I'm on Slade's unmade bed, leaning against his pillows. He's sitting on his throne, playing one-handed with his sticks so that they snap back and forth between being parallel to each other and forming a cross in his hand. The sticks make a sharp clicking noise each time he switches.

I couldn't care less about Fahrenheit 451, but Slade's having a bad day, and I need a way to distract him. With Yuze's help, we'd sent out emails to fifteen clubs asking to use their facilities. The twelfth and thirteenth rejections arrived today.

"Admit it's a horrible book." I reach over and run my fingers slowly down the side of Slade's neck, teasing him.

"I can't. It's brilliant." He leans my direction while still clicking his sticks back and forth.

"If you love it so much, then name your band after it someday. But in the meantime, I don't want to read it." I rub his Adam's apple with my thumb.

"Jojo," he murmurs while looking at my mouth, "you don't have to read it if you don't want to."

"And be cut out of your process? Wow. That hurts." I sit back, twirl one of my curls between my fingers, and give him a smile full of invitation.

"Jojo . . ."

"No one's home but Vinnie." And he won't bother us. Slade hid tiny candies all over the apartment for him to find Easter-egg-style.

"Panozco could show up at any time," Slade says somewhat desperately. "We're going to get caught."

"Not in this exact moment, we aren't." I crook a finger at him.

He drops his sticks to the floor and leaps across the bed at me, whispering my name, "Jojojojojojojojojo . . ."

I laugh and throw my arms around him as we crash backward.

***

Day 97 of 162 of the China Assignment
Changde City, Hunan Province, China

"Are you free?" I whisper into the phone the moment Slade answers. He always answers when I call, and I only call when it's important.

"Hold on a second. Let me hide something to keep Vinnie busy." The line goes silent for a long moment and then Slade comes back. "Parents fighting again?"

I relax with the sound of his voice. I'm overreacting to the fighting. I know this. They aren't even mad at me. "Quentin's homeschool adviser says he's getting C's in both biology and math."

"They blaming you? He refuses to let you help him."

"No. They're just mad."

My dad's been under a lot of pressure from MSS. The search for possible draco-reptiles isn't going well. It's not even that, though. My parents seem to look for excuses to fight.

Slade and I sit in silence. I hear the soft tap of him hitting a stick on one of his practice pads. I picture him playing one-handed so he can hold the phone to his ear. The tapping makes me think of him saying my name. It helps.

"Slade?"

"Yeah?"

"What are you afraid of? I mean, other than being separated from Vinnie and the entire country of China."

"I'm not afraid of China."

I snort-laugh, because he so is.

"Beer," he says abruptly. "Alcohol. But beer smells the worst. Like mold."

Chapter Thirty-Three

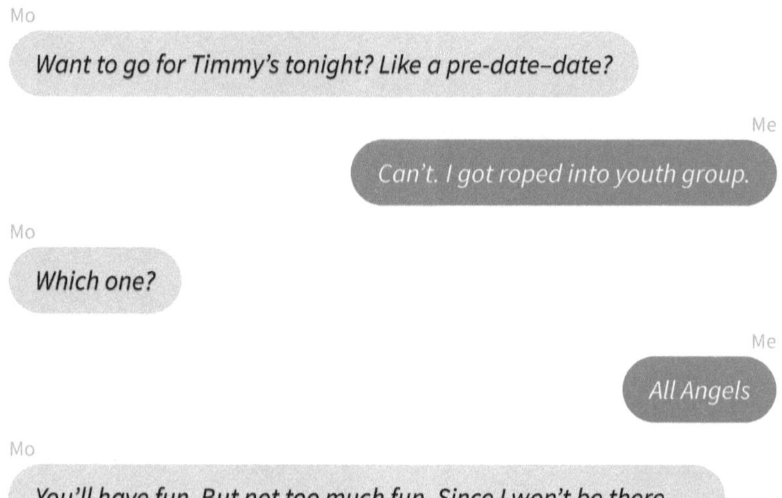

So not inviting him. I shouldn't even have told him. Apart from the whole I-was-no-longer-into-him thing, I couldn't risk him asking questions I needed to keep quiet about.

Like that check.

Which Mo couldn't actually question, since he didn't know it existed. Didn't matter. The check was a carrot that the hamster that lived in my brain was chasing on its wheel of paranoia, and I couldn't stop thinking about it. (Did hamsters even eat carrots? No idea.)

Only one thing kept me from completely freaking out.

Dad hadn't signed the back of the check before putting it in the bin for future shredding, meaning he hadn't deposited it. Thus, it was safe to assume Dad wasn't hand-in-hand with the developers.

Mo

Hopefully, at that point, I'd have new info on Brady that I could casually run by him. Going out with Mo just one more time had its upsides.

I changed into skinny jeans and a bright yellow tee for youth group. A friendly, cheerful, but not-too-forward outfit to charm Brady.

He texted me that he was two minutes out, and I hurried downstairs. When I opened the front door, Slade was walking up the drive.

I jumped back inside to hide.

"Jojo, I can see you."

I reluctantly stepped out onto the porch. "What are you doing here? And without a car?"

"I walked over. Our rental's a block over."

"I didn't realize."

Slade stared at me, all focused and intent. Little curls of anxiety twined around my internal organs. Hadn't he skewered me enough?

He gave an upward chin-nod. "Why did Panozco and your father borrow my car?"

"What?" I asked, startled. That was why he was here? How did he even know?

"Jojo, what's going on?"

"Nothing," I said quickly. "What even makes you think that?"

He sighed, ducked his head to the side, and ran a hand through his hair. "I told Panozco I found a hundred bucks on the passenger floor after he used my car. He said he'd been alone, it was his, and took my money."

"Maybe it was his?"

"It was mine. He never carries cash. Which means there was a second person there, and Panozco was covering for them. Since you were freaking out about it, I'm guessing the second person was your dad. Again, what's going on?"

I wanted to tell him. Just unload it all and ask him to help.

Also, that had been a lot of words for him. He wasn't struggling to talk to me at all. Nor had he on our drive home from the party. In any other moment, realizing this would've been a gift of utter happiness wrapped in a bow of life-is-good. Right now, it was yet another obstacle.

"Can't chat right now," I said. "A friend's coming to pick me up."

"The bonehead?" Slade's lip turned up in a sneer.

"No. And don't call him that. Mo's a nice guy."

Slade opened his mouth to say something else, something likely disparaging, but a brown SUV pulled up to the curb, saving me. I locked the front door of the rental and brushed past Slade.

He turned with me but then froze. "How many guys are you dating?" His voice went all cold and pissed, judgmental.

The weight of it pressed into me, sending me right to the edge in a way Slade always seemed to do.

I.

Could.

Not.

Do.

This.

"I'm going to youth group. That's all." I hurried down the drive, counting backward by sevens in my head.

Slade followed on my heels. "You don't go to youth group."

"Brady invited me. He's a nice guy and—"

"Is this revenge? You're going to force me to watch you date the entire town now?"

The pain hit. The tears gathered. My throat clogged. My breath stalled. No amount of counting would help. I was going to have a meltdown. Chernobyly.

Which was so unfair. How come he always got to yell and I always had to cry? Just once, couldn't we switch?

And it wasn't only Slade. It was Mo. And my parents. And siblings. And Bob. And the dracos. And Lei. And the entire gossipy town of Gander. Pretty much every person in my life, because they all endlessly buried, smothered, suffocated me. Even while I went out of my way to never do the same to them.

For some reason, that thought banked my waterworks and, for the first time in my life, what replaced it ran hot.

"Revenge? How can you even say that?" I never got mad. Ever. I didn't know how, but this was Slade, and if there was anyone I could safely release some wrath on, it was him. Which made zero sense but was also the truest thing ever.

"You play games."

"One game," I snapped back. "There was only ever one game, Slade, and as hard as I tried, you absolutely won it." I walked around the front of Brady's car and waved to him, forcing a friendly, cheerful expression to cover the anger seething underneath. Brady glanced from me to Slade and went all wide-eyed with alarm.

"I didn't win," Slade said, his voice rising as he followed me. "You win. You always win."

"You abandoned me."

Slade went rigid. His nostrils flared. His jaw clenched so hard the tendons of his neck showed.

Good.

I turned on him. "You walked away without giving me a chance. You just left."

"You don't get to put what happened on me." His hands balled into fists. "You screwed it all up. I'm the one who paid."

Fire pounded in my chest, behind my eyes, in my ears, on my tongue. The pain didn't shrink me for once, but built, expanded, pushed my edges. I rushed him, both hands out, and plowed into his chest with my bodyweight behind it.

He shifted back half a step and shoved me away.

"You think I don't know?" I yelled. Burning tears spilled down my face. Stupid, useless tears. I couldn't even get mad without crying. "Because I'm aware. All of it was my fault. Every bit of it. The entire mess in China. That you ended up separated from Vinnie. That I hurt you. That you hate me. I'm aware. I'm aware that you're aware. Every freaking moment of my life, I'm aware. It was all me and nobody but me. That's why I've been trying so hard to fix it."

"Fix it?" he yelled right back. "You've been trying to screw with my head. You've been screwing with my head since the first day I met you."

I shoved him again, but this time he was ready and I bounced backward, forced to catch myself. "All I ever wanted was your attention. That's it. Sum total. No other games."

"All you do is play games. Then. Now. Forever."

I threw my hands in the air. My cheeks burned with tears. "If you believe that, then why are you even here? Why do you keep showing up? What do you want?"

"I told you what I want. What I've always wanted."

"For me to shut up? To grovel and apologize some more? To live the rest of my life drowning in guilt? What?"

"You, Jojo." The words exploded between us. "I want you." His voice dropped, slowed. "Or at least I want the person I thought you were in China."

Slade's knife struck again, and this time it was dull, jagged, and tore rather than sliced. I felt it happen, was aware of the carnage left behind, but the pain didn't follow.

Not yet.

A breeze slid across my skin, cooling the damp on my face, chilling my cheeks, stripping me of my anger. Slade's chest rose and fell in heavy jerks. His hands hung at his side, fists still balled. He watched me, warily.

I rubbed my wet face on my sleeve and looked away, to Brady, who was sitting in his car, his mouth wide open.

Which led to the realization that the front curtain of our neighbor's window was pulled back, the house next door had two people standing on the porch, and there were five dracos sitting in the nearest tree listening in and not bothering with invisibility.

I squeezed my eyes closed, making yet another tear drip down my face. If the entire town hadn't already heard that Slade and I were standing in the street screaming at each other, they soon would.

"I need to go," I muttered.

"Jojo . . ."

"You win. We're both done." I got in Brady's car and slammed the door.

(This was what I got for letting myself be real.)

***

Brady and I didn't go to youth group. I sobbed for twenty minutes while he drove around and handed me tissues. Which, all things considered, wasn't that long for what should've been a major meltdown. Either Brady was a calming influence, or I was getting better at being skewered.

"Everything with Slade is just so messed up," I finally said. "I shouldn't have told him I was done. I didn't mean it. I could never mean it."

"I thought you were with Mo?" Brady said it cautiously.

I started to cry again.

"I'm not. I mean, everyone thinks I am. Starting with Mo. Slade definitely thinks it. I should've been clearer about that, but Mo's been telling everyone I'm his girlfriend, and I can't seem to stop it. I'm terrible at getting people to listen to me, especially when they're mad. Or nice. Or people that just exist in general. Nobody ever listens to me. I still shouldn't have told Slade I was done. Even if he wants me to be."

Brady handed me another tissue.

"I'm a horrible person."

"I think you're just really sad." He patted me on the arm.

I was. I had been. For a long time. Possibly my entire life.

Brady drove us outside of town. The sun descended over the hills in the distance as we pulled into a gravel lot fronting a pond. The sunset reflected on the water, and trees dotted the shore. It was gorgeous. Perfect.

My tears turned into a high-pitched, slightly frantic, possibly unhinged giggle. Oh, the irony. "I don't suppose you have any interest in making out?"

Brady's eyebrows shot for his hairline.

"Sorry." I sniffed back a mix of tears and hysteria. "That was a joke. A bad one. I'm starting to lose it here."

"I should take you home."

"I don't have a home."

"Would you like to be my friend? You seem like you could use a friend."

"I'm a terrible friend, just ask Slade." I laughed again, but it was a little less unhinged. Brady *was* a soothing presence. "Also, your hatred of dracos would be a problem."

Brady blinked in surprise, and his cheeks pinked. "I don't hate dracos. My dad pays me to help him at the rallies, and he only does the rallies because the church needs money, and with the publicity around the shuck, we're getting large donations. An occasional rally keeps the donors happy."

"That's a horrible reason to do them."

He looked down at his hands. "I told that to my dad, but he ignored me."

I looked at Brady, so sincere and kind and a little like me. "I'd love to be your friend."

Chapter Thirty-Four

Day 103 of 162 of the China Assignment
Changde City, Hunan Province, China

I head to Slade's apartment right at 3:45 p.m. as I still do most days. The door is unlocked, since he's expecting me. I start to push it open but pause at the sound of yelling. Dr. Panozco. Getting louder and heading my direction. I thought he'd left already or I wouldn't have come over.

I press against the wall of the hallway as the door jerks inward and Dr. Panozco storms out. He sees me, glares, and keeps going. My knees go quivery.

Another voice comes from the apartment. Slade's mom. The door is still wide open, so I hear her perfectly. "I need to say something and I need you to hear it."

"He shouldn't be drinking. Not in front of Vinnie." Slade's voice is low and oddly calm, considering Dr. Panozco's fury.

"It was one beer."

"And I didn't say a word. I didn't even look at him."

"You didn't have to. Slade, you do judgment like a chicken does eggs."

I shouldn't be listening in on such a private conversation. Slade would hate that, only there's no way for me to escape without walking in front of the open door.

His mom continues, "Try harder not to upset him. He's good to me. And Vinnie."

"He's not good. He's pretending."

"He's trying."

"Mom, he's not."

I glance longingly at the elevators on the far side of the door. I hear movement, Slade putting on his Chucks, and then his mom's voice again, lower this time, softer. "Slade, I'm not good at this. I say the wrong things, but I really do want what's best for you and Vinnie. It's all for you two."

"That's BS. The only reason either Vinnie or I even exist is because you were trying to hold on to Dad. Now you're trying to hold on to this guy. Don't put that on me. Or Vinnie."

Oh, Slade . . .

I hear him coming my way and lean harder into the wall. He steps out, shutting the door behind him, and presses his eyes closed. His hands hang loose at his sides, no drumming, tapping, or hammering for once. He isn't nearly as calm as he sounded.

I hurt for him. I hurt as if it's me hurting. It ripples through my body and makes my stomach churn, but I don't know what to do. Does he even realize I'm here?

He takes a deep breath, the air shuddering through his nose. His jaw is clenched tight.

Fear builds within me, the kind that chokes my throat, stalls my lungs, and makes me fall apart. The kind that hasn't happened since the first day I met Slade.

That dark place inside of him? The one where he disappears to whenever he's upset? It's as if he's waving it back and forth, banner-like, between us. And its name is Rage.

If Slade falls apart, explodes, yells, I'm going to fall apart too, and it's going to be bad. Maybe the worst meltdown of my life. And he'll see it.

He extends his hand my direction, fingers open. An invitation. He knows I'm here.

I go weak with relief and slide my hand into his, intertwining our fingers. He squeezes our palms together.

"I used to think," he says softly, evenly, calmly, "that she was the most perfect person on the planet. The best mother. The greatest one ever." He shakes his head. "She's not. She's just really screwed up."

***

Day 113 of 162 of the China Assignment
Changde City, Hunan Province, China

Tears stream down my face.

I sit between Slade's knees in the stairwell, turned so that my arms are folded on his thigh with my chin leaning on top. With one hand, he pulls yet another tissue from a box and hands it to me. With his other, he holds a paperback copy of his latest English book, another one he really likes and is reading to me.

I mop at my drippy face with the tissue. I've cried from the first page of the book until now, when the seventeen-year-old protagonist has just been told by his doctors that they're sending him home to die from leukemia. Slade strokes my hair.

He's distracted at least. Our second round of emails to clubs isn't going any better than our first.

"Enough for today?" he asks softly.

"I'm such a sap."

He wraps his arm around my shoulders and pulls me back against his chest, pressing his cheek into the top of my head. "Can I show you what I want to write my essay on? I found a quote I like."

"Of course."

He flips through the book and holds up a page of solid text detailing the day-to-day life of being a dying kid. In the middle, just kind of shoved between being force-fed and having a bedpan changed, Slade has circled a short sentence in ink.

"'Some things I don't understand,'" he reads quietly and then looks right at me, studying me as if I'm the enigma.

Which is silly. Slade gets me. Of course he does. "That makes no sense."

"It makes sense." He puts the book down and wraps me back in his arms. "Do you remember when you asked me to tell you something I've never spoken of before?"

"You told me about making it with a band."

"I want to tell you something else." He says it without explaining the quote, which still seems nonsensical to me. "Something I've never talked about. Ever. To anyone. Can I tell you?"

"Anything."

Chapter Thirty-Five

I dreamed I was curled in a tight ball in the muddy bottom of an ocean cove. The cold of the water pricked at my edges like a million icy pins. I could see the surface above where there was light and heat and the shadows of friendly dracos circling, but I lacked the ability to get there and needed to protect the small bits of warmth in my center. There were watchers all around me. Eyes above and below and hidden in the mud. They were coming for me, but I was too fragile to do anything but sit there and wait for them to eat me. I needed help.

"Hey, Joey?"

I blinked and looked around, still half immersed in the dream and feeling thin-walled and brittle. I hugged my penguin and checked that my memorials were all on my dresser in their assigned places.

Where was I exactly?

Norway?

"Joey, wake up."

Quentin's voice. Or at least a suspiciously soft, kindly version of Quentin's voice.

"Go away." I pulled my pillow over my head and held tight to my penguin.

"Slade's outside. He wants to talk to you."

My heart gave a dull lurch.

Right.

Newfoundland. Slade. Our argument the night before. Which, based on his attitude, Quentin had heard about. "Tell him I'm not home." I was so done with being skewered.

"It's seven in the morning."

"Tell him I'm asleep."

Quentin stood there for a moment.

I kept my head buried. "Please?" It came out all teary-eyed.

"On it." He shut the door.

I flipped to my stomach and tried to go back to the dream, which hadn't even been that good, just vivid and kind of vulnerable. I got up after a full hour-of-not-sleeping later but only because my list of problems that I didn't want to deal with was getting longer by the second.

The sibling chat had gone crazy, I had ten tons of texts I really didn't want to look at, and my Slade-has-contacted-me alarm was shooting fireworks everywhere.

I stared at it and then caved and read his messages.

7:07 a.m. – Slade Adler (DO NOT CONTACT. You've been blocked. If you do it anyway, you'll feel worse than you already do.)

Jojo, come talk to me.

7:09 a.m. – Slade Adler (DO NOT CONTACT. You've been blocked. If you do it anyway, you'll feel worse than you already do.)

I realize not everything you did in China was an act.

7:25 a.m. – Slade Adler (DO NOT CONTACT. You've been blocked. If you do it anyway, you'll feel worse than you already do.)

I'm heading to work but will come by on my break.

I threw on leggings and a hoodie, grabbed a stale bagel from the kitchen, and fled the rental. No way was I letting Slade skewer me again. (I did take the time to remove the descriptive tag from Slade's contact info. It was annoying to actually have to read it.)

The moment I was out the front door, Ramoth threw a rock at me, hitting me on the shoulder.

"Ouch, that hurt." I clutched at my shoulder. Temeraire did a flyby, snatching a hunk of my hair and tugging it so hard that I yelped. For some reason, he now wore a leather harness with gold-fringe epaulets at the shoulders, as if he was a ranking member of a draco military. A beige draco, one I hadn't seen before, squawked at me from a tree in a high-pitched car horn way. I'd been too much of a mess to deal with the dracos last night and had kept my window shut. Apparently, they were offended. (But what happened to invisibility?!)

"I'm sorry," I said to them, even though what I really wanted to do was pick up that rock and throw it right back at Ramoth to teach her that being tagged hurt. "Friends aren't supposed to attack each other. Friends are supposed to always be nice."

Ramoth threw another rock. This one missed. Had to hand it to the dracos, they were always one hundred percent real about how they felt.

The yellow phone rang.

"Do not complain to me about your boy problems," Bob announced the moment I picked up. "I'm completely uninterested . . . No . . . Absolutely not . . . She has no obligation to . . . Fine . . . I'll tell her. Ramoth says that if you want her to be nice, you should've explained all the yelling with the Adler boy yourself, rather than forcing her to figure out what it meant via me. Which, by the way, I wholeheartedly agree with."

I rubbed at my forehead.

"Saphira," Bob continued, "that's the beige one, says the Durand boy drove around in his truck looking for you last night, and this was a *nice* thing for him to do."

Saphira did the high-pitched squawk again.

"She also says to tell you that the Durand boy would never yell at you the way the Adler boy did. She insists you're best off committing yourself to the Durand boy immediately. Are you happy?"

"I'm not really looking—"

"Can we move on to what's important here?" Bob demanded.

"Are you even talking to me?"

"No! I mean, yes! I've a house I need you to break into. The dracos say they've found an unlocked window you can climb through, just like you did to get to the rowboat. Actually, they may have broken the lock themselves. It's unclear. Also, not a single one of the dracos approves of your interest in the Forester boy. Who, by the way, you owe me information on. Regarding his anti-draco activities, that is, not how your date went."

I rubbed my head again.

"Hey, Bob? Can you ask the dracos if the shuck is okay?"

"What do you mean?"

"Nothing. I had a weird dream about it, that's all. It seemed sad and scared."

Bob went silent for a long moment. "Ramoth says the shuck complains too much, and you should be dreaming about her rather than it. I'll ask Maur once he's awake, as he's more reliable about these things."

"Thanks. Send me the address for the house with the broken window lock. I'll text you about Brady, although there isn't much to tell." I shoved the phone away from my ear and began walking without paying any attention to the direction or the non-invisible dracos who followed. I just needed to move.

Several minutes later, Bob sent me not just an address but a photo of a sprawling summer residence located in a neighborhood north of town, way too far to walk. I'd need someone to drive me.

Which, as a problem, I would take. A nice, normal, no-craziness problem I could solve on my own.

But not by asking Mo. Or Stella, who'd tell Mo. Brady would be my pick, but he'd said he was working today. We'd ended up hitting it off and were going to hang out with his church friends on Friday. None of which helped me in the moment, but for which I was deeply grateful. (And rambling. Because stress.)

I texted Bob what I'd learned about Brady and his dad while I walked over to Tabby's and Isa's rental. Maybe I'd get lucky and this time Isa would be the one with a dental appointment.

When I arrived, Isa stood outside, the keys to her family's car in her hand. Darn.

"Well, that makes things easier." Isa looked me up and down. "I was coming to find you."

"Why?"

"I'm well paid," she said, dryly.

I started to offer her my most friendly smile but then stopped. Isa wasn't about to be charmed either way.

She shook her head. "Lei texted me like fifteen times because Stella keeps contacting her. Stella's concerned because Mo's freaking out because you aren't answering your phone. Rumor has it that Slade followed you home last night, murdered you, and dumped your body where it'll never be found. Also, your brother asked Tabby to check on you. Someone named Desi thinks you might be having a nervous breakdown."

I leaned my forehead against the front post of her rental house, resisting another bout of unhinged giggles.

"Are you?" she demanded. Isa wasn't a nice person.

"No. I just need a ride."

"Great. I'll drive you wherever you want, just as soon as you send out a mass text notifying the entire world you're fine, so that they stop bothering me. Start with your boyfriend. And by that I mean Mo, since there's confusion on who you're actually dating."

***

Bob's directions took us to the cabin from the photo. It was fancy compared to anything else I'd seen in Newfoundland, with lots of gables, windows with carved trim, and a roundabout driveway that in Florida would've been lined with palm trees. The surrounding forest had been replaced with paver stones and a curated lawn.

I didn't send any texts. I pretended to do so for Isa's benefit, but I'd powered off my phone to avoid Slade and had zero desire to turn it on now to find out if he'd continued texting me. Per Bob's instructions, I directed Isa down a dirt lane next door to the house.

"What are we doing here, exactly?" Isa demanded.

"A friend of mine works for the family that owns the house. He's not supposed to have visitors, so I'm sneaking in through the back." (Today's excuse was much better than my last one.)

"Why not just text him?"

"His mom took his phone."

"I guess I'll wait here."

Perfect.

I called Bob on the yellow cell once I was out of Isa's line of sight. "So, what exactly is my goal here?"

"Your dracos will be there in a moment."

My dracos?

They were totally mine.

Ramoth and Temeraire flew in, twisting and turning between the trees to get to me. Temeraire wore the harness with the epaulets again, and Ramoth carried another black bag that she flung at me. Inside was a pile of coin-sized black disks.

"Covert surveillance devices," Bob explained. "Top of the line. Your job is to hide them around the house. You brought gloves, right? You don't want to leave fingerprints."

I'd brought gloves. Fingerprints as a problem had occurred to me, since this was all highly illegal. (Was it wrong that I found doing a B&E a stress reliever and fun?)

"So, I'm bugging someone's house. Whose?"

"I'm not telling you in case you get caught."

"I thought you said this would be easy."

"It will be. But better cautious than cavalier."

The back of the house had a huge patio made of more pavers and stone flower beds filled with yellow daisies and a life-sized topiary of what might be a minotaur. Or one of those California redwood trees that you could drive a car through. It was hard to tell.

Beige Saphira perched on what was either the crown of the tree or the minotaur's horns. Ramoth barreled into her and knocked her off. Temeraire whipped around and whacked Ramoth with his tail. Ramoth also fell off, taking a good lot of the leaves of the crown/horn with her.

"Uh . . . Bob?" I whispered, staying inside the shadows of the tree line. "We have a problem."

"Yes, they're fighting over a lawn ornament. Nothing I can do about it. The concept of *possessive control of territory* appeals to them."

"No. I mean, that's fine." Or at least sort of it was. "It's just that the back of the house has a camera on it. If I go out there, I'll be seen."

"Huh. The dracos didn't warn me. How are you going to disable it?"

"Me? It's two stories up." It sat at the roofline, giving it a wide view of the patio and making it impossible to reach.

"Well, I can't do it."

I glanced around, looking for anything that might help.

Nothing.

Except the dracos.

One draco, especially. Who loved to throw things. Only any rock she could carry was unlikely to do much damage. Same for Temeraire and Saphira. Hmmm . . .

"Bob? Crazy idea, but could you ask the dracos to poop all over the camera? Like cover up the lens?"

"They'll love that." He didn't sound pleased. I didn't blame him. Pretty sure encouraging this was a terrible idea.

Ramoth launched herself up, leaving Saphira and Temeraire to fight over the topiary. She snapped her wings wide, beat upward, and banked sharply, bringing herself even with the camera. Once lined up, she spat lavender crud out her butt.

She missed entirely and got the side of the house. I got hit with the smell of sulfur and rotting corpses.

"Oh, gross, gross, gross. Hey, Bob, Ramoth was a misfire. Can Temeraire try?"

"Stick me on video and turn the phone so I can watch."

"You want to watch dracos pooping?"

"In order to advise them how to aim better," he snarled.

I snort-laughed. This had to be yet another one of the weirder moments of my life.

Temeraire perched on the camera. His turquoise crud dripped down the sides, creating a mess on the ground and missing the lens. Saphira's poop exploded everywhere, hitting everything except the lens.

"Bob? This isn't working. I'll go back to town, get a disguise, and—"

"Hold on, the dracos are calling in reinforcements."

"What does that mean?"

Much sooner than I would've thought possible, I was hit by a violent wind and the *shu-shu-shu* wingbeat of a large draco. Maur dropped from the sky and released a refrigerator-sized chunky, yellow mass. It coated the roof, filled the gutters to leaking, and snapped the camera off the side of the house.

Effective.

Also entirely disgusting.

I squeezed my eyes shut, pinched my nose with one hand, and covered my mouth with the other, fighting the heaves.

"Well, that worked," Isa said from behind me. Her voice was all nasally.

I jumped, hitting my head on a tree branch.

She had tissue stuffed up her nose. "You should've prepared in advance for the odor problem. Also, wouldn't it have been easier to have the dracos just rip the camera off the house?"

It totally would've been.

Isa handed me a tissue. She also already wore gloves. "When whatever we're doing here is accomplished, you're going to put me in contact with Bob a.k.a. Robert Minh Quan, who very clearly isn't actually a wyrm-netter but a magic-handler, and if there's magic involved, then I'm in. What are we supposed to do next?"

I put the yellow phone to my ear. "Did you get that?"

Silence.

"Bob?"

More silence.

And then so quietly I could barely make it out, "I refuse to speak until she's signed a nondisclosure agreement. I'll get one prepared."

"Not helpful!" But neither would I be breaking my NDA if I put Isa to work. It wasn't like I'd told her myself. I poured half the black disks into the pocket of my hoodie and handed the bag with the rest to Isa. "We're going to hide these inside that house. They're bugs."

"Whose house is it?"

"I don't know."

"You're really not that good at this." She flashed me a sneering smile.

For once, I didn't flinch or wince or gather up my tears. Instead, I did my best to curl my own lip. Likely made me look ridiculous but felt great. "Come on. Let's do this and get out of here."

Ramoth had returned to the topiary. She and Temeraire faced their butts at each other, tails lifted, in a skunk-life stand-off.

"Ramoth," I called, "you have to tell me which window is unlocked. Have Temeraire and Saphira go to the front of the house and keep watch for us, 'kay? And pass the word that when we get back to the rental, absolutely no one poops in my bedroom, no excuses."

"They understand you?" Isa asked incredulously. "And they come into your house?"

I didn't bother answering.

All three dracos flung themselves into the air. Ramoth went over to a railing on the far side from where the yellow sludge still dripped from the roof. Isa and I headed her way. The window by the railing was missing a locking mechanism entirely, which seemed suspicious. I looked to Ramoth, who bobbed her head as if I'd just given her the world's greatest compliment.

Isa boosted me through and then I pulled her. The room beyond was an all-white master suite. I hid a bug in a fake plant in a corner.

"You take the downstairs," I said. "I'll go upstairs."

The stairs were marble and wrought iron, a total mismatch to the exterior of the house, the surrounding native forest, and Newfoundland in general. I hid a couple of bugs in a private movie theater and then a home gym. (Not that it seemed likely any serious conversations would happen in either.)

The third room was an office. Lots of steel, glass, and leather furniture. I went to the desk and dropped a disk into a jar of pens.

Where I paused.

The pens were all matching with a swirly company logo and the initials RBS.

I slammed the phone to my ear. "Bob? Whose house is this?"

He didn't answer.

"Isa's not here. You can talk."

Still nothing, but the house fit the two people I'd seen.

I jerked open the top drawer of the desk, less interested in leaving the bugs than verifying the owners. The drawer held office supplies, none personalized. The next drawer held a leather binder with the same swirly initials engraved on the front in gold.

I picked it up, my hands shaking. My dad had a binder like it, made of plastic. I flipped the cover open.

Yup.

Checks.

Oversized, fancy-papered, rich-people checks with duplicates behind each one so that there was a record of every transaction. They matched the check I'd found waiting to be shredded back at the rental. I flipped through the duplicate pages looking for the check to my dad.

There it was. His name and seven hundred and fifty thousand dollars. Underneath it was a second check. Same amount. Payable to Dr. Panozco.

"Joey?" Isa called out, her footsteps pounding up the stairs. "The dracos are banging on a window trying to get my attention. I think someone is coming. We need to get out of here."

CHAPTER THIRTY-SIX

Day 113 of 162 of the China Assignment
Changde City, Hunan Province, China

"When I was fourteen," Slade starts, speaking softly into the top of my head. "I stole my mom's car. She'd just found out she was pregnant with Vinnie, and I was so sick of it all. My parents. My life. Everything. And then she randomly decides to add a baby? I was so effing mad.

"My cousin Ben was staying with us. He wanted a Slurpee and knew how to drive. So after my mom went to bed, I stole her keys. We snuck out. Isn't that dumb? We were just stupid kids."

The door above us on the stairs opens. We both sit up and separate for a moment while two women walk past. The moment they're gone, I lean back into him and he into me.

"It was midnight on a Thursday. Absolutely no one else around. Ben told me to find us some music, so I was messing with the stereo. One moment, I was looking for something better than eighties love songs. The next, there's this huge crash. Like a building collapsing. Or two trains colliding. The world goes crazy. I'm thrown around and hit my head. Then it just stops. I'm sitting there in silence. My seatbelt locked. The car, reeking of alcohol. The windshield, gone. Ben missing. I have no idea what happened."

Tears stream down my face. Slade hands me a tissue. I'd heard gossip that he'd gone to juvie for killing someone. Lei Tien texted me about it months ago, but I'd thought she was just trying to cause trouble.

"All I could think about was how my mom would ground me from going to the studio with my dad for stealing her keys. So I pulled them out of the ignition. Put them in my pocket. Got out. I wasn't even scared. It was all just totally surreal. Then I saw Ben. He was face down on the street in front of the car. He . . ."

Slade's voice breaks off. I wrap my arms around him, hugging him as tight as I can.

He clears his throat. "My mom made me do Scouting, so I knew CPR. I wanted to help him. But he was all twisted, and I knew he was dead. Bodies just don't do things like that and survive. When the police arrived, I was sitting there next to him, soaking in a spreading puddle of his blood."

"Oh, Slade."

He gives a small shake of his head. "It wasn't Ben's fault. We'd been hit by a drunk driver. The guy left a nearby bar and plowed through the first red light he'd come to. Only there was alcohol in our car too. It wasn't ours. My mom had emptied the house into the backseat to take to my dad's because of her pregnancy. The accident shattered the bottles. I was drenched in it. Since I had the keys, looked older than I was, didn't have an ID, and refused to talk, they arrested me."

"It wasn't your fault."

He shakes his head again. "It wasn't. It was just a big, effing, meaningless accident because some a-hole had to go on a drinking binge. The police took me to juvie and did a tox-screen that came out clear. Their investigation showed I hadn't been driving, and I was released to my mom. Ben's funeral was a week later. No one blamed me. He was a year older. He'd been living with us because his parents couldn't control him."

"You feel guilty anyway." I hug him tighter.

"I just wanted to tell it to you. I wanted you to know."

"I'm glad you did."

"My mom told me not to ever bring him up. That it was over. The past. And I needed to move on. I don't want to be like that. I admired him. I still do. I want to remember him forever. Will you help me?"

"Of course."

Day 120 of 162 of the China Assignment
Changde City, Hunan Province, China

Slade's cousin had wanted a dragon tattoo on his upper arm with the tail snaking around as an armband. Slade wants to get the tattoo himself as a memorial. Which I totally get. Memorials are important. Also, having a mission to get the perfect tattoo distracts him from not being able to play his drums.

The tattoo can't be on his arm. It has to be on the back of his shoulder so that Panozco won't see it. I hate every example Slade shows me.

He shows me a lot. Hours of looking online, and there isn't a single one I approve of. So we go to tattoo studios.

"None of these is you," I say as we stand inside our fourth studio, looking through yet another book of designs while holding hands. Part of my hesitancy is that even in China, the simple, black images he can afford just aren't good enough. Slade is vivid and complicated, and any tattoo he gets has to be vivid and complicated too.

Part of it is the designs themselves.

"You're just not a dragon guy. Dragons are too done already."

"It's not about me."

"But it's your body. It has to match."

"Jojo. It'll match."

I purse my lips. It won't, and I really don't want him to get something permanent unless it's perfect. And beautiful. Like him.

"Also, the location," I continue. "You never take your shirt off. No one will see it on your shoulder."

"That's the point."

"Now, sure. But ink is eternal, and some day you'll want people to see it."

"I won't."

Which is so him. And yet . . .

"If it's on your shoulder, not even you will see it." I raise our joined hands and quickly kiss the back of his before he can pull away. "I think it needs to be here. And not a full dragon but just a part. An eye."

He quirks a brow at me. "Yeah, Panozco will never notice a giant eye tattooed on the back of my hand."

I kiss his hand again, grabbing a bit of skin between my teeth, tugging on it, right where the eye would go.

"Jojo," he murmurs, half in protest, half in . . .

Well . . .

Not protest.

I grin, loving how easy it is to get his attention even when my doing so makes him uncomfortable. "You should wait until we can do it right."

I trail kisses over the back of his wrist, which gives me an even better idea. "You need a full sleeve. In color. Bold with lots of details. So that you can see it, and I can see it, and it'll look amazing in motion when you play your drums. Then you and I will always remember Ben, but no one else will know what it means. It'll be our secret."

Chapter Thirty-Seven

Texts from Slade that downloaded when I turned my phone on to take a picture of the checks before fleeing the Ricketts's house:

I'm outside. Come talk to me.

Jojo . . .

Please come talk to me.

I'm off work at five. Will you meet me somewhere?

I recognize that ghosting me is payback but come on.

If you know something about Panozco, you have to tell me. Even if you're mad at me, you owe me this.

***

Isa and I ended up at her place for the afternoon. Bob emailed her a nondisclosure agreement that she signed without reading. Then she took the yellow phone into the backyard for a private chat with Bob. I tried sneaking over to listen, but Saphira landed on my head, which Ramoth objected to. (As did I.) I managed to overhear Isa bargaining with Bob over spells in trade for helping with the investigation, but that was it.

Tabby and their mom were both gone, so I was alone inside the house. Something was bothering me. (Other than feeling like Dad and Dr. Panozco were my personal Pompeii and Herculaneum right before Vesuvius exploded.)

If I looked at what had happened so far, here was what I got:

- *Nighttime visits to the shuck prior to my arrival*
- *Theft of Thaddeus's boat*
- *Use of Thaddeus's boat for another nighttime visit*
- *Popping of CMSRC tires in the middle of the night, probably to keep as many scientists in Gander as possible. Also, canceling of CMSRC bus by Dr. Panozco for the same reason*
- *Blowing up of CMSRC research vessels*
- *Developers come by the house to pressure Dad*
- *Dad and Dr. Panozco drive out to Trinity at night*
- *Checks to Dad and Dr. Panozco from the developers*

It was all building toward something. Something big, and it felt like a math equation on the world's hardest exam that I couldn't puzzle through enough to begin solving.

I started to open my phone to look at the photo of the checks to see if they were dated before or after the borrowing of Slade's car, but I had an unknown voicemail, so I went for that first. (Sigh. It seemed fated that I'd never actually get to talk live to Sasha.)

"Hey Joey, Bob told Ari and me that you had a dream about the shuck. Ari thinks the dracos are trying something similar to his dreamscape spell on you so that they can talk to you directly. Ari doesn't think it'll work, but if you start having strange dreams, that's what's happening. We're not quite sure how the shuck got involved, other than Maur told Bob that it's feeling left out because it can't follow you around or turn invisible or practice being territorial the way the dracos can. We don't think the shuck is in immediate danger, but possibly it's trying to manipulate you for some reason. Sounds crazy, but that's magic for you. Also, Bob is trying to limit the number of dracos around you, but they're having trouble with the concept of *taking turns*. If you end up with more than say ten hovering, fifteen at the most, do tell Bob."

Fifteen?

Fifteen!

I looked out the window where Ramoth and Temeraire were dropping pine cones on Isa's head while she talked on the yellow phone. Saphira dug at a hole in the ground for some reason. If there were more dracos out there, they, at least, were sticking with invisibility.

***

"Wake up," Isa said. "We're now partners."

I sat up on the sofa, rubbing at my eyes. I'd taken a nap just to see if the shuck would show up again. It hadn't.

"Bob gave me a way to talk to the dracos through one of his spells, but they flipped out thinking that he was replacing you with me and got all butt hurt. They pretty much hate me." She said it with pride. "They've agreed to let you and me be partners, though. So catch me up on your love life. The juicier the details, the better."

"What . . . ?" I blinked at her in confusion. "So, you can talk to the dracos now?"

"Yes."

Was it wrong that I was jealous?

"Don't ask how," she continued. "It's a weird spell, and I don't understand it. But I will. Either way, it's none of your business beyond knowing that the dracos have agreed to work with me, but only if I answer all their questions about your dating life. And let me tell you, Bob couldn't have agreed faster."

"Or we could just not. You don't even like me."

"You're growing on me." She smiled, showing off her teeth, and I got the distinct impression she was enjoying herself. "Ramoth says you usually leave for the pizza place right about now. Let's head there so that you and Mo can do something dramatic to get the dracos' attention and force them to come to me with their questions."

I glanced at the clock over the mantel. Crap, I was going to be late. (And crap, crap, crap on the rest.)

Mo came rushing over the moment Isa and I walked into Pizza Utopia, concern written all over his face. Isa took a seat at a table, observing us, and Mo led me back to his uncle's office. I should've prepared something to say to him, but I hadn't. I, once again, hadn't thought of Mo at all.

Huge mistake on my part. This wasn't the kind of situation where impromptu was a good idea.

A sheaf of papers on top of a filing cabinet in the back corner randomly slid onto the floor in a giant mess. A pen on the desk began to roll back and forth until it too hit the floor. I spun around, pretending to knock into the desk myself as if I was the one causing the disruptions. But at least the dracos had finally remembered to go invisible.

Mo sat down on the desk so that we were the same height. His hands were in his lap, his shoulders slumped, his brows drawn together, his lips downturned. He looked like a kicked puppy again.

A jacket hanging over the desk chair slid slowly over the back as if being pushed to make room for a draco to perch.

"I'm so sorry I didn't text you back and made you worry," I said to get all Mo's attention on me before he noticed Pizza Utopia was now haunted. "I got overwhelmed, just flooded, exhausted, trounced, swamped, knackered, overcome, and turned my phone off. Please don't ask me to talk about it. Last night was awful, a nightmare. I'm moving on and don't want to think about it anymore."

Mo dipped his head. "I can understand that."

"It was stupid. Everything just fell apart."

Another pen rolled off the desk violently, as if shoved. It hit the floor with a clatter. Someone didn't like my answer. (Ramoth. Guaranteed.)

"I'm glad Brady was there to save you." Mo reached down and took my hand in his, but loosely, as if expecting me to pull away. "I wish it'd been me."

I couldn't imagine anything worse than Mo being there.

"The thing is . . ." Mo continued, "are you still wantin' to go out with me? Because yeah, I'm jealous again. But that doesn't mean you're obligated to do Thaddeus's boat photo, and draggin' you to a family shed do was pushy of me anyway. Stella, who watches out for me, thinks you're not over the Adler guy. If that's true and you don't want to date me, I'd rather you just tell me upfront."

I stared at him. My mouth may even have dropped open.

Tell him? Upfront? Be honest? Open? Real? Just like that? Someone actually asking me to do so? Maybe even listening when I tried?

Mo suddenly became the nicest guy I'd ever met. (Even if he still had boundary issues.)

And yet . . .

It wasn't Mo I wanted to be upfront with. Even with everything that had happened, it was still Slade. It would always be Slade.

Slade, who never played games, never even flirted. He just put himself out there, bared everything he was to me. Even when we'd been yelling at each other, he'd been real. Painfully real. I wanted to call him, ask him to find a stairwell where we could sit together like we used to do, and dump all of my problems on him. No yelling this time. No fighting. Just us.

"We have a great time together," I started, stumbling a bit on the words, not quite sure how to go about getting real with Mo and telling him I'd rather we just be friends.

Then what he'd actually said sank in. "Wait. Thaddeus found his boat?"

Mo gave me a blank, confused look. "No. Buysco is replacing it."

"Buysco Superstore is replacing Thaddeus's stolen boat." I said it as much for myself as for Mo. "That's really nice of them."

Mo nodded. "They're good people. But you don't have to go with me to the giveaway. Joey, it's okay if—"

"Buysco replaced all the tires for CMSRC, didn't they?"

"Well, Canadian Tire and a couple of small places pitched in as well, but Buysco took the lead and covered the most. About our date . . ."

Buysco was involved somehow.

It was a stretch. A long one. Longer than Australia's Dingo Fence or America's Keystone Pipeline or even Russia's Trans-Siberian Highway. My crazy brain was possibly reaching too far.

It also fit.

Buysco Superstore was connected to the tires and Thaddeus. My dad had handled the tire replacements, so he was connected to Buysco too. Panozco wasn't that I could tell, but the Buysco parking lot was even where I'd seen the anti-draco rallies taking place.

I looked at Mo, who rubbed at his chin as if totally confused by the direction of our conversation. (Understandably.)

It would be wrong on every level to go to the boat giveaway and family night with Mo without coming clean that I didn't want to date him. Only if I told him the truth, there was also a good chance he'd uninvite me. I mean, who'd want to take a former not-actual-girlfriend to meet their parents?

I really needed to go to that giveaway.

Mo was the only connection I had.

His please-just-be-upfront hung over my head, a megaton bomb just waiting to drop if I made a wrong move.

I did it anyway.

"I want to go with you." I squeezed Mo's hand.

He jumped to his feet and threw his arms around me. I let him do it. He kissed me, and I didn't object even though it was worse than last time, like being facially attacked by a giant squid. Half a point on my scale of zero-to-Slade.

I still didn't stop him. I was a T.E.R.R.I.B.L.E. person.

Another sheaf of paper went flying and then a lamp fell over.

***

7:25 p.m. – Slade

I don't want to talk to you in front of the bonehead, but if you don't text me back, I'm going to walk into the pizza place and do it anyway. You've got half an hour.

7:29 p.m. – Me (deleted)

I don't know anything more than you do about why Panozco and my dad borrowed your car.

7:33 p.m. – Me (deleted)

I don't know anything. If I talk to you, you're going to skewer me and make me cry and I don't want to do that anymore.

7:41 p.m. – Me (deleted)

Feels pretty crappy to be ignored, doesn't it?

7:48 p.m. – Me (deleted)

Slade? Can I call you later? Just to chat? I really miss you.

7:50 p.m. – Me (sent)

I don't know anything more than you do about why Panozco and my dad borrowed your car.

8:01 p.m. – Maxwell

Joey, either start answering Desi's questions on the sibling chat or she's going to make me shut off your cell service. You know I have access, right?

Chapter Thirty-Eight

Day 122 of 162 of the China Assignment
Changde City, Hunan Province, China

I don't hear the knock, just my mom's footsteps and the front door opening.

"Hello, Mrs. Partridge," Slade says slowly, painfully. It hasn't gotten easier for him to talk to anyone but me. "Is Josephine home?"

"It's a little late," my mom replies.

I hop off my bed to go save him.

"Hey, Slade," I say with a grin. He's standing in the doorway, looking uncomfortable, holding his tablet, and struggling to find what to say next. "Mom, did you know Slade's taking Quentin to the gym three times a week? They're lifting weights for PE credit."

"Door stays open," My mom says as I drag Slade through the apartment to my room. I shut the door.

Slade pushes it back open.

I throw my arms around him anyway.

"Your mom's right there." He goes all stiff, and his voice sounds like someone's got a rope around his neck, strangling him.

"You're no fun." I haven't seen him all day, and I missed him so much. The world's dreary when he's not around.

He turns the tablet so I can see it. "Can you check the translation of this email? It's garbled." His eyes have an odd, eager glow to them.

I look at the email. The translation app did make a mess of the message. "Should we ask Yuze for help?"

Slade shakes his head. "Just read the translation."

"Apologies for the late reply. Spam filter. Open to the suggestion. Have soundproofing. Come by Thursday to chat." I look at Slade and frown. Then my eyes go wide as I get it.

"Someone said yes!" I throw my arms around him a second time, squealing with delight. It's been several months since we started sending out emails to clubs. We contacted every place we could. I'd given up hope. "We have a place for you to play!"

He picks me up off my feet and twirls me in a circle, kissing me quickly before putting me back down and taking a step back.

***

Day 125 of 162 of the China Assignment
Changde City, Hunan Province, China

The club is perfect. Small enough to be intimate, with lots of soundproofing to keep from annoying the neighbors. A guy in his thirties runs it for his grandfather, who lives in one of the back rooms. The guy agrees to let Slade use the space for a small fee as long as we're out by four each day. He even gives Slade a cubby to store his kit so that we can keep it there.

Day one is spent going back and forth on buses between our building and the club to move the kit.

Day two is set up and tuning, which includes a side trip to a music store as two of the stands wobble, and a snare strap needs replacing. My fix-it skills come in handy.

On day three, Slade gives me a set of earplugs, puts on his headphones, apologizes because the sound is only going to be mediocre, and begins to play.

I immediately sink down in the middle of the floor and shove the earplugs to the side. Eleos on an altar, Slade behind a real kit compared to him on his practice pads is like the Atlantic compared to a mud puddle.

His mouth spreads wide, his eyes glimmer with joy, his arms whip around so fast his sticks are nearly invisible. His entire body, his entire self, engages in a way I couldn't have dreamed possible. He exudes passion and energy and even anger. No wonder he's been having such a hard time not being able to play. This is how Slade releases all the emotions he buries deep within himself. (I'm supposed to be doing Calculus homework, but forget that.)

I soak it up, stealing every bit of him, fitting it inside myself every way possible, holding tight to this whole new side of him, going so gooey it's a miracle I don't leak.

Hours later, he lays his sticks down on top of the bass drum. I'm still sitting on the floor, absorbed by him. "I think I might be dead." Awe tinges my voice.

"Yeah?" The edge of a smile twitches the corner of his mouth.

I jump to my feet. "Slade, there's no possible way you won't make it as a musician. You're going to be the next . . ." I pause, trying to remember his favorite drummer, the guy he likes so much from Tool.

"Danny Carey." Slade gives a pleased chuckle.

"Him," I agree. "Tomorrow, can we bring a speaker so I can hear the rest of the music too? You make me want to dance."

Chapter Thirty-Nine

Hey, I'm sorry I worried you all. Yes, Slade and I had an argument. I didn't tell you because I needed some space to work through it.

I'm not getting back with him or anything like that. We've both agreed we're done, and I've decided to take some time for myself.

Don't listen to Quentin. He doesn't know what he's talking about. There's no need for an intervention. Desi, you don't need to fly out. I haven't felt like having a meltdown in ages.

If that changes, of course, I'll reach out to you guys first.

I believe you that you don't know why Panozco borrowed my car, but if there's nothing going on, why were you so jumpy?

Do I have to back you into a corner again to get you to respond?

***

I knew little about Buysco beyond what was common knowledge. Big box store that sold everything and anything. Prolific across North America. The largest store in Gander.

Internet research added that it was listed on the New York Stock Exchange and headquartered in Vermont. It originally grew out of a family-owned business from the 1970s called Scofield Timber and Freight that served New England and Quebec. The Gander store opened twenty-ish years ago.

I didn't tell Bob about Buysco. I wanted to but didn't want him leaping to any conclusions I couldn't handle.

The next day, Bob gave Isa and me another assignment. He wanted us to plant more listening devices in various places around Gander. The Ricketts I could understand, but his list was pretty extensive, which seemed a waste of time. Bob was possibly a bit of an over-thinker, like me.

On the other hand, planting the bugs would keep me out of the rental and free of Slade. I agreed without complaint.

All Angels Church was Isa and my first stop, which felt like a betrayal of Brady, but we did it anyway. A women's Bible study was going on in one of the side rooms, so the church was unlocked. We left bugs in the vestibule, two offices, and in the back corner of the central podium. (Bob was sure to love listening in on Dad's playing.)

"Too easy," Isa said, as we walked out. "Now tell me more about your upcoming date with Mo."

"The dracos heard all about it themselves."

"Yes, but they don't get nuance or subtext at all."

Seven dracos, all about Ramoth's size, circled above us.

"They'll just have to wait to witness it," I said.

Our next stop was a dry cleaner, where Isa planted a bug in the crack between the register and the counter. Then a realtor's office where I couldn't talk us past the receptionist but managed to slide a bug into her desk plant. Next the hardware store. With this one, I chatted my way into the back office by asking questions about a mouse problem we were having at the rental and the most humane options for solving it. Isa hid a bug in a bookcase while the manager showed me several websites of mouse traps.

As we walked back to Isa's car, the dracos appeared again. Twelve this time.

"Can you tell them to turn invisible?" I said to Isa. "Someone is going to notice."

"When they go invisible, they can't see each other and have flying accidents."

Guess that explained that.

The dracos suddenly bolted at top speed in twelve different directions. I glanced around, but there wasn't anything obvious to have startled them.

Final stop was the Ricketts's main offices. I'd saved this for last intentionally. While at the hardware store, I'd filled the pinhole microphones of a handful of bugs with caulking to muffle anything Bob might overhear about my dad. The moment we drove up to the Ricketts's offices, I knew it wouldn't be needed.

The location wasn't where Slade picked up his deliveries, but a stand-alone steel building centered in an empty parking lot on an industrial road. There were no cars in the parking lot, and even at a distance, the place looked dusty and unused. It was the right address. The front had a large sign with the usual swirly lettering.

Isa parked, and we walked to the front to scope it out. The dracos circled again, coming in close to each other and then scattering and then coming in close and scattering again like they were yo-yos.

"What are they doing?" I asked Isa.

"Trying to figure out how to be *hard-to-get*." Isa knocked on the glass front door of the steel building. It looked like it hadn't been opened in a while.

"What does that mean?" I turned on my cell light and cupped my hands to the glass to peer inside. I could make out a seating area and a reception desk. It was all bare, no computer or phone or anything else to indicate it was in use.

Isa peered in next to me. "Ramoth doesn't like you avoiding Slade. I told her you were playing *hard-to-get* as a form of flirting."

"Don't tell her that. I'm not flirting with Slade."

"As if I care. What matters is what Ramoth thinks. It keeps the peace between the dracos if they believe both Slade and Mo are on equal footing with you."

I folded my arms and gave Isa a direct look. "I'm not flirting with Slade."

"Again. Don't care. But also, don't tell Ramoth. She gets pissy about him being slighted. Saphira wants you to play hard-to-get with Mo too. She's taken over Team Mo after deciding Temeraire wasn't being possessive enough."

"I'm not going to—"

"Trust me, this is way better than the other project they're working on."

"Which is?" I glanced at the sky again.

"None of your business. The building is clearly vacant. Could they have moved?" Isa stepped back from the building. "Or is it possible it's not a real company?"

"Slade works for them. It's a real company."

The dracos did another round of wildly flying off in different directions and then looping back together.

"Let's call Bob," Isa said and put her hand out for the yellow phone. I handed it to her.

"Shell company," Bob said. "I've got several myself. All legal, but they do need a physical address. I use—well, never mind how I do it. Many of them exist to cover up money movements and avoid taxes. Laundering and such, so this could be relevant."

Money laundering!?

The moment Isa and I were back in the car, I pulled out my phone and pretended to text while she drove but really opened up the photo of the checks. The address was the one for the empty building. The date was the night Dad and Dr. Panozco had driven out to Trinity.

And there was a third check.

I'd been in such a hurry when I'd taken the photo that I hadn't noted it before. It was below the other two and written in a different hand. The writer hadn't pressed hard, and the backup copy was faint and hard to read.

But not so hard that I couldn't make out the words Celsius Burns, LTD, or that the amount was for one point five million dollars.

***

5:30 p.m. – Slade

I just searched Panozco's office and found an uncashed check to him for $750K from Rickett Brothers and Sons. The company I work for. WHAT IS GOING ON?

5:59 p.m. – Slade

Apparently, we're doing this again. I'll come by the pizza place tonight.

6:18 p.m. – Me

I don't know why Panozco got a check. My dad got one too. He didn't cash his either. Don't go to Pizza Utopia. I'm not working.

6:18 p.m. – Slade

I'll be by your place in ten minutes.

6:18 p.m. – Me

I won't be here.

6:19 p.m. – Me

I have a date.

✳✳✳

For my date, I wore a nice pair of jeans, a blousy print shirt, my brown leather jacket, and sandals. Stylish and cute, very meet-the-parents appropriate. I even talked Quentin into making butter tarts to take with me. I might be drowning in guilt over letting Mo think I was still into him, but I wouldn't embarrass him.

I was prepared. I looked good.

I was shaking in my sandals. That third check . . .

Slade didn't know.

He wouldn't be pestering me if he did. Someone else, like Dr. Panozco, had to be using Celsius Burns as a front.

What that meant in any practical sense, I had no idea. But when things fell apart, which they would, the band and Slade would get blamed, and it'd be the end of Slade's dreams. If I didn't stop that from happening, it'd be my fault.

Thank you, paranoia.

Everything else aside, I *had* to protect Slade. (I mean, and my dad. And the shuck.)

Mo pulled up outside the rental. I raced out to the passenger side of his truck but then wasn't strong enough to open the door. He came around to help me and used it as an excuse to try to kiss me. I turned it into a hug that hopefully kept him from noticing how frazzled I was or that the neighbor's tree had a good twenty dracos sitting in it. Ramoth let out an unhappy squawk. Saphira did cheerful loop-the-loops high above us in the sky.

Mo drove us to Buysco. This had better be worth me using him.

A section of the parking lot was cordoned off, and a speedboat with racing stripes sat on a trailer on a big platform. On top was a giant red bow. In front was Thaddeus in his Buysco vest.

"Thaddeus is getting an upgrade," I commented.

"A grand one." Mo brought his truck to a clanking halt and then came around to let me out. "They asked us to replicate the old photo as a marketing op for the company." He leaned in to try to kiss me, but I pretended not to notice and skirted past him out of the truck.

"Hey, Joey." Brady walked our way. He wore a Buysco vest too.

"Brady, my new friend." I waved in his direction. "You said you had a job, but I didn't realize you worked here."

"Everyone either did or does, right, Mo?" Brady nodded Mo's way.

"I thought you used to work for Canadian Tire?" I asked Mo.

"I switched after the original photo op. Buysco gives amazin' internships to former student-employees, and the owner said I should throw my name in. Hey, Brady, Thaddeus is wavin' me over. Mind stickin' with Joey so she's not alone?"

"Sure. I've got half an hour before my shift starts."

Mo leaned over as if to kiss me before leaving. I again pretended not to notice and turned to Brady. "Let's watch from over there." I pointed the opposite direction Mo needed to go.

"You seem better," Brady said cautiously as we walked.

"I am better. Hey, who is that old guy with Mo and Thaddeus?" It was the same old guy in a suit who had been in the previous photo.

"Oh, you didn't know? That's Cyrus Scofield."

"Scofield?" I paused, trying to remember how I knew that name. "Scofield, as in the family who started Buysco?" It hadn't occurred to me that the original family might still be involved.

"He's got a house in Nova Scotia but comes up here occasionally, mostly because of our airport."

If Buysco was connected, what were the chances this guy wasn't?

"Do you know him?" I snapped a photo of the boat and the three people now sitting in it.

Brady shook his head. "I met him once, but he wouldn't remember me. I just work in the paint department."

"Come on, let's go introduce ourselves."

We had to wait until the photographers were done, and that took a while. I studied Mr. Scofield. He was older, sixty-something, short and round. He reminded me of the guy in the KFC advertisements. White hair, rosy cheeks, fluffy goatee, merry in all ways. He was gracious to the cameramen and Mo and Thaddeus. He joked with them and laughed a lot.

First impression: Friendly grandpa-type. If I didn't think he was linked to my investigation, I would like him.

The moment the photo op was done and Mo and Thaddeus helped Cyrus down the ladder, I beelined over. Brady hung back.

"Joey, c'mere and meet my future boss," Mo said, taking my hand. "Or at least my future boss's boss's boss's boss, since I'll be startin' out at the bottom. Joey, this is Cyrus Scofield, who offered me an internship once I graduate. Cyrus, this is Joey Partridge, the grandest girl in Newfound-land."

"Mo will do a great job for you." I pasted on the biggest, most fawning, flattering, ingratiating, friendly smile of my life. "You won't find a better employee."

"Bless your heart, aren't you just the sweetest thing?" Cyrus smiled back at me, his voice jovial and welcoming, and topping my friendliness by a meter. "You're a Partridge? That name rings a bell. Why does that name ring a bell?"

"My parents are CMSRC."

Cyrus tapped his knuckle against his chin. He wore a huge ring on his finger made of diamonds and rubies. The way he smiled at me gave the distinct impression he already knew who I was.

"Dexter Partridge is your dad? I met him when we helped with the vandalized tires. Lovely man. Very lovely. Good Canadian stock. Just like you. You're a good egg, Joey Partridge. I like you. Mo's lucky to have you."

"See," Mo said, pointing at me and then himself. "Mr. Scofield gets it." Did he?

Mr. Scofield motioned one of the photographers over. "Come get a few photos of the three of us together. I'll have one of my people send copies to you kids. Just because I like you so much."

Second Impression: No one in this situation, other than Mo, was being real. Pretty sure I'd found my suspect.

***

Mo's house wasn't just a house. It was a home. It had white clapboard siding with dormer windows on the second story, and cherry-red trim around the front door. A huge tree with a swing grew in the middle of a recently trimmed lawn. Three kids' bikes lay in a pile on the drive.

Mo's family was a dream-come-true. His dad teased me and pulled one of my curls. His younger sister asked where I got my clothes. His mom offered me home-cooked food that tasted amazing. His cousins and aunts and uncles and grandparents all joked with me, told me stories about Mo, and complimented me on the butter tarts. A true utopia. (No pizza present.)

I tried to be real with Mo's family in every way I possibly could while also not acting too much like his girlfriend. Pretty sure this was the worst kind of fake of all, but I couldn't come up with anything better.

The moment the family event ended and Mo drove me back to the rental, I shoved the truck door as hard as I could and hopped out. "Thanks so much for an amazing evening."

"Hold on a sec," he said, starting to get out on his side. "I'll walk you to the door."

"No need. I've got it. You don't want to be late for closing up Pizza Utopia." Before he could say anything else or corner me into another kiss-attempt or make me feel even worse about using him, I hurried to the front door and went inside.

When I got to my room, Ramoth was curled up on my bed. Temeraire was on the coveted back-chair spot. Saphira sat on my windowsill, her head tilted, her reptile mouth curved just enough to make her look smug. I took this to mean she'd witnessed my evening of avoiding Mo and defined it as playing hard-to-get.

I shrugged off my jacket and dropped it on the seat of the chair. A piece of paper fell out of the pocket, and I snatched it up, thinking of Aristotle. It wasn't from Aristotle. The paper had been ripped from a spiral notebook, and the handwriting was different. Quavery, as if the writer was either nervous or trying to hide their penmanship.

Your phone is bugged.
Buysco is behind it.
Don't tell anyone.

I rubbed my eyes to make sure I wasn't seeing things. I wasn't.

I sat down. Ramoth crawled over to settle in my lap, craning her long neck up to look me in the eye. I could almost hear her asking what was wrong. I put my finger over my lips and gave a small shake of my head, hoping she'd understand. Then I placed my phone face down on the bed and covered it with my penguin. I nudged Ramoth backward and reached for the yellow phone. It shouldn't be bugged. I hoped.

I took a photo of the note and texted it to Bob while all three dracos watched me avidly. They knew something was up.

Bob

> *Go somewhere your personal phone can't overhear and call me.*

I snuck out of my room as silently as possible. Ramoth followed, but the others stayed put. My parents were in Trinity, so I went to their room and shut the door.

"Where did the note come from?" Bob asked.

"I don't know." I told him about my evening, the photo op at Buysco with Thaddeus's boat, dinner with Mo's family, and my suspicions of Cyrus Scofield. (Things were getting too serious not to share.)

"So the options are Mohmmedidrees Durand, Brady Forester, or a member of the extended Durand family."

"Yup." No one else, including Cyrus Scofield, had gotten close enough to me to slip a note in my pocket. "I think it was Brady. Before we became friends, he acted weird around me, and I never really figured that out."

Then I had another thought.

"It was Lei." I stood and paced the room as I spoke, suddenly filled with a needling, vibrating energy.

"Lei Tien was there as well?"

"No. I've been avoiding her. Lei couldn't have given me the note, but she talked me into putting an app on my phone. That's how it got bugged."

Only, how would Brady know that? And what was Lei's connection to Buysco?

"Didn't her mother invent the spectrometer that burst into flames and caused the fire in the women's Airbnb?" Bob asked.

She had. I hadn't previously considered that the fire might be related to the shuck. Possibly a huge overlook. "Are you thinking Dr. Tien destroyed her own invention? My parents say she's in the process of getting world-wide patents and is likely to make a bunch of money. The spectrometer works."

I had yet another thought. Just as good as the first. Possibly even better. "Dr. Tien's spectrometer marks raw magic. That's what it does. CMSRC would've been using it to locate the exact spot where the shuck sits underwater. The research vessels that blew up would also have had her spectrometers on them. What if the goal of blowing up the boats was to destroy the spectrometers without making it obvious? Bob, is it possible the shuck isn't there? That someone took it and is trying to hide that fact by destroying the equipment that would find it?" I remembered my dream and the awareness of watchers.

Bob went silent and then, "I'm asking Maur." He came back a moment later. "Maur says no. The shuck is definitely still in Trinity Cove."

Darn.

I mean . . .

Good. And not just because the thought of the watchers hurting it was so horrible. The entirety of the seadragon species depended on that shuck surviving. And maybe this was shallow and shortsighted of me, but I now felt like I knew it.

I returned to pacing. The answers were close but too far to grasp. "Could it be the opposite? Someone took out the spectrometers because there's something else in Trinity Cove that can't be discovered? Something magical?"

Bob went silent a second time. "Maur says no again. The veradracos have been keeping out any underwater creatures big enough to damage the shuck. The shuck is drawing smaller creatures, and the dracos are allowing those. Things like draco-krill and minuscule draco-fish. Maur says they become the food source for the newly hatched seadragons."

"Would these small creatures attract magic-handlers?"

"Anything allowed into Trinity Cove by the veradracos is too small for a handler to bother with."

Maybe I was wrong about the spectrometers being related.

The jittery energy coursing through me didn't think so.

Trinity Cove and the shuck. Lei and her mom and the spectrometer. The developers and their checks. Cyrus Scofield and Buysco. Dr. Panozco and my dad. Thaddeus's boat. Brady.

Something big was on the horizon. Right there. Just out of view.

"I sent the note to Aristotle who will research the Buysco angle," Bob said. "The dracos will triple their guard over the cove. Don't do anything to give away that you know your phone is bugged. Let me figure out a way to keep it from sending any more information, and then I'll send Ramoth over in the morning with a bag to collect it. I've got a spell that should trace the bug back to whoever is tracking you. That alone will give us a lot of information, and we can decide what to do next."

I'd bet every single one of my college acceptance letters it would trace back to Cyrus Scofield.

"And . . ." Bob continued, sounding suddenly uncomfortable. "Good job for getting us this far. You're not as useless as I anticipated, and I do give credit where credit is due."

CHAPTER FORTY

Day 126 of 162 of the China Assignment
Changde City, Hunan Province, China

I sit on the floor of the club, legs crossed, Slade's wireless speaker next to me. "Play music about dancers."

"Warm up. Then practice. Then I'll play for you." His eyes have a sparkle and his foot is already tapping, eager to begin.

I wrinkle my nose at him. From experience watching him on his pads, warm up and practice will be boring to watch. He stops a lot, repeats the same groove at different speeds and volumes, changes things, starts over, stops again. I work on Chemistry homework for the first couple of hours.

Then the speaker bursts into Lady Gaga. I startle and drop my tablet. "Slade!"

He gives me a chin-nod. "Dance, Jojo."

I jump to my feet, taking the speaker with me. I'm stiff as I've been so absorbed in Slade that I never looked for a local studio and haven't danced in months. I keep things easy for the first couple of songs, stretching as I move. His playing is irresistible, and song by song, I loosen up and enjoy myself. The music and his emotions pound the air, just as they had the day before, but this time I'm part of it, a participant rather than a listener.

I toss off my sweater so that I'm down to a cami and denim skirt. Slade watches me.

Slowly the music changes.

Not the sound or the tempo or anything else that concrete, but something more personal. My heartbeat matches his rhythm. His arms fly, and I do too. It's like we're one thing, not two, forming a dance between us, and it's amazing. I sing along to the music, and his playing gets so full of me that I feel it in my muscles, my bones, my soul.

Our gazes lock. His cheeks are flushed, his lips parted, his eyes laser-focused and intense.

The music stops. Abruptly.

I still, my breath coming too fast, sweat beading my skin. I take a step in his direction.

He stands. His sticks fall to the floor.

I drop the speaker on my foot. He knocks into his hi-hat, making it clatter. I launch myself in his direction. He races mine.

He plows into me, walking me backward until I'm crowded into the wall. Zero space between us, shared air, his mouth devouring mine, mine inhaling his. This isn't kissing. It's joint incineration. There's no place where I start and he ends. There's just us.

And then there's a loud crash as something hits the wall next to Slade's head. A chair.

We both jump. Slade lets me go and spins around. An older man in a felt hat yells at us in Mandarin while shaking his pointer finger our direction.

Slade goes all tense and shoves me behind him. I start to shake, panicked because of the yelling but also because this is exactly the situation most likely to upset Slade.

The man yells himself out and then with a huff returns to wherever he came from. Slade and I stand there for a long moment, and then Slade turns to face me. I latch onto the edge of his tee with both hands.

"You okay?" he asks, and his voice is all funny. Not calm at all. He presses the back of his hand to his mouth.

I start to panic. "I'm okay. Are you?"

He gives a jerky nod. His breathing is rough and coming in spurts. He's going to get upset, yell just like the old man. This is Slade's worst nightmare come true, and it feels like it's all my fault for wanting to dance.

Slade drops his hand to my waist and leans his forehead against mine, making a sound that is half-guffaw and half-chortle.

Ummm . . .

What?

"Slade, are you laughing?"

Another guffaw-chortle bursts from him.

"You are laughing. Slade, you don't laugh." Not like this. Not in moments like this.

He goes off in earnest. His whole body jerks and spasms. Tears run down his face. I laugh too, just because he is.

We stand there clinging to each other, our laughter filling the room, our foreheads pressed together. My anxiety slips away. I've never been so happy in my entire life.

Chapter Forty-One

I dreamed of the shuck again. It sat on the muddy floor of the cove, but this time the water and sky above were dark, and rather than me being the shuck itself, I rested cross-legged next to it.

"Hi." How exactly did one charm a glowing orb? Also, I wasn't having trouble breathing, nor was I cold. There was something comfortable about being here, communal even.

"So, I'm Joey. Sasha Clems said you wanted to communicate with me, but that this spell was unlikely to let you do so. I seem to be able to talk to you, so good job on that. I hope you can understand me. Ramoth and the others have always been able to."

It sat there unresponsive.

"You're very pretty. Love the mix of purple and blue lights. I can see why people sneak in just to get a glimpse of you."

I looked around for clues as to what it wanted or additional conversational topics. Nothing but dark water. "I guess I could tell you a story about my love life. That's what Ramoth likes. I don't mind telling her, although to be honest, I'm not crazy about Isa or Bob being involved. Shall I tell you a secret? Something just between you and me that I haven't told Ramoth or Temeraire or Saphira?"

Still nothing from the shuck, but instinct said it was interested.

I lowered my voice. "Mo Durand is the worst kisser ever. Like, grosses me out when he even leans in. I'd way rather kiss Brady. Or Ramoth. Or Lei. Slade, for sure, even though I shouldn't go there. No amount of pretty locations with trees and water will ever make up for just how bad Mo is at kissing." I shuddered for effect.

And then the shuck and the water and the communal feeling disappeared, and I woke to dracos yanking my hair in multiple directions. I jerked upright, which pulled my hair even harder. One of the dracos, Temeraire, fell off the bed with a thump.

That's when the first smoke detector burst into high-pitched screams. Seconds later, another joined it. And then a third. I leaped from my bed into a cloud of smoke that sent my nose burning and my lungs coughing. "Out the window, all of you." I grabbed Ramoth and threw her bodily in that direction. The other two followed. I couldn't go that way myself. The branch would never hold me. Also, I needed to get my brother.

"Quentin!" I yelled and dropped to the floor, crawling to the door. Our parents were in Trinity, so it was just us.

The hallway was filled with more smoke and heat and a deep roaring from somewhere below. I lapsed into coughing. Quentin's door burst open, and he half-fell, half-jumped to the floor next to me. "There's a fire. We have to get out of here."

"I know."

We crawled together toward the stairwell. More smoke rolled up from below, making it hard to see or breathe. The stench of it singed my nose hairs, and the heat burned against the bare skin of my arms and legs and right through the thin covering of my PJs.

Quentin and I slid on our butts down the stairs, holding tight to each other. Even with the thick smoke, light came from the direction of the kitchen. It must be fully engulfed.

"Hold your breath and we'll run for it." Quentin grabbed my hand and pulled me to my feet. I managed a single deep breath, which tasted more like smoke than oxygen, and raced with him to the front door.

Thank Eleos, I'd fixed the sticky lock.

We burst through to fresh air and cold and a cacophony of dracos flying wildly around the front yard screaming bloody murder. Quentin dragged me across the street to the neighbor's tree, the one where Ramoth and the others always gathered to spy on me.

From the front, our rental didn't look so bad other than the glowing windows, but flames were shooting up the back above the roofline, and a column of smoke reached for the night sky. The kitchen was directly below my room. If it wasn't yet burning, it would be soon.

Along with all my belongings.

One moment, I had a heart and lungs and intestinal system, the next, my entire body caved in. I threw my arms around the tree.

My penguin. My duvet. My clothing. My statue of Eleos.

My bell from Peru. My star from Japan. The nesting dolls from Russia. My blue sweater. The mug from Gander I'd bought just weeks ago. The photo of Slade, Vinnie, and me that I kept in the back corner of the lowest drawer where no one but me would see it. Every single item I owned, except for the purple daisy-print, cami-and-shorts PJs I currently wore, would no longer exist.

Sirens blared in the distance. They seemed unreal, more background noise in a WWII documentary about air raids than anything connected to reality. RCMP showed up with flashing lights. A firetruck followed. The neighbors' doors opened. People yelled. The firemen hooked up a hose to a hydrant. Flames shot upward above the house.

I pictured my memorials one by one, flick-flick-flick in quick rotation, each sitting in its own special spot on my dresser. Melting. Flaming. Crumbling. Right before my eyes.

My breath frayed. My skin went clammy. I slid down the tree, the bark scraping the inside of my arms. I was drowning. I was dying. I was so beyond *threshold* the hamster in my brain ran itself straight into heart failure.

I slumped to the ground. Something cold pressed into my face. There was noise. Yelling. Yelling scared me. Where was I? Toronto? Only in Toronto, I'd been in a washroom. Washrooms didn't usually have trees.

"Quentin, where is she?" someone roared.

Even if I was in a washroom, I had to hold on to the tree or I'd fall over and get another head wound. Only, I already fell. I might already be dead.

Someone pulled me upright and pressed me backward against the tree trunk. I couldn't hold my head up and slumped forward.

"Quentin, how much smoke did she inhale?" Slade's voice.

"Same as me."

A sob tore upward through my chest, and I convulsed. Tears gushed down my face, snot ran from my nose. I couldn't see. Maybe I'd gone blind.

Slade lifted my chin and pried my mouth open, shining a light in my face.

Relief swept through me that he was here.

Only he couldn't be here.

Slade couldn't see me like this. He just couldn't. I tried to turn away, but he held me in place.

"Her throat looks good. Quentin, go find a paramedic and get yourself checked."

"Aren't you a paramedic?"

"You're not my problem."

I was the problem. This was my problem. He. Could. Not. See. Me. Tears dripped off my jaw, splattering my chest.

"Once you've been checked," Slade continued, "run to my car and grab my jacket. She barely has any clothes on."

Slade scooped me up and twisted around so he was sitting against the tree, and I was on his lap. I fell against him, and he took my hand, wedging it between our bodies, pressing it to his heart. But it wasn't my hand. It was just this lump of clay that used to be connected to me but no longer was.

"Jojo, you're having a panic attack and you're hyperventilating. I know it's scary, but we're going to fix this, 'kay? We just need to get your breathing back on track. Feel my chest rise? Breathe with me. In through your nose. Out through your mouth."

He started counting, in one-two-three, out one-two-three.

I couldn't do it. My nose was too clogged. My lungs didn't exist. There was no air. The world started to spin.

"C'mon, don't pass out." He lifted my chin again. "Look at me. Look in my eyes."

I did. I loved his eyes. I managed a shaky breath.

"Good. Do it again."

I did and then a second and a third and a fourth. My hand became a hand again.

And then his conversation with Quentin sank in. "You can't be a paramedic."

"Well, I am. Or in training. Keep breathing."

I pulled back from him, shaking my head, my voice rising, hysteria coming in strong.

"No. No. No. No. You can't be a paramedic. You have to be a musician, Slade. You just have to. It's already happened, hasn't it? It's already over. They took your band from you, and I didn't stop them."

Quentin wrapped a jacket around me from behind. "Desi wants us to take her to an ER and get her sedated. Right now."

"Jojo, you need to calm down. You're freaking yourself out. Breathe."

"Everything's gone." The words tumbled out around fresh sobs. "My penguin. My statue. My clothing. Your band. You. It's all just gone. There's nothing left."

"Uh," Quentin interrupted, "Desi thinks—"

"Tell Desi to shut up." Slade ran his hand up my back under the jacket and my PJs, pulling me into his chest. "Jojo, I'm right here."

"Your band—"

"The band is fine. We've got gigs scheduled all fall and plans to start writing our own stuff. Your belongings will have to be replaced, but you're great at finding things you love. You're going to be okay."

I wasn't. This wasn't, but I caved into him anyway, giving up, curling my arms around his back, leaning into the solidness of him, the steadiness he always radiated. I wiped my tears and my snot on his shoulder and buried my face in the side of his neck. He smelled like sweaty Slade, like he'd just spent a couple of hours playing his drums Slade. It was a wonderful smell. The smell of China, of him, of kissing, of having ground beneath my feet.

It wouldn't last.

Nothing in my life ever did.

***

The firemen got the fire out. One of them wanted to check me over, but Slade pulled out his wallet to prove he was a paramedic-in-training in Toronto and got them to leave me alone. I stayed buried in his neck, managed to stop crying, and pretended none of this was happening.

Slade gave an RCMP officer his number and rental address and told them he'd take Quentin and me to his mom. He wanted to carry me to his car, but I pulled myself together enough to walk. We held hands.

I didn't look at the house. I couldn't. But I overheard someone say the entire backside, which would include my room and my stuff, had been cremated.

The drive to the Adlers' rental took twenty seconds. Slade really did live right around the corner. The lights of the house were all on, and his mom was outside loading Vinnie into a car.

"Stay here." Slade jumped out to go talk to her.

"He's coming back, right?" I asked Quentin in the back seat. It was a stupid question, but my brain was still way past *threshold*, and my hamster MIA.

Maybe the destruction of our rental and my stuff would make my flipping out not so unreasonable to Slade. Maybe if I held it together going forward, he'd think I was just having a bad day and not look further.

Quentin shoved his phone at me. "Desi wants to talk to you."

"Absolutely not." I batted the phone away.

"Solomon's trying to find Mom and Dad," Quentin continued. "Max is trying to find a flight out here. If you don't talk to Desi, she's going to make me take you to an ER."

"No Desi. No ER."

Slade returned. A wave of relief engulfed me so thoroughly I went lightheaded.

"CMSRC is evacuating everyone to a motel for the night while the other houses are checked." He tossed a duffel bag in the back next to Quentin.

We ended up at a low-budget place with a bunch of other CMSRC families. Slade's mom stood outside a room with an open door. She'd beaten us somehow.

"Quentin, grab my duffel and help your sister." Slade jumped out again. "I've got to get Vinnie and convince my mom to let us share a room, which will go better if you're taking care of her rather than me."

Ten minutes later, Slade's mom showed Quentin, Slade, a drowsy Vinnie carried by Slade, and me to a double room. The curtains were burlap, the comforters geometric patterns, and the artwork paintings of icebergs in jewel tones. Hideous, but not the worst I'd ever seen.

"Partridges in that bed," Slade's mom said, giving me a long, wary look that she then slid to Slade. "Adlers in this one."

"Of course," I agreed, my voice only shaking a little.

Slade told Quentin to take a shower and borrow whatever he needed from the duffel. Quentin came out wearing sweats that were way too short on him and a Razor band tee.

If I wanted to change out of my damp, sooty, purple daisy-print PJs, I'd have to wear Slade's stuff too.

Since I no longer owned any clothing myself.

Hysteria did a hit-and-run takeover of my brain.

"Breathe," Slade said and started in my direction. I put a hand up to stop him and pulled myself together, even though what I really wanted was to throw myself at him. Wanted it like Jason wanted his fleece, medieval Christians wanted the Holy Grail, Hitler wanted to take over Europe. (Okay, the last was going too far even for me.)

I couldn't do it. If I did, he'd know. And when he left again, him knowing would make everything that much worse.

It was the single most awful shower of my life. The tiny bottle of motel shampoo wasn't near enough to suds up my smoke-saturated hair, and the conditioner was even worse. I carefully folded my filthy PJs for safe-keeping and grabbed a pair of navy boxers from Slade's duffel that fit if I rolled the waist. I put on a Celsius Burns tee. Maybe he'd let me keep it.

Slade took a turn in the shower, and I climbed into bed. Quentin had lined the center with pillows, a Partridge family tradition in moments when we had to share. They smelled all wrong, like chemicals. My arms ached to hold my penguin, and the towel I put down to keep my hair from making the bed all damp was scratchy. I blinked back more tears.

When Slade came out, he glanced my direction for a long moment and then turned off the lights before sliding in next to Vinnie.

My head immediately started churning.

Slade was right. I was good at finding things I loved. I'd just have to use that talent to replace my memorials and clothing and then everything would be okay. I'd go to every country we'd lived in and search out the same vendors and the exact same items.

It'd take months, years.

I didn't have months. Or the money to fly around the globe. I was going to have to move to either Yale or MIT empty-handed. Nothing to prove I had a place in the world. Not even a passport. Was I Canadian? Was I a person? Did I exist?

I *knew* I was being irrational, but the pressure was squeezing me down. I tried counting backward from ten but couldn't remember the second number. I shoved my hand into my mouth and dug my teeth so deep into my knuckles my wrist ached.

"Quentin," Slade said from the far side of the room, breaking the weight of the darkness. "I'll give you fifty bucks if you'll switch places with me and keep your mouth shut about it."

"Dude, I'm not listening to you make out with my sister."

"I'm not going to—look, she's starting to hyperventilate again. So either you're going to help her breathe, or you're going to let me do it."

"I'm fine." It came out all ragged.

Quentin rolled out of our bed, and Slade took his place. He left the pillows between us but slid his hand underneath to catch mine and tug it back so that my palm was pressed into his heart. He was solid under my touch. A rock, and I wanted this. Needed it. Even knowing it was going to lead to more hurt.

I focused my attention on the rise of his chest, the evenness of his breathing, his heartbeat. I shifted to touch my bare foot to his. When he didn't pull away, I moved my other foot over as well, tangling us together.

Time passed. Quentin fell asleep. The air-conditioning unit kicked on, filling the dark with a rattling hum.

Without pills, sleep was going to take a while.

Slade slid his free hand under the pillow and pressed it against my collar bones so that the U of his thumb and fingers cradled the base of my neck. His other hand still pressed mine to his heart. Our feet were still tangled. We were all connected to each other in multiple places.

"Jojo? Today wasn't your first panic attack, was it?"

I tensed.

"Back in Toronto, when you came to my dad's place and I punched the wall. You had one then too." He spoke slowly, not struggling but thinking it through, puzzling out what he knew of me, finding pieces and uniting them.

I squeezed my eyes closed. I bit down on my lip. My pulse flailed against his fingers around my neck.

Which was why he'd put his hand there. He was doing his para-medic-thing and monitoring me. *Oh Jeez.* I flushed with humiliation but I didn't get hysterical.

"And back in China," he continued, his voice going even slower. "With the MSS guy and the business card and you throwing me under the bus. You were having a panic attack then as well, weren't you?"

I didn't answer.

"You had one the night I drove everyone home from the bar and yelled at you. And when we had the fight in the street. You have them all the time."

The room was entirely dark. Quentin snored and the air conditioner buzzed. The chemicals from the bedding stung my nose.

Slade stroked my neck with his thumb.

"Why didn't you tell me?" he asked quietly.

The familiar pressure built, the explosion-waiting-to-happen, the shrapnel, the shreds of everything that scared and hurt me.

If he'd given me half a chance after China, I would've blabbed. I would've fought not to, but I would've done it anyway.

"Jojo?"

I pinched my eyes tighter and clamped my teeth together. It was too much. It wasn't his business. The words burst out anyway. Too fast. Too loud. A little angry. "Because I knew what would happen. What did happen. You thought I was perfect in China. The moment I wasn't, you walked away."

He stilled. His chest paused in its rise and fall. He pulled his hand back and went deep into himself.

I'd upset him.

Good.

Slade returned his hand to my neck, not stroking but still monitoring. We stayed that way for a long time in the dark with the pillows between us, the hum of the air conditioner the only sound. When he finally spoke again, it was barely audible, and there was a good chance he thought I was asleep.

"Well, shit."

Chapter Forty-Two

Day 134 of 162 of the China Assignment
Changde City, Hunan Province, China

"Hey, did you guys get the email about the MSS lecture?" Quentin asks as he opens the fridge.

Slade and I sit at the kitchen table. He's wearing a Danko Jones tee and drawing our latest idea for his sleeve tattoo, a massive tree with a draco hiding in the branches. This would be idea number forty or so. Slade's a terrible artist, but since I'm even worse, he gets to do the drawing. He doesn't care that he's bad. He just keeps trying.

Now that we have the club, we spend most of our day there. I make him break for lunch and homework. (Or he won't bother with either.) Then he's back at it until the four o'clock deadline. He's so obsessed with playing that he's leaving Vinnie home with his mom too. I work on my homework while he plays, which is good since I've spent so much time helping him that I'm behind. Occasionally, I dance to distract the both of us for a while. We have a pretty great life. China is the best place I've ever lived.

At the moment, I'm painting his toenails black.

"You want to go over to the MSS offices with us?" I ask Quentin. "Or meet us there?"

The lectures by the MSS officer overseeing the CMSRC assignment have been a regular event we're forced to attend. Our parents had to agree to them as part of the job assignment. The lectures are fine, all about Chinese culture and behavioral expectations. At the last one, the MSS officer in charge started yelling and threw a paperweight at his assistant. Stressed me out, but I handled it with Slade next to me.

"I'll meet you." Quentin shuts the fridge without taking anything. He looks at me finishing up Slade's pinky toe. "You guys are weird."

"She gets into trouble when bored." Slade doesn't look up from his drawing as he says it, but I grin at him anyway. It's a lot of words for him in front of Quentin. Slade's starting to talk more lately. He even asked Yuze to pass the peanuts last night.

He holds up his drawing for us to see.

"It's great," I say automatically, even though it looks more like a green and brown space alien than a tree.

"Worse than the last one." Quentin opens a cupboard. "You should ask Solomon to help when he gets here. He, at least, knows how to draw." (Yes, my siblings are all coming for a visit. So not looking forward to that.)

"I really like it." I put Slade's foot on the ground and grab the other one. "But what if instead of a full tree, you just do a branch? One that twines around your arm. And then have a draco face behind the branch peeking through and breathing fire or something?"

"You think he's capable of drawing that?" Quentin asks.

"A branch," Slade murmurs while pulling out a fresh paper. "Good idea."

Chapter Forty-Three

I woke the next morning, groggy and slow to remember where I was. I'd dreamed of the shuck again, but the dream was hazy and undefined. I'd been underwater, and a voice had shouted *hurry, hurry, hurry* at me repeatedly.

I looked around the motel room. I was alone, and everything I relied on to hold myself together had been destroyed. Even more . . .

The thing I'd feared for all of this time had happened. Slade now knew.

I didn't freak out.

I was too numb to do so.

I dragged myself to the washroom to find my hair had gone all poodle-with-its-paw-in-an-electrical-socket to match my Joey-is-wrecked general mental state. I doused my head under the shower, but without hair products or at least a good dozen hair bands, it was going to poof again as it dried.

Slade's duffel bag was still there, so he must not have high-tailed it back to Toronto and away from me first thing this morning. I didn't want to see him, like really, really didn't want to.

I borrowed sweats and then a button-up shirt to go over the Celsius Burns tee to make it less obvious that I no longer owned a bra. Someone knocked on the door, and I peeked out the window.

Isa.

I let her in.

"Bob says to tell you he's grateful to you for finding the connection to Buysco and the spectrometers. He gives you full credit for figuring it out, which is making the dracos super happy for some reason, but he won't risk you getting killed, so you're fired."

Not my biggest problem at the moment. "Hey, can you drive me out of here? I really need out."

"You think my mom let me keep my keys after someone just tried to kill you? Because no other CMSRC rental was touched. And why aren't you running off with Slade? It's clear as day that the two of you are crazy, madly in love with each other."

I winced. "We aren't." We weren't. "Have you seen my parents?"

"Your mom was here earlier but headed over to meet RCMP at your house. Back to Slade—"

"The dracos put you up to this, didn't they? That's why you're here."

"Five minutes ago, Slade walked up to Quentin in the motel breakfast room and said, and I quote, 'Quentin, I'll give you two hundred bucks if you'll answer some questions about your sister.'"

I stared at her.

It made sense in a Slade kind of way. Especially if he was now feeling guilty about our fights. Slade had always been an excellent overprotective watchdog with Vinnie, and he'd gone all-out on his paramedic-thing last night. There was a good chance he was now going to Desi-me.

"Crap." I collapsed onto the bed, burying my face in my hands.

"Quentin replied that Slade should talk to your elder sister, and they went off together to call her."

Even worse.

"Which is frustrating the dracos. They can only hear his side of the conversation, and he's not saying much. The dracos want you to interpret. They think she's yelling."

She likely was.

Isa put her hands on her hips and stared down at me. "What exactly happened between you two last night?"

"Nothing. He hates me and . . ." Not even I believed that anymore. "It's complicated. Everything's fine. I just really need out of here." Who else had a car? Brady? He'd be my first pick, but I'd no way to reach him.

Stella? Same.

But there might be a way to reach Mo.

I scooted around Isa and went to the desk in the corner. It held a phone and one of those books full of motel instructions.

"Please tell me," Isa continued, frowning, "that you aren't so stupid that you don't realize Slade's crazy, madly in love with you, worships the ground you walk on, and would willingly spend the rest of his life staring adoringly at you while you sleep. The last being both romantic and creepy, but it's also true."

"I'm not stupid." I rifled through the motel book, looking for a list of local restaurants. Mo'd said he was going into Pizza Utopia this morning. He should be there.

Isa stepped over to stand in front of me. "You really don't realize it, do you?"

I gave her a wary look and picked up the phone receiver.

"How exactly did you interpret him loudly announcing the whole, 'You, Jojo. I want you. The way we were in China'?"

"You know about that?"

"Everyone knows. Back to my point. You do realize what he was actually saying was that he's crazy, madly in love with you, worships the ground you walk on, and wants to spend the rest of his life staring adoringly at you while you sleep, right?"

Her words were yet another knife puncturing my chest, cracking wide my ribs, uncovering the shredded mess that was my heart. Gossip hadn't gotten the words right. Slade might now feel guilty and obligated, but he didn't want the real me. He'd been clear about that. I dialed the number in the book.

"Aye?" Uncle Gerald answered.

"Hey, this is Joey. Is Mo around?"

Isa lunged for the phone, but I pulled back just in time.

"What are you doing?" she demanded.

Mo came on. "Joey, are you okay?"

"Can you come get me?"

"You're at the motel by the airport, yeah?" Mo asked.

"I need to sneak away without anyone knowing. Can you help?"

"Give me ten. There's an alley out back. I'll borrow Uncle Gerald's truck so I'll fly under the radar and meet you there."

"Ten minutes. Thank you so much."

The moment I hung up, Isa grabbed my arm, none too gently. "Slade is going to flip. So is Bob."

"Don't tell them."

"Because you just disappearing is so much better?"

She had a point. "Tell Slade I left with Stella."

"How can someone so smart be so incredibly blind? Joey, don't do this. You need to talk to Slade. Like, really talk to him because I'm right about how he feels about you. I'll pin him down first, explain things, tell him what to say to you so he doesn't screw it all up. Then he'll make how he feels clear and take you wherever you want to go. If you run off with Mo, you're going to ruin everything."

"Ramoth will survive." And Team Mo would be thrilled. I looked around the room, automatically searching for my phone before remembering that it no longer existed, and even if it did, I couldn't use it since it was bugged.

"But will you?" Isa demanded. "Someone is trying to kill you."

I paused at that. Then shook my head. She was wrong on this too. Both she and Bob.

They were right as well. No way had that fire been accidental. "If someone had wanted to kill me by lighting the house on fire, they would've pulled the batteries from the smoke detectors first. It wasn't me they were after, it was . . ." I paused, but the answer was obvious. "My phone. I was going to give it to Bob so that he could figure out who was listening to me. They destroyed it." Along with every other belonging of mine. Overkill much? I shuddered. "Cyrus Scofield is behind it." He was definitely a person who enjoyed overkill. But how had he known I was going to give my phone to Bob? No one should've been able to overhear our conversation.

Unless the entire house was bugged.

The entire house must've been bugged.

Just like Bob had Isa and me do to the Ricketts.

"Look," Isa said. "Bob said not to tell you this because there isn't any proof, but Aristotle's convinced Cyrus Scofield had the seadragon killed back in California in the first place. And that he was behind the ransacking of Sasha Clems's house and had a member of BIMD on his payroll."

Which made me pause.

It lined up in some indecipherable way with the other clues, especially what Bob and I'd speculated about the spectrometer and not wanting CMSRC searching the cove.

I looked to Isa. "The shuck's okay, right? Nothing bad happened last night?"

She shook her head. "Did you have another dream? Because Bob checked first thing on hearing about the fire. The shuck is fine. He thinks it's sending you dreams because it's bored."

I wasn't so sure I agreed. Even more, regardless of me being a personal mess, this wasn't over. The shuck needed me. My dream last night felt like it was asking for help. Slade and my dad needed me too.

Isa's eyebrows scrunched all consideringly. "What aren't you telling me?"

And then suddenly I knew what to do next.

"Tell Slade I'm fine. Tell him I'm not freaking out in any way, and he doesn't need to worry about me. Tell him there's something I need to do, and I don't need his help. Tell him . . ." I hesitated. The next was a lie, and he'd know it. "Tell him I'll text him later."

"Don't do this, Joey."

I headed for the door. "And whatever you do, don't let Slade follow me."

***

I snuck out of the motel room and back to the alley. Isa didn't stop me, and I didn't run into Slade or anyone else. My challenge was that the alley was gravel and apparently a great place to dump bottles, which then got smashed. Twice, I had to stop to remove glass chunks from the bottom of my bare feet.

Mo pulled up in a gray truck and got out. "Joey, I've been worried sick. I wanted to come find you, but everyone said to leave it because CMSRC had you locked up and—" He looked me over, noticing my outfit. "—and that." He finished with a big, dark finality that left Slade's name unspoken but between us. (At least he was nice enough not to comment on my poodle hair.)

"It's not as bad as it looks." I smiled at him and touched his arm, being flirty. "He was the only one with clothes to borrow from and—"

I halted mid-word.

I couldn't do this.

It wasn't fair to Mo, it wasn't fair to me, and it was way past time to stop being unfair. I dropped my hand and started over, blurting.

"Mo, I need your help. I really, really need it. I've got a problem to solve, and I can't handle it on my own. I also can't date you anymore. I've been dating you for all the right reasons but also all the wrong reasons, and I have anxiety issues I don't talk about but that are out of control right now. I didn't tell you about my anxiety before, but we've been on three dates, and as fun as it's been, I don't owe you an explanation. But as you can hear, I can't keep my mouth shut when I get stressed, which I am right now. I hate talking about it and I'm telling you, which is huge for me. I do like you, but that doesn't make us right for each other. Really, we're all wrong. For dating, that is. I'm so sorry, but it's best if . . ."

I trailed off because Mo's eyes had glazed over. He rubbed at his face. "Are you like dumpin' me?"

"Yeah." It just about killed me, but I met his gaze.

No sad puppy eyes or anger or hatred. Just confusion. "And if I don't want to be dumped?"

"I do it anyway and still ask you to help me."

"Does this mean you're back with . . ."

My eyes widened in alarm. "No. No way. He's the one I'm trying to hide from."

Mo frowned and rubbed at his face again. "Got it." He set his jaw. "I'll help you. Whatever you're needin'. If for no other reason than I really hate that guy."

"Thank you," I said, intentionally ignoring the fact that he seemed to care more about besting Slade than me. "Can I borrow some money? I need shoes and a change of clothing but am pretty much destitute at this point."

"Sure. Where do you want to go shopping?"

"Buysco. Definitely Buysco."

Chapter Forty-Four

Day 139 of 162 of the China Assignment
Changde City, Hunan Province, China

"So, Slade," my brother Solomon says from across the table of an upscale restaurant in Changde's high-end district. "Tell us about your future plans." He sends Slade an assessing, not-terribly-friendly glance.

Max looks up from his rice plate to observe Slade too. Desi looks at me. Next to her, Slade's mom goes stiff. Yes, my siblings flew across the world to scope Slade out. Thank you, Quentin. Pretty sure Madame Menace offered him more money to tattle than I'd been paying him to keep quiet.

Slade and I are seated on opposite ends of the table per his choice. He also moved away from me when I tried to sit next to him in the van ride over and hasn't looked at me once all evening. I get it. There's nothing more important to Slade than privacy, especially when it comes to me. It still hurts.

"No plans yet," Slade says slowly. His expression is blank. Nothing there. Not even any of his speech-tells, even though it has to be torture for him to speak in front of all these people. He turns to Vinnie, who is playing with a child's puzzle box.

"You're in twelfth year, right?" Solomon asks. "What are your thoughts on college?"

"I. Don't. Know." Slade doesn't look up.

I bite down on my lower lip to keep from helping him. Slade won't want me to and doing so would draw more attention to him.

"Acceptance letters should be coming out right about now." Desi looks Slade up and down while frowning.

Slade picks up Vinnie's spoon and offers him a bite of vegetables.

Desi's right. Slade should've started applying to colleges right about the time we met, and he's never mentioned it.

"Solomon, do you still like living in North Carolina?" I ask in an attempt to change the subject.

"Not that college is your only option," Desi continues. "There's the trades, of course."

I glare at her.

But no way has Slade not thought about what he wants to do after he graduates. Slade isn't impulsive. He considers things, makes deliberate choices. He must have ideas.

He just hasn't mentioned them to me.

I could be devastated by this, but I'm not. It's a good thing. A really good thing. I never allow myself to think more than a week ahead of where I am and always act as if the next move, next assignment, won't ever happen. Doing otherwise would destroy me.

With Slade . . .

Nope.

There's plenty of time.

The here-and-now is so good, so consuming that I don't need a single thing more.

Slade realizes this about me even though I've never talked to him about it. That's why he hasn't shared his thoughts on the future.

It all makes absolute sense.

Chapter Forty-Five

Buysco looked exactly as it had last time. Glass front, cement siding, massive green roof, parking lot in need of repaving. Typical big box. I wanted it to be different somehow, but it wasn't.

No dracos followed us that I could tell. They were too busy obsessing over Slade and Desi's Joey-gossip-fest. We were on our own.

After parking Uncle Gerald's truck, Mo ran around the side to get the door for me. He glanced down at my bare feet and then the distance between us and the front entry. "Piggyback ride?"

"Definitely."

Once indoors, he put me down. Plan time. Such as it was.

Cyrus Scofield knew everything I knew. All the clues, the checks I'd found, my suspicions of him. Therefore, there was no reason to not just confront him. Or not *confront*, since even with Mo backing me, I was never going to be a confrontational person. But *talk*, at least. And do it in a public enough way that the entire town would know Mo and I were here.

Shopping first. For several reasons.

"Heyo, Mo and Mo's girlfriend," A guy in overalls called out to us as Mo grabbed a cart.

"It's Joey," I said.

The guy gave me a bewildered look.

"My name."

He shrugged, not really caring.

"Ouch, easy now," Mo said as the guy walked off.

"That wasn't about me dumping you." I took the cart from him. "I hated being your nameless girlfriend even when I was your kinda-sorta girlfriend."

I started my shopping in the hair department, grabbing the best of the frizz-relief options and a bunch of scrunchies. From there, we went to women's clothing, where I didn't allow myself to think about everything I'd lost while I picked leggings, a tee with a picture of a giant sunflower, and socks. I made Mo wander off while I hit women's delicates.

Mo returned the moment I was done, bringing Cyrus Scofield with him. Exactly as I'd hoped would happen. Mo was predictable. So was Cyrus Scofield, even if I barely knew him.

"Look who I found," Mo announced. "He's compin' you a new wardrobe. Just like with Thaddeus's boat and CMSRC's tires. Isn't that grand? Cyrus is good people."

"Yup, he is," I agreed.

"Least we can do," Cyrus said. "Buysco is here for you, Miss Joey Partridge. I've always liked you." He smiled wide. His cheeks went round and rosy, as if he didn't know that I knew that he knew. (He was *really* good at this.)

I paused, not sure I could match him. If he yelled at me . . .

"This shouldn't have happened to a nice girl like you," he continued, laying on the charm and making me relax. Maybe he would yell, but not at first. At first, he was going to butter me up. It's what I'd do. What I was doing.

He took my elbow and pulled me away from the cart. "Let's go find my managers to take care of you. You deserve our best."

I smiled, giving it my all. "That's really nice of you, Mr. Scofield. I have some questions for you, actually."

"I love questions. Wardrobe first, though."

Mo gave me a happy thumbs-up. I grabbed his hand. No way did I want to get separated.

Cyrus guided us through the store. I made a point of waving at every person we passed. Every person greeted Cyrus and Mo back by name. Several even stopped to commiserate with me about the fire. A guy wearing a fishing vest slipped me some cash. The last person we saw, right before we headed from the store to the back area, was Brady, wearing a Buysco vest and stocking paint.

I ignored him entirely, pretending I didn't see him. No need to drag Brady into this any more than he already was. (But I'm glad he was there. If Mo and I disappeared, I trusted him to say something.)

"This way, this way." Cyrus led us through an area of workers opening large shipping boxes. I greeted each one of them too. They greeted us back. We stopped at a door marked *private offices* where Cyrus punched a code into a keypad.

Leaving the more open area of the store wasn't my preference, but it also made logical sense.

Just inside was an open box of small metal mouse traps sitting on a table. They were oddly shaped, and I recognized them. I'd seen one recently, although I couldn't place where or why.

Cyrus led us down a hallway to another door with a keypad. Mo and I followed him inside, right into a circle of six security guards, all clearly waiting for us.

They weren't regular security guards, the kind hired at minimum wage. These guys were professionals, big, muscular, and with guns on their hips. One of them stepped behind us, blocking the exit.

I had a flashback to China and threw my hands in the air while my intestines turned to mush. "I didn't do anything."

"What's happenin' here?" Mo asked, puzzled rather than alarmed. "You lot new to town? Why don't I know you?"

"Terribly sorry about this." Cyrus gave Mo a hearty pat on the back. "You're a great kid and your internship offer stands, but your girlfriend knows too much and talks too much. The two of you are going to stay here until that damned shuck hatches."

I tried to pull myself together, which was hard with all the people and guns and stern expressions surrounding me.

Wait?

What had he said?

"Hatches?" I slowly lowered my hands and my panic ebbed. "You want it to hatch?"

One of the guards grabbed my arm and slapped a handcuff around my wrist. I started shaking but fought it. This was too important.

"Clever girl." Cyrus pinched my cheek, sounding delighted. "Not quite clever enough, eh? Of course, neither is Aristotle, who should've figured it out by now. Give it some time and you'll get it. And call me in a couple of years once you have some college under your belt. I'm happy to offer you an internship too."

The guard snapped the other side of the handcuff around Mo's wrist. Another guard snagged his phone. Cyrus headed to the door.

"I have questions." I threw the words at him in the best non-confrontational, friendliest tone I had. "Can't you just answer them? Please?"

"You'll figure it out," he replied.

"But everyone saw us walk back here. If we don't return, the entire town will know Mo and I disappeared while with you."

Cyrus clapped his hands together in delight. "Disappeared? My, you do have quite the imagination, don't you? Let's see how the next couple of hours go. No one will think twice about you hanging out here for a couple of hours."

Hours? He expected this all to be over in mere hours? That made no sense. But also, Cyrus was enjoying this. He was baiting me and thought it was fun doing so.

"What are you talkin' about?" Mo demanded, finally realizing something was off.

"Joey will explain everything once she figures it out. In the meantime, I've got work to do."

"What work?" Mo asked.

Exactly. What work?

Only then I got it. Like a giant math problem that wouldn't tie together until suddenly it did. (In all fairness, Cyrus had dropped several huge clues.)

Either way, I now knew what was going on. And it was bad.

CHAPTER FORTY-SIX

Day 139 of 162 of the China Assignment
Changde City, Hunan Province, China

"Jojo?"

We stand on the street outside the restaurant with our families. The van to take us back to the apartment building waits for us, the driver next to the open door. I glance hopefully at Slade. It's the first time he's acknowledged me the entire evening, and I want him to.

"Check the driver," Slade whispers.

"'Kay." Alcohol use and driving completely freaks Slade out. (For good reason.) And I have a better nose than him.

I sidle over to where the driver is holding the side door for my mom. Slade takes Vinnie's hand and follows.

Almost immediately, I get an alcoholic tang up my nose. Not beer, something harder.

I nod at Slade.

"Is something wrong?" Solomon asks.

"Vinnie and I. Are taking a bus," Slade says.

"What about me?" I burst out, startled, hurt, rejected that he'd left me out.

"No, you aren't," Dr. Panozco says at the same time.

"So something is wrong?" Desi gives Slade a pinched frown.

"The driver's been drinking," I say quickly to defuse the situation. I glance at Slade's mom for backup. She should get what's going on here.

She's frozen, her face a statue of panic, one hand half-raised in the air. Only she isn't looking at her two sons. Not at Slade, who's face-to-face with a personal demon and clearly freaking out. Nor Vinnie, who is hiding behind Slade, looking scared. She's staring at Panozco as if her fear is less for her children and more about how her husband is going to react to them.

I suddenly get why Slade stays so close to Vinnie.

"Have you been drinking?" Solomon asks the driver.

"No. Of course not. Never." The driver frantically shakes his head. Liar.

I turn to Dad for backup. He also has an excellent nose, but he's looking the other direction and paying no attention to any of us. I glance at Slade's mom again. She continues to stand there dead-still.

"Get in the van, son," Dr. Panozco says.

My stomach churns at the tension in the air. At the anger in Panozco's voice. At Slade's mom's lack of movement. At all the attention being on us. Words build, an explanation, backup for Slade, but before they spill out, Slade swings Vinnie onto his shoulders and grabs my hand to tow me determinedly in the other direction.

I wheeze out a breath of relief that he hadn't left me behind, even though, realistically, Slade can't. He has no idea how to get back to our building on his own.

Chapter Forty-Seven

The moment Cyrus and the guards left, I started hopping up and down, filled with a frantic energy. "No way, Mo. No way. No way. No way."

Mo grabbed me by the shoulders, holding me in place. Since we were connected by the cuffs, he took my hand with him. I latched onto his forearm, holding tight.

"Talk to me, Joey."

I choked on a laugh that was headed to hysteria-land, but for once not in a bad way. "Mo, did you watch Sasha Clems's livestream?"

"Of course. Who didn't?"

Actually, me. Not live, anyway, as I'd been taking a multivariable Calculus final at the time. I'd watched it after. Several times. Clips still appeared in my social media streams on a regular basis. (None of which was relevant to the current moment, but I was so keyed up my head was spinning.)

"Remember the part of the livestream," I spoke quickly, probably too quickly, "when Sasha was standing on the hook of land and different groups pitched her to buy her semis? Several magic-handlers were there, including one who had a spell that made her cough whenever anyone lied."

"That was deadly funny."

"Totally." I needed to pace around, that's how hyped I was, but Mo held me tight.

"Isa said that Bob said that Aristotle Montague-Smith-Montague said that Cyrus Scofield has a BIMD agent on his payroll." I glanced around the room. We needed to get out of here. I needed to tell all of this to Bob, not Mo.

Which made me laugh. Any other moment, there'd be dracos with me who could tell him, but the dracos were way more interested in Slade and my love life. (Which wasn't funny at all, but I was having a moment.)

"Who's BIMD?" Mo asked.

"American group related to the FBI. Deals with magic." I pulled free of Mo's grip and towed him over to the door. Locked.

The room was mostly empty space. No windows, just the one door, and the only piece of furniture was a metal desk shoved in a corner. I headed there.

"One of the BIMD agents also pitched Sasha as part of her livestream, but a second BIMD agent said the first agent's pitch wasn't from BIMD. Do you remember if the coughing-lady coughed when he said that?"

"No?"

I didn't either.

The metal desk had three drawers. I jerked them open one by one, not even sure what I was looking for.

"Wait, wasn't that the superhero plan?" Mo asked, finally catching on. "He wanted the semis so that someone could swallow it and become an uber-magic-handler."

"Exactly," I crowed. "No one took the guy seriously. The only person to have swallowed a semis and not died is Aristotle himself, and he was like three years old when he did it. Which must be why Cyrus thought Aristotle would figure it out first."

The drawers of the desk were all empty.

"But Cyrus wasn't even there," Mo said.

"He didn't have to be. The BIMD guy's pitch wasn't Cyrus's real plan. Everyone knows swallowing a semis doesn't work." I gave another wild laugh. It was all so dead obvious. "It's not common knowledge, but Aristotle didn't swallow a single semis, he swallowed two. When he survived, handlers tried to duplicate what he did, but everyone in their experiments died as well. Aristotle's always been considered an enigma because of it. CMSRC has even asked to study him, but he's always declined. But what if Aristotle didn't swallow two semis? What if he swallowed two of something newly hatched?"

Saying it out loud struck me with a whole new level of giddiness. I bounced up and down on my toes again.

I was right.

This had to be it.

Even though no one, including the Handlers' Alliance and the draco-scientists, had ever considered this as a possibility for Aristotle's surviving.

But Cyrus had.

And with that, every last bit of excitement flashed out of me in a puff of smoke worthy of last night's fire. I shoved the last drawer of the desk closed.

"He's going to trap them and sell them." My voice went all shaky. I pictured that box I'd seen in the hallway. The one holding what I'd thought to be mousetraps. I *had* seen one of those before. I'd picked it up from the floor of the shed holding Thaddeus's boat.

Thaddeus's boat, which the dracos had said had gone out several nights in a row, not just the night before the research vessels blew up. Cyrus's people must've filled the area around the shuck with traps. They'd used Thaddeus's boat because . . .

Because . . .

Because . . .

It wouldn't set off alarm bells if it was seen?

Everyone would just think it was a local having a prank?

Seemed a stretch, but I was definitely on the right track overall.

It also explained needing to destroy the spectrometers since the only possible bait for the traps was seadragon food, meaning raw semis. No way would the CMSRC scientists using spectrometers have failed to notice a whole ton of unmoving semis just sitting there on the ocean floor. CMSRC would've investigated, discovered the traps, and realized what was going on.

"Cyrus is going to trap the baby seadragons," I said to Mo, "and sell them so that people can swallow two and become magic-handlers."

"That's crazy. Who'd go for that?"

"The rich people sitting out in their yachts." My voice sped up again as another piece fell into place. "Mo, that's why they're there. Magical-creatures don't live long in captivity. Cyrus has to catch the baby seadragons and transport them to the buyers super-fast. And if all those rich people end up handlers, it'll upend the entire world order. Here, help me move the desk so that it's under the vent in the ceiling."

Based on what Cyrus had said, he expected all of this to go down today. Within hours, even. Which meant the shuck must be on the verge of hatching, and he somehow, someway, knew. Possibly, the shuck had even been trying to tell me it was time in my dream last night.

We had to get out of here. Bob and the dracos had to hear this. We had to stop Cyrus's evil plan.

The ceiling was old-style panels resting on dropped aluminum framing, the kind found in stores and buildings and older-type apartments worldwide. I'd replaced such panels any number of times in my life.

"Help me climb up on the desk."

Mo obliged, holding up his arm where we were still attached.

"The dracos have to move the shuck," I continued, once I was up. "As soon as possible. They have to get it out of Trinity Cove and into open water where it can hatch safely away from the traps." Only the dracos couldn't touch it. Their bodies would absorb the magic, killing the incubating seadragons. Sasha Clems had said so in her TV interviews. It's why Bob and the dracos had needed her help in the first place.

The vent was attached to the frame by six screws. With nothing better to use, I started in on the nearest with my fingernail.

"Let me help." Mo climbed up to work a second screw. Luckily, they weren't overly tight, but it still took forever to get them free. Once we had all six out, we lowered the vent face.

Only to discover the vent was fake. Nothing beyond but a small open space and a black camera connected to electrical wires. It dropped toward us, swinging.

"Wow, he really is good," I muttered. "And now Cyrus knows that I know." Although that didn't likely change anything. He'd seemed convinced I'd figure it out. I grabbed the camera and jerked downward. The wires ripped out of the back with a satisfying snap.

"What now?" Mo asked.

No idea. The aluminum supports above us were too flimsy for our weight, and there didn't appear to be anywhere to go anyway. We needed rescuing.

It'd be a while before the town started to wonder if something was wrong.

Which left Isa. Possibly, my abrupt exit from the motel without telling her where I was going had been a mistake.

Mo climbed down from the table. I attempted to jump down next to him, but he put his arms out to catch me, which pulled my cuffed hand, knocking me off balance. I face-planted into his chest.

"I'm supposed to be graceful," I muttered into his shirt.

"Sorry, sorry." He threw his free arm around my waist. "I keep forgettin' we're connected."

The door to the room burst open, and Slade and Isa rushed in.

"This isn't what it looks like," I blurted and then slammed shut my mouth because they were also handcuffed together. As were Lei and Stella behind them. All followed by more of Cyrus's guards with guns.

No rescue in sight.

Chapter Forty-Eight

Day 147 of 162 of the China Assignment
Changde City, Hunan Province, China

"Jojo?"

I jump, slam shut my laptop, and jerk around to face Slade all in one motion. "You scared me!"

He walks into my room and over to my memorials. He picks up the photo of Vinnie, him, and me, puts it down, and taps my bell from Peru.

Mom and Dad left to take my siblings to the airport forty-five minutes ago. Before that, Desi and I went to lunch. A long lunch where she'd done all the talking and said the most awful, upsetting things about Slade. She'd covered a laundry list of medical and mental health diagnoses that she's convinced he could have but has no right or experience to even suggest. Half of them I hadn't even recognized. The research I'd been doing before Slade interrupted didn't help.

Which leads to another thought.

Slade, Quentin, Maxwell, and Solomon went to the gym during Desi and my chat. Seems likely Slade received a lecture as well. "What did my brothers say to you?"

Slade sits on my bed and presses his thumb into his temple.

Something has definitely been said. "It was bad then?"

"No."

"What does that mean?"

"It was . . ."

"Bad." I move over, touching my knee to his and taking his hand. It's the first time I've touched him since he dragged me away from the restaurant. (Dad finally paid attention, caught the smell, and threw a fit demanding a new driver. Pretty sure Dr. Panozco yelled at Slade that night anyway.)

"My brothers are idiots."

"Your brothers are protective."

"Overprotective, and in all the wrong ways. What did they say?"

Slade picks up my e-pen and taps out a rhythm on my thigh.

"You have to tell me."

"They called you a fragile porcelain flower," Slade mutters, "and said they'd spend the rest of my life suing me for minor financial infractions if I broke any of your petals."

I laugh. It sounds just like Solomon and Max. "They're all talk. I'm so sorry."

Slade doesn't laugh. He also still doesn't look at me, just keeps tapping. "They think I'm going to hurt you."

"You're not."

"If I were them, I'd think so too."

"Why? Because you aren't like them? Slade, I don't want you to be like them. I want you to be you. I like you."

He leans over and kisses me. Thoroughly. Something he rarely does without me flirting, cajoling, teasing him first.

He wraps his arms around me so I can rest against him.

"They're good brothers." He hesitates, thinking it through. "I want to be them. For Vinnie."

"They were awful to you."

"Because they love you."

Chapter Forty-Nine

The guards shut us in and left. Mo and I stayed on one side of the room. He massaged my hand and whispered something into my ear that I ignored. Yes, I was freaking out. I'd told Isa not to let Slade follow me.

I'd.

Told.

Her.

I mean, there were other things freaking me out too. And I shouldn't have expected Isa to listen.

Mo nuzzled my neck.

"Mo, stop trying to piss off Slade." Isa and Slade stood on the far side of the room. Lei and Stella were by the door. Everyone had taken a corner. (Lei's fauxhawk was now bright green, the Buysco color green even.)

Slade death-glared Mo. I shoved my elbow into Mo's side to get him to back off. But also, Isa was right. Mo's affection was way more about Slade than me. Even as getting rid of Slade just became my biggest priority. Yes, this was paranoia again. No, I didn't care. That check to Celsius Burns that no one but me knew about was going to get him blamed.

"They took your phones?" I asked, just to be certain.

"Yup," both Lei and Stella answered.

"Can you get us out of here?" I asked Isa.

"Nope."

"What about the spell that knocked Maur backward? Couldn't you take out a wall or something?"

"It only works on living things. Unless someone volunteers to get thrown bodily through a wall, I can't help. Also, Bob told me that Aristotle figured out Cyrus Scofield's plan not long after you left." She went on to explain everything that I'd told Mo, adding in the checks to my dad and Dr. Panozco, which Slade had told her and Bob about, and Bob had told

Aristotle. Aristotle thought Cyrus had been buying access to the cove. Once Isa had worked all of this out with Bob, she'd set Quentin and Tabby to forestalling her mother with a promise to Quentin that she'd let him take Tabby on a date if he succeeded. (He was so going to succeed.)

Isa'd figured my obvious destination was Buysco, so she and Slade had started for here when Lei and Stella showed up trying to find Mo. Since Isa couldn't get rid of them, she'd brought them along, and the four of them had gotten captured by the guards the moment they'd walked into the store. They hadn't seen Cyrus at all, which meant he must be on his way to Trinity.

Basically, it was all a giant mess that I had to get Slade out of before Isa, Bob, and I fixed the rest.

Mo rubbed my arm and smiled down at me all concerned-like. "Babe, your anxiety is getting bad, isn't it? How can I help?"

Isa shoved Slade on the arm. "Go talk to Joey. Tell her what I told you to say. It's the quickest way to keep Mo from doing his touchy-feely thing and make the dracos happy."

"No." Slade continued to glare at Mo.

Evil as it was of me to be grateful for this, there was no way Slade could talk in any real sense in front of all these people.

"Seriously, Babe," Mo said, smirking and running his hand up my shoulder. "I'm here for you, yeah? I'm your guy."

Isa pointed a finger at the empty desk. "Just shut up already."

I jumped.

Isa continued. "Slade's not playing hard-to-get with Mo. Slade's being broody and territorial. No . . . No more definitions . . . You absolutely understand the concept of *territorial* . . . Yes . . . Mo is also being *territorial* . . . No, they are not going to start fighting, and that definitely wouldn't be fun to watch." She gave first Mo and then Slade a hard look and then returned to glaring at the desk.

"The dracos are here," I said, but rather than relief that we had help, I tensed even more.

"No . . . Absolutely not," Isa said to the table. "Nobody but you thinks Joey getting kissed is going to calm her down."

"I'm calm." I really wasn't.

"Babe, do you need kissing?" Mo asked.

"Definitely not and stop calling me that." I pulled away from him again. All of this was going down a really steep hill of how-do-I-end-up-in-these-situations?

Mo stepped closer to me, wrapping his free arm around my side. I elbowed him, but he held tight.

"Hands off." Slade moved my way.

"Don't you give orders to Mo." Stella jumped forward, hit the end of where she connected to Lei, and jerked to a halt. (Had to give Stella credit. She was an excellent best friend to Mo.)

Isa glared at the table again. "Yes . . . Stella is now being territorial too."

"Can you all stop yelling at each other?" My voice went high and shaky.

Slade stepped back and dropped his death-glare to the floor.

"I'm kissin' Joey now," Mo announced with a snide look in Slade's direction.

Isa spun to glare at him. "Before or after you admit you bugged her phone? Because the dracos don't want to witness you kissing her, not even Saphira. Not after what you did. The dracos are all aboard Team Slade now. Team Mo sank."

"Mo didn't bug her phone." Now Stella glared at Isa. "I already told you that."

"He did." Lei took a deep breath. "Joey, the app I had you download really was to keep you from annoying Slade. I owed you after what happened in China, and the app seemed like a good idea. But if it wasn't me who bugged your phone, it had to be Mo—"

"It wasn't Mo," Stella said again, louder.

"Mo had your phone in his hand the first time I met him, remember?" Lei said.

"You're looking a little pale there, Mo," Isa said snidely. "You have anything to add?"

"No."

Slade shifted his attention to Lei. "Tell. Her. About China."

"Lei wasn't in China," I said.

Lei's shoulders slumped. "I'm so sorry, Joey. It was my fault no one believed Slade was innocent of defacing the business card. It was all so stupid, and I never meant for anything bad to happen. I should never have said anything, but you kept gushing about how great he was and how happy you were when I'd met Slade first."

"Wait," Stella said, turning to her. "So you're bi?"

"I'm not attracted to him." Lei gave a shudder. "Gross. I wanted a best friend. Like you and Mo. My mom came to me as the only other person in CMSRC who knew Slade, and asked if Joey was telling the truth about the accusations by the Chinese government being false. I said he was manipulating her, and she was covering for him. That's why no one in CMSRC ever believed Joey. I'm so, so sorry."

"China was my fault," I said, "not yours."

"Wrong important point," Isa cut in. "Joey, look at Mo's face. He's totally guilty."

We all turned to stare at Mo.

He looked down at his feet, his shoulders hunching.

"Mo, you didn't actually . . ." Stella said. "You *would never . . .*"

He glanced guiltily at her and then back down and then to me. "I didn't know about any of this until right now. The app was to protect you, Joey. That's what Cyrus told me. Because of your brother."

"Quentin?" I craned around to look at Mo. He'd actually done it?

"Mo, I'm going to kill you," Stella said. "Boundaries, remember?"

"Your other brother," Mo said to me. "The one that's roommates with the magic-handler. Cyrus was worried the handlers were goin' after your family. He asked a couple of us to try to get a tracker on your phone and stay silent about it to not tip off the handlers."

Isa laughed. "Mo, you're one seriously gullible dude."

"Were *you* spying on me this whole time?" I asked.

"No." He frantically shook his head. "I would never. Cyrus said it was in case you got kidnapped or somethin'."

Then I had another thought. "Brady was asked too, wasn't he?" It explained how weird Brady'd been at first and that he knew about Buysco. Unlike Mo, Brady hadn't gone through with it.

"Probably," Mo admitted. "I'm so sorry. I thought I was helpin'."

"And that's why you asked me out? To get an app on my phone?"

"No way, Joey." His voice went all earnest. "I liked you for you. I still do. You're cute and funny and we have a great time together. I totally would've hit on you regardless of the tracker thing. I'll hit on you right now if it'll help. I'd love to kiss you if that's what you need."

"Don't. Touch. Her." Slade stepped forward again.

"Don't touch *him*," Stella growled at Slade. "It's *my* job to kill him for this."

I stared at Mo, not sure what to think. I mean, I believed him. He'd clearly been conned rather than actively trying to hurt me, and since Cyrus had likely conned my dad, it seemed unfair to blame Mo for falling for it. Also, I'd let him kiss me and gone on that third date just so I could spy on Buysco. I didn't have the moral high ground here. And most of all, like him, I was a person who regularly did and said stupid, witless, addle-brained, moronic, foolish things too.

I turned to Mo. "You've always had my best interests at heart. I forgive you, but don't ever do that to anyone again."

"He won't," Stella said. "I guarantee that one."

"She's right," he said. "Lesson learned. I won't. Never. Ever."

"I believe you." I looked to Stella. "Please don't kill him. Violence helps nothing."

Isa whacked her own forehead. "Well, that didn't work. Slade, go talk to her so we can end this Mo thing and get out of here."

"No," he replied sharply.

Isa glowered at the table. "I'm not saying that . . . Get out of my head or I'm going to . . . Fine . . . Yes . . . I'll tell them." She sighed dramatically.

"Ramoth?" I called out, trying to take control of the situation.

"Who's Ramoth?" Lei asked.

"Draco," Isa replied. "She's sitting on the table. So are Temeraire and Saphira. Just accept it."

Between one blink of the eye and the next, my three dracos appeared on the metal desk. Temeraire even wore his little harness with epaulets again. So cute.

"Ramoth," I quickly said, "can you tell Bob we need to move the shuck?"

"That's the draco that ruined my runners," Lei announced right over the top of me. "Wait. Are dracos doing magic? Does CMSRC know?"

"You named one of the dracos Temeraire?" Mo asked at the same time. "*His Majesty's Dragon* is like my favorite book ever."

"It's true," Stella said, "it's his favorite book. I'm burning it once we get out of here."

Temeraire squawked at Mo and fluffed his wings, making his epaulets stand out, but not in a friendly way.

Isa rolled her eyes. "The dracos named themselves. And taught themselves magic. It's a long story."

"Ramoth, we really need to—" I tried again.

Isa pointed sharply at the dracos. "I'm not telling him that . . . Or her . . . No. That's not going to help because . . . No deal! No more deals! Joey isn't going to—" She threw her hands in the air. "Fine, I'll tell them." She turned back to me and put her free hand on her hip. "Ramoth and the others want to make a deal."

"Dracos don't make deals." Lei stared between them and Isa.

"These do," Isa replied. "My fault, actually. Either way, the dracos are annoyed that Slade won't talk to Joey. They're excited about that conversation and primarily came along to witness it. Since it isn't happening, they want to make a deal for something that interests them just as much. They feel strongly Joey needs to get kissed."

"I'll do it," Mo announced.

"Joey needs to get kissed by Slade . . . No . . . Don't make me say that out loud . . . Fine . . . I'll say it." Isa sighed dramatically. "He's apparently really good at kissing, and you're not. Which they know because—"

"Maybe we should all just—" I quickly muttered, knowing exactly what was coming next. The shuck was a total traitor.

"—Joey said so," Isa finished. "At length."

Mo stiffened next to me. I turned bright red.

Then from the depths of my utter embarrassment, I got an idea. A really good one. One that might solve everything.

Slade was going to hate it and possibly go back to hating me.

Perfect. (I mean, sort of. Or not really, but I couldn't worry about that right now.)

I turned to my dracos. "Ramoth, I'll make a deal with you. I'm an excellent kisser, and I'll kiss Slade just so you can see me do it. I guarantee it'll be a good one, but it can't happen here. You and the other dracos have to free us. Only then can Slade and I have the greatest kiss ever to be called a kiss."

Ramoth's eyes brightened with interest. Temeraire raised up on his back legs. Saphira whipped her tail around in excitement.

"Jojo . . ."

I kept my attention on Ramoth so I wouldn't have to look at Slade. "It'll be a redo first kiss, and as I've told you, first kisses need to be done right.

We need to go somewhere outdoors, somewhere pretty, with trees and water and sky."

Ramoth bobbed her head. She knew the details of every first kiss I'd ever had.

"Jojo," Slade said louder.

"Someone tell me this is a joke," Stella groaned.

"The dracos love it," Isa announced. "Every draco within flying distance just started this direction to witness your epic kiss."

"There's more." I held up my hand, joined to Mo's. "I can't kiss Slade attached to another guy. Especially as Slade's going to need some convincing. He might even fight me. We may need to tie him to a tree or something."

"I'm not—" Slade started.

"Because," I said, raising my voice. "My final condition is that after I kiss him, we're going to Trinity Cove, Isa and I and Lei and Stella and Mo, if they'll come. Once there, we're going to move the shuck to keep it safe from Cyrus's traps. But not Slade. He gets left behind at the pretty spot with the trees and the water."

"Jojo, what the—"

"Ramoth says yes," Isa yelled and threw herself sideways, shoving hard into Slade and taking both of them to the ground. "Everyone on the floor. Maur is going to take out the back wall."

***

The wall crashed in as the base of a light pole came through like a wrecking ball. Chunks of cement, siding, and drywall flew in every direction. Ceiling tiles rained down, and the room filled with a cloud of dust that reeked of sulfur. Mo dove over the top of me. The light pole took out two more sections of wall in quick succession, opening up the backside of the room.

"Enough," Isa yelled from somewhere under the cloud of dust. "Ramoth, make Maur stop . . . I don't care if he's having fun. He's going to hurt us."

"Can't breathe." I pushed at Mo. He weighed a ton.

Mo rolled to the side, jerking my arm near out of the socket in the process. "We've got to clear out of here," he said.

"Where's Slade?" I searched where I'd last seen him.

"Jojo?"

"Here. Are you okay?"

"Stay put. I'm coming."

There was another screeching crash that sounded like Maur dropping the light pole on someone's car. The dust cleared enough for me to see Slade helping Isa to her feet. I spotted Lei and Stella. The back wall of the room was now steel I-beams with cement rubble piled everywhere and a dusty view to a parking lot beyond. No Maur, so either he'd left or (hopefully) had done his damage while invisible. Mo and I headed toward the open air.

"Jojo, stop."

I didn't. But neither could I hurry. Bare feet and a recently demolished wall went together about as well as a beach umbrella and a Gulf Coast hurricane.

Slade and Isa caught up to us where the wall had been turned into foothills of debris.

"You aren't. Ditching me."

"I told you to talk to her." Isa shoved Slade so that he bumped into me.

My foot landed on a jagged chunk of concrete. I snatched it off the ground, hopping on the other foot and hurting that one as well. No way was I making it over the remains of the wall quickly. Which I needed to do. Cyrus's guards would be on their way. Not to mention the town.

"Can you carry me?" I asked Mo.

"'Course." He turned so I could get on his back, but that put our handcuffed arms crisscrossing between us.

"Maybe if we—" I started.

Slade ducked his head under my free arm and threw me over his shoulder fireman-style. My head hung down his back, my hair everywhere, including my mouth. I sputtered, trying to spit it out.

"Hold her steady," Slade ordered Mo. "And keep up." Alarms sounded in the background and sirens in the distance. No time to fuss.

I grabbed the back of Slade's shirt as he climbed over the rubble, jumping from one concrete pile to another. My stomach rammed into his shoulder with every leap, but I stayed in place. Both Isa and Mo helped by putting hands on my back.

Once on the other side, Slade didn't put me down but kept going, not stopping until we reached his car. He bent forward, sliding me back to my feet, and latched onto my arm.

"You aren't. Ditching me." His eyebrows were pressed together, his jaw set.

"I am."

He fished out his keys. An RCMP SUV pulled into the parking lot, lights flashing and sirens blaring.

But also . . .

Slade couldn't actually drive. Not with Isa attached to his left hand. She'd either have to sit on his lap or hang out the window. Even if he drove with his arm crossed over to the passenger's side or had Isa drive, he couldn't get the both of them into the car without letting go of me.

I sent Mo a quick, be-ready-to-bolt look. (Mo and I were going to have the same driving problem.)

Slade unlocked the car and then tossed the keys to Stella. "You drive." (Darn it.) He turned to Mo while still holding tight to me. "Get in the back. Slide all the way over."

"Don't listen to him!"

Slade tightened his grip on my arm. "Jojo, get in the car."

A firetruck and more RCMP vehicles entered the parking lot. We had no choice but to do as Slade said. For now.

Once Mo and I were settled, Slade slid in next to me and Isa climbed onto his lap. (Nothing in life had ever made me more aware that I wasn't wearing a bra than sitting in the middle seat of a small car squashed between two boys with broad shoulders.)

As Stella pulled us out of the Buysco lot, Slade put his free hand, palm up, on my leg. An invitation.

I wanted to. I soooo wanted to.

I ignored his hand.

"Where are we going?" Stella asked.

"Trinity," Slade said.

"We have to follow the deal," Isa said. "Thanks to Joey, we need a pretty place with trees and water. It also needs to be large enough to house a bunch of nosy dracos of various sizes as they are all on their way."

"You're not. Ditching me," Slade said for the third time.

Isa patted him on the chest. "You have no one to blame for this but yourself."

CHAPTER FIFTY

Day 158 of 162 of the China Assignment
Changde City, Hunan Province, China

"It's a beautiful story. Both romantic and deeply brooding." I hold up my tablet to show Slade my second-favorite line from his latest English assignment. The assignment I'm having to nudge, badger, hassle, pester him to work on. Left to his own devices, Slade spends every second he can at the club. I also have to pester him to eat.

"He's a blowhard. She's a headcase." Slade sits behind me in our spot on the staircase. One hand is around me, one twirls a stick like it's a baton. "Creep" by Radiohead plays on Slade's speaker. Yes, he's making a point with the music. I like the song, so no complaints. It too is romantic and brooding in its own way.

"It's a masterpiece," I say. "And a classic. You just don't get it."

He snorts.

I read the line on my tablet. "'My love for Heathcliff resembles the eternal rocks beneath: a source of little visible delight, but necessary.'"

He puts the stick down and pretends to cough into his hand. "Headcase."

I dramatically sigh in objection. It's important to me that he gets this. I flip over to my very favorite quote. "'Whatever our souls are made of, his and mine are the same.'" I touch Slade's arm. "You can't hate that line. It's gorgeous. Perfect."

He stays silent for a long moment. "It's alright." He switches the music to Natasha Bedingfield's "Soulmates."

Chapter Fifty-One

Stella drove us to a clearing in the forest with a pond and a large sign full of bullet holes.

Private Property
No Trespassing
Violators will be Prosecuted with Buckshot

"Slade can't get hurt." Otherwise, it was a gorgeous location. The water was deep and dark. The trees were leafy. The nearest one even had a heart carved into the trunk at head height. All of it was worthy of a first kiss.

That said, kissing Slade might not be as easy as I'd implied. From his perspective, there was nothing less romantic than handcuffs, four extra people, and a large quantity of dracos avidly staring. Also, he still had a steely determined look in his eyes.

I had to do it anyway. For him.

"No call to worry about safety," Mo said, enjoying himself. "The house is kilometers away, and Old Man Coates is three-quarters deaf. He won't notice Slade's here." He pushed his door open and helped me out. Slade and Isa exited the opposite side, Slade never taking his attention off of me.

"What's that noise?" Stella asked, looking up at the sky.

I looked too. Something thrummed the air, getting louder by the second. And not just a sound, but a pressure.

An elephant-sized emerald draco skidded over the trees and landed in the water. It was followed by a cloud of smaller dracos. They dropped onto the large one's back, onto the shore and the trees. There were hundreds of them. (Seriously? My love life wasn't that interesting.)

Ramoth, Temeraire, and Saphira claimed the top of Slade's car.

"Shoot," Isa said. "They finally worked out how to teleport. Bob was hoping it would take them longer." She looked at Ramoth. "No . . . The correct word is teleport . . . Joey doesn't care about your stupid book . . . None of that is relevant at the moment . . . Fine, I'll tell her." Isa turned to me. "Ramoth wants you to know that they figured out how to teleport from Ramoth's book, the one she named herself after. So the credit for figuring it out goes to her. The concept of *credit* being their latest obsession."

I petted Ramoth's silky back scales. "Of course, Ramoth gets credit. Ramoth is super smart."

"You're only saying that," Isa said, "because you don't yet realize that learning to *teleport*," she glared at Ramoth, "means every single draco on the entire east coast of Canada will be arriving in the next few minutes."

Maybe Ramoth was too smart?

Slade started around the back of the car, heading my direction, bringing Isa with him. "I'll talk. To her."

"No, you won't." I yelped, scurrying backward. If there was one way for him to halt my epic kiss, that was it.

Another wave of dragons landed around and on top of the first. They knocked into each other, swatted their tails against the ground, fluffed their wings into leaf-laden branches and each other, but also left a circle of empty space for the humans. A few, of various sizes, wore harnesses like Temeraire's.

"My mom would pay to be here," Lei said, her eyes wide.

So would mine.

"Jojo. I will. Talk to you." The line between his brows was deep, and he had crevices on both sides of his mouth.

I turned my back to him. Not happening.

Maur circled above, banking lazily first one direction, then the other.

"Isa," I asked, "if all the dracos are here, who's guarding the shuck?"

"Yeah, Bob's a little upset about that. The faster you can get the kiss taken care of, the quicker they can teleport back to Trinity. But not too fast. You promised them a good one."

"Jojo—"

From out of nowhere, a horse-sized draco swooped down from the sky and dropped a giant mess of tangled green wiring on top of Slade and Isa, knocking them into each other.

"Christmas lights?" Lei asked. "Why are the dracos carrying around Christmas lights?"

"Not helping," Isa yelled. "Stay away from the transfer station. That's garbage . . . No, I can't . . . I'll explain the concept of *garbage* later . . . Or ask Bob."

Even more dracos arrived. Squabbles broke out. Flames were shot. Slade shoved the mess of lights to the side and headed my direction again, stalker-like. "Help me," he said to Isa, "talk to her."

"Don't help him," I snapped back.

"The dracos want to hear what he has to say," Isa said, "but they really like the tree-tying idea and want to do that first. From their perspective, the Christmas lights make total sense. People wrap them around trees all the time."

"I didn't mean the tree thing literally." I backed away from Slade and Isa, pulling Mo along. Which was counterproductive to the actual kiss, but the thought of Slade talking was sending my pulse pounding and my stomach churning.

An orange draco came low overhead and dropped a fishing net over the top of him.

"Better," Isa yelled up to the sky. Then to Slade, "Don't say I didn't warn you. You should've done it when I told you to."

Slade shrugged off the net. "Jojo."

I backed into the water, stepping on a sharp rock that made me hop around yet again. Mo put his arm around me. Stella picked up the net.

A coil of rope large enough to tie off a boat dropped from the sky. The rope missed Slade and Isa.

"The dracos are loving this," Isa said. "Joey, they especially want to praise your skills at playing hard-to-get."

"I'm not—" I started but gave up.

"I'm so being the one to tie him to a tree." Stella picked up the rope and slung it over her shoulder. "Mo would never have done the phone thing if it wasn't for you."

"Pretty sure they hadn't met yet when he bugged Joey's phone," Lei pointed out.

"Whatever," Stella replied.

"Ramoth?" I looked frantically around for her in the thousands and thousands of dracos. She winged over to settle on the tree with the carving. It was in the cleared circle of space left for us humans and the only tree not drooping with dracos. "Slade's going to say mean things and make me cry. You've seen what I'm like when I cry. If I cry, there'll be no kissing. I won't be able to do it. Even if I try, it'll be a bad kiss."

"Jojo, I won't. Make you cry."

"You always make me cry. Every. Single. Time."

He winced, and then a pony-sized pink draco plowed into him from the side, knocking him to the ground and sending Isa sprawling to her knees.

"Ow, you imbeciles," she screeched. "Not me."

Stella threw the net over Slade and leaped across his chest, holding him in place.

Mo dropped a foot on Slade's shoulder. Lei sat on his free arm. A handful of smaller dracos, including my three, piled on top, burying Slade under a crowd of net and wings and people.

"Don't hurt him!" My voice cracked as my anxiety sprinted straight for the cliff of *threshold*. I swung around Mo and fell to my knees behind Slade, pulling at the net to free him.

"Don't hurt me," Isa said, all disgruntled. "Slade's fine, Joey. You do realize that taking him out is what you want, right?"

"No, it isn't." I mean, it was, but not like this.

Slade's and my eyes met. He drew his brows together all con-cerned-like. His furrow deepened. "Jojo, breathe," he said, painfully slow. "I'm here. You're fine."

"Can I punch him?" Mo asked.

"No!" I shoved into Mo, hitting him on the side of the leg. He lost his balance and stepped off of Slade's shoulder.

Slade stayed motionless, his gaze on me steady, his eyes golden, his lips parted, his expression soft. (For him.)

Gone was the angry boy he'd been after China. Or even the paramedic who'd taken charge and gotten me through the night.

He was suddenly my Slade.

My best friend.

My everything.

And he was looking at me like I was everything to him.

Slade wasn't going to skewer me.

He was going to forgive me.

"I'll. Cooperate," he said, looking at me but speaking to Isa, each word forced out by brute willpower. "But I talk. First. Tell the dracos. A deal. For the kiss."

Chapter Fifty-Two

Day 161 of 162 of the China Assignment
Changde City, Hunan Province, China

Slade and I walk into the MSS conference room for yet another lecture. We follow Quentin to the back corner as usual. There are thirteen scientists' kids total, but I barely know them. Slade is enough.

At the front of the room, a guard stands at attention with his legs apart, shoulders straight, hands behind his back, and a rifle hanging across his chest. The gun is a new addition to these meetings, but not the first one I've ever seen. Part of living overseas.

"Something's off here," Slade whispers to me.

"My dad said MSS is upset at the lack of signs of a draco. Possibly, we're getting the brunt of that. I'm sure it's nothing."

The scary MSS officer walks in with four more guards, also carrying guns. "Field trip," he yells, startling everyone in the room. "To your feet."

I jump up. We have to go. It's expected.

Slade follows more slowly. "Jojo, your parents know we're here, right?"

I nod. They're in town at the moment. "I added it to the family calendar."

"Do everything they say." His voice is intense. "Something is definitely off."

The guards load us into vans and drive us across town to an abandoned building with missing exterior walls, broken windows, graffiti, and cyclone fencing. Slade's right. Something is really, really off.

We walk single file up a creaky staircase and into an empty cement room with no windows. Slade is behind me, close enough that I can hear the rustle of his clothing and tread of his shoes as he walks. I focus on that as best I can.

The back wall of the room has red dots spaced out on the floor, one per kid. The dots are too far apart for me to hold either Slade's or Quentin's hand, which I desperately want to do. Several kids start crying.

"Dishonor!" the MSS officer screams as he walks in.

I flinch. So do several other kids.

"Disgrace!" He switches to Mandarin. Everyone except Slade pays rapt attention, even though most of us have no idea what the officer is saying. Slade stares at the ground, completely blank.

The MSS officer steps in front of the kid closest to the door, a Malaysian girl. He pulls out a folder and shoves it in her face. The girl bursts into sobs. The MSS officer moves to the next kid.

"No matter. What's. In there," Slade whispers, his words choppy, a struggle. "Don't react. Just take it."

I look to him, wanting to make eye contact, needing him the way I do when my parents fight, but his attention is solidly, determinedly on the floor.

The officer goes down the line, yelling and holding up the folder to each kid. I get tenser with every step nearer to me he gets. The room goes cold. My skin, hot. It's hard to breathe. I keep looking at Slade. He doesn't notice.

The officer gets to Quentin, and I'm shaking so hard my brain feels like it's in a blender. I'm dizzy. My stomach rolls. I glance at Slade one more time. Slade still stares at the floor. He's gone deep into himself. Away.

Quentin's gaze moves from one side of the open folder to the other. "Oh," he whispers.

At his word, the MSS officer balls his fist in Quentin's direction.

"Don't hurt him," I scream.

The MSS officer's attention abruptly turns to me. He lowers his fist and steps over, yelling in Mandarin again. I'm trapped by the sound, caged, imprisoned, the walls of which are shrinking around me. Nausea rises. The room darkens. He yells so forcefully his spit hits my face like tiny, sharp darts. I'm going to die.

The officer holds up the folder. It blocks the force of his yelling, and I manage a breath.

The right side of the folder is a blown-up copy of a business card. It's been colored in, making the logo look like a penis with scabs. The other side of the folder holds one of Slade's tattoo drawings.

My chest hollows out.

Tree branches with leaves going every direction crisscross over dragon scales. Or at least that's what it's supposed to be. It actually looks more like razor wire dripping green goo over an abstract background. The green is the same color as the scabs on the penis. The shapes are similar too.

The MSS officer abruptly stops yelling. He watches me silently, eyes turned to crevices, face drawn inward.

"You know something," he says, spitting the words into my face again. "Talk."

Chapter Fifty-Three

How was I supposed to let Slade talk? It would be torture for him to even try, and that wasn't taking into consideration the tied-up part.

Isa and Lei helped untangle Slade from the net so that he could get to his feet and line himself up against the tree with the heart carved into it.

"You can totally do better," Stella muttered to me as she circled the rope around his arms and torso. A dragon tagged her in the back of the head with a pine cone.

I crossed my free arm over my chest, pressing my hand into my middle. Then I uncrossed it and recrossed it and finally just locked my fingers around the hem of my (Slade's) shirt so that I'd stop fidgeting. If Slade did manage to get the words out, what was I supposed to do? I had to leave him here. Absolutely had to, but I already didn't want to. My whole brilliant ditch-Slade plan was a disaster. (This wasn't even my Slade-paranoia this time.)

"Maybe we should all just—"

"No talking," Isa said. "Not until everything is just so, per your rules even."

Pretty sure she was enjoying herself.

Once the rope was wound from Slade's shoulders downward so that only his head and hands were free, the dracos crowded in. One of them pulled Mo around the back side of Slade and the tree, as far as Mo and my linked hands would allow. Statement made.

I ended up an arm's length in front of Slade. I couldn't bring myself to look at him and stared at the carving just above his head. It was old, more scar than words, but inside the heart I could make out *Michael loves Becca*. I randomly wondered if Mo knew them and if they were still together.

"Great," Isa said. "We're set. Slade, you're up."

"What if instead we . . ."

"Jojo. Look at me." He spoke haltingly. His crevice of concentration was dug between his eyes, and a vein in his neck ticked. Seeing him struggle killed me.

"You hate talking." My voice went high. "So don't. And you said you were done with me. So just be done."

He shook his head but not in denial, more trying to shake the words down from his brain. "I. Was. Wrong. And. I'm sorry."

"Don't you apologize." I screeched the words. "That's my job."

The dracos crowded in closer.

"Jojo, I've spent. The last weeks. Being pissed. And taking it out. On you. After China. I took it out. On you. But after China. I had a right. To be pissed. The things you said . . ."

"I deserved your anger." I couldn't look at him. Were Michael and Becca now my parents' ages and married with three kids, two dogs, and a home?

"You knocked me over," he continued. "I needed. To not talk to you. After. To have space. To avoid being hounded. By you. To deal with it. The things you said—"

"What did she say?" Lei asked.

"Hush," Isa said. "The dracos don't like interruptions."

One of them nudged me in the back, knocking me forward, making me take a step closer to Slade, closing the gap between us halfway.

"But not in Toronto," he continued. "I had no right. To take my anger out. On you. In Toronto."

"You didn't know about my anxiety. It wasn't your fault. I didn't tell you."

"I knew."

"You didn't. Not until last night."

He pressed his lips together, straining. "I knew. That you. Got overwhelmed. That you. Had hang-ups. About your stuff. That you. Had a drawer. Full of medications. I knew. But I didn't connect it. I didn't understand . . ." He clenched his jaw, fighting but unable to finish. He looked to Isa.

"So here's what happened after you took off with Mo," Isa said, jumping in with glee. "The dracos made me go hunt down Slade and Quentin to get Desi on speaker phone so that they could hear the conversation. From that and with additional information from Quentin, it became clear to everyone, especially Slade, that back in China, he let you take care of him, solve all his problems, do his homework, babysit his brother, and generally make his life easier without it ever occurring to him that he was supposed to be taking care of you back." She looked at Slade. "You agree that you were a clueless, self-absorbed, artistic idiot who was raised by wolves, right?"

He gave a chin-nod in her direction without taking his eyes off of me.

"But you weren't." I looked back and forth between the two of them. "Slade, I liked taking care of you and you were wonderful to me. I was happy."

"I—" he started.

"I'm sure he was wonderful, but he was also oblivious," Isa inserted again. "Joey, you were so busy being in love and trying to please him and everyone else around you that you missed that you were in an eighty-twenty relationship and everything in China was about him. That worked just fine until the mess with the business card. A situation you were entirely unequipped to handle, which is not a slam on you, as we've all got our issues. But if Slade had been paying even an ounce of attention to your needs, he would've recognized that you were falling apart. Quentin saw it. Quentin understood you needed help, and he's an even bigger idiot than Slade." She paused for breath. "So while, yes, you screwed up in China by talking too much, Slade also screwed up and let you flounder because it never occurred to him to do otherwise."

"Jojo, she's right. I didn't know. That I was supposed to do things. For you. And then I got mad. At you. I was wrong. I was cruel. I am. So, so sorry."

I shook my head. "I don't understand any of this."

"The dracos have decided," Isa announced, "that Joey and Slade can share the blame for China. Not that the dracos get the concept of *sharing* or *blame* exactly, and Bob may have watered the whole thing down by relating it to credit and making it a positive."

It was all too much.

A draco shoved me hard between my shoulder blades. I put a hand out to catch myself on Slade's chest, and then stayed there, pressing my fingers into a gap between the rope over his heart. His chest rose and fell under my hand.

"Jojo. I am sorry. That I made you feel. Like you had to be perfect. I'm sorrier. That it took this long. For me to realize. That you are. Perfect. You always have been. Even when things fell apart."

Tears welled in my eyes. I pressed my hand harder into his chest. His heart beat against my palm. "I hurt you."

"You did. And I hurt you back. We're not going to do that anymore, 'kay?"

"'Kay," I whispered.

With those two small words, everything changed. I changed. The air around us definitely changed. (This may have been the dracos crowding closer and closer.)

An orange draco nodded. So did several others. As did Isa and Lei.

Slade shifted under the ropes, like he was trying to reach out for me even though he couldn't. I ran my hand down to touch my knuckles to his, intertwining us in a backward handhold.

"Let me," he continued, his struggle worse again, each word a battle, as if the next part was the hardest of all. "Prove. That. I can. Do better. For you."

My pancreas and my spleen and my liver all turned warm and soft. I bit down on my lip.

Isa jumped in. "Dude, we talked about this. Repeat after me, 'Joey, I'm crazy, madly in love—'"

"No," I burst out. "Slade, no."

Isa glared at me. "The dracos really want to hear him say it."

Slade ignored Isa and focused in on me. His forehead wrinkled and he briefly squeezed shut his eyes. "Please. Give. Me. Another. Chance."

The most beautiful words of my life. Words I couldn't ignore or wipe away or run from. Real words.

I wasn't bowled over by happiness shooting everywhere. The rest of my organs stayed just regular old organs. No butterflies showed up. Instead, the nervous, crazy-making, paranoid part of me just . . .

Quieted.

Isa cleared her throat. "The dracos still want him to—"

"Shut up, Isa." Slade kept his attention on me. "Jojo?"

I let go of his hand and slid mine over the ropes to his shoulder. I rubbed the knobbiness of his Adam's apple with my thumb and trailed my fingers around the back of his neck. "Kay."

"'Kay," he agreed.

And it was done.

I caressed his jaw, the barest bit of stubble prickling my fingertips. I ran my thumb to his lower lip and tugged at it, giving myself a chill up my own chest. "Can I kiss you now? Not even for them." I tilted my head to the circle of human and draco faces pressing around us. "I just really want to kiss you."

"Please."

"Not while attached to me," Mo announced.

"She isn't." Isa smirked. "The dracos fixed that the moment Slade started talking. Joey's now attached to me."

I ignored them and leaned forward to brush my upper lip against Slade's lower, the barest of strokes. A touch. A glance. A reintroduction. A greeting.

Someone clapped.

Mo bellowed about being handcuffed to Slade. Stella let out a string of expletives. The dracos hooted and squawked and flapped their wings.

I leaned in again, pulling myself closer and brushing against his lips. Slade took over, kissing me through and through, as if we were the only two people (or non-people) present.

And it was good. So good, so familiar, so right. Better than China. Better than any kiss I'd ever experienced in my entire life. On a scale of zero-to-Slade, we were Slade-times-infinity. His mouth, his touch, his heart, his soul merged into mine, into me, into we.

"Wow, that actually is a pretty great kiss," Isa said.

Slade pulled back and ran his mouth across my cheek to rest next to my ear. "Jojojojojojojojojo . . ."

"Sladesladesladesladeslade." (It didn't have the same effect.)

"You were right," he whispered just for me to hear. "What you said about me in China. Some of it anyway. I want to tell you. Take me with you. So I can tell you."

I ran my fingers through the tips of his hair. "No."

CHAPTER FIFTY-FOUR

Day 161 of 162 of the China Assignment
Changde City, Hunan Province, China

"I-don't-know-anything," I say, slurring the words all together. It's either speak or die on the spot. Those are my choices.

"Talk, girl." The MSS officer smiles, bearing small, vicious teeth.

"Slade drew the picture on the left." The words come out fast. I have no control. It just happens. Anything to keep my heart beating, my lungs pumping, my brain alive. Words, words, and more words, my only anchor in a category five storm. "His cousin died in this horrific car accident. Like, really horrific. There was alcohol. And blood. And Slade was covered in both and taken to jail. He feels really guilty about it and lives in terror of something like that happening again, especially to his little brother. He doesn't trust his mother with his brother at all, which I totally understand since she only even got pregnant with him to trap his dad into staying with her. Desi thinks he has PTSD over the accident. I don't know how Desi found out about the accident, other than maybe Slade's evil stepfather told her.

"Desi could be wrong. She also thinks he could have autism spectrum disorder or ADHD or bipolar disorder or antisocial personality disorder or a speech disorder or aphasia from the accident. That's a lot of ors, so likely Desi was just throwing things out to scare me. Also, Desi has a PhD in physics, not psychology, which doesn't give her the right to diagnose someone she barely knows or use Slade's mental health as a fear tactic. I told her that, but she just kept throwing out more options for things she thinks are wrong with him.

"I looked each of them up, and autism or expressive language disorder or a word-finding disorder or even selective mutism seem the most likely. I'm probably wrong, as none of them fit perfectly, and I know even less about *these things than Desi. But several can be genetic. If he has one of those, and only a real therapist should diagnose him, his little brother probably has it too."*

I pause for breath and realize everyone is staring at me.

Including Slade.

He's sheet-white. One of his fists presses to the center of his chest, the other to his mouth. His eyes blink wildly, and he shakes his head back and forth, staring at me as if he has no idea who I am.

Which freaks me out even more. "He expresses himself in ways other than words."

"Thank you." The MSS officer gives me a courteous bow. "For naming the artist." He snaps shut the folder with Slade's drawing, grabs Slade by the back of the neck, and throws him to the cement floor.

Chapter Fifty-Five

Stella drove us to Trinity on a dirt road that cut through a number of private properties, several forests, and a rocky area that nearly destroyed Slade's rims. Good news, the route bypassed security in a way only locals would know about. Bad news, it took forever.

Slade hadn't liked me leaving him behind, but he hadn't argued, just made me promise to come back. Mo, who the dracos had indeed handcuffed to Slade, had been less accepting, even after Stella announced it was a fitting punishment for bugging my phone. (Stella was having a much harder time forgiving him than me.)

I was good. No. I was more than good. I was happy. I had an idea, and it *would* work.

"We're going to the house with the stolen rowboat," I told Isa, Stella, and Lei. (Girl power!) "We'll push the boat down to the water. Maur will pick it up, dive down, and scoop up the shuck without touching it. Then he'll fly the boat and shuck out to the open ocean and gently deposit it where it can hatch safe from Cyrus's traps."

"Straightforward and simple," Isa said, sounding almost, but not quite, impressed. "I like it."

"Won't work," Lei said from the front seat. "One of my mom's friends did her dissertation on draco air bladders. Maur isn't capable of diving underwater. Dracos float."

"So there are a few issues," I replied. "But it's still what needs to happen. Isa, can you ask Bob and the dracos how to solve the floating problem?"

"We've got a bigger problem," Stella announced right as we got a view between the trees to Trinity Cove.

Several dozen Buysco delivery trucks were lined up along the road just above the hook of land where Sasha Clems had done her livestream. Guards in military-like uniforms unloaded the backs, pulling out grenade launchers, large rifles, and powerboats. I'd figured on Cyrus and his people being here, but not so much in these quantities. The military weapons hadn't been on my radar at all. (Also, pretty sure we'd just discovered how the stolen rowboat had been transported.)

"Dracos are not bulletproof," Lei said. "We can't put them in danger."

"Definitely not," I agreed. "Isa, can you use your pushing spell to shove the Buysco people out of range so Maur can safely dive?"

"I can, but my mom's going to ground me for life when she finds out."

Stella parked us by the boat shed, and we crept down to spy out our adversaries from a grouping of dense trees.

A guard used bolt cutters on a barbed fence between the road and the water. Another backed a quad with a boat trailer. Cyrus, a guy in a suit I didn't recognize, and a handful of guards walked out onto the hook, ignoring the many KEEP OUT signs posted along the shore and on buoys in the water.

"The shuck hasn't hatched yet, has it?" I asked Isa. Cyrus and his people seemed in a hurry.

Before Isa could answer, Ramoth dove in with lots of flapping of her wings. She held a black bag in her claw.

The last time I'd seen her, she'd been with Slade. "You really do have the whole teleporting thing figured out, don't you?"

Ramoth preened and handed me the bag.

Isa snatched it from my hand. "The shuck hasn't yet hatched."

"Cyrus must think it's about to," I said. "They're preparing to collect the traps. Why isn't CMSRC and RCMP stopping him?"

"See the guy in the suit next to Cyrus Scofield?" Stella pointed to a tall man with wavy brown hair, the one I didn't recognize. "Politician. Privy council, I think."

We all stared.

Hmmm . . .

That might just explain my dad's involvement. I could totally see him bending over backwards to help someone so high up in government. Which meant access to Trinity *was* the point of involving him and Dr. Panozco. My dad wouldn't need to be bribed in this scenario.

Isa opened the black bag and pulled out another yellow phone. "The dracos have now decided that the shuck is indeed about to hatch, although whether it actually is or whether they are just saying that because Joey asked is unknown."

Ramoth gave out a screeching squawk.

Isa glared in her direction. "Well, if you knew it before she asked, then you should've told me. Since you didn't, she gets credit."

Ramoth cocked her head at me as if for moral support.

"Of course, you figured it out first," I told her. "Ramoth gets credit."

Ramoth blew small flames Isa's way in a very clear *I told you so.*

Isa rolled her eyes and explained our plan and its problems to Bob via the phone.

I rubbed the itchy spot behind Ramoth's left wing. "Hey Ramoth, could you pretty please remove our handcuffs using your magic? We need to get started on moving the boat so we can save the shuck. I'll give you full credit."

***

Once unhandcuffed, Stella and I boosted Lei through the same unlocked window that Isa and I'd used to access the shed before. Lei then opened the front door.

The boat sat on a wheeled metal trailer. The ground outside sloped toward the water, so it should be easy to move once we got it rolling. We lined up along the back, including Ramoth, who sat on the back edge.

We pushed.

The boat didn't budge.

"Are the wheels blocked?" Stella peered around the corner at the tires. I did the same on my side. A wooden wedge was shoved in front of a wheel. I removed it.

It still didn't budge.

Isa joined us. "Bob and I have the floating problem figured out. I can use my pushing spell to force Maur underwater, but the timing is going to be tight if I also have to rid us of the Buysco guys too. Joey, Bob wants to talk to you."

"Let's do this first." I scooted over so that Isa could help push. Still no movement.

"I'll ask a few of the mid-sized dracos to help," Isa said.

"Or we could just wait for Mo and Slade to arrive." Stella said it all casually, as if it was no big deal.

The rest of us turned to stare at her.

"What?" she asked with a shrug. "Did you really think they wouldn't follow?"

"We left them in the middle of nowhere without a car," I said.

Stella shrugged. "Slade's in the middle of nowhere without a car. Once Mo stops freaking out, he'll steal Old Man Coates's beater. He's done it before."

"Why didn't you tell me that?!"

"Why did you dump Mo for Slade?"

Fair enough.

"Joey, talk to Bob," Isa said, shoving the yellow phone in my face.

I pushed it away. I had to get that shuck moved before Slade arrived and ended up getting blamed.

The rowboat sat there taunting me with our inability to move it. Ramoth rubbed her claw back and forth on the back edge.

"We need to shift the weight of the boat backward," I announced. "As is, the weight is on the tongue, but it needs to be on the wheels. Physics 101. Lei, climb up on the back with me to adjust the weight. Isa and Stella, you guys push."

It worked too well. The boat careened out of the shed and downhill, Lei, Ramoth, and I screaming and holding on for dear life. We broke through the tree line and hit the water with a splash. Ramoth burst into the sky. Every single person across the cove looked in our direction.

Time to move even faster.

"Remove the tie-downs," I yelled to Lei. We had to get the boat free of the trailer so that Maur could pick it up.

"Joey," Isa called. "Bob says he really needs to talk to you before this goes any further."

"Not now." I squeezed the latch of a tie-down, loosening the strap so that I could unhook it. (That I knew how to do this was due to Duarte and his boat.)

"I have no idea how to get this thing off," Lei said, tugging ineffectively at a tie-down. I pushed past her to take care of it. Stella climbed into the boat to help.

"Joey," Isa said. "Isn't that your dad over there with Cyrus? And Dr. Panozco?"

I looked while undoing another tie-down. Cyrus and the politician now stood with two other people. It was indeed Dad and Dr. Panozco.

My hand slipped on the tie-down, my grip going suddenly slack. No. No. No. Everything had been going so well. (Relatively speaking.)

"Talk to Bob." Isa threw the phone at me. I caught it and put it to my ear.

"Why didn't you warn me about the bribery checks, Josephine?" Bob said loudly and on speaker. I pulled the phone back from my ear. "Do you realize how much work that might've saved me? I shouldn't have had to learn about it from one of your boy toys. It's a lead. And a trail. Something I could've followed ages ago. Money talks."

"My dad just showed up," I said quickly.

"You want to protect your father," Bob continued. "Admirable, but not helpful. That neither your father nor Kyle Panozco deposited their checks means something. Did you ever think of that? Lack-of-money talks too."

"Of course, but right now—"

"Do you know who else should've talked? You. About the third check. The one that Aristotle only found after we used a spell to hack the bank that the other checks were written against. See what you've done? Now I'm hacking banks. You've entirely ruined my personal ethics."

"I'm sorry," I started, hating that he was yelling at me but also getting annoyed. "About my dad—"

"The third check was deposited. And into a shell company. Does anyone recognize the name Celsius Burns?"

Isa, Lei, and Stella all turned to stare at me, specifically at Slade's tee.

"Nope," I mumbled and buttoned Slade's over-shirt to hide it.

"Don't bother lying," Bob said. "I know who it connects to. It's a shell company owned by another shell company, which is owned by a third shell company, which is owned by a beneficial trust. The beneficiaries of the trust being Kyle Panozco, Lauren Panozco, and Vinnie Adler."

"Not Slade?"

"Not Slade Adler, although the shell company that deposited the check in the name of his band appears to have been set up by him, and he's the one who deposited the check."

And there it was. The disaster I'd always known would happen.

"Slade has nothing to do with any of this."

"Which no public investigator is going to believe. Not when he works for the company the funds were drawn on and is the only connection between RBS and the Panozcos."

Crap.

Crap. Crap. Crap. "We have to prove he's innocent."

"Unless he isn't innocent," Bob said.

I glanced wildly around at the others. "Slade'd never do something like this."

Across the cove, the quad backed the first of the powerboats into the water in a more controlled way than we'd managed. My dad and the others stood on the hook looking in our direction, waiting.

Which gave me another idea.

"Ramoth?" I crouched down to talk to her. "I need you to help me save Slade. Could you make yourself invisible and take this cellphone over to those people across the way so that we can record them talking? You'll have to do it without them knowing, a bit like a game of hard-to-get but more hard-to-see-or-hear. If you succeed, you'll get credit for saving him. And . . ." I tried to think of what else would appeal to her. "You'll be showing how territorial you are over him, because those people want to take him away from us."

Ramoth's eyes widened with excitement, and she reared back on her hind legs.

"Now you've done it," Isa announced. "Every single draco is demanding to be the one to save Slade. Are you absolutely sure he's innocent?"

"A thousand percent." Absolutely no doubts there. Just like in China.

"I've got a better idea," Bob said via the phone. He cleared his throat, and when he spoke, he did so like a grouchy general giving an order. "Temeraire. And all other dracos who currently believe themselves to be members of the British military. Report to my house." He dropped his voice. "And here I thought all those hours making harnesses were a waste, but I'll attach cameras with listening devices to the harnesses and send the dracos to spy . . . No, Ramoth . . . Any dracos not currently enrolled in the British military will just have to wait . . . Yes, the dragons in your book wore harnesses, but I don't have time to outfit anyone else."

I gave Ramoth a quick hug. "Don't worry. We'll find an even better job for you."

Lei shook her head. "Cyrus isn't going to randomly talk about Slade."

True. "I bet I can get him to do so. He and I get along really well." I infused my voice with a confidence that was overly ambitious. "Then once the dracos have his admission recorded, I sneak off, Isa takes care of the people with guns, and Maur moves the shuck. That'll work. And Ramoth can go with me to help."

Chapter Fifty-Six

The easiest way across the cove was Thaddeus's boat. It took ten seconds of me being alone on the water to discover that I'd no idea how to row. Isa sent invisible dracos to push me across. Ramoth perched on the bow, her neck extended, her wings spread. She looked like a lavender figurehead, pointing our way.

We reached the hook, and four of Cyrus's guards pulled us onto land. Ramoth squawked and jumped backward, crashing into my chest.

"Ramoth, fly away so they think you've left and then make yourself invisible so they can't hurt you and return, 'kay? That's what I need you to do."

She leaped for the sky.

"Josephine," my dad called out. "Keep out of the water. Just this morning we recorded the temperature at 12℃."

"I'll be careful." No need to make him worry.

A guard dressed in all black and sporting a combat helmet offered his arm to help me climb to dry land.

"Thank you so much." I smiled at him, nice and friendly. He smiled back. See, these guys weren't inherently monsters.

I hiked up the rise to where Cyrus and the others waited, stepping on enough rocks to make my feet ache. Wiry grass scratched at my ankles.

"Josephine," my dad said, frowning. "You lack footwear and your outfit is entirely inappropriate. You've let your personal grooming standards lapse. I find this irresponsible in a situation where you represent CMSRC."

"I'm sorry. As soon as this is over, I'll take care of it."

He wore his white lucky shoes. "Is it because of the fire?" he asked. "Your mother drove over to deal with it. The fire's probably her fault. I think she may have left her hair gadget plugged in and—"

"Miss Partridge!" Cyrus cut off my dad and threw his arms wide to embrace me. "I see you figured it out. You are a bright one."

"I did, but I have questions."

Cyrus took my hand and placed it in the crook of his arm, turning me away from my dad. "Have you met the Honorable Ronan Murphy?"

The politician with the wavy hair gave me a broad smile. "You must be Dr. Partridge's daughter. What a delight to meet you."

First impression: He seemed friendly.

Second impression: Don't put all my eggs in my own first impressions.

In the background, the empty rowboat floated away from the hook of land, meaning dracos were pushing it. All part of the plan, but I needed to hurry things along on my end.

"How do you know my dad?" I asked the politician.

"Why, everyone in Newfoundland knows your dad, sweetheart." The politician smiled, exposing overly whitened teeth.

"Great man, your dad." Cyrus clapped me on the shoulder.

Dr. Panozco made a humphing noise as if he didn't agree.

"Is that why you wrote him the check for seven hundred and fifty thousand dollars?" I asked. "That's the part I don't understand."

"What check?" the politician asked just a little too quickly.

Cyrus chuckled. "Exactly. What check?"

"The one he didn't deposit. From the Ricketts. Dr. Panozco got one too."

"I never got a check," Dr. Panozco snapped back.

"Yes, you did," my dad said. "We both did. On the night the Honorable Ronan Murphy had us drive to Trinity to meet with the Prime Minister."

"I wasn't there," Cyrus said. "I have no idea what anyone is talking about."

Liar.

But also the Prime Minister? This was good stuff and explained so much. Yes, my dad knew the Prime Minister. Yes, he'd drop everything, borrow a car, and sneak out at night, if he thought that's what the Prime Minister's security team wanted him to do. Yes, he'd wear his lucky shoes to do it. "You met with the Prime Minister?" I asked my dad.

"He had to cancel," he replied sadly.

"Last-minute emergency," the politician jumped in. "Something to do with Russia, the Americans, and the Bering Strait."

"The Ricketts regretted wasting our time," Dad continued, "and offered financial remuneration. Only the amount was inappropriately high. It would've looked like a bribe. Dr. Panozco and I agreed not to deposit the checks."

"Very wise of you." Cyrus nodded.

"But why was the Prime Minister coming here?" I asked. "Dad, why are you here now?"

"To protect the shuck, of course," Dad said. "With the help of Buysco's security team. We're working together."

"Protect the shuck from whom?"

"The magic-handlers," Dr. Panozco broke in, looking at me sternly down his nose.

Cyrus beamed at me. "It's always the magic-handlers, eh?"

I beamed just as hard back at him. "Is it?"

Dr. Panozco continued, "The magic-handlers have a devious plan to capture the newly hatched seadragons as a way to increase their magic-handling capacities. We're here to stop them."

That's what they believed?

It did make a certain amount of sense. Even I'd wanted to blame the handlers at one point. Easy way out.

"What about Celsius Burns?" I asked. "Why did they get a check?"

"Who's that?" Cyrus asked with another smile.

"Never heard of them," the politician said.

Dad shrugged, also in ignorance. His was real.

Dr. Panozco looked at his feet. No way did he not know the name of Slade's band.

I turned back to my dad. "These people are lying to you. The magic-handlers aren't involved. The person planning on capturing the baby seadragons is Mr. Scofield. By giving him access to Trinity, you're helping him do it. Mr. Murphy must be working not for the Prime Minister but for Buysco."

Dad stiffened. "Josephine, you will apologize immediately. The proper title is the Honorable Ronan Murphy."

I automatically turned to the Honorable Ronan Murphy and opened my mouth to apologize. Then I snapped it shut. As much as I wanted to appease Dad, his missing my point was more important.

"Dad, it makes no sense that the Prime Minister, the government, and RCMP would turn security over to a superstore owner. Or ask land developers to be your contact with the Prime Minister. It's all fake. These people are scamming you."

Dad frowned. "Mrs. Ricketts is the Honorable Ronan Murphy's younger sister. That makes it nepotism, not a scam."

Seriously hoped the dracos had gotten that. "But—"

Cyrus clapped me on the back again, his voice filled with mirth. "Oh, the imagination of children."

"My sincerest apologies." Dad nodded at the Honorable Ronan Murphy, then Cyrus, then Dr. Panozco. "Josephine is going to remain silent from here on out. She's known to talk too much. Her elder sister insists it's related to an anxiety disorder, although there's no sign of anxiety on my side of the family, so it must come from her mother."

Out in the water, the rowboat was now in the middle of the cove. Only, instead of floating loose, two boys sat inside. Slade and Mo, working together on the oars and bringing themselves in my direction.

No!!!!!

Why had Isa let this happen? And Stella. Stella should've been all over stopping Mo.

I turned back to Cyrus, speaking quickly. "Back to Celsius Burns. You had the Ricketts write a check for a million and a half dollars. It was deposited into a fake company that Dr. Panozco has the power to draw on."

"What?" Dad turned to Dr. Panozco. "The Ricketts suggested such an amount, but I made it clear it crossed a boundary and I'd have to notify CMSRC if they pushed it. A direct donation would make more sense."

Yay, Dad!

"And thus, no such check ever happened," Dr. Panozco said. He glanced at Cyrus.

"It did happen," I said.

Slade and Mo rowed closer to the hook. I'd minutes to finish this up. "There was a check. I saw the backup copy. Even more, Robert Minh Quan found the bank account where it was deposited."

"Robert Minh Quan?" Dad asked, his attention turned. "The famous draco-biologist who studied the collapse of the Stellar sea lions due to feeding on *Draco decapodiformes*? That Robert Minh Quan?"

Of course, Dad would remember Bob as the scientist he used to be and admire him for it.

"Brilliant man," Dad continued. "Utterly brilliant. I was hoping to chat with him while we're in the area. He did his undergrad at Yale."

Cyrus stepped between Dad and me, his gaiety turned all the way up but edged like a knife.

My chest tightened. My blood pounded. I kept going anyway, blurting, but the right words. "Dr. Quan says Cyrus Scofield and Buysco are behind the checks from the Ricketts. Mr. Scofield set up a fake company called Celsius Burns as a way to give money to Dr. Panozco in trade for the two of you providing access to Trinity."

Dad turned to Dr. Panozco, looking puzzled. "Dr. Quan had an impeccable reputation back before he died, I mean, left his field of study."

"I would never take a bribe," Dr. Panozco announced. "The idea is ridiculous. The only way I'd ever accept funds from a third party was if the funds were intended for research. In particular, the project on draco-lice in the sub-Antarctic. Even Dr. Partridge, the female Dr. Partridge, that is, has said the draco-lice project is vital for furthering our understanding."

"If I recall correctly," Dad said. "We talked about that. I had to convince you that taking the checks personally rather than having the donations made directly would break CMSRC rules."

I held my breath and let Dad ramble, which he did, going into detail about the conversation between Mr. Ricketts, the Honorable Ronan Murphy, Dr. Panozco, and himself on the night they were supposed to have met the Prime Minister, but instead spent several hours at a defunct theme park just above Trinity working out the details of how to protect the shuck from the supposed magic-handlers using Buysco security.

So.

Much.

Blurting. (Until this exact moment, I'd never realized I'd inherited that particular trait from my dad.)

But not a word about Slade or anything that would prove him uninvolved.

The rowboat ground onto the shore below us and was immediately surrounded by guards. My time was up.

"Joey," Mo called out. "We need to—"

Slade leaped over the side of the rowboat, jerking Mo by their linked handcuffs. Mo's left eye was bright red and swollen shut.

Chapter Fifty-Seven

"Oh, look, my favorite two people." Cyrus threw his arms wide as if he was going to race down and hug them.

The guards, not so much. A group approached Slade and Mo. Slade ignored them and came straight at me, pulling Mo behind him. Mo, who'd very clearly been punched.

"You hit Mo?" I asked, half-horrified, half-flattered. (I mean, assuming it was over me.)

Slade gave me a steely, determined look, took my hand in his, and turned on his heel to tow both Mo and me back to the rowboat. The guards formed a line to block the way.

"Son?" Dr. Panozco joined the guards. "What's going on?"

Slade circled to the left. The guards cut us off, bringing us to a halt. Slade elbowed Mo. "Talk."

"Josephine," my dad took my other arm so that I was strung between him and Slade, "what are you doing with Dr. Panozco's stepson? And why is he handcuffed? Did he ever apologize to you? He was supposed to apologize."

"He did, Dad. A really good one too."

"Well, that's excellent news then."

More guards arrived. Slade glared over his shoulder at Mo. "Talk. To her."

"There's a snag with the plan," Mo said, with a quick glance to Cyrus. "Isa's sayin' you need to come back and—"

"And there it is!" Cyrus exclaimed, clapping his hands together in delight. "A plan. With a known magic-handler. And a known miscreant, who has recently escaped police custody." He smiled pointedly at Slade, the handcuffs, and then the guards. "Grab him."

No. No. No.

The guards rushed in, breaking my connection to Slade. A guard did a single-handed chop on the back of his neck. Slade went down.

Terror washed over me so cold it felt straight off an iceberg. I ripped free of my dad, throwing myself toward Slade, screaming his name. This was China all over again.

A guard grabbed me around the waist. It was even the nice one who'd helped me before. He didn't seem so nice now.

Mo landed on top of Slade, flattening him with an ooof of air.

Cyrus turned to my dad and Dr. Panozco. "That boy," he pointed at the unmoving Slade, "is working with Isabella Maldonado-Flores, whose grandmother is the head of the Mexican American magic-handling family. If there was a check for one point five million made out to the miscreant's rock band, it must be from them. He's conned Dr. Partridge's daughter and this nice local boy into helping him. I understand Dr. Panozco's stepson has even done this before. In China."

"Slade was innocent in China!" I screamed as tears poured down my face. "He's innocent now."

Mo rolled off of Slade. Slade pushed himself slowly to his knees, turning to look at me. Our gazes locked and held. His mouth moved, but he made no sound. I heard him anyway. *Jojojojojojojojo . . .*

It was enough.

He was okay. I wasn't alone. I took a deep breath. Then another, and wiped my face on my (Slade's) sleeve. This was bad, but we still had options.

Right?

I couldn't think of any, so I kneed the guard holding me but missed my goal, getting him in the upper thigh. I stomped down on his toes, but barefoot vs. boot was a no-go.

"I'm tellin' you he's innocent," Mo said, from where he sat sprawled next to Slade. "Mr. Quan found proof Slade couldn't have deposited that check."

A guard pointed a gun at Slade's head. I began to shake. I elbowed the guard who held me, but he was wearing body armor and didn't appear to notice.

"It. Was. Time. Stamped," Slade said. "The deposit. To Celsius Burns."

A different guard whacked him on the back of the head with the butt of a rifle. I screamed again. Slade went down again. A guard dropped a boot on the back of his head.

"Don't hurt him!" I fought my guard to get free, but he held tight.

"Mr. Quan hacked the bank," Mo said, "trying to find connections between the Ricketts and Buysco. The check from the Ricketts was deposited by a burner phone from Gander that appears to have been purchased by Slade, but it wasn't. Nor could it have been Slade who used it. The deposit happened while Slade was in the middle of performing with *Carrie: The Musical*, which was recorded. Joey and I were even in the audience that night. There's no possibility Slade deposited that check."

Slade's cheek was smushed against the ground under the guard's boot, warping the shape of his face, but he looked at me anyway and mouthed my name. *Jojojojojojojojo*. Letting me know he was okay, because he understood I needed to know. Because I couldn't do this alone. Because *we* were a *we* again. (Or at least *we* would be if *we* survived this.)

I pressed my palm to my own heart and took a deep breath.

"Well, it wasn't me," Dr. Panozco announced, glancing at Cyrus again. (Which meant it *had* been Dr. Panozco.)

"Best made-up story I've heard in years," Cyrus said. "I can't tell you how much I enjoy a good drama. Mohmmedidrees, you've earned an internship on creativity alone. Corporate office, if you want it."

"There's a connection between Buysco and the Ricketts?" Dad asked several beats late.

"There isn't one. That's the whole point." Cyrus patted Dad on the shoulder, all kindly, or better said, condescendingly.

I stared at Cyrus. And then I had a thought, a relatively calm one even. About Cyrus.

"You have no reason to do any of this." I motioned to my dad, Mo, the crowd of guards, the water where the shuck lay. "I mean, you're going to make a ton of money and that's likely your first motivation. And power and fame, since you'll get that too. But you already have all those things. So deep down inside, that's not what it's about for you. I bet you aren't even planning on swallowing the baby seadragons yourself."

"Are you going to psychoanalyze me now? How lovely. A true gift." He put a hand on his breastbone and smiled broadly in invitation. There may even have been deeply moved, if fake, tears glistening in his eyes.

"You destroyed my Gander mug, my mango-on-a-stick, my clothing, the research vessels. You wrapped my dad, Dr. Panozco, and even Mo around your fingers. Rather than use one of your own boats to set the traps around the shuck, you stole Thaddeus's and bought him a new one, making a huge deal about it. You targeted Slade and his band even though they had nothing to do with anything, and there was no benefit to doing so other than upsetting me."

I paused, working the truth of it all out in my head. I looked to Slade again. He slid his hand out and turned it palm up on the ground. An offering. An understanding. A promise.

Again, it was enough.

"You just like to play games," I said to Cyrus. "I bet you're even the donor behind the anti-draco rallies."

"And you like to play games too!" He puffed out his chest, thrilled with the idea. "We're exactly the same."

It'd been Slade that had called me a game player, and I hated that Cyrus knew. He was also wrong.

"I've never once played a game or faked anything or made another person squirm or created drama just because I wanted to intentionally injure someone for my own entertainment." Not even with Mo. "And that's why you do it. You like the money and the power, but even more, you enjoy manipulating and hurting people."

Cyrus's eyes narrowed but then he abruptly switched to his widest, most fake smile yet. "Nice try."

And then suddenly, I'd had it. Like red-hot, Joey-is-angry had it. With Cyrus for destroying so many things and people for the fun of it, but also with all the rest of them. (Helped that Slade and my dad were now cleared.)

With Dr. Panozco for letting Cyrus say horrid things about Slade when none of it was true.

With my dad for being so smart and yet falling for Cyrus's games anyway.

With the guards for hurting Slade.

With the politician for . . .

I glanced around. The politician had snuck off and was back at the main road quietly slithering toward the parked cars. With the politician for being pond scum.

"Ramoth," I yelled. "I'm *done* being nice, and I'm *done* talking to these people. I need you and the other dracos to take care of them for me. Absolutely everyone here, other than Slade, Mo, and me, gets covered in poop."

And two more things.

"Dad? I'm picking which college I go to based on what I want, with no more input from you or Mom or anyone else. And Cyrus? If you know nothing about any of this, especially those checks, then how did you know Celsius Burns is the name of Slade's band?"

Chapter Fifty-Eight

Cyrus got hit dead-on in the face by turquoise poop. Panozco got beige. My dad, orange, and the politician, who'd made it within a meter of a black SUV, got dumped on by Maur.

There was screaming. Lots and lots of screaming.

Dracos took out the guards one by one, the poop arriving like a rainbow of rancid rain from a really angry god. (Eleos, I hoped, although she was supposedly a compassionate, empathetic god.)

Ramoth, fully visible again, dropped onto the helmet of the guard holding me and sank her claws into his face. He shrieked and let me go. I pinched my nose and leaped toward Slade as she pooped lavender down the back of the guard's exposed neck.

The guard with his boot on Slade's head sagged suddenly backward, dripping fuchsia.

"Are you okay?" both Slade and I called out at the same time.

"I'm fine," we both answered.

"They hit you," I said, launching myself his direction as he and Mo pushed themselves to their feet.

Slade caught me and kissed me, quick, to the point, and super reassuring. "I can take a hit. It wasn't that bad."

Pretty sure he was lying to keep me from freaking out, but this wasn't the moment to argue. Around us, draco poop continued to fall. Cyrus and Panozco took the worst of it, getting hit multiple times from multiple directions. If the smell hadn't been so abominable, it would've been funny. They looked like losers in an oversized game of poop paintball. (Guaranteed the dracos were loving this.)

"Isa needs you," Slade said, grabbing my hand even though it meant he couldn't pinch his nose closed like Mo and I. "Tell her." He nudged Mo with his elbow and towed us through the hacking, vomiting, color-coated guards toward the rowboat.

"The dracos are refusin' to let Maur transport the shuck," Mo said all nasally. "They each want to do it themselves, even the small ones. Somethin' to do with credit."

"Seriously?" My voice came out all nasally too.

"Isa needs it sorted."

Slade picked me up single-armed and swung me into the boat.

"How am I supposed to do that?" Only then I got the best idea. A really good one. Slade was going to hate it.

"Ramoth!" I yelled at the top of my lungs. "Tell the dracos that Slade and I will go in the boat with the shuck. Maur will carry us. Every other draco, and you can invite as many as you want, come along as guards, like the guards Cyrus uses, or like guards in the British military. Every single draco gets a job and gets credit for saving the shuck. But Ramoth, you get the most important job, and I'm trusting you especially to do it. You have to make absolutely sure, like a thousand percent, that Maur doesn't drop us."

***

Flying with Maur was exciting, thrilling, pure-exhilaration, and beyond cold. And that was with Maur having dumped all the excess water after the shuck told him it would be fine in the open air for the trip. (Thank goodness, because Ramoth's solution was to heat the water for Slade and I via draco flame. Just no.)

I crouched on the floor toward the front, ignoring the burning cold wind on my cheeks. Slade pressed against my back, his arms around me, his hands latched onto the bench so that I was encircled by him. His knuckles were bone white, and he breathed quick and shallow into the back of my head, and not just as a way to avoid eating my hair.

The shuck sat at the back of the boat. It looked exactly like it had in my dreams, an oversized glassy, colorful ball of black, blue, and purple that pulsed with internal light. The light had an odd, disjointed movement. The baby seadragons?

Ramoth, Temeraire, and Saphira flew closest to us. Thousands of other dracos formed a backdrop. The noise and the smell and the occasional burst of flames were gloriously horrific.

We flew over a knot of several hundred luxury yachts. I waved. Slade grabbed my hand and forced it back to the bench.

"Don't let go," he yelled.

Maur took us north, following the rugged coastline.

We reached an area of rolling, peaty grasslands ending abruptly in ragged cliffs above the ocean. A squat, red-and-white-striped lighthouse kept guard across a wide bay from us.

Maur descended, and the boat hit the ground, jolting my teeth in their sockets and slamming me backward. Slade held tight to the seat, keeping us from being ejected.

"Are you okay?" we both asked at the same time.

"I'm fine," we both also answered.

The wind and odor disappeared as Maur took off into the sky. The other dracos followed, even Ramoth, which was part of our deal. Slade and I alone would push the boat and the shuck into the ocean so that the dracos couldn't fight over credit.

"That was fun!" I shifted in Slade's arms to check on the shuck. It seemed the same.

Slade stood, pulling me up next to him, his face ashen. "When this is over, we're walking back to civilization."

I kissed him on the tip of the nose just because it was there. "I don't have any shoes."

"I'll carry you."

He helped me over the side of the boat and onto what looked like a bedding of soft moss and lichen. It wasn't. It was some kind of twiggy undergrowth that only looked soft. Felt like walking on a mat of spiny twigs. I leaned on Slade and shifted from one foot to the other, trying to find an easy way to stand.

The yellow phone rang.

"Push the boat to the edge of the cliff," Bob said without preamble. "But don't shove it over. A pod of *Draco porcopiscus* followed the veradracos. If the shuck goes in now, a porcopiscus will eat it whole. You have to wait until it hatches so that the majority of the seadragons can escape."

Sometimes the natural world sucked.

I explained what we needed to do to Slade. We (Slade) pushed until the front third was hanging over open space. Once the boat was in place, I worked my way along the side to look over the edge. Best to be sure we wouldn't be dropping it onto rocks or a shoreline.

Slade grabbed me around the waist and towed me in the other direction.

"I just want to check that—"

"No." He bent forward and slung me over his shoulder fireman-style like he had back at Buysco.

"Slade!"

"Jojo, you're not falling over that cliff."

"I won't—"

"Not caring."

Guess we had to trust that Bob and the dracos had it covered. "Can you at least hold me face up?"

Slade swung me around to the front, bride-style. I threw my arms around his neck and kissed his ear.

He hiked us up a ridge above the boat and sat down on the edge so that I could settle between his knees. I leaned back against his chest, and he wrapped an arm around my shoulders and one around my waist, just like he used to. Tears welled in my eyes. Not a deluge but a creeping, drawn-out swelling, coming from the center of my chest as my heart inflated against my other organs, squeezing the moisture and every emotion in my entire body upward. Sitting against him, like we used to do, touching, was every bit as meaningful as kissing him. "Why did you punch Mo?"

"That's what you want to talk about?"

"Definitely."

He sighed. "He swung first."

"And . . . ?" Because there was more. I could totally tell.

"He used your name."

"He called me Jojo?"

Slade said nothing, so I turned and kissed him while running my fingers over the shaved parts of his head, getting a feel for the soft prickliness. (That I loved that he'd hit Mo for using my nickname was likely wrong, but there I was.)

"Can I talk about me now?" he asked. "I want to tell you."

"I want to know."

He chin-nodded. "I got tested. After China. For those things you said. I didn't do it for myself. I did it for Vinnie."

"Slade, I'm so, so sorry. I should never have—"

He kissed me to shut me up. Very effective. Then he tucked my chilled fingers under his arms and turned me back around so we were sitting in our usual way. "Your sister didn't know what she was talking about."

"I could've told you that."

"I don't fit perfectly in any one thing other than a general language disorder that doesn't match an exact profile. The doctor said I could probably get an autism diagnosis if I did more testing, but I'm not going to do that unless Vinnie needs me to. I don't care."

"How come no one caught it before?"

He breathed slowly into the top of my head. "We moved a lot when I was a kid, touring with my dad and staying with relatives. I could always talk to my parents, so they didn't see it, and it's not like I never talked. I just didn't do it much. As long as I could talk to the people I wanted to talk to, I didn't try very hard with anyone else."

I hugged him tight.

"I've been going to speech therapy in Toronto, and it's helped. I can talk to the guys in the band most of the time. And I talk at work, because the job's repetitive and for some reason giving orders is easy for me, so I give orders a lot. The therapist helped me figure that out and taught me some other techniques. It's better than it was."

"It's way better. You're doing great."

He rested his chin on top of my head. "It's still hard at times, and I don't want that for Vinnie. My therapist says some of my problems are likely because I didn't get help when I was a kid, and my head just adjusted on its own. I'm trying to convince my mom to give custody of Vinnie to my dad and me so he can start young."

"After everything Panozco did? I bet she leaves him."

"Let's hope, but it causes a problem. Jojo, I can't follow you to Yale or MIT or wherever it is that Desi lives. I have to stay in Toronto."

The phone rang. Before I could answer, Bob's voice boomed from behind us. "It's hatching. Stop gushing at each other and go push the boat."

We jumped to our feet.

The exterior of the shuck was dissolving and caving over from the top down, like a candle melting. Slade swung me into his arms again and raced us to the boat.

"I'll move to Toronto." The words came out disjointed as I bounced. "I want to go to U of T anyway and stay put and have friends that last and join a dance team and be near you."

"No more romance," Bob announced from right next to us again. "Get the seadragons into the water." (Apparently, the dracos weren't the only ones with an invisibility spell.)

Slade put me down behind the boat. As the shuck melted, masses of colorful worms with filmy water-wings spilled out. Millions of them. Tiny, but still so cute with stubby little heads, big eyes, and long sinewy tails.

It meant the shuck was at the end of its life or magic or whatever. Sentient or not, my heart beat heavy for it for a moment, and I swallowed a lump of loss. It'd been on the verge of being my friend. That it had tattled to the others about Mo's kissing made that seem even more true.

"You did great," I murmured to its remains, a single tear welling in my eye. "You get full credit."

"Push," Bob yelled.

Slade and I (and possibly Bob, but mostly Slade) pushed.

The boat slid over the edge, tumbling down the cliff until we heard a loud crash and splash. I stepped toward the edge. "Just one look. I promise not to fall over."

Slade made a grab to stop me, but I was ready and jumped sideways. One of my feet landed on a particularly prickly plant. I tripped in the direction of the cliff, and Slade scooped me up once again and jogged us backward.

Right as he set me back on my feet, the dracos returned en masse, filling the sky above us. The noise of them made me wish for earplugs. Their wind sent my hair flying into Slade's and my faces. The smell made me pinch my nose again.

I fought to pull my hair into a knot as Ramoth, Temeraire, and Saphira landed on the ground in front of us, wings flapping, tails swishing with excitement. "Yes, you all get credit," I said and smiled at them one by one. "Lots and lots of credit."

Slade wrapped his arms around me. I climbed on the top of his Chucks to save my feet and slid my arms under his.

"Jojo?" Slade yelled into my ear above the noise. "Isa and the dracos were right. You need to hear me say it."

"Hear what?"

"That I—"

The surrounding air went suddenly, eerily silent. The dracos were still flying above, but the sound was gone. As was the smell. Ramoth settled on the top of Slade's head.

"Don't hurt him!"

"It's fine," Slade said. But of course that's what he would say.

Slade turned me around in his arms so we faced each other. Ramoth swished her tail down the back of his neck and gently combed through his hair with her front claws.

"I want you to come to Toronto," he said. "I want this, us, to work out." He gazed right into my eyes. "Because Jojo, I *am* mad-crazy in love with you. I always have been, even when I was angry. I worship everything about you. I can't help but stare at you, sleeping or not. I have no idea what adoring looks like, but give me a chance and I'll figure it out."

A slow smile spread over my face. I flooded with gooeyness. Honey and molasses and melted chocolate and maple syrup. All of it surrounding a bone-deep contentment.

I leaned into him and kissed him once again. It was a really good one. Again. And not just due to our oh-so interested audience and Ramoth craning her neck so that her head was inches from ours. "Slade?"

"Hmmm?"

"I'm crazy, madly in love with you too. But even more, I really, really missed you."

Chapter Fifty-Nine

Five Days Later
Hiking distance from Spillar's Cove, Bonavista Peninsula, New-foundland

Robert Minh Quan hated his name, or at least the formal version of it. Being called Mr. Quan, or worse, Dr. Quan, brought back memories of a life he couldn't have and wanted back.

Bob stomped out of his invisible house without glancing at the rolling ocean view below or the obnoxiously cheerful red-and-white lighthouse across the bay. He settled in an invisible Adirondack chair facing the opposite direction. He'd had the chair specially made with slots in the back to accommodate his wings. Wings that he'd resent less if they did anything other than get in the way and force him to sew his own clothing.

"Just call me Bob," he muttered to the rolling grasslands and the larval seadragons fighting for their lives somewhere down below against a host of other magical-creatures that had come to feast on them. Nature sucked. But it was what was supposed to happen.

"And walk a little faster. I don't have all day."

Actually, he did. Now that the latest disaster was over.

He sat in his chair invisibly waiting for over an hour. This one was an even slower walker than his last two (and only ever) visitors. When she finally came up the path toward his invisible house, she was dressed entirely in black. Black dress, black tights, black boots that looked ready to take her into combat, and a black expression on her face.

She was followed by half a dozen of the smaller dracos, who threw twigs and rocks at her to nudge her in the right direction. Invisible or not, every draco in the vicinity knew exactly where Bob's house was.

The girl strode right past his chair, complaining out loud about the dracos and her dislike of hiking. She had a terrible attitude, way worse than anyone else he'd worked with so far.

In response, Bob remained silent and allowed her to walk straight into the side of the house, her head thumping hard. She fell backward onto the prickly ground and yelped.

Inside Bob's head, the dracos released peals of what was likely meant to be human laughter but sounded like chickens being plucked alive.

"So you made it," he grumbled, even though deep down, he liked her. She had spunk.

She jumped to her feet and spun around, unable to locate him. Which was good, and one of the things he'd wanted to discover with this visit. She had a spell going that should tell her exactly where he was. That it wasn't working meant his counter-spell was effective even with her this close. Which might be an important defense for him in the near future.

Bob waved a hand and let go of the magic of his invisibility spell.

The girl stared, mouth gaping rudely open. He let her do it just to get it over with.

"I figured it was something like this," she said, shocked but not as badly as either Aristotle or Sasha had been.

"You don't like blue?" He let her get a full view of his reptilian scales, frog-like face, wings, and general non-human-ness.

"Spell gone wrong?" she asked, stepping toward him. One of the dracos dropped a pine cone on her head.

"I have a job for you," he said. "Something only you can do and that I'm willing to offer compensation for."

"If you're paying in spells, I'll do it."

Typical impulsive teenager response. He explained that he needed someone who could get access to the secret boarding school for magic-handler youth, and once there, find a specific book. "If you succeed and the book has what I need, I'll make you a joint heir of all of my spells along with Aristotle."

"How much do you have?" she asked, her eyes going wide with excitement. Greedy and right to the point. He'd take it.

"Aristotle gets the technology spells as you couldn't handle them. Everything else you share." He listed off a few of his choicest. Spells she'd be sure to want.

"And this spellbook I'm to steal?"

"No stealing needed, and it's not a spellbook. You'll take pictures of the pages I need and send them to me. Specifically, a chapter on reversing damaged spells."

She nodded in sudden understanding and then looked past him at the ocean. "Only problem is that my mom will never let me go. I had to slip sleeping pills into her breakfast to sneak away today."

"Then she hasn't thought the situation through. She may even decide to send you on her own once she's had the facts laid out for her."

Isa frowned. "She won't. She hates that school. It's one of her many reasons for cutting the magical world from our lives."

"So, neither one of you has thought this through."

She frowned harder.

Teenagers could be so oblivious. Bob stood up, letting her see the wings, the extra joints in his legs, the sheer bloody nuisance that was his dragon body. "We just ruined plans that took Cyrus Scofield over twenty years to bring to fruition. We humiliated him in doing so, and that's not even counting the viral video of him being covered in draco dung. Josephine might've been the one to make it all happen, but he won't go after her. She'd be too easy for him to squash, no challenge, no fun, no reward. Cyrus Scofield is going to turn his anger on the people he thinks were behind her. Meaning me. And very possibly you."

Isa stared at him. Her face scrunched as she slowly got what he was saying. "I'll do it. Convince my mom. Find your book. And if Cyrus comes after me, I'll welcome the fight."

He nodded. "I thought you might."

She nodded back. "Thank you, Mr. Quan."

Bob winced.

CHAPTER SIXTY

Eight Weeks Later
Margaret Addison Hall (Margad), University of Toronto

The knock at my dorm room comes two minutes early. My heart beats wildly in my chest, and I force myself to take a deep breath and do one last check in the mirror.

Slade and I had three days together in Newfoundland before my family had rushed off to Tonga for a draco rat infestation and Slade returned to Toronto. Tonight, we reunite and go on our first-ever official date. Then tomorrow, he's taking me to meet his band. I'm brimming over with anticipation.

Lei spent the rest of her summer (err . . . winter) in Peru with her mom and is now at the University of Florida and loving it, even if her romance with Stella didn't work out. The twins' family ended up in Japan, although I haven't heard from either of them in a while. There may be some bad feelings there, as Quentin and Tabby's date hadn't gone well. Without the rest of us present, Quentin quickly realized they had nothing to talk about and ghosted her.

Bob published the dracos' videos of our conversation on the hook. The CMSRC commissioner wasn't happy with the publicity, but the rest of the Canadian government was thrilled. Aristotle and Sasha sent me multiple voicemails and even several magical notes telling me how great I'd done. She and I never did manage to connect directly.

Cyrus disappeared. The politician was disgraced. The Ricketts are being audited by the Canadian Revenue Agency. My dad was hailed as an upright and patriotic CMSRC scientist. Mo and Stella became local heroes, making international headlines along with me. (Slade stayed out of it.)

Brady and my friendship didn't get a chance to go anywhere, but I sent him a long text telling him how great he was and pointing out that he, the quiet, unassuming, church-kid, was the single person to realize something was off about Cyrus Scofield from the beginning.

Dr. Panozco was able to prove that after depositing the money into the Celsius Burns shell company, he donated every penny to Antarctic-lice research, and that his donation happened before the events at the cove, so his intentions had always been good. Since no one came forward to demand the funds back and CMSRC wanted the money, Dr. Panozco got his hand slapped for not following CMSRC procedure but nothing worse. Shocking, I know.

Slade's mom didn't leave him, but she did agree that Vinnie needed help and that she'd look at options for having him live in Toronto. Yay!

My parents gave in gracefully about U of T, mostly due to Desi. After her and Slade's phone conversation back at the Gander motel, she swung a one-eighty and became his biggest fan. Go figure, but I wasn't complaining.

Ramoth, Temeraire, Saphira, and I had a standing date every Sunday afternoon where they teleported in and I told them everything interesting that had happened to me that week. There was a good chance they'd show up tonight as well, hopefully not with too many of their friends and staying invisible.

I look at myself in the mirror one last time. Slade said to wear something dressy, so I purchased a Southern-belle chiffon wrap dress with ruffles at the hem. The whole thing is light, fluffy, way-girly, and not me. I saw it and just had to have it anyway.

"You're here," I say and throw open the door for Slade.

I'm greeted by the largest bouquet of red roses I've ever seen. Like Miss Universe big, with a massive bow that trails to the floor. "You didn't have to buy me flowers." A giant, totally surprised, pleased, best-door-open-I've-ever-done grin spreads across my face. "But I'm so glad you did."

Slade turns to the side so that we can see each other. Behind him is a group of my floor-mates, several with cameras up. Slade's totally made a spectacle of himself, which he has to hate but also knows I'd love. I go all gooey. Butterflies burst their cocoons in rapid succession.

I tug him into the room and shut the door so we're alone. I asked my roommate (a.k.a. new best friend) to make herself scarce for an hour. She can meet Slade another time. Tonight, he's all mine.

He wears a dark suit, crisp white shirt, and navy tie. His hair is pulled back with a hair band. The sides are fresh-shorn, and his hoops are in. The last at my request. They so need exploring.

"You look amazing," I whisper, so happy I can barely contain it.

"Pretty sure that's supposed to be my line." He studies me all intense-like. "You're beautiful, Jojo."

I grin even harder and reach for the roses so that I can drop them somewhere, anywhere, and throw myself at him. He pulls them tight against his chest.

"The flowers need to go with us. For later."

"Later?" I ask.

"Later," he agrees. "First, we're going to take a couples dancing lesson, and then we're eating Chinese noodles on a blanket by the lake while we discuss your dreams and mine and how we're going to make both of them happen. Then I have a gift for you that's hidden in the roses. Will you cooperate in holding off on the roses and the kissing until later?"

He's never given me a gift before. I glance at him through my lashes, loving every bit of this. "Self-control when it comes to you isn't really my thing."

"I'm not complaining, but—"

I dart around the roses and nail him right on the mouth. It's supposed to be a quick peck, since he asked me not to, but once touching him, I can't stop and back him against the wall. With his arms full of roses, he can't fight me off. It's perfect. Meaning the kiss, of course.

I pull away first for once. "Later, Slade." I blow him a flirty kiss, backing toward the door, knowing he'll follow.

"You're evil." The ghost of a smile tugs at his lips.

"And I talk too much. And I have anxiety. And I make a mess of pretty much everything. I'm probably going to make a mess of your life. It's what I do. But I'll fix the broken light switch in your bedroom, and I'll love your little brother and your band and you. Most of all, I'll make you happy."

"You already do."

I slide my lower lip between my teeth and wrap a curl around my finger, smiling right into his eyes. Then I bolt for the door. He and the roses chase right after me.

Chapter Sixty-One

Day negative 1 of 162 of the China Assignment
Air China Flight 063
Vancouver International Airport

Slade was pissed. He was always pissed but today was different. He'd specifically asked Panozco to book the tickets so he'd be seated next to Vinnie on the plane. He'd practiced in advance, asked politely, and wore a button-down shirt to do it.

Yet here he sat, irritated, waiting for the start of a thirteen-hour flight in an aisle seat in the back of the lower deck while Vinnie was a floor above with Mom and Panozco. Neither of them would play games with Vinnie or make sure he was comfortable when he fell asleep or think to take him to the washroom every couple of hours. If Vinnie had an accident, Panozco would blame him, he'd cry, and Slade wouldn't be there to help.

Panozco was an ass. His mom was a tool. Slade loathed them both, right along with the entire world and everyone in it. His loathing was this giant raging ball of fury that he beat out daily to keep anyone from noticing.

And it couldn't be noticed. Not even when Panozco sat him down before boarding the plane for another one of his lectures on what a gift Slade was getting by living with them and warning yet again that if he messed with either the local girls or the CMSRC girls or embarrassed Panozco in any way, he'd return Slade to his dad faster than Vinnie could down a baggie of goldfish. Slade's loathing was so strong in that moment he envisioned his fist landing against Panozco's face.

But he hadn't said a thing. He couldn't.

It was like there was this conduit between his head and his tongue, and the moment he tried to talk, his body revolted and squeezed down on the conduit until the words had to be pulled through one-by-one via sheer, painful resolve. Panozco wasn't worth the battle.

Someone touched him on the shoulder. A slender girl with wild curly hair motioned to the empty middle seat. She was hot in a unicorn-attracting kind of way. Not his type, even if he wasn't taking Panozco's warnings seriously. He stood to let her by, and that would've been the end of it, except she turned her back and shimmied to get past, giving him a full-body brush. Her wild hair ended up in his face, and her girl-smell all over him. Yet another thing to piss him off. He sat down and turned up his music, crossed his arms, closed his eyes, and ignored her.

Or at least he tried to ignore her.

The girl was restless. She moved around in her seat, rearranging how she sat, getting stuff out of her bag on the floor and then putting stuff back. Each time she turned her head, her hair flew in all directions, mostly onto him. She also kept unintentionally touching his arm with her elbow. Her girl-smell ended up everywhere.

The plane took off, and she continued to fuss. Then she went so still that he cracked an eye to see if she was okay.

She was doing some kind of ridiculously hard math work on a tablet, holding it with her left hand and using an e-pen with her right, all of which made her low-cut shirt gape, giving him a perfect view down the front.

Holy—

Her bra was light blue and lacy.

Decent guys didn't look down girls' shirts. Halfway decent guys didn't either.

And yet it wasn't like she'd ever know. In another twelve hours, they'd arrive in Beijing. She'd go on her way to wherever she was headed. He'd go find Vinnie to make sure his mom and Panozco didn't lose him on the way to the next flight. Slade was unlikely to ever see this hot girl again.

He snuck more peeks down her shirt, making good and sure she didn't notice. His anger eased up.

The base of her neck did this little tremor, like she was making a noise in her throat as she worked on her math. Sound was Slade's thing, so he turned off his music to hear it but couldn't over the noise of the plane. He snuck a few more looks down her shirt.

He was so not a decent guy.

She put the tablet away, pulled out a brochure of some sort, and flipped through it. Disappointingly, her shirt stopped gaping.

That's when he recognized the brochure. He had a matching one somewhere in his luggage.

"You're CMSRC." The words burst from him without a struggle for once.

She jumped and turned. Her hair ended up all over the place again.

Their eyes met, and hers were a pale blue, the same color as her bra. She had this pert, upturned nose, freckles, and soft, plump lips. She bit down on her lower lip, intimidated by him but trying to hide it.

He sneered to encourage her fear, an auto-habit to avoid conversation. She didn't look away or shrink in on herself or make any of the other petrified defensive move he was used to. Instead, she said something he didn't understand and smiled.

Her smile was full of softness, easiness, lack of judgment, warmth, friendship, genuineness. It was wildly attractive. Hotter than her appearance or her bra. Compelling even, because no one had ever looked at him like that before. For the first time in his life, Slade wanted to talk to someone he didn't know. To her.

He shouldn't. On pain of pissing off Panozco. Of being separated from Vinnie. Of terrifying this cute, friendly, decent, unicorn-attracting girl who was likely to hate everything about him.

He did it anyway. His brain even cooperated.

"I don't speak Chinese."

✳✳✳

Thank you so much for reading *Partridge Up a Pear Tree (and Dragons)*. If you have a moment, please consider leaving an honest review in one of the usual spots. It really does help.

I'm aiming to release my next book (Isa's story!) in early 2027, sooner if I can make it happen but no promises. To receive notices for that and my other releases, head over to my website to join my occasional newsletter: www.racheltaylorthompson.com.

Happy Reading!

~Rachel

P.S.I bet you want to know what Slade hid in the roses, right? I suppose I'd better tell you!

Buried in the roses is a bracelet with a plaque meant to be worn on Joey's left wrist. On the plaque is engraved the word *Permanence*. Slade also added *Permanence* to his sleeve on the inside of his right wrist. When the two of them hold hands and line everything up just so, her bracelet and his ink touch.

Terms

Acronyms:

BIMD: Bureau of Investigations, Magical Division – US federal organization

CMSRC: Canadian Magical Sciences Research Council – Canadian governmental agency responsible for studying all things draco and solving draco emergencies worldwide. Canada is the worldwide leader in draco research and protection.

MSS: Ministry of State Security – Chinese federal organization

RCMP: Royal Canadian Mounted Police (Mounties) – Do not wear red serge, boots, Stetsons, or ride horses outside of parades.

Magical Terms and Dragon Definitions:

Magic-handlers: Humans with special DNA that allows them to turn semis into spellbooks and use those spellbooks to perform magic. It's believed the first handlers were created by ingesting semis and not dying.

Magic-handlers' Alliance or Handler's Alliance: Worldwide magic-handler organization. Currently leaderless. Magic-handlers group themselves into families based on geography, language, and shared ethnic heritage.

Semis: Source of magic in the form of a jewel that is held within a magical-creature's body. The semis allows the creature to live and to defy the normal rules of physics and biology. A semis also contains the DNA of the magical-creature and is part of procreation. Combining two semis of the same species perpetuates the species. A semis is harvested by killing the magical-creature. A semis can have a magical form of sentience.

Shuck: Egg-like object made from two semis of the same species. Functions as an incubator for developing magical-creatures. Each shuck incubates many thousands, if not millions, of baby magical-creatures, depending on the species.

Spellbooks: Created by magic-handlers from semis. Spellbooks both contain magic and channel magic through the body of the magic-handler. Because of historical overharvesting of magical-creatures, most powerful spellbooks were created to solve problems prior to the Industrial Revolution and are no longer useful.

Spellbooks can go awry as part of their creation and often do in dangerous and unexpected ways. Spellbooks can also go awry if stolen from the magic-handler who owns them. Most spellbooks are stored by magic-handlers in fourth-dimensional libraries. Magic-handlers access these libraries via magic when they need to pull on their spellbooks.

Structure of Dragon nomenclature: Each dragon species has a latinized convention, a local language convention, and colloquial nicknames. Choice of nomenclature depends on the human and their relation to the magical world.

For example, a honey bee with a semis would properly be called a *Draco apis* or a bee dragon. A squid with a semis would be called a *Draco teuthidis* or squid dragon.

Traditional flying dragons are properly called *Draco verus*. They have multiple nicknames, the most common being veradracos or truedragons. When the term *draco* or *dragon* is used without added identifiers, the speaker is usually referring to Draco verus.

Wyrm-netting: Phishing by magic-handlers to gain access to magical-creatures and their semis.

Acknowledgments

Partridge is the twelfth book I've written over twenty years of plunking away at my keyboard. It's also, by far, my most beloved.

This is partly because Joey's blurting is an extreme version of what I did as a teen. Whenever an authority figure would put pressure on me, I'd blab my heart out to get them to stop and throw everyone and everything under the bus. I had this one friend that I endlessly got into trouble, and yes, I *still* feel guilty about it all these years later!

It's also partly because I fell so in love with Newfoundland. And partly because researching Slade sent me down a rabbit hole of music I'd previously hated but now listen to non-stop. (Tool. Iron Maiden. Three Days Grace. Breaking Benjamin. Papa Roach. Danger Kids. Primus . . . Okay, I'll stop now but in the last month I've seen both Ghost and Linkin Park in concert, and one way or the other, I'm going to see Tool and Danny Carey someday.)

But most of all, I love *Partridge* because it's a second-chance story of hurt leading to regret and ultimately understanding and healing. Forgiveness and shared-grace strike my heart like absolutely nothing else. (Also . . . my own marriage may have come about via second-chance . . .)

All of that said, this was a bear of a book to write. Left to my own devices, I created a massive pile of ideas and characters that absolutely and utterly didn't work. It was bad. Unbelievably bad. Just ask my writer friends, who had to listen to me complain and bang my head against the wall day-after-day, week-after-week, month-after-month. Joey and Slade and Ramoth and the story *should have* worked. It *had* to work. I desperately *needed* it to work. But it didn't work, and I had no idea why.

In walks Natashya Wilson, editor extraordinaire. I handed her a giant pile of words in the vague shape and smell as what Maur dropped on the politician. A whole ton of her time and a novella-length editor's report later, she explained the heart of the issues and pointed me toward fixing them. She was universally right about everything. A million thanks to Natashya!

(Just in case you were wondering (because I would be), the fundamental problem was that Joey wasn't in the driver's seat of the story. Which, in hindsight only, was dead obvious. Sigh.)

Partridge is also a very detailed book covering places and areas of expertise that I knew nothing about when I began. So many people assisted me in getting the details right. (And if there are errors, they are all mine.)

In no particular order, but with a huge amount of gratitude, I send my utmost thanks to: *Robert Kingett* (Slade's speech disorder), *Samantha Kassé* (especially for help figuring out Mo's personality - www.samant hakasse.com), *Fiza Abbas, beta reader and developmental editor* (and the best asker of thoughtful questions – fizabbas.com), Colin Glavac (NFLD details, especially the word 'deadly,' which I LOVE but likely misused anyway), Jamie Barry (Slade's speech disorder and for making me think deeper about human psychology), Rowan Sanan (for such a great outside view of my characters that they felt new to me again), and a small group of Canadian, Chinese, music, and other experts that asked to remain anonymous, including the person who told me to just let Mo have his accent.

Thank you to Stephanie White (whiterabbitediting.com), who last minute threw on a red cape and saved me and the book from a true copyeditor disaster. Not sure the book (or I) would ever have made it to the finish line without her.

Thank you to a Newfoundlander named Wish, who I met while visiting the Silent Witnesses Memorial outside of Gander. Wish spent a good hour and a half telling me about the Memorial and letting me pester him with questions about Gander, the airport, the weather, and all things Newfoundland. Then I ran into him again at Lake Gander, and he let me pester him all over again. A lot of the best small details in the book come from Wish, my favorite being the Dover's Fault joke. (Also, Joey's hair was inspired by the statue of the small girl at the Memorial. Go look it up. It's great hair!)

Thank you to the cruiseship band Delorean based out of Mexico. You hopefully didn't notice me, but I ditched my extended family every night on a ten-day cruise so I could sit directly above you guys, looking down, and absorb all the minor details of your performances that a regular audience wouldn't notice.

A whole ton of thanks to the many battery/front-ensemble/percussionist students who inspired me to write about a drummer. Yes, I secretly made notes about the things you did and said and all the quirky little ways you play with your sticks. Yes, I stole several of them for Slade. Yes, your instructors and band directors deserve a whole ton of credit too.

Thank you to all the authors who inspired me as a teenage English student to love literature, and then those same authors who inspired me again as I re-read their books to help with my own teens' English class assignments. More thanks to the authors who inspired my dragons (and me!) with their fabulous fantasy novels. My Maur, Ramoth, Temeraire, Saphira and the others all fly in the shadows of giants.

And thank you to my family. Because . . . well . . . just because.

~Rachel